HIDE AND SEEK

Andrea Mara

PENGUIN BOOKS

TRANSWORLD PUBLISHERS

Penguin Random House, One Embassy Gardens,
8 Viaduct Gardens, London SW11 7BW
www.penguin.co.uk

Transworld is part of the Penguin Random House group of companies
whose addresses can be found at global.penguinrandomhouse.com

Penguin
Random House
UK

First published in Great Britain in 2022 by Bantam Press
an imprint of Transworld Publishers
Penguin paperback edition published 2022

A CIP catalogue record for this book
is available from the British Library.

ISBN 9780552177993

Typeset in ITC Giovanni by Jouve (UK), Milton Keynes.
Printed and bound in Great Britain by Clays Ltd, Elcograf S.p.A.

The authorized representative in the EEA is Penguin Random House Ireland,
Morrison Chambers, 32 Nassau Street, Dublin D02 YH68.

Penguin Random House is committed to a sustainable
future for our business, our readers and our planet. This book
is made from Forest Stewardship Council® certified paper.

To Elaine, with love.

1

June 2018

Ten seconds.

That's how long it takes for Sophie to disappear.

That's how long it takes for me to realize that she's not in our front garden. That she's not behind the car and she's not behind the gate and she's not behind the pillar in the porch. That she's not in any of her small selection of favourite hiding spots.

That Sophie's not here at all.

'Sophie? Sophie!'

I'm confused. I'm not worried. Not really. She knows not to leave the garden. I'm almost certain she knows not to leave the garden. Our rules for Hide and Seek are simple: I count to ten, she hides somewhere *very* nearby, and I search. Sometimes I have to pretend I can't see her, to make the game last longer. Like when she huddles behind the cherry blossom: a tree whose trunk is far narrower than even three-year-old Sophie. And then I walk up and down past it, eyes straight ahead, calling her name, just as I'm calling it now.

Only she's not behind the cherry blossom.

She's not anywhere.

'*Sophie!* You can come out now – the game's over!'

This is why I don't like Hide and Seek. This is why she's not

1

supposed to hide anywhere other than our own front garden. Could she have gone inside the house? I glance back, but the front door is closed, the key in the pocket of my shorts. The side passage maybe? The back garden? The shed? A lurch of worry takes hold. The shed is full of trouble – rakes and trimmers and hammers and weed killer. Did Mark lock it last night? Could Sophie have—

'I think I've found something of yours.'

The voice comes from the garden next door. I look over to see a woman nodding pointedly at the dividing wall – at something on her side, out of sight from where I'm standing. Something, or some*one*.

'Sophie?' I'm at the waist-high wall in three strides, and there she is, crouched down in this stranger's hydrangeas. 'Sophie! Come out of there. You can't just go into other people's gardens.'

She looks up at me, all blue eyes and freckled nose and butter-wouldn't-melt mouth.

'Did I win Hide and Seek?'

'No, because you left our garden without telling me, and you shouldn't do that.' It sounds sharp and I can feel the woman looking at me. 'Now, say sorry to . . .' I glance up at our neighbour.

'Frances Burke. Fran.'

'Say sorry to Fran for going into her garden.'

'I don't mind visitors,' Fran says to Sophie, 'but you must ask your mum first. OK?'

Sophie nods and walks across Fran's lawn towards her gate. She doesn't say sorry, but I'm choosing my battles this evening. I say it instead.

'Sorry about that – I got a fright when I couldn't find her.' I laugh to show her I'm not the kind of mother who panics over losing sight of her child for half a minute. Even if that's exactly who I am.

Fran nods. She's in her early fifties, tall and solid, sweating in the evening sun, with wisps of fair hair escaping an untidy ponytail. She's wearing an olive-green t-shirt and the kind of too-long boot-leg jeans I haven't seen on anyone since 2008. Her feet are in brown leather sandals with thick buckled straps and she gives off an air of sensible practicality.

'Of course. I don't have children but I can imagine. Is it just the one you have?' She nods towards Sophie, who is making her way slowly along the footpath from Fran's front gate to ours.

'No, two older ones as well – Emily is eleven, and Ben is nine. Both inside finishing homework.' I realize I haven't introduced myself. 'Sorry, I'm Joanna, by the way.'

'Lovely to meet you, and welcome to Rowanbrook.' She nods towards our house. 'They're grand family homes. The previous owners did a nice job smartening up the outside to sell it.'

'They sure did. It's the inside that needs work . . . someone was clearly fond of a dark palette. But nothing we can't fix over time.'

'Exactly. And it's a great neighbourhood, very friendly.'

'Oh, that's good to hear – we haven't really met people yet.'

'Well, now you've met me. The people on your other side are gone already to their place in Marbella, so you won't meet them till September.'

'Are you here long yourself?'

Sophie arrives beside me, slipping her hand into mine.

'My whole life,' Fran answers. 'Apart from a brief escape to a flat in Harold's Cross.'

'Wow, that's a long time!' I tell her, before realizing how it sounds. Fran doesn't seem to mind.

'It is. I came back to look after my mother – just for a few weeks until we figured out a long-term plan. That was twenty-five years ago.'

'Wow,' I say again, trying to gauge if this is a sad story or a happy story or most likely an it-is-what-it-is, perfectly fine story.

'When my mother passed away, she left me the house, so here I am, still watering her rose bushes. Just me and him.' She nods towards a huge black cat who's watching from the porch. She laughs. 'That sounds a bit maudlin, doesn't it? Like I'm a lonely cat woman. I took voluntary redundancy from work a few months ago, so all this' – she sweeps her hand around the garden – 'is a relatively new pastime. What do you do yourself?'

'I'm a psychotherapist. Was. Still am. Sorry, not yet used to my new status.' Sophie lets go of my hand and wanders back towards the gate. 'I'm a psychotherapist but my current contract just came to an end, so I'm taking some time out with the kids.'

'Well, I hope you'll be very happy here. It's a grand place for kids.'

'It does seem lovely. Speaking of kids, I'd better get Sophie in before she disappears again. Imagine losing your child in a game of Hide and Seek in your own front garden.'

'It would be ironic, I suppose, after what happened here.'

'After what happened here?'

'To the other little girl.' Fran jerks a thumb at our house.

'Who?'

A funny look crosses her face. 'Oh, it's nothing. Forget I said it.'

'Something happened to a little girl here?' I prompt, curious, but suddenly uneasy too.

She purses her lips, then, decision apparently made, moves closer to the wall.

'I suppose you'll find out anyway if you google it. It happened back in the eighties – a whole heap of kids playing Hide and

Seek one morning, down there on the green.' She indicates with her hand. 'Only one poor little thing hid somewhere and was never found.'

'Wait. I've heard that story. Lily . . . Lily Murphy was the child's name?'

'Yep. Awful time. Everyone searched and searched, but she was never found.' She lowers her voice. 'Obviously after a point, they were looking for a body.'

'Jesus.'

Fran nods. 'Can you imagine? Mary and Robbie, those were her parents, living a perfectly normal happy life, all destroyed by a simple game of Hide and Seek. That's why what you said about your daughter struck me as ironic. Same game, similar age, and same house too.'

'*The same house?*'

'Yes – the Murphys lived here in the house you've just bought.'

'Oh my God.'

'I take it the estate agent didn't mention it . . .'

'The estate agent didn't say a word . . . That's . . . Wow. I don't know what Mark will think.'

'Your husband?'

'Yeah. Actually, you might know him – he grew up here in Rowanbrook. Mark Stedman?'

'Mark Stedman,' she repeats, and her expression changes but I can't read it. Is it nostalgia? Surprise? Irritation? 'No, I don't remember the name.'

None of the above, then.

Fran tilts her head. 'But if he's from here, surely he must have been aware that you were buying Lily Murphy's house?'

'No. He'd have said I'm sure he wouldn't have bought it if he'd known.'

'Right . . .' Fran tails off, then smiles. 'Too late now anyway,' she says brightly, as though we're talking about buying the wrong kind of cereal or full-fat milk. 'So, we should swap numbers – are you in the Rowanbrook WhatsApp group?'

'No, I didn't realize there was one.'

'Did you not – well, you got a mention there already, you know. You're famous.'

'Really?'

'Ah, I'm exaggerating. When the house went up for sale, someone in the group shared an old article about Lily's disappearance. I think people were curious to see who would buy the house. That's all. I'll send you an invite link to the group if you like, what's your number?'

I call out my number and she keys it into her phone.

'Grand, I'll get that to you now.'

'Thank you. I'd better head in to check on Emily and Ben. Actually, we're having a small housewarming on Friday evening. Come along if you're free? Around seven?'

A small hesitation. Then a half-smile. 'Lovely. I'll be there.'

'Great! It was nice to meet you.'

'You too,' Fran says, turning back to her gardening.

As a general rule, I wait until the weekend to open wine, but when the sun is out that rule gets shapeshifty. You never know how long the heatwave will last. What if it rains for the month of July, and there are no more wine-in-the-garden nights? That's how I explain it to Mark when I open the bottle of rosé that Wednesday evening, balancing glasses on our slightly rickety garden table. I don't really need to explain it to him, he doesn't overthink the way I do, and he's happy to take the proffered drink without a dissertation on the rights and wrongs.

'So, I met one of our neighbours tonight and discovered something about this house.'

'Oh?' He takes a sip of wine and reaches instinctively for his phone before remembering not to.

'Do you know the name Lily Murphy?'

'Yeah . . .?'

'It's *their* house. The Murphys lived here.'

'What?'

'Yes. You didn't know? Even though you used to live in Rowanbrook?'

'Well sure, but we lived three rows over. And we moved across to Oakbrook a bit before it happened, I think. God. Are you certain?'

'Yep. The solicitor sent us details of all previous owners, but I hadn't bothered to read it. I went back and checked after talking to Fran, the neighbour. The names are there in black and white. Mary and Robbie Murphy. You really didn't know?'

'No! I'd have said.'

'You'd heard of Lily Murphy though, right?'

'Yeah, of course . . . though it's hard to remember now which bits I heard in real life and which bits I know from newspapers.'

'But you've never mentioned it, in all our years together?' I ignore the little voice saying I'm in no place to criticize.

'I suppose it just never came up.' He looks across the garden at the back of our new home. 'It's a bit weird though, knowing they lived here.'

'Weird and sad. Three years old, never seen again. Same age as Sophie.'

I pick up my phone and type 'Lily Murphy Missing Child' into Google. The first search result is from Wikipedia and the second is a thirty-year-anniversary newspaper feature. Both are accompanied by thumbnail images and I zoom in now on the first photo. Little blonde curls, big blue eyes, snub nose, dimpled cheeks, startled smile.

Familiar smile.

Something lurches inside me. I blink and my mouth is suddenly dry.

'God, yeah,' Mark is saying. 'Same age as Sophie. When you put it like that . . .' He picks up his empty wine glass, stands and stretches. 'I can't believe they never found out what happened to her.'

I hardly hear him as I stare at the photo.

I don't know how it's possible, but I think I *do* know what happened to Lily Murphy.

I think I killed her.

2

June 2018

MY PHONE BURNS IN my hand, the screen glowing in the unfolding dusk; the photograph sucking me in, freezing me to the spot.

Lily Murphy. Three years old. Hide and Seek. Never seen again.

Sweet wrappers. Books and notebooks. Foil packets. Little vials. The turn of the key. And her *age*. My mind is whirring with memories I've been pushing away for years. I think I'm about to be sick.

'I'm going to lock up now,' Mark says. 'Are you coming?'

Like a sleepwalker, I move across the cool, dark grass, into our new home. Forever home. Last known address of Lily Murphy.

In the living room, Mark puts on the TV and finds a football match as I open my Mac. My hands are shaking but he doesn't notice. I need to tell him. But not yet. Not now. And it could be nothing.

A coincidence. My guilty conscience. Her ghost.

I google again, and click into Wikipedia:

Lily Murphy (born 5 May 1982) was a three-year-old Irish girl who disappeared in Rowanbrook, Edenvale, Co. Dublin on Monday 1 July 1985. Lily is presumed drowned but her body has never been recovered.

1985. When I was nine. When she was three. *Oh God.*
I swallow and keep reading.

Disappearance

*Lily Murphy (fair hair, blue eyes, 95 cm) was last seen at
approximately 11.30 a.m. on Monday 1 July 1985, near her
home in Dublin. She had been playing with friends on a green
near where she lived, in Edenvale, Co. Dublin. The children
had started a game of 'Hide and Seek', moving from a wooded
area at the back of the green into a nearby building site. The
building site had been abandoned after the construction company,
VB Holdings, went into receivership. The building site was only
loosely secured and local children had been playing there for
weeks (citation needed). Lily Murphy's mother, Mary Murphy,
was nearby, watching the children, along with some other women
from the neighbourhood. At approximately midday, most of the
children returned from the woods but Lily Murphy did not. A
child who had been with Lily brought the group of adults to where
they had been hiding, but Lily had disappeared. A search ensued,
but the child wasn't found. Gardaí (police) were called, and the
search continued throughout the day, and on into the days and
weeks that followed. Officials and locals believe Lily Murphy to
have drowned in a shallow river that runs along the back of the
woods, but no body has ever been rec—*

'Mum!' The shout makes me jump as the living room door
bursts open. Emily, red-faced and angry, hands on hips. 'Mum,
can you *please* tell Ben not to go into my room.'

Ben comes thundering down the stairs behind her. 'I didn't!
But she went into mine and messed up my *Minecraft* figurines!'

'As if I'd go near your *Minecraft* figurines. Which, by the way,
are only for babies.'

'They are not. What would you know? You can't even play *Minecraft*.'

'I'd rather literally die than play *Minecraft*. Anyway, I wasn't in your room. Your room is gross. All spidery and creaky and dark.'

'This whole house is spidery and creaky and dark,' Ben says, his voice rising in indignation. 'It isn't just my room, you know!'

'*Guys!*' I stand up. 'You're far too old for this kind of bickering. Back upstairs and quiet now, Sophie's asleep.'

Mark doesn't take his eyes off the match as the kids slope out of the room and up the stairs. I sit back down and top up our glasses.

'Can I ask you a bit more about Lily Murphy?'

He turns down the volume on the TV. 'Sure. Why though?'

'I'm just a bit jittery after hearing about it. Realizing the house has this tragic past, I guess.' My attempt at nonchalance sounds forced to my own ears, but he just nods.

'I really don't remember much of the detail – we had moved across to Oakbrook and I was away in Irish College when it happened. When I came back, I remember everyone's parents were worried and kept talking in whispers. For me and my mates . . . I guess it seemed like a bit of excitement at first. That probably sounds bad. But we didn't really get it. I was sixteen, and fully caught up in myself. Obsessed with rugby and discos and impressing the girls.' He grins. 'Though obviously none of my other girlfriends were a patch on you.'

'Actually, speaking of old girlfriends, Fran next door says she doesn't remember you, but she had a funny look on her face when she said your name. Any story there? Fran Burke?'

Mark's mouth drops open. 'Fran Burke lives next door?'

'Yep. That's who told me about Lily. So you knew her?'

'Yeah, I remember Fran. We even hung out for a while when I . . . well, when I used to live around here.'

Mark's cheeks flush and I wonder if he and Fran dated. He has an old-fashioned habit of keeping his past relationships to himself, as though I'll somehow be jealous of his exes from twenty years earlier. It is as endearing as it is silly.

'Well, I've invited her to the housewarming on Friday, you can reintroduce yourself then.' I nudge him with my elbow. 'But anyway, did locals have any thoughts on what happened? Like, Wikipedia's saying people believed she drowned?'

'Yeah, I think that's what the police thought. Actually, I remember Mum and Dad saying everyone except the parents believed she drowned, but in that kind of *knowing* way. Like they pitied the parents for losing their child, but pitied them for being naive too?'

I nod. I can imagine this very easily. Mark's parents haven't changed over the years.

'Would they remember, do you think? Could I ask them?'

'If you want. Dad's getting forgetful . . . although it's often about stuff Mum's asked him to do, and only when it suits him. He'd probably have a good memory for things that happened years ago.'

'I wonder how they didn't realize this was the house?'

Mark shrugs. 'Same as me, I suppose. Rowanbrook's huge. We lived in a different part. My parents knew the Murphys, but thirty-three years later, I don't know if they'd remember which house it was.' He picks up his phone reflexively and puts it down again. 'And you know what Mum's like, caught up in her golf and her book club and who wore what when. I doubt she paid much attention when I sent her the link to the house.' He laughs. 'Imagine, all these years, desperate for us to climb the property ladder, *desperate* to have something she can show off about at golf, and when we finally trade up for the "big" house, she's too busy to click the link. But yeah, you can ask her all that tomorrow night. She might remember more than I think. What about you?'

'Me?'

'Do you remember it from the news back then? Of course, you were probably still in the womb.' He nudges me with the remote control. 'My child bride.'

I force a smile, cycling back through the lies I've told him. 'Very funny. I would have been nine, so still living in London, and it wouldn't have made the news over there.'

He goes back to the match and I go back to my Mac, clicking into the Images tab on Google. Her face fills my screen – black-and-white photos, colour photos, pictures taken with her parents, pictures on her own. All different but all the same – blonde curls, blue eyes, snub nose, and those dimples. The longer I stare, the more familiar she is. Inside my head, images and memories are skittering like pinballs. *Wrappers. Syringes. Books and notebooks. The locked room. The key.* And now we're living in her house. Am I about to be found out? It would be no less than I deserve.

3

June 2018

IT'S THURSDAY AFTERNOON AND I'm standing in the yard of Edenvale National School, Sophie's hand in mine. The mundanity of this daily ritual is both calming and surreal. How am I here, smiling and waving at familiar faces, while inside my head, images of Lily Murphy flash like a manic home movie? And yet, what else can I do. I'm Joanna Stedman: PA-member, barbecue-holder, advice-giver, gin-drinker. I am my Twitter bio – psychotherapist, mother, wife, reader, runner, coffee-fiend. I'm the go-to person, not the fall-apart person. On the outside, at least.

'How's the unpacking going?' says a voice in my ear.

'Adana! How are you?'

'Shattered, this one barely slept last night,' Adana says, rocking a buggy gently back and forth. 'I *love* the new hair, by the way. Did you go darker, as well as shorter?'

'Yeah, I figured if I've finished up in the clinic and moved house, I may as well have new hair too, even if it's just for the school run.' That's when I remember something. 'Adana, you went to school here in Edenvale, didn't you?'

'I sure did.'

'Do you know anything about the little girl who went missing from here years ago, Lily Murphy?' I manage to keep my

14

voice surprisingly even. 'It turns out she used to live in our new house.'

Adana's eyes widen.

'Oh God, Joanna. Really? Well, I guess all houses have history . . .' She blows air into her cheeks. 'That poor family. Remember they interviewed the father on TV? Heartbreaking. Oh, you were probably still living in London back then?'

'Yeah . . . But you lived here, didn't you?'

'Yes, right here in Oakbrook at that point, so everyone knew about it.'

The twin housing estates, Rowanbrook and Oakbrook, were built in the early sixties, one on either side of a broad, tree-lined avenue in Edenvale, in South Dublin. Luxury homes for families who wanted suburban quiet, huge gardens and a choice of golf courses, but without drifting too far from the city centre's glossy department stores and buzzy restaurants. Edenvale National School was in Oakbrook, and most kids from both estates went there, including Mark and Adana. By the time I met Adana at university, she'd moved from Oakbrook, and now lives just down the road in Dún Laoghaire.

'What do you remember?' I ask her now. 'Bafflingly, Mark hardly remembers anything. And clearly did not know the house we were buying once belonged to Lily Murphy's parents.'

'I remember it being a big thing back then, but I'd be blurry on the details now.' Adana tilts her head. 'And, in Mark's defence, I'd have had no idea which road in Rowanbrook they lived on, not to mind which house. Plus, he'd moved by then, hadn't he? He was living over here in Oakbrook.'

I nod to confirm this as Liz Landry, another mum from the class, arrives and stands beside us. She's taller than me even in her trainers, which I notice are that vegan brand everyone seems to have these days. Liz is an estate agent, and always gets the school-gate uniform just right – her dark brown hair is impervious to the breeze and she's wearing giant silver earrings with grey tassels that almost reach her collar bone, and lipstick in a perfect shade of pink. I glance down at my shorts and flip-flops. Four weeks into stay-at-home motherhood; four weeks out of smart work dresses, and I'm still figuring out my own new uniform. As yet, nothing feels quite me.

'Joanna,' Liz says, 'did I hear you're moving house?'

'You did – we're in already, two weeks now.'

'Is it Rowanbrook?'

I nod.

'That's where we are too – which cul-de-sac are you on?'

'Oh, I didn't realize! We're on Rowanbrook Drive. Where are you?'

'We're Santa Cruz, one of the older bungalows just after you turn in from the main road, on Rowanbrook Grove. Had you much work to do on the house?'

'It's got a few quirks and the decor is a bit bleak, but nothing we can't live with. We're blessed really.'

'Well,' Adana says, lowering her voice, 'except for the whole disappearing-child thing.'

'The what now?' Liz asks.

I fill her in, repeating everything I've just told Adana.

'Oh my God, I'd heard the story, but I had no idea they lived in Rowanbrook. Jesus.'

'Same,' I tell her. 'Actually, Liz, you're an estate agent, right?'

'Part-time now, but yes,' Liz says.

'Shouldn't our estate agent have told us the house had a history?'

Liz scrunches up her face and nods in a way that says *in theory, yes*.

'Legally?' I ask.

'No, not legally. Ethically, yes. *We* would always tell. There's no point in having a sale fall through at the last minute because someone finds out there's been, say, a violent death.'

Adana must see the worry in my face. She touches my arm. 'Look, all houses have a history and often we just don't know about it. It'll be fine.'

I nod with a certainty I don't feel. 'It'll have to be! And look, it's still the perfect house for us, nothing changes that.' Even as I say it, I know it's not true. The creeping unease I've been feeling since last night is spreading.

Any response Adana has is swallowed up by a bubble of noise bursting across the school yard, as kids pour through the doors. Ben bounces over, leaning his blond head in for a kiss. Emily follows shortly behind, dark ponytail bobbing. No kiss, and I know better than to try.

'Mum, I'm walking home with the girls, 'K?' Emily says, turning away before I can answer.

'See you at home, cross at the lights!' I call after her.

'When can I walk home on my own?' Ben asks.

'When you're Emily's age.'

'But I know the way, I'd be fine. It's not like I'm going to get kidnapped or something.'

Adana raises her eyebrows. 'Try telling that to Lily Murphy's mother,' she mutters under her breath. Then, louder: 'Joanna, am I still calling in later for a cuppa?'

'Definitely.'

At home, the house is stiflingly hot, with afternoon sun streaming through the narrow kitchen-diner windows. Somehow, despite this, the kitchen still feels bleak and austere and almost forbidding. Maybe it's the colour on the walls – a deep pine green, so dark it's almost black. The sooner we brighten this place up, the better, I think, moving towards the kitchen counter, where the kids are arguing over who can use the toaster first.

'I'll do the bagels, you guys go out and have a bounce on the trampoline,' I tell them, wondering if it's really awful that I want a bit of peace already, when we're only in the door from school.

As soon as they're outside, I haul the ancient sliding door shut and switch on the radio to catch the news. The heatwave permeates every headline – a possible hosepipe ban on the way, a drowning in a lake, and a gorse fire that spread to a farmhouse, killing its two occupants. Wincing, I switch off the radio and eye up the six unopened boxes by the kitchen-diner windows. But unpacking is unending, and my heart's not in it today. Instead, I go back to my Mac.

After a morning googling, I know the Wikipedia page off by heart and her image is branded on my brain. I've read the thirty-year-anniversary pieces and the few newspaper reports from 1985 that have been uploaded online. I know all of it. And yet, I keep searching and staring. Wondering if Lily Murphy can really be who I think she is. Was.

A shriek from outside pulls me back to reality. Through the window I can see Emily yanking Sophie away from something – they're down at the end of the garden, and the trampoline is in the way, so I can't see what. I shut the Mac and rush outside. Mark's voice is in my head as I run. *Calm down, you're such a panicker, the kids are fine!* But Mark's not here.

'What's going on, what's all the shouting?'

As I draw near, I realize Sophie's face and hands are covered in big, black blotches.

Emily stands back, relinquishing her grip on her little sister.

'What on earth – my God, Sophie!'

'Coal,' Emily says. 'She bit into it. Or tried to.'

'Coal? Where did you get coal?'

Sophie points to the far corner at the bottom of the garden, a shadowy spot obscured by low-hanging branches and tangled brambles. I make my way there, and the girls follow closely behind. It's only when I'm almost on top of it that I see it. Nestled into the trees, camouflaged by surrounding foliage, sits an old coal bunker. I move closer, noticing that the somewhat decrepit fence that divides our property from our absent neighbours' property comes to an abrupt end a few feet from the coal bunker, leaving a gap big enough for the kids to get through. And just beyond the coal bunker, there's another gap, this time in the fence that borders the back of the garden. It's quite hidden by dense evergreens, but if anyone can find an escape route, it's Sophie. Making a mental note to remind her not to leave our garden, I brush loose branches off the top of the coal bunker before lifting the cover to peer inside. It's still half full of coal. There's something unsettling about that – as though some long-gone owner left suddenly. Unexpectedly. I shake myself. This is the Lily Murphy story spooking me. Of course people don't take coal with them when they move house. I lower the cover, noticing that it's almost as high as my waist, and I wonder how Sophie could have got at it.

'She opened the hatch at the bottom,' Emily says, reading my thoughts.

Sure enough, there's a sliding metal hatch at ground level, currently open.

I turn to my youngest child.

'Sophie, why would you eat coal?'

'I didn't,' she says, the black dust on her lips belying her words. 'I just licked it.'

Back inside, after googling 'Is coal poisonous' and handing now-cold bagels to the kids, I revert to Wikipedia, as if it's going to say something new this time. But there's nothing new. Nothing that answers any of my questions at all. A disappearance. A commonly held belief that she drowned. Devastated parents who wouldn't give up. And a little girl who, the more I stare, looks just like the one in my nightmares.

4

June 2018

'MUM, ADANA'S HERE,' EMILY calls from her position at the bottom of the stairs, directly opposite the front door.

'Well, can you let her in?' I'm in the kitchen, my hands covered in a sticky, doughy scone batter.

Emily obliges, and Adana arrives into the kitchen giving me a sardonic smile.

'I see you've fallen for the "stay-at-home mums are always baking" myth.'

'Well, I figured I could try once a week – I never did any baking when I was working, and the kids were always saying they wished I was at home so we could bake together.'

'Mmm. And where are those wannabe bakers now?' she asks, pushing her fringe out of her eyes.

'Emily's on my phone, Ben's on the trampoline, and Sophie's trying her best not to lick coal. I see your point. Where are your gang?'

'Dave's working from home. I told him it was clock-off time and he was in charge,' Adana says, lifting a half-unpacked box of cookware from a kitchen chair and sitting down. 'So, how's stay-at-home mammy-ing going?'

'Good. Well, you know, fine. It's a bit quiet when they're at

21

school and then it's very loud when they're at home. It'd be nice if there was some kind of in-between.'

'I think the in-between you're seeking is your old job – adult company, not so quiet, not so loud. Fewer sticky handprints. I'd say you're loving the new house though? All the space?'

'Kind of . . . It's almost eerie here on my own in the mornings. I think if I paint the walls, it'll feel better. Less creepy.'

'Hmm. Is this about the decor or what you found out about the missing child?'

I consider my options. Adana is my oldest and closest friend; ever since we sat at the back of Theatre M in UCD, cogging notes off each other just before our Second Year exams. The first person I ever let into my life – though it's probably more accurate to say she forced her way in, insisting on befriending the studious loner. In theory, I can tell her anything. In practice, this extends to childbirth stories, office gossip, and complaining about how much time Mark spends on his phone. So, no (*God, no*), I can't tell Adana that I think I killed Lily Murphy. Jesus. Even thinking those words makes me ill.

'I suppose it's a bit about Lily Murphy,' I say instead. 'It's surreal. Like, her mother probably sat here, right in this very spot.'

'Or not,' Adana says, matter-of-factly. 'Isn't this part an extension?'

'Well, yeah, but I don't know when it was built. Anyway, you know what I mean. It's eerie.'

'Those poor people.'

'I know. How would you ever get over that?' I glance out of the window at Sophie and Ben. 'Right, I'll make that coffee.'

'Can I use your laptop to google her story?'

I slide the Mac across the table and open a new tab for her. By the time I'm back with two coffees, she's already on to the second page of search results: more anniversary pieces, a cold-case feature, some Reddit threads, a true-crime forum post, and a renewed appeal for information.

'Sorry,' she says, 'I skipped ahead – do you want me to go back to the Wiki page?'

'No, I read it four hundred times this morning, I know it off by heart.'

Adana nods and clicks 'next' at the bottom of the screen.

At the top of the third page, there's a website called Deep-Dive.ie with an article dated 3 May, entitled 'What Really Happened to Lily? For the news you can't get in the news, this is Deep Dive'.

'Might be some crackpot,' Adana mutters. 'Doesn't even give a name.' But she clicks in anyway.

It's almost thirty-three years since Lily Murphy disappeared near her South Dublin home. The media won't cover it this year (it's just the ten-year anniversaries now) but is there anything new to say? Did they say everything back then or are there gaps; little gaps like the ones between newly built houses, or bigger gaps, wide as a river?

They said she's believed to have drowned. Is that because it's the only explanation or the simplest explanation?

What about the questions nobody ever asked at all?

Which neighbour was interviewed multiple times by gardaí but kept hush-hush? Why did local gossip focus on strangers and not on those who lived inside Rowanbrook's leafy enclaves? What about those whispers – only ever whispers – that some of the people there that day knew more than they disclosed? And worst of all, is there any truth to the story of Lily Murphy and the locked room?

*

23

The locked room.

My chest tightens and my breath feels suddenly shallow. Adana glances up.

'Are you OK? You're white as a ghost!'

'I . . . I—'

'Joanna?'

Deep breath.

'I'm fine. Just . . . just thinking about that poor little girl, and the idea that someone locked her somewhere . . .'

Adana looks at me quizzically, unconvinced. But in all the time we've known each other, I've never told, and today is not that day.

'It sounds like this Deep Dive person might know some more details about the story. We could ask them?'

I nod and click to the comment section at the end of the blog post. It's just the default comment functionality, but it's worth a try. I start to type:

> Hi, I've just read your blog post. I've recently moved into the house Lily Murphy used to live in and am curious about her story but also finding it a little unsettling! I would like to find out more and would be interested in emailing you directly if you'd be open to that?

I put my email address in the mandatory field and hit submit.

Adana is already moving on to other things – the heatwave, the plague of homework, and the way the sun makes you want a glass of rosé even though it's only Thursday and not yet six o'clock. I smile and nod and play my part, just as I always do. But I can't get the memory out of my head: a little girl, blonde hair, dimpled smile, and a locked room.

5

It was only when Mark arrived in from work and wondered if he'd have time for a shower 'before we have to leave' that I remembered we were due at his parents' house at seven. Susie and Tom Stedman, matriarch and patriarch of the eight-strong Stedman family, and the last people I want to see tonight.

But now we're here, sitting on their back patio, drinks in hand, and Susie is giving a running commentary on everything they've had done with the garden.

'You need to hire a gardener for your new house as soon as possible,' she says to Mark. 'Shouldn't they, Tom?'

Tom nods. 'What you need is a good strong fellow from Eastern Europe. They're the ones to get for the gardens.'

Mark and I exchange a glance. But there's no point in saying anything. Tom thinks we're all far too politically correct these days.

'Yes,' Susie says. 'I have a man you can borrow. I'll bring his details when we come over for the housewarming tomorrow night.'

I quite like our unruly flower beds and we can't afford a gardener, but I leave it to Mark to respond. When it comes to Susie's unsolicited advice, it is *always* easier to let Mark do the talking.

This is why she likes me so much and has no idea what's going on inside my head.

'Mum, you can't really say "I have a man you can borrow" – it sounds a bit . . . like you own him?'

'Pah. Don't be silly. Joanna understands, don't you, Joanna?'

I nod and smile, and sip my gin.

'I'm sure you had a whole team of gardeners when you were little,' she continues, glancing down as she crosses one delicate ankle over the other. Susie is very fond of her delicate ankles. 'The upkeep on those grounds would have been extraordinary. Am I right?'

Oh God, here we go.

'Well, I wouldn't say a whole team . . .' Her face drops in disappointment. 'But yes, we definitely needed a gardener,' I add, to make her happy.

'There you go!' Triumphant. 'Now, I know this garden isn't anything like what you were used to as a child, Joanna, but even so, it's worth making the effort. Did your parents garden much themselves?'

Mark tenses beside me. He rarely brings up my parents. Susie, though, did some kind of psychology course ten years ago and believes in confronting sensitive topics at every opportunity.

'Not really. They both worked a lot and when they weren't working, they were travelling or hosting parties. Not much time left for gardening, I'm afraid.'

'It must have been so glamorous.' Susie sounds wistful. 'I can just imagine the parties and London society life.' She shakes her head. 'Nothing like that around here. Dublin in the eighties – well, we were a little drab.'

'I can't imagine you were ever drab!' I tell her, because it's what she wants to hear but also because it's true. I've seen the photos. 1960s Susie with long, dark lashes and Brigitte Bardot hair. 1970s Susie with feathery layers and huge floppy sunhats. 1980s Susie with a smart blonde bob and brood of children. She was a chameleon to each decade, and she was never drab.

'You *are* sweet, Joanna. And we had some good times, didn't we, Tom? Dinners and dances and trips to Marbella. It wasn't all grey and dismal.'

'Yeah, those trips to Marbella were *amazing*,' Mark says, with exaggerated emphasis. 'Oh, wait, I wouldn't know. You never brought us.'

'Oh, Mark, you had plenty of holidays. Marbella was just for your dad and me. That's allowed.'

Mark shakes his head at me in mock exasperation. 'Imagine if *we* did that: booked a babysitter for a week and headed off to Spain without the kids. Great life they had!'

Susie makes a clicking noise with her tongue. 'It was different back then. You didn't have all these creches and car seats and not leaving your child outside the shop. It's all gone very politically correct.'

Mark and I exchange another hidden eye-roll. This is why we don't let Susie and Tom mind our kids.

'Yep,' says Mark. 'Back then you could just leave your six kids with a babysitter who hardly knew her left hand from her right, crossing your fingers she didn't lose any of them. Remember the one with the blonde straggly hair?'

'She wasn't *that* bad,' Susie says, but her cheeks are pink now.

'Mum, she literally forgot me at the park one day. One of the neighbours found me and brought me home. Ines O'Brien, wasn't it, who brought me back? The Spanish lady?'

'And aren't you fine? No harm done.'

'And still you kept using the same babysitter – for years after! I could have been a statistic. A child on a missing poster.'

This is my in. I take a sip of gin to coat my throat. 'Speaking of missing children, we found out that Lily Murphy, that little girl who disappeared in 1985, used to live in our new house. Did you know the family?'

A beat. And now it's Susie and Tom exchanging a look.

'Your house is the Murphys' old house?' Susie says. 'My goodness . . . gosh, of course . . . when you said it was Rowanbrook Drive, I should really have made the connection. That's quite . . . unsettling.'

'So you knew them back then?'

'Well, yes. Everyone knew everyone. And *everyone* knew Robbie and Mary. They were the golden couple of Rowanbrook. He was *very* handsome, all big warm grins and dimpled cheeks.' She smiles fondly at the memory.

'I guess that's where the little girl, Lily, got her dimples,' I say, keeping my tone casual.

Susie tilts her head. 'Are dimples hereditary? They're hardly rare. Anyway, yes. They were the golden couple. Mary was beautiful. *Stunning*. A bit exotic, I suppose.'

'Exotic?'

'She was from California. They were like a Hollywood couple, but no airs and graces. Robbie was the friendliest man you could meet, threw the best parties. And Mary – she could come across as shy but it was more that she wasn't a chatterbox like the rest of us. And a little nervous about fitting in, I think, though she hid it well.' She sighs. 'Gosh, we used to have great fun at those parties.'

'So you were friends?'

'Yes, we were friends.' Susie shakes her head. 'I never realized it was the same house . . . goodness, Mark, you sent me the link and everything. But it looks quite different?'

'Yeah, I think the outside used to be grey, back in the eighties. It's been done up since, the whole lot plastered over and painted white. Not much done to the inside though,' he adds with a rueful smile, 'that's been left to us. Speaking of inside, I'm going to get a beer – anyone like another drink?'

Susie and Tom are both fine. I ask Mark for another gin and tonic, and to check on the kids, who, after a perfunctory 'how's school?' quiz, have retreated to their grandparents' TV. Getting them up tomorrow morning will be painful – especially Sophie – but Susie insists on inviting us in the evening time, so that her days are free for golf.

I turn to Susie. 'What do you remember about the disappearance?'

She shakes her head. 'It was a dreadful time. Police asking questions, locals gossiping, lots of finger-pointing. The poor little thing drowned, no doubt, but it didn't stop people spreading rumours.'

'What kind of rumours?'

'That a local man was involved – questioned by the guards. Victor O'Brien was his name. Poor Victor, God rest him. He and his wife were friends of ours. Tom was great pals with Victor.' Tom nods, on autopilot it seems, and Susie keeps talking.

'Victor was married to Ines, our Spanish neighbour who found Mark in the park that time. It was all nonsense, of course, Victor had nothing to do with it.' She tucks a white-blonde strand behind her ear. 'There was also an altercation between a neighbour called Eddie something and Robbie Murphy, Lily's father. Robbie ended up with a broken arm or sprained wrist. I remember he had his arm in a sling that morning, during the search.' She purses her lips. 'Dreadful. Luckily for him he was left-handed or he'd have been off work for weeks on top of everything else. And he had a *very* good job. An accountant, but not one of those regular ones – a super-successful one. A high-flyer, that was Robbie.' She shakes her head. 'Such awful, uncouth behaviour in a grown man. Eddie I mean, not Robbie,' she adds quickly. 'Now, I'm fairly sure the child drowned, but if not, my money would be on Eddie.' She looks around, checking the kids aren't in earshot perhaps, before continuing. 'The most dreadful rumour was that there was something between Robbie Murphy and a local girl.' The glint in Susie's eye belies her 'most dreadful' claim. 'I can't remember her name now. Tom, do you remember?'

Tom frowns in concentration. 'Small girl, the pretty one?'

Susie nods. 'Yes, that's her.'

'Can't think of it. Gorgeous little thing, she was.'

'Yes. Anyway,' Susie continues, 'the other rumour was that it had something to do with a young fella called Gavin. He was always hanging around; I mean literally, just hanging around outside the Murphys' house. There'd been some break-ins too, including one at the Murphys', so her disappearance was linked with that by some people. Mostly because there was little or no crime back then, so it seemed logical that there must be a connection. The police never confirmed it though, so . . .' She shrugs, a delicate movement in her neat red blazer, as Mark arrives back with a gin and tonic for me.

'All OK with the kids?' I ask.

'Yeah. Emily has a bit of a headache but she'll be fine.'

Susie starts to get up. 'Oh, the poor thing. I'll run in and get her some paracetamol.'

I put my hand up. 'No, she's fine, honestly.'

Susie shakes her head. 'I don't know why you always want to suffer on – there are no medals for it, you know. And God invented paracetamol so we don't have to put up with pain. At least let me give her a spoon of Calpol. I have an old bottle somewhere.'

'Please don't. She'll be fine with a glass of water.' The 'old bottle of Calpol' is another reason we don't let Tom and Susie babysit. Susie has a loose relationship with use-by dates and dosage when it comes to medicine, even with other people's children.

She hovers above her chair. 'Sometimes I think you forget that I had six of my own. I know what I'm doing.' She sits down. 'Anyway, back to Lily Murphy. What else do you want to know?'

I take a sip of my gin and try to think what to ask next. None of what Susie's said sounds in any way familiar – I don't remember anyone called Victor or Eddie or Gavin from my childhood. This puts a few more weights on the *I didn't kill Lily Murphy* side of the scale. I'm still guilty of taking a life, nothing changes that. But maybe she wasn't Lily. The images I've been staring at for twenty-four hours are skewing perspectives, that's all. Distorting memories.

'I'm not sure what I want to know, really . . . I'm just morbidly fascinated, I guess. Strange to think of such a tragic story taking place right there in our new house. Those poor parents.'

Susie reaches across and pats my knee. 'I imagine it's making you think of your own childhood. It's like a reversal of your story, isn't it – they lost their child, you lost your parents.'

Mark stiffens again.

'I can't help thinking losing a child must be worse,' I tell her, and I mean it.

'Be that as it may, it doesn't diminish your own experience. There's always someone who has it worse, but losing your parents at such a young age and in such horrific circumstances . . .' Her voice cracks. God, she drives me mad sometimes, but she means well. I put my hand on hers.

Mark clears his throat. 'I'll go check the kids again, see if Emily's feeling OK. And Ben and Sophie were arguing over what to watch so I better make sure they're not killing each other . . .'

'Tell them to mind the couch, won't you?' Susie calls after him as he disappears inside. 'No feet on the furniture.'

She turns to me. 'Those beautiful kids of yours. You know, spending time with my grandchildren is one of my greatest joys in life.' She says it without the slightest hint of irony. 'I'm sure you must be sad that your own mother never got to meet her grandchildren.'

If only you knew. 'Of course. But you more than make up for it, Susie. The kids are lucky.'

She preens, batting away the compliment. 'Goodness, I just do what any grandmother would do.' A pause. 'Joanna, you look a bit wan tonight. Are you OK?'

'I'm fine. It's just this whole Lily Murphy story . . . it's unsettling.'

'I'd say try to forget about it if you can. I push it out of my head any time it pops in – it's just too sad. And especially when she was their only child.' She pauses again. 'That must have made it extra hard for you too, Joanna, when you lost your parents. Being an only child.'

I nod into my gin, unable to speak. I wasn't always an only child. Not until I killed my sister.

6

'Now, who wants an Aperol Spritz?' I'm brandishing a jug of orange-coloured fizz and wearing my brightest hostess smile. This is the well-practised version of Joanna my friends and family are used to. Guilt clings to me permanently, like stale smoke in my hair, but I'm very good at disguising it. From the patio doors, I take stock. The sun has already dipped below the tall trees at the back of the garden, but strings of solar lights are coming to life and the buzz of noise has risen. Someone – Mark or one of the kids presumably – has put music on. It looks normal and lovely and welcoming and warm. How a housewarming *should* look. And I will act the part, because that is what I do.

Fran from next door, dressed in a Hawaiian shirt belted over a long green skirt, eyes up the jug.

'What on earth is that?' she asks, holding out her empty wine glass.

'You'll love it.' I step closer to pour, taking in the surfboard-and-palm-tree print on her shirt, and the brown leather belt with the rather incongruous rhinestone buckle.

'Go on, so. At least I don't have far to get home. I can't remember when I last had drinks with the neighbours.'

'Oh, really? What about the people who lived here before us?'

'It's been rented mostly over the years – expensive corporate rentals, people staying for a few months before finding somewhere more permanent. Since the Murphys lived here, I never really got to know anyone.'

'When did they sell up?'

'Not *they* – Robbie dropped dead of a heart attack just before Christmas of '85. The more dramatic neighbours said he died of a broken heart, once he accepted Lily was gone.' Fran shakes her head, her drop-pearl earrings catching the evening sunlight. 'Mary never accepted it though. As far as I remember from my mother, she sold up because she couldn't afford the house after Robbie died, but she still came back, searching and hoping, even though the whole world knew the poor child had drowned.'

'Oh my God, that's awful. What a sad history this place has had.'

We both turn to look at the house. The peeling paint and rust stains that fleck the back wall are at odds with the freshly painted front exterior, and suddenly make the house seem neglected. Neglected and sad. I shiver despite the warm evening.

'Ah, look, I'm depressing you,' Fran says. 'You go and see to your guests, I'll finish my orange cocktail and go inside to snoop through your living room bookshelves. Good plan?'

Good plan. I move down the lawn to a couple of would-be Aperol Spritz drinkers – Liz Landry and a woman I don't know.

'Joanna, the house is gorgeous!' Liz says. She's wearing a long, monochrome wrap dress and huge black hoop earrings. 'And the garden! Ours is tiny, I'm very jealous.'

'Thanks, Liz, we're delighted.'

Liz turns to the woman beside her. 'Joanna, this is Cora, another Rowanbrook resident. She lives next door to me. We were chatting at the gate when I was on my way over and she decided to come along too.' Liz's eyes widen in a *hope that's OK* way.

I smile and nod and shake Cora's hand, wondering what kind of person invites themselves to a housewarming, but then again, the more the merrier.

'So, Cora, have you lived in Rowanbrook long?'

Cora begins an extraordinarily protracted story in which she lists every single place she's ever lived, while we listen politely. She's in her early forties, I reckon, with faded sandy hair in a mass of curls framing her small face. Her navy t-shirt is pulled at the neck as though it's been warped by too many washes, and over it, she's layered a pine-green denim jacket. She wears no make-up, and her small eyes dart from me to Liz and back while she tells her story, as though unsure (quite rightly) of her listeners' interest.

'So, in the end,' Cora eventually concludes, 'I'm back in my parents' old house, God rest them. I'm only there a month, but it's as though I never left.'

Just like Fran next door, I think, wondering if Cora was here when Lily Murphy disappeared. I examine her face again. Definitely early forties. And something else. Something familiar? Or is it just because I've been standing here listening to her life story, staring at her face for too long?

'So, to some extent, you're a newbie, like me,' I say, raising the jug of Aperol Spritz. 'Cheers to that.'

Liz raises her glass. 'I'm just delighted to have a party that's in walking distance – I'm always envious when I see neighbours in and out of each other's houses for wine. Now I have a wine buddy.'

I grin and clink the jug against her glass. I've known Liz since Ben started school, but only from the occasional class coffee morning or end-of-term night out. The trouble with working long hours is you never get to do the school run, though that novelty quickly wears off, I'm learning. We bonded on our first class night out over a shared love of gin cocktails and a shared antipathy towards school dress-up days.

'How mean of your neighbours to drink wine in each other's houses and not invite you!' I say now.

'Rowanbrook can be a bit closed to outsiders and I'm the blow-in.' Liz takes a sip from her glass. 'Only here ten years. I expect by the time the kids are graduating, we'll be getting the invite for Christmas Day eggnog.'

'Is it really like that?' I ask, lowering my voice.

'Ah, it's nice here, but I'm delighted to have someone my own age nearby and the kids will be able to play on the green together. Lots of elderly people on our road, so my kids are constantly complaining there's no one to hang out with. As if we should have known that back when we first viewed the house.'

'Out of interest – and not that I'm obsessing over houses and macabre histories or anything,' I say with a grimace, 'but was it easier to buy the house because you're an estate agent? I guess you know all the insider secrets?'

'Hmm. In general, it makes it easier to rule places *out* – to read between the lines on the brochure. But same as anyone else, when you find the house you love, you just *know*. In my case, I didn't buy at all – my husband bought it, and I simply moved in. I liked the house and decided to marry him. There's worse reasons to marry someone, you know,' she says with a wink.

Cora looks taken aback. 'I can't tell if you're serious or not. You're only joking, aren't you?'

'Well, let's just say, it was supposed to be one of my colleagues showing my now-husband the house that day, but I switched things so I could do it. And here I am, ten years on, mistress of said house, in all its single-storey, slightly cramped, mid-century glory. Girls, you never know when a tiny and slightly sneaky manipulation of a work schedule can change your life.'

'And what happened to your colleague,' I ask, 'the one whose place you took?'

'Oh – he had a wife, a house and three kids already – I'm fairly confident I didn't do him out of anything. Though my husband is *very* good-looking, so who knows,' she says, grinning. 'It could have been my colleague ensconced with him in Santa Cruz instead of me.'

Cora still looks unsure about how to take all of this.

'I love the house name,' I say to Liz. 'I'd quite like to choose a name for our house. What made you pick "Santa Cruz"?'

'We didn't, it was called that by a previous owner – a nod to where she was originally from, I believe. But it's nice, isn't it. Makes me think of sun.'

And with that, Cora is off on a very long story about a coach tour holiday she did ten years ago and why she'd never do it again.

I hold up the jug of certainly-lukewarm Aperol Spritz when she reaches the end.

'Can I get either of you a drink?'

They're fine, they say, raising their glasses, and I go back up the garden, through the back door into the utility room to get more ice.

As I stand at the freezer, scooping ice cubes into the jug, I glance through the doorway to the kitchen. Fran from next door is standing by the sink, staring out through the kitchen window, at something or someone in the back garden. She tilts her head, squinting, as though not quite sure what she's seeing. Trance-like, she reaches into her bag and pulls out her phone. Slowly, she lifts it, frames something in the shot, and clicks. I stand up straight and step closer to the doorway to get a better look. Instinctively, I move silently, taking care not to disturb her. I crane my neck, trying to look through the window, to see what she can see. My angle is off, and I can't improve it without moving closer, but I can make out at least some of what's in the photo. A pear tree, strung with lights. Falling dusk. People. Liz and Cora, just outside the kitchen window. Emily, sitting on the grass, scrolling through my phone. Beyond her, some couples from the next road over, chatting under an apple tree. Just behind are Susie and Tom, deep in conversation with Mark, who has Sophie by the hand. And beyond them, Adana and Dave with their kids. Why is Fran taking photographs of my housewarming guests? And, I wonder, looking at my new neighbour, which of them has provoked the deep frown on her face?

7

GEORGE EZRA IS SINGING about bikini bottoms and lager tops when I go back outside, and I can see Ben standing by the speaker, singing along. I'm not entirely sure the lyrics are appropriate, but I choose my battles. So 'No' to Instagram (Emily's greatest earthly wish) and 'No' to playing *Minecraft* in bed (something Ben claims everyone in his class is allowed to do), but no comment either way on George Ezra's bikini bottoms. Besides, my mind is still on Fran's photograph and the expression on her face as she looked through the kitchen window.

I spot Adana standing on her own now by the trampoline and walk over to join her.

'Thinking of having a go?' I ask as I draw near.

'With *my* pelvic floor? No chance. Are you enjoying meeting your new neighbours – did you ask any of them about Lily Murphy?'

Her name makes my skin prickle but I keep my expression neutral. 'I met a woman called Cora who lived here in Rowanbrook when she was a child, though I didn't ask her about the disappearance. Yet. I asked Mark's mother about it last night.' I fill her in on the back-then gossip about Victor O'Brien and Eddie Something and the Small Pretty Girl.

'You're a right little Nancy Drew, aren't you,' Adana says with a grin.

My attempt to match her smile falls short. 'I suppose I just want peace of mind.' I glance around. 'The whole thing is making me feel sad about the house, and a bit . . . spooked. So I just want to know that what they think happened is what really happened. That she fell in the river. That it was an accident.' *That it wasn't me.*

'But what if she didn't fall in the river?' Adana asks. 'What if you find out something even worse happened? Do you really want to know?'

That, I think, as I notice Fran still looking out of the window, is a good question.

Susie is bearing down on us, one hand aloft in greeting, the dewy lawn sucking her kitten heels.

'Joanna! We are *loving* your party. Tom's just taking a little break inside, so I thought I'd do the rounds. So strange to be back in this garden, all these years later . . . I remember the parties Mary and Robbie used to have. Gosh, they were happy times. And always the best food and drink. You know how some people hide the good wine when they have guests?'

I nod, hoping this isn't a reference to Mark and me, and the ten-euro-a-bottle supermarket Malbec we bought for tonight.

'Well, Robbie and Mary were the opposite. Best wine, best whiskey. Super hosts. I remember once they even hired staff to cater. Just neighbourhood girls but still, believe me, nobody did that in the eighties.' Her gaze travels the breadth of the garden again. 'So strange to think back on everything that happened . . . Anyway, we won't dwell.' She turns to Adana. 'Adana, isn't it? We met at Emily's tenth birthday party?'

'Yes, nice to see you again, Mrs Stedman.'

'Oh, don't be Mrs Stedman'ing me – I'll feel ancient! Where are you from originally, Adana?'

I wince, knowing exactly what Susie means, but it doesn't faze Adana.

'We're just down the road in Dún Laoghaire, near Joanna's old house, but I'm from here originally – I grew up in Oakbrook.'

'Yes, but I mean—' Susie looks her up and down, then decides against what she was about to say. 'Oakbrook is where *we* are! I'm absolutely thrilled to have Joanna and Mark so near. Actually, why don't you both join my Edenvale Ladies' Book Club? We're looking for new members in the locality.'

Adana's eyes widen and I hide a smile.

'Honestly,' Susie goes on, 'you'll love it. We're reading one about this girl who disappears and her husband's trying to find her. I can't think of the name. First Tuesday of the month, eight p.m., rotating around the houses. Oh.' She stops and looks at me. 'That's your you-know-what time, isn't it? Your' – she lowers her voice to a whisper, although Adana, the only other person in earshot, can still hear her perfectly – '*therapy?*'

'Yes. It's OK to say it.' I smile. 'It's not a secret. Adana knows.'

'It's different now, I suppose,' Susie concedes. 'Back in my day, only people on American TV shows went to therapy. But after what you went through, I'm not one bit surprised. Although . . .' She pauses. I brace myself. 'You'd think she'd be done by now? Dr Kinsella? That she'd have, you know, cured you? I mean, she's a *doctor*, after all. Are you sure you're going to the best person? It's been years . . .'

So much for her psychology course. 'Well, she's a therapist with a doctorate, as opposed to a medical doctor, but either way, it's not really about *curing*. I was sent to grief counselling after my parents died, and all through my time at boarding school.' This is a story I know off by heart. 'And then it morphed into just regular therapy. You don't have to be ill to go to therapy.'

'Of course. And you know best, being a therapist yourself.' She stops again and I can almost see the thoughts rolling through her head: *Why can't Joanna just fix herself?* 'Anyway,' she goes on, 'I'm sure it's money well spent. Mark was saying the fees are quite high – will you need to cut back now you're not working?'

This makes me squirm. Has Mark really been telling his mother about the payments? Susie continues without waiting for my answer.

'You might cut back in time, I suppose. But anyway, we often move book club to Wednesday if someone can't come. Will I keep you posted? I will.' Susie's superpower is answering her own questions. She lifts her glass to clink with mine. 'Isn't it absolutely gorgeous to be outdoors at this time of evening. I know we're supposed to be against climate change and all that, but I'd love this heatwave to last for ever. Although' – she lowers her voice – 'did you hear that awful news story about the gorse fire? Two people dead, asleep in their beds. I just—' She stops abruptly and puts her hand over her mouth. 'Oh, goodness, I've done it again, haven't I? Sorry, Joanna. The last thing you want to talk about is people being killed in fires.'

Even Adana, unflappable Adana, is uncomfortable now. I can feel it emanating from her.

'It's OK! Honestly, Susie, it was all so long ago. I'm fine.' I reach to touch her arm. Smoothing over. Fixing. Placating. Because that is what I do.

8

'MUM, BEN WON'T LET me watch anything on the den TV and Sophie's watching *PAW Patrol* in the sitting room – can I have your phone?'

I pass it to Emily as Mark stands at the sink, shaking his head with a faux-mournful expression.

'You know, when we were small, there were only two TV channels, and we all watched the same thing on Saturday mornings. It was called *Anything Goes* and—'

'Dad, stop! We know already, you've told us a gazillion times. You do get that only having two channels doesn't actually mean life was better back then, right?' She sweeps out of the kitchen, head already bent over my phone.

Mark shrugs. 'They don't know what they're missing. Life was easier back in two-channel land.'

'Yes, yes, and the summers were hotter and everyone played outdoors from dawn till dusk, I know the drill.' I dig him gently in the ribs. 'Speaking of childhood – did you get to meet Fran last night? Reintroduce yourself?'

'No – I saw her across the garden and I recognized her, but I never got the chance to say hi. I'm sure I'll see her around if she's only next door.' He fills a glass of water and swallows half of it. 'God. I'm getting too old for parties. Anyway, I'd better start cleaning up the garden.'

As Mark gathers empty bottles from the lawn, I start the even less appealing task of sorting out the attic. Christmas decorations, suitcases, winter clothes and old kitchen chairs 'in case we need them' are sprawled all over the place, thrown up here when we moved in. Now, there's no space near the hatch, and I need to move things to the eaves. I'm an hour into the task when I come across a battered cardboard box, deep in a dark corner where the roof meets the floor. It's not one of ours, as far as I can tell. Pushing aside thoughts of spiders and mice, I lift the lid and shine my phone inside. Lying face down across the top is a picture frame. It's big – about twenty inches square – and heavier than I expect when I turn it over. At first it looks like it's a painting, but actually it's a photograph, I think, bleached by time. A photograph of a pier, stretching out into the ocean. The kind you see on the west coast of America. There's no glass protecting the photograph and it's thick with dust. I set it aside and turn back to the box, which appears to be full of books – paperbacks and hardbacks, titles I recognize from the seventies and eighties. Mostly American authors, at least at first glance. And a video tape. A blank one used for recording from TV. I pick it up, squinting at the handwritten label: *Lily Age 3, 1985*.

Downstairs, I stare at the video cassette, wondering. Will it tell me anything – confirm that I had nothing to do with Lily's disappearance? How can I play it? I'm googling 'transferring film from video tape to digital' when the doorbell rings. Emily answers, and when I come out to the hall, I find Fran standing on the doorstep, holding out a corkscrew.

'I found it in my pocket. Sorry. I'm not usually a thief.'

'Oh, no worries – thanks for bringing it back!'

She passes it to me, but I fumble, and both the video cassette and the corkscrew clatter to the hall floor. Fran picks up the video and Emily, rolling her eyes, picks up the corkscrew.

'Old home movies?' Fran asks, handing back the cassette.

I hold it up so she can see the sticker on the front.

'I found it in the attic. I think it's a video of Lily.'

'Have you watched it?'

'Well, no. I don't have a video player.'

Fran's eyebrows go up, as though it isn't actually 2018 and it isn't unusual to still possess a video recorder.

'Do you not? How do you watch videos?'

'We don't, I suppose. We have Netflix and there are DVD drives in the TVs . . . Why, do you have one?'

She nods. I wait, but no invitation is forthcoming.

'Do you think we could . . .'

Still nothing.

'. . . watch it in your house? If you're not busy?'

A small sigh. I'm not sure if it's because I'm being too direct or she has no interest in watching it, or something else, but then she nods and beckons me to follow, which is how, after shouting back to Mark that I'm popping out for a few minutes, I find myself making my first visit next door.

Fran's house is a replica of ours on the outside, but completely different inside. Where our ground floor is gloomy and dark, Fran's is a rainbow of twentieth-century hues: bottle-green carpet in the hall, with stripy red-and-cream wallpaper on the walls, while in the sitting room, the carpet is dusky blue, and the walls deep pink. There are piles of newspapers and magazines on both armchairs and on the small glass-topped coffee table that sits in the centre of the room. A floor-to-ceiling built-in shelving unit is home to knick-knacks and souvenirs from

Fran's – or someone's – trips abroad. I spot a small gold Eiffel Tower, a green Murano glass vase, and a 'Los Angeles' snow-globe (perhaps appropriately) without any snow. Books fill the top four shelves and I'm not surprised now that she wanted a look through our books last night. My eyes scan the covers while my neighbour goes out to put on the kettle. Fran has eclectic tastes. I spot the distinctive orange spines of Penguin classics dotted between familiar contemporary crime titles, along with non-fiction books on everything from American history to Roswell to the JonBenét Ramsey mystery.

I step away from the bookshelves as Fran returns from the kitchen and gestures for me to take a seat. This is no easy task – one side of the couch is home to a stack of newspapers, and the other holds a camera and a photography magazine. I remove the camera, placing it carefully on the floor, and am reminded of the photo Fran took through the kitchen window last night. I open my mouth to ask her about it but can't find the right words. And maybe Fran is just someone who likes taking photos. With the lights and the drinks and the falling dusk, it was, no doubt, a pretty picture. This gives me an idea.

'Last night seemed to go well and we were blessed with the weather – I've no photos though! Such a lovely, sunny evening and I forgot to take even one picture.'

'Ah well, I'm sure your friends took some,' Fran says. 'People are always snapping away on their phones. I don't get it myself. Dozens of photos of the same thing, then they never look at them again. Give me a proper camera any day, and proper printed photos.' Fran points at the wall above my head. I turn to see a dozen framed images of a variety of blond boys, one tall red-haired woman, and a somewhat awkward-looking girl I recognize as Fran.

I nod, disappointed my brainwave hasn't paid off, and watch as Fran pulls her glasses down from the crown of her head and puts the video in the recorder. I half expect to see an old box-shaped television like we had when I was a child, but Fran's one nod to modernity is a sleek flat-screen TV.

It flickers to life and the video recording begins to play, opening with a handmade sign in red marker on what looks like a page pulled from a copybook. It reads *Lily's 3rd birthday!* and I feel a creep of unease as we watch. The camera swings away from the page and hovers on a windowsill above a kitchen sink. The picture blurs but we can still make out the objects on the sill – a souvenir plate on a stand, a porcelain Alice in Wonderland, and a little white lighthouse with a green band at the top. The picture clears, then blurs, then clears once more as someone corrects the focus, and now the camera swings to a group of people at a kitchen table. A small girl stands on a chair, eyes wide as a cake is carried towards her. Her blonde curls reach just below her ears, pinned back from her forehead with a pink hairclip. Her dress is red with white polka dots and short puffed sleeves. Her hands – tiny hands – reach up as though to catch the cake. Laughter from those around her. *God. God. Oh God, oh God. That face. That little face.* White noise pumps in my ears now and I have to force myself to concentrate. It all matters. Any one of these people could be the link.

'I remember this,' Fran says. 'I think I was there that day. I wonder will I see myself. Goodness.'

We watch and wait and I'm staring at Lily, but it doesn't tell me anything really, and then the person holding the cake comes into focus, visible in side-profile. Tall and slender, dark hair in a bun, wearing a long turquoise-blue dress and a wide smile for her daughter. I shiver. *Mary.* I've seen photos of her online and to that extent, she's familiar. The distraught mother, searching desperately for her missing child. But not beyond that. She is not, I think, a person from my past.

The camera jerks down, showing a man's shoes, then up again. A male voice says something inaudible. More laughter. The camera pulls back, panning across the wider group of people as they sing 'Happy Birthday'. I lean closer. To Lily's right is a child of seven or eight, with a mass of springy curls the colour of sand, and a tiny, freckled face. She's wearing a red spotty dress quite like Lily's and a matching bow in her hair. Her gaze is not on the camera but on Lily. To her right stands a thin woman with dark hair. Like Mary, she wears it in a bun, but on her, it's severe, pulling her features, making her sharp. She's staring, unsmiling, at Mary. Fran points at the woman.

'That's Ines O'Brien, the one giving Mary dagger-looks.'

Ines O'Brien, I think, the Spanish woman who brought Mark home when his babysitter forgot him at the park. Married to Victor O'Brien, who was questioned by police. I stare at Ines as on screen, she stares at Mary. There is something there. Something familiar. Maybe.

Beside Ines is a fair-haired, bearded man with his hands in his pockets and an impatient look on his florid face.

'The man with the beard is Victor, Ines's husband. And that's Cora,' Fran says, pointing at the small, curly-haired girl with the bow in her hair. 'Their daughter.' She glances at me as though waiting for a reaction, then continues. 'Cora was with Lily the day it happened, hiding with her. She's never mentioned by name in the reports, but that's who they're talking about. The last person to see Lily alive.'

The last person to see Lily alive. Or was that me? I clear my throat.

'Cora. I met her.'

'Really?' Fran looks at me over the top of her glasses.

'Last night, there was a woman called Cora at the party, maybe you saw her? It must be the same person – it's not a common name, and the Cora I met grew up here.' I squint at the TV, doing calculations in my head. 'She was in her early forties, which'd be about right.'

'God, I haven't seen Cora O'Brien in thirty years, I'm not sure I'd recognize her. Why was she at your party?'

I look at Fran. There's something in her tone that I can't quite place.

'She's living back here. She inherited her parents' house and moved in last month. I got the blow-by-blow account at the party. You didn't see her?'

Fran shakes her head. Again, I can't help feeling I'm missing something.

'A mum I know from the school is her neighbour, and Cora kind of tagged along with her. *Has* to be her.' I look at the TV screen again, at the small, pale child. It *must* be.

I turn my attention to the other people in the video.

'So, I assume the woman holding the cake is Mary?'

'Yes, no mistaking Mary. She was always beautiful. They made a very good-looking couple, herself and Robbie. And people loved them. Loved being around them. Probably helped that they were generous and always had the best parties. Best baby-sitting gig around too.'

Mary's turquoise dress seems to shimmer around her, the thin straps delicate against her neat, tanned shoulders. With her oversized sunglasses on the crown of her head, she looks every inch a California girl beside her less glamorous neighbours.

'I wonder did it bug them,' I say.

'What?'

'Mary. People don't always like *different*.'

'Tell me about it,' Fran says. 'Try being the tallest girl in the class your whole life. A carthorse among show ponies. Or the only one at the family wedding who hasn't found a husband.' She puts 'found' in air quotes.

That's not it, I want to say, there's *different* and there's enviable, exotic different. People being people, this effortlessly elegant interloper may have ruffled some feathers.

We watch the screen as the camera moves to the other side of Lily. Two girls who look about twelve or thirteen are craning their necks to see the cake. The girl nearest Lily is auburn-haired, and tanned in a way I always envied when I was a kid, her nutmeg skin bronze against a bright pink t-shirt. The next girl, small, blonde, pretty but perhaps less striking than her friend, seems to have accepted her fate at the end of the line, furthest from the action.

'Aren't they a bit old to be at a three-year-old's birthday party?' I nod towards the screen.

'Ah, back in the eighties you invited every child in the estate to your parties. Was it not the same for you?'

'I was in boarding school, so it was different, I suppose.' The words come so easily, I don't have to think any more. 'Do you know the girls' names?'

'That's Aoife,' Fran says, pointing at the auburn-haired girl. 'And the little blonde one is Ellen. Aoife lived up in the Grove, where the bungalows are, and Ellen lived here, on the other side of your house. They were both there the morning Lily went missing too. They used to play with my twin brothers, so I'd see them in and out. Everyone knew everyone back then,' she says. 'You could just call in to people without arranging it a week in advance. Not like now.'

The camera moves beyond Aoife and Ellen, and I can see a blonde woman facing away, chatting to someone off-screen. Is the blonde woman Mark's mother? If Susie was friends with the Murphys and a regular at their parties, it quite possibly is her, but I can't tell for sure. Now the camera sweeps back to Lily.

'It's weird watching it, and a bit . . . unsettling?' I say. 'They look so happy; they have no idea what's about to unfold. God, it's sad.' I sit silently, aware of the understatement, staring at tiny Lily as she leans forward to blow out her three candles; at Mary's smiling face as she kisses her daughter's head. They are more than a story the estate agent tried to hide, more than a hazy memory in my head. They were real people, and just weeks after the video was filmed, one of them was gone.

9

May 1985

TINY FLAMES TURNED TO smoke, where candles burned just moments before. Mary leaned forward to kiss her daughter's head.

'Smile for the camera!' Robbie was saying. She turned and smiled, the only person on this side of the table. The guests were lined up on the other side, tin soldiers flanking Lily. Singing for supper. Waiting for cake.

'Shall we cut it, Lilybug?' she asked her daughter.

'Yes!' came the unsurprising response, as Lily clapped still-baby hands.

Gently, Mary slid the knife through white frosting. With deft strokes, the cake was sliced into neat wedges and passed around to eager hands. Aoife and Ellen, two ponytailed teenage girls, took their slices to a corner of the kitchen and huddled together the way girls that age do. Cora O'Brien nibbled her slice around the edges, making it last as long as possible. Fran Burke inhaled her slice in two quick bites and stood expectantly, perhaps waiting for more. At seventeen, Fran was a little old to be at a child's birthday party, Mary thought, but Robbie said they should invite everyone. And thankfully, it seemed to be a success – the guests were smiling, the cake was good, and she hadn't messed up any of Rowanbrook's unwritten rules. She glanced over at the windowsill, at her souvenir plate and her Alice in Wonderland figurine and her lighthouse. Her touchstones from home. A life with rules she could follow. But today was going OK.

'Is your mom gone back next door?' Mary asked Fran now, looking around the kitchen.

'No,' Fran replied, her mouth full of cake, 'she went out to the garden to chase down the twins – here she is now.'

Della Burke rushed into the kitchen, sweat on her brow.

'Did I miss the singing? Sorry!'

'Don't worry, Mary will cut you a slice,' Robbie said, and Mary passed her a plate.

'Thanks. The twins were fighting over a football – I had to stop them before one of them put it through the window.' Her cheery voice belied her harried expression.

Della had five children, of which the twins were the youngest. She'd always wanted three children, she said, and the fourth pregnancy was a surprise. Even more so when it turned out to be twins. And even more still when her husband walked out, just before the twins turned one, leaving her a lone parent of five.

A tall, blond boy – one of Della's sons – darted in through the back door, yelling, 'Cake! There's cake!'

Mary didn't know which one he was. There were three sets of twins in Rowanbrook, all called John and Paul. The Pope had a lot to answer for.

'You were as well off missing it, Della, this lot are terrible singers,' Tom Stedman called from the other side of the kitchen, winking.

Mary smiled and shook her head. 'The singing was beautiful. Now, who's for jelly and ice cream?'

A chorus of 'Me!' rose up among the younger guests, as Mary took a tub of vanilla ice cream from the icebox and a jar of jelly from the cupboard. It didn't make a whole lot of sense to her as a dessert, but Robbie had been adamant that ice cream and jelly was a staple at his own birthday parties growing up. She spooned ice cream into small plastic bowls, topping each one with a dollop of strawberry jelly, and began passing them around.

Aoife scrunched up her nose. 'Why is there jam on the ice cream?' she asked.

Susie Stedman sidled up. 'Oh. That's very unusual. Probably an American thing.'

Aoife put her bowl back on the table.

Mary frowned. 'But Robbie said ice cream and jelly is a dessert here in Ireland?'

Susie began to laugh just as Robbie arrived over to see what was going on.

'What's wrong?' he asked.

'I don't think the dessert is too popular . . .' Mary trailed off.

'It's supposed to be jelly though, not jam?'

Fran came to the rescue. 'Jam is called "jelly" in America.' She turned to Mary. 'I think Mr Murphy meant what you would call "jello".'

'Oh.' Mary felt her face redden.

Susie laughed again. Robbie shook his head and put his hand on Mary's shoulder. His fingers felt hot and heavy on her bare skin.

'There's plenty of cake and ice cream to go around. Nobody needs jelly. Or jam!'

He pulled her in for a kiss, picked up a bottle of wine and a corkscrew, and walked away smiling.

'It's a fantastic birthday party, Mary,' Susie said. 'Lily's having a great time and that's the main thing.'

Mary nodded. Susie was right. The dessert faux pas wasn't a big deal – as long as Lily was happy, that was all that mattered.

'Imagine, three years old already,' Susie went on, shaking her head in wonder. 'Must be time for a baby brother or sister!'

Susie had six children, the younger three of whom were there that afternoon, racing around Mary's kitchen. Susie had also brought her babysitter, Cynthia. Cynthia was ostensibly there to help Susie with the children but as far as Mary could see, she'd spent most of the afternoon topping up her own glass and laughing with the dads.

Mary shook her head, smiling at Susie. 'Oh, I think one baby's plenty for me.'

Ines O'Brien, who was retying a bow in her daughter Cora's hair, made a clicking noise with her tongue, and Della threw Mary a pointed look. Mary's face heated up again. *Dammit.* She shouldn't have said that in front of Ines.

'Ines, would you like some cake?' She held out a plate. Peace offering.

'No, thank you, I never eat cake,' Ines said, her Spanish accent laced with disdain. She lit a long, slim cigarillo and moved to the open patio door.

Mary looked at the remaining slices. 'Ellen,' she called, and a blonde head turned her way. 'Is your mom going to stop by for some cake?'

Ellen shook her head and went back to her huddle with Aoife. Ellen lived next door, but her parents kept themselves to themselves. Her mother always matched Mary's wave with a nervous wave of her own, though never accepted invitations to drinks or dinners or card nights.

She's intimidated by you, Della had said once. *Lots of the neighbours are.*

Mary didn't think she was in any way intimidating and said so.

It's because you don't look and sound like everyone else; because you float while the rest of us straggle, Della had explained.

ANDREA MARA

That wasn't quite accurate, but Mary knew what she meant. Her American accent stood out from the South Dublin inflection of the other Rowanbrook residents. Her long sundresses and rope flip-flops were at odds with her neighbours' A-line skirts and sensible Scholl sandals. And her lipstick – well, unless it was a dinner dance, no one else wore lipstick at all.

The exception to all of this was Ines O'Brien. *She's like a cut-price Mary Murphy*, Della had said once. Mary had shushed her, laughing. It wasn't true. Sure, they were both 'other' – one American, one Spanish – but apart from that, they were quite different, Mary reminded Della. Ines was far more glamorous, for a start. Expertly applied make-up, with perfectly painted eyebrows in thin arches above long-lashed eyes, and deep red lipstick in a permanent pout. Her jet-black hair was darker than Mary's and made her look far more groomed. *More vampiric, you mean*, Della said, and Mary laughed again. They shouldn't laugh, Mary thought now, looking over at where Ines stood alone, smoking by the back door. It couldn't be easy turning up at something like this, knowing everyone knew your business.

That was all down to Ines's husband, Victor O'Brien, and his friend, Tom Stedman. People said women gossiped, but as far as Mary could tell, the men of Rowanbrook were just as quick to share family secrets. Their own and other people's.

In this instance, the secret belonged to Ines and Victor. And according to Della, who always knew everything, Ines never wanted anyone to find out. Of course, it came down to alcohol, as it almost always did in Rowanbrook, from what Mary could see. Whiskey and vodka, lowering guardrails and loosening tongues.

With Victor and Tom, it had started with a round of golf, followed by quite a few drinks in the club. Tom had made some off-the-cuff comment to Victor about having more kids. Commenting on other people's procreation choices was something

56

Tom and Susie did on a regular basis – incapable, with their brood of six, of understanding why everyone didn't want the same. Victor, three pints and four whiskies in, had apparently broken down, and told Tom that he and Ines couldn't have any more children. They'd tried, when Cora turned two. They'd gone for tests when Cora was four. But there was no possibility. His voice had cracked at that point, Tom reported back, and Tom had found himself awkwardly hugging his neighbour at the Edenvale Golf Club bar, commiserating with him over another round of whiskies.

Victor got embarrassed then, brushed it off, apparently. Said he didn't mind too much. That it was more Ines than him who was upset. That Cora was enough. That Ines saw it as a failing on her part. That the doctor said lifestyle changes would help. Less alcohol. No smoking. *But*, he'd shrugged, taking another gulp of whiskey, *you know Ines.*

Of course, Della pointed out, you couldn't really blame Victor for confiding in Tom. Even men need to open up sometimes. But then Tom went home and told Susie. And Susie told the babysitter. And Cynthia, who babysat for quite a number of Rowanbrook families, told everyone. Where was Cynthia now, Mary wondered, as Susie's three-year-old son Luke upended a glass of cordial. She glanced around the kitchen as she wiped up the spill. Robbie was cleaning frosting from Lily's chin, and Cora, beside them, was still nibbling on her cake. Victor O'Brien, barely hiding his disinterest behind his beard, had joined Ines by the patio door – the two stood side by side, not speaking, as Ines blew cigarillo smoke towards the garden. Meanwhile, Susie was chatting to Della, oblivious to her child's mishap. Mary stood and moved to the sink to squeeze out the cloth, looking through the kitchen window as she did. She spotted Cynthia out in the garden with Tom Stedman, her head thrown back in laughter, her straw-coloured hair cascading to her hips. She reached out and touched Tom's elbow in what looked like a *you're so funny* gesture. Tom *was* funny, and never more so than when he had the attention of the twenty-nine-year-old babysitter. Mary ran the water to rinse the cloth and outside, Cynthia ran her hand through her hair, her lean, brown arm ropey in the sunlight. Mary had a sudden urge to feed her. Cynthia never seemed to eat. When Fran next door babysat, the bowl of treats was always empty by the time Mary and Robbie arrived home. When Cynthia babysat, even during the day, there was never any evidence that she'd eaten anything at all. Lily, though only three, already preferred Fran, and Mary did too. Fran wasn't a particularly enthusiastic or energetic babysitter and she never tidied up after herself, but Cynthia . . . well, there was something brittle about her. Sharp but distant. Disconcerting.

Mary glanced over at Susie, who was still chatting to Della. If Susie was irritated by her husband's flirting, she showed no sign.

Robbie was twisting a corkscrew into another bottle of wine, while holding court with the Bowmans, a couple Mary didn't know very well. The husband seemed to be asking Robbie for something but his voice was too low for Mary to hear.

'I'll see what I can do,' Robbie said, as the cork finally popped. 'Leave it with me.'

Mr Bowman clapped Robbie on the back. 'You're a gentleman and a scholar.'

'You're a *lifesaver*. Gavin needs a bit of focus for the summer,' the wife added, her hand on Robbie's arm. Mary wondered what exactly they were asking. Gavin, their sixteen-year-old son, with his headphones permanently clamped to his ears and his hands permanently stuffed in his pockets, could certainly do with a bit of focus, but she wasn't quite sure where Robbie came into it.

Susie sidled up to Mary. 'I caught the end of that – what's Robbie doing for Gavin Bowman?'

'I have no idea,' Mary said. 'I'm curious too.'

'Mark's in school with Gavin,' Susie whispered. 'I wouldn't be his biggest fan. Good-looking boy but . . . anyway, whatever Robbie is organizing for him, he's a saint. You're married to a saint, you know that, Mary? You do, I'm sure.'

Mary glanced over at Robbie, who still had Mrs Bowman on his arm. People had no idea what other people's lives were really like, she thought, before turning back to Susie.

'And you are married to the most charming man in Rowanbrook,' she said loyally, smiling at her friend.

'Don't I know it,' Susie said darkly, before rushing to stop Luke grabbing a third slice of cake.

Mary looked around the kitchen. Happy guests. Full drinks. Half-eaten cake. Smiling birthday girl. It was all in hand. Over by the back door, Ines had finished smoking her cigarillo and was searching for somewhere to extinguish it. Mary took an ashtray from the kitchen shelf and brought it to her neighbour.

'We must go now,' Ines said. 'I must finish packing for my trip. Thank you for inviting us.'

'Are you off anywhere nice?' Della asked, coming up behind Mary.

'Spain, to see my mother. One month.'

Mary could sense Della's jaw drop. Della hadn't had a holiday since before the twins were born.

'God, isn't that grand for you. And who'll mind Cora all that time?' Della asked, nodding towards where Cora was fixing something in Lily's hair.

'Cynthia will take care of her after school, and Victor will of course be there every evening and weekend.'

'Goodness, she'll miss you!' Della said.

'She will be fine. It is not good to spoil children with too much attention. They will never learn to be in the world if we wrap them in wool. It is just four weeks.'

Ines gave a little shrug, as though disappearing for a month at a time was a perfectly usual thing to do. For Ines, it was. For as long as Mary had lived in Rowanbrook, Ines had flitted in and out as took her fancy – health farm stays, shopping trips to New York, visits to her family in Spain, and even one memorable month-long trip to the Maldives.

On cue, Cynthia arrived in through the patio doors. She was smiling but it had a glazed quality, Mary thought, as though she was smiling at nothing at all.

'Ah, yes, Cynthia,' Ines was saying. 'Just the person. You will be there when Cora arrives home from school tomorrow, yes?'

For a moment, the smile slipped and a small line creased the bridge of Cynthia's nose.

'Oh yes! Of course. Three o'clock. I *love* Cora. We'll have the best time.' She looked at her watch and her eyes widened. 'Is it after five? Shit.'

'Are you running late for something? I'll give you a lift if you like?' Tom Stedman called from the other side of the kitchen, jangling his keys. Susie was busy tying her son's shoelace and didn't look up.

'Oh, if you could!' The big smile was back – less glazed now, more focused.

'We will go too now,' Ines said, and Victor, following an unspoken command, walked over to take their daughter by the hand.

'Thank you so much for coming,' Mary called from the porch, waving off her guests. Ines, Cora and Victor walked in single file down the driveway, with Ines admonishing Cora for eating a second slice of cake. 'You will be a fat little pig, and you do not want that.'

Cora's head hung low. Victor strode on, oblivious. Mary winced. Poor Cora.

Further down towards the gate, just ahead of the O'Briens, Mary could see Cynthia leaning on Tom's arm as she stumbled in her heels and almost crashed into a familiar figure coming in the opposite direction. Ruth Cavanagh. Striding up Mary's driveway. Mary sighed inwardly.

'Ruth, hi,' Mary said, wondering, as she took in the scowl, what she'd done to upset her difficult neighbour this time.

'Another party?'

Mary nodded. Robbie's 'invite everyone' didn't include Ruth Cavanagh.

Ruth shook her head, and her light blue eyes narrowed behind her glasses. 'You'd better make sure none of those children cross into my back garden. My peonies and foxgloves were destroyed last summer by children sneaking in.'

Ruth's house was right behind Mary's, with their gardens backing on to one another, but their relationship revolved solely around Ruth's deep disdain and frequent complaints.

'I'm sorry to hear that,' Mary said. 'I don't think—'

Ruth cut her off. 'Children today have no manners. When I was teaching, if anyone carried on like that – slipping through the back fence, trampling flowers, muddying up my path – they'd get a clip around the ear.'

They're too damn scared to call at the front door, Mary thought to herself. Della had told Mary that her twins rang Ruth's doorbell once, looking for their football, and she threatened them with a wooden spoon. After that, they skipped the niceties and went straight for the garden fence. Mary didn't say any of this to Ruth.

'We'll remind everyone to stay in our garden,' she said instead.

Ruth stood for another moment, as though about to say something else. Tall and thin, her hair was styled in a severe, dark grey bob and Mary could never tell what age she was. There had been a Mr Cavanagh once, though he'd died many years earlier. Some said Ruth wasn't a widow at all – that Mr Cavanagh had upped and left a joyless marriage – but that seemed a little mean, Mary thought. Surely the woman wouldn't have lied about her own husband's demise.

'Fine,' Ruth said eventually, and stalked off, her burgundy A-line skirt stiff in the evening breeze.

Della's voice came from behind Mary as she watched the dramatic departure.

'She's just jealous she wasn't invited. Like the wicked fairy from *Sleeping Beauty*. Ignore her.'

'You're right. We've had a perfect day, and I won't let Ruth Cavanagh ruin it,' Mary said, putting the encounter firmly out of her head.

10

THE BAR IS CROWDED though it's early still, and at first I don't see Adana waving at me from a booth near the window.

'You were in another world,' she says as I slide into the seat opposite. 'Got you a G&T.'

'Thanks.' I take a deep swallow and it settles me in a way that is good and not good.

'All OK?' She looks at me quizzically.

'Yeah.' I consider for a moment – what I can say, and what I can't. 'I'm just a bit unsettled after something that happened this morning.' I fill her in on finding the video tape and Fran's somewhat reluctant agreement to watch it in her house. 'It was odd sitting there, seeing Lily blow out candles and knowing it would be her final birthday.'

Adana sucks air through her teeth. 'God. When you put it like that . . . Though I suppose there's a small chance she's not dead.'

I saw her body. The words flash through my mind before I can stop them. I take another deep drink.

'Anyway, we are being *horribly* morbid,' Adana continues. 'It's Saturday night and we're here to have fun.' She takes a sip of her red wine and grimaces. 'This isn't going down very well. I think I had a few too many at your housewarming.' She pulls a pack of paracetamol from her bag and pops two in her mouth before offering the packet to me.

'I'm fine, thanks.'

'As always. Joanna Stedman, woman of steel. You know, it's not a sign of weakness to take a painkiller. Or to admit you have a hangover every now and then.'

I smile. 'Mark was feeling fairly grim this morning. Reckoned it was that one past-its-sell-by beer he had, not the six before.'

'Mark's *mother* is quite something, isn't she! Not a whole lot of filter there?'

'Susie doesn't believe in filters, no.'

'I wanted to ask' – a pause, a sip, another grimace – 'were you OK with what she said? I mean, the fire?' Adana, who is never ruffled by anything, is suddenly awkward. 'It's just, you don't talk about it, and I'm never sure whether to bring it up.'

'It's fine. Susie does that – she likes exploring the gory details but doesn't want to be seen to be nosy.'

'But it must be hard for you?'

'Not any more. It all happened such a long time ago . . . I don't know if you ever get over something like that, but you can't let it define you either.' That's my go-to line for explaining why I'm 'actually fine'. 'And Susie means well. It's healthy to talk, and all that.'

'Do you want to? Talk, I mean? Tell me what happened?'

I push back in my seat and nod, though this will be for Adana, not for me. I've told this made-up story so many times over the years I know it word for word and can narrate it on autopilot – distanced, unemotional. A fiction that almost seems real to me now.

'Sure. Most of it you already know. The house caught fire late one night, after a party. My parents had a lot of parties – they'd put my housewarming to shame.' I smile. 'I was never allowed to join them – they weren't those kind of parties and they weren't those kind of parents.'

'So, no kids bouncing on the trampoline while Mammy serves wine with one hand and orange cordial with the other?'

'Definitely not. Anyway, I was away at boarding school when it happened. That particular night, the party went on late, and soon after the last guests left, the house went up in flames. They said it was a cigarette. That simple. My dad, having a nightcap, fell asleep, cigarette fell on to the rug. He was so drunk he slept right through it. My mother the same, only she was upstairs in bed.'

'Jesus. I knew most of this from when you told us that night in college, but God, it's just so . . .'

That night in college. Sitting in the bar in UCD, eking out our last pints, Adana, Mark and me. The flickering candle between us. The realization that I couldn't keep fobbing off these new friends whose homes I'd been to, whose parents I'd met. *Mine are dead.* It came out of nowhere. *I live with my grandmother. She's not well. She doesn't like visitors.* End of story. But no, not end of story.

How did they die? Of course they were going to ask that. Six pints in, they were never not going to ask that. A fire, I said, watching the candle flicker between us. Regretting it as soon as the words were out. Explaining to Mark and Adana why they hadn't seen it in the papers. *We lived in London. It wouldn't have been in the papers over here.* The fictional trust fund and made-up boarding school, to explain how and where I lived. The presumption of wealth that I didn't dispel. The big house of my stories, so beautifully different from reality. The big house that burned to the ground. They haven't asked much about it over the years but it comes up every now and then, usually over drinks. Like tonight. And then I try to keep it vague.

'Yeah. A lot of what happened after is blurry. It was decided that it was best to keep me at boarding school and then, as you know, I came to Ireland for college and lived with my grandmother until she died. And look – didn't I turn out OK?' I force a smile. I hate this. I do it on autopilot every single time I'm asked. But I hate it. Especially with Adana. And Mark. Jesus. Mark.

Now Adana's eyes are uncharacteristically damp. 'You are *amazing*, you know that? God, look at me, getting soppy after one drink. That's it now, back to giving out about everyone for the rest of the night. Another G&T?'

I nod, and as Adana leans out of the booth to signal a waiter, I notice a familiar figure on the other side of the bar. A welcome distraction from the fire that never was and the guilt that never wanes.

'Oh, my neighbour Fran is here. I should go over and say hi in a bit.' Craning my neck, I try to see who she's with. She's in a corner spot, and I can see her in side-profile, elbow on table, hand under chin. To her left, facing us, is an ash-blonde woman in her early thirties. She's telling a story, it seems, gesturing with her hands, laughing. There's something familiar about her. Her eyes? Her smile? The way she moves? I shake my head. This is silly. I'm seeing familiar everywhere now.

'Oh, by the way, did you see there's a new Deep Dive blog post?' Adana is saying, tapping on her phone screen. She slides the phone around for me to read.

Little Whispers
It's been a long time since anyone asked any questions about Lily Murphy – is the story about to unfold again? Will fresh eyes see what nobody saw before?

Someone knows something. To be more accurate, a number of

people know a number of things. And some of them are still there, in Rowanbrook, tending their gardens, greeting their neighbours, old and new. But now, there may be little whispers and new questions and fresh eyes.

Watch this space.

DD.

The air around me thickens as I read it a second time, gin swirling in my stomach. I look up at Adana. 'What do you think they mean by fresh eyes? Reopening the case?'

She gives me an odd look. 'I assume it's about the comment you left on the blog? Saying you're interested in finding out what happened?'

Of course. Shit. I *do* want to know. I want to know that Lily and my sister were not the same person. That I'm not the one who killed Lily. But if I'm wrong, I can't have anyone else find out. The blog comment was a mistake. As I scroll on Adana's phone, searching for my comment and for a delete button, I feel someone's eyes on me. I glance up and see Fran looking over, but when I raise my hand to wave, she turns away. Perhaps she didn't recognize me.

Our drinks arrive and I pay, still scrolling on Adana's phone. There's no delete button on the comment. *Shit.*

'Are you OK?' Adana asks.

'Yeah, sorry, don't mind me.' I hand back her phone.

'I was thinking,' Adana says, looking down at her screen, 'we could try searching on some true-crime forums? See if we can find any Lily Murphy theories there?'

'Yeah, good idea.'

Fran and her companion are standing now, gathering bags and jackets.

'I'm just going to say hi to my neighbour before she goes,' I tell Adana and begin making my way across the bar, dodging around a group of Italian tourists who've just walked in. But by the time I get there, Fran's table is empty. She and her friend have left half-eaten meals and half-drunk drinks and two fifty-euro notes. A baffled-looking waiter picks up the money.

'They didn't even ask for the bill,' he mutters, and begins clearing glasses. The main door swings shut behind them and I stand staring, wondering what caused Fran to leave in such a hurry.

11

FRAN PRESSED THE MURPHYS' doorbell and stepped back, almost falling off the doorstep in the process. Behind her, her best friend Zara giggled just as Robbie Murphy opened the door, smiling briskly at the two of them.

'Come on in – Mary's upstairs getting ready, and Lily's watching television. Come through.'

'Thank you, Mr Murphy,' Zara simpered, with another small giggle.

'Thanks,' Fran said.

Lily was in the living room, sitting on a cushion on the floor, watching *Road Runner*. Fran winced. *That constant beep-beep.* Lily didn't seem to mind, but then, she was three. *Road Runner* wasn't aimed at jaded seventeen-year-olds. She perched on the edge of the couch, while Zara stood by the floor-to-ceiling bookshelves, smiling at Robbie.

'So, ladies, how are things? Studying hard?' Robbie asked.

'Absolutely,' Zara said with a coy dip of her chin. 'Nearly done with the exams though, and then we're off on our J-1 to America.'

'J-1?'

'It's a work-travel visa. We're spending the summer in Virginia Beach.' She grinned. 'Doing as little work and as much

69

travel as possible.' She turned and ran her hand across a row of books. 'You must be a great reader, Mr Murphy. I don't think I've ever seen so many books in one place.'

Fran groaned silently.

'The non-fiction books are mine – the ones on accounting and history and politics. You young ones would be bored to tears by them. The novels are Mary's. I'm not into fiction but she loves it.'

Zara pulled out a hardback history of World War II.

'I'm the same,' she said. 'I much prefer non-fiction.'

Fran stifled a laugh. The only non-fiction Zara ever read was *Jackie* magazine.

Robbie beckoned Fran through to the kitchen then, and Zara put the book back on the shelf to follow.

'Fran, can I ask you to heat that milk for a bedtime drink for Lily, in half an hour?' he said, pointing to a small saucepan on the hob.

'No problem, Mr Murphy,' Zara piped up before Fran had a chance to answer. 'Are you and Mrs Murphy off anywhere nice?'

'A dinner-dance in the Burlington, the only reason you'll catch me in a monkey suit.' He touched his bow tie and winked.

'Well, I think it suits you!' Zara said, giggling again.

Fran bit the inside of her lip. She should have come on her own. Young-free-and-single Zara was generally a liability. Humiliated-after-a-break-up Zara was a disaster waiting to happen.

'Why thank you, Zara, you're most kind. Right, I'll see how Mary's getting on,' Robbie said, leaving the kitchen.

Fran threw Zara a look.

'What? I just told him he looks nice!'

'I know what you're like, but even you have to draw the line. He's about forty.'

'He's not, he's thirty-three, and he's a lot more handsome than any of the other men around here. That dimple . . . The floppy hair . . . Those dreamy eyes . . . And his lashes!' Zara did a faux swoon. 'He looks like Rob Lowe, don't you think?'

'Not one bit,' Fran said, though now that she thought about it, maybe he did. Zara had been obsessed with Rob Lowe ever since they'd watched *The Outsiders*. *If only that girl spent as much time on her books as she does mooning over film stars*, Fran's mother Della used to say. She was worried about their upcoming summer in America, afraid Zara would be a bad influence. *Here's hoping*, was Fran's response to that, though only in her head.

They walked back into the living room and flopped simultaneously on the couch, just as the doorbell rang.

'Should we answer it? While they're getting ready?' Zara asked.

Fran shook her head as they heard the sound of footsteps on the stairs, then the front door being opened, and a voice that was familiar though indistinct.

'Is that *Gavin*?' Zara mouthed. 'Why would he be here?'

Fran had no idea. Gavin Bowman was 'born trouble' according to Della, and for once, Fran had to agree with her mother. Her twin brothers were obsessed with Gavin, of course. Looked up to him like he was some kind of idol. And the girls in their group – Ellen and Aoife – seemed to hang off Gavin's every word. She scooted sideways along the couch, listening. Sporadic snippets filtered through. 'Office' and 'lesson' and 'cash'. And then, inexplicably, 'lawn mower'. That was unexpected. Gavin spent most of his time hanging around the green, smoking – he wasn't the odd-job type.

The sound of the front door closing sent Fran scurrying back to the middle of the sofa and Zara into a fit of silent laughter. Now they could hear Mary coming down the stairs.

'Who was that?' she asked, her voice carrying through to the living room.

'Gavin Bowman. Remember his parents asked if he could do work experience in my office?'

Fran and Zara exchanged looks. Neither of them could imagine Gavin working in an office. They stayed stock still on the couch, listening through the closed door.

'Oh, that's right. Will he start soon?'

Robbie laughed. 'Yeah, but not in the office.'

'Oh?'

Another laugh. 'I told him I promised his dad work experience but didn't specify what *kind* of work. So you, my dear, have a new gardener.'

'I don't understand?'

'Ah, look, I'll bring him into the office for a week at some stage and throw a bit of cash his way. But for now, he's going to cut the lawn here once a week, do a bit of tidying up. You should have seen his face.'

'Are you sure he's OK with this? I don't know if—' Mary's soft voice was harder to hear than her husband's and the last few words didn't make it through to the listening ears in the living room.

'He'll have to be,' Robbie replied. 'I need the garden done; he's looking for work experience in my office. Nothing is for nothing, right? Now, we'd better get off to this dinner.'

The living room door opened, and Fran and Zara made a great show of looking at *Road Runner* with Lily. Mary greeted them in that quiet, slightly aloof way she had about her. She looked beautiful in a long green sparkly dress, silver shoes, and a matching silver hairband. Actually, Fran thought, she looked like a film star; like Natalie Wood or Audrey Hepburn, her hair all swept up in a bun, her tiny arms and tiny waist. Fran thought about her own rather thicker arms and waist, and instinctively sucked in her stomach. She was the unhappy recipient of her mother's strong, sturdy figure, while Mary, no doubt, came from a long line of wasp-waisted women.

'There are candy bars and cookies in the kitchen,' Mary said. 'Please help yourselves after Lily goes to sleep.'

Fran and Zara exchanged a look.

Candy bars. Cookies. Nobody said cookies. They were *biscuits*, for goodness' sake.

'I'm fine thanks, I'm not really into chocolate,' Fran found herself saying, while Zara threw her a look of surprise.

'Since when? You ate two Marathons in college yesterday!' said her so-called best friend.

Mary, serene with her half-smile, bent to kiss Lily. Or 'Lily-bug' as she called her, a nickname that made Fran cringe every time.

'Oh, Zara,' Robbie said suddenly. 'I keep meaning to ask, would your Aunt Ruth like any help in the garden? Cutting back trees and hedges? I can't imagine it's easy for her managing on her own.'

'That's so thoughtful of you!' Zara said, clapping her hands together. Fran winced.

'Not at all, mention it to her anyway. We'd better go, Mary,' Robbie said, turning to his wife, and the pair, as beautiful as any Hollywood couple, said goodbye and left.

'He is *so* good-looking,' Zara said as the front door closed.

'Zara, I'm all for "plenty more fish in the sea" et cetera, but seriously, stop about Robbie.'

'All I'm saying is, objectively speaking, the man is attractive. I may be broken-hearted but I'm not incapable of noticing other fellas.' She smirked. 'And he was eyeing me up earlier, before Mary came in – didn't you notice?'

Fran most certainly had *not* noticed. She put her finger to her lips and pointed her toe at Lily. 'Keep your voice down.'

'She's lost in *Danger Mouse*, she hasn't a clue what we're saying. Should you be getting her to bed?'

Fran pulled herself off the couch. Zara was good at eating Kit Kats and choosing videos, but not so keen to help with the *babysitting* part of the babysitting.

Lily's wailing began an hour later, when Fran and Zara were twenty minutes into *The Amityville Horror*, a film choice Fran was wholly regretting.

'I'll pause it while you go up,' Zara said, slipping off the couch and reaching towards the video recorder.

Fran put her finger to her lips, head cocked, listening. 'She sometimes goes quiet after a minute . . .'

Zara shrugged and moved to a mahogany cabinet on the other side of the fireplace.

'What's in here, I wonder,' she said, opening a door. Fran shook her head. Zara knew exactly what was in there.

'Leave it, Zara.'

'Bacardi. God, aren't they fancy with their Bacardi?' She unscrewed the cap.

'Ah, Zara, stop, will you?'

Zara took a mouthful, scrunching her eyes closed as she swallowed. She coughed and took another swig.

'Come on! Like, we're in charge of a child.'

'*You're* in charge of a child. And doing a questionable job, I'd say,' she said, pointing towards the ceiling, through which they could still hear Lily's intermittent wails.

'Please just put it back. What if they smell it on you when they get home?'

'I won't *breathe* on them. I promise I'll stay at least three feet away from Robbie all the way home.'

'What are you talking about "all the way home"?'

'When he's walking me back to my house. He'll have to, right? I mean, you're only next door, but I'm a good ten-minute walk away.'

Fran rolled her eyes. 'You can stay in my house.'

'Nah, I'd better go home. Robbie won't mind walking me. It won't be the first time. And I'm great company. I'd say I'm a lot more craic than Mary anyway.' She picked up a bottle of whiskey just as Lily broke into an almighty roar. 'I wonder what this is like?'

'Don't you dare,' Fran hissed, as she left the living room. Between raiding the drinks cabinet and simpering over Robbie, Zara was well on her way to getting Fran fired. Next time, she was coming on her own.

12

IT'S MONDAY MORNING AND the bed linen needs changing and I'm trying not to think about Lily Murphy, but she's everywhere. The new house – the forever home – feels big. Too big, and too quiet, and as I walk from room to room, it's almost eerie. Like the ghosts in the cracks in the walls are listening too.

I move through the silent landing to Sophie's room. *Lily's room*. I'm sure of it, though I can't say why. It's colder in here – maybe because the window is smaller and west-facing, with no morning sun. Embossed wallpaper, beige curtains and a cream wardrobe suggest the previous owner used it as a guest bedroom. I stand in the centre, looking around, wondering what I can do to make it more *Sophie*. A few pictures would help, and a new lampshade. And maybe it wouldn't be a huge job to strip the walls and paint the room? I kneel and tug at a corner of the wallpaper, down by the skirting board where no one will notice. It comes away easily, but underneath there is more wallpaper. A wave of nostalgia sweeps over me as I spot the familiar Holly Hobbie illustrations. I remember the same wallpaper from my own childhood – a friend's bedroom, I think. Not mine. My bedroom had bare, cream walls; no pictures or posters allowed.

I sit back now, staring at the paper. Perhaps this means I'm right – the room *had* once been Lily's. And I'm swamped now, overwhelmed with the memory of a small, trusting face and big blue eyes. She knew I'd never do her harm. And then I did.

On Monday night, Mark is late home from work. The kids are already upstairs, and I'm on the couch, deep in Google, when he joins me.

'Do you want to watch that new thing with the subtitles?' he says, picking up the remote. 'Apparently it's brilliant once you get halfway through the second season.'

'You go ahead – I have some research to do.'

'Research?'

'Yeah,' I say, not looking at him. 'A DIY project.' My cheeks heat up at the fib as I angle the Mac screen away and shift towards the end of the couch, not entirely sure why I'm lying. Then again, 'I'm googling Rowanbrook residents to see if one of them is the link between Lily Murphy and me' isn't a great opener either.

I started earlier with Mark's parents, but there was nothing of interest and little I didn't already know. A fifty-year wedding anniversary announcement in the *Irish Times*, highlights from Tom's career with Bank of Ireland, and an occasional photo of Susie in magazine society pages. But nothing that suggests I ever met them before that first time Mark brought me home for Sunday lunch. I try Victor O'Brien and this is where it gets morbid. Less than a year after Lily went missing, he drove his car off a bridge. *Well* over the limit with alcohol, traces of cocaine too, and driving through the worst storm the country had seen for years; nobody could say if it was deliberate or not. The date jumps out at me. 19 March 1986. The same year and maybe even the same month my sister died, though I only remember it was near Easter. I turn that over, wondering. But staring at Victor's photo – his ruddy face and thick beard and humourless frown – I can't see any connection. Next up is Ines O'Brien, Victor's wife. Cora's mother. Like Susie, she appears occasionally in magazines. Unlike Susie, Ines does not smile. In every photo, she looks somehow . . . hard. At war with the world. I find a small piece in a newspaper feature on bilingual homes. She was half-Spanish, it says, spending much of her time back home in Málaga with her mother, and raising Cora to be fluent in Spanish. That gives me an idea. I flick through the Rowanbrook WhatsApp group member list, and find Cora's number. I hesitate. This is like commenting on the Deep Dive blog – asking questions that could indeed lead to answers for me, but also to awkward enquiries from other people. Then again, Cora seems like someone who might talk without worrying unduly about why I'm asking.

With her number saved to my Contacts, and a quick glance at Mark, I start to type.

> Hi Cora, this is Joanna here, from 6 Rowanbrook Drive. I hope you don't mind me messaging! (I'm assuming this is Cora O'Brien who I met at our housewarming, please excuse if I have wrong number.)
> We're still settling in and trying to get to know the area. I was wondering if we could meet for coffee some time and you could show me the ropes – tell me a bit about the neighbourhood and who's who?

As soon as it's sent, blue ticks confirm Cora has seen it. *Cora is typing . . .* my phone tells me. And then as Mark suggests *Spotlight* for the third week running, because he keeps forgetting we've seen it already, the reply pings through.

> Hi Joanna. Yes it's me! I'd love to meet for coffee. I lived here when I was a child as you know. I know area v well. I can tell you

about the Residents' Association. I just joined. You should too!
We can meet tomorrow morning. I'm off work but no plans.
There's a cafe in Edenvale called The Sugar Tree. See you there
at 10? Looking forward to it! Cora.

Tomorrow morning. Cora is keen. Then again, so am I. I tell
her I'll be there and go back to Google. There's no point in
searching under Robbie and Mary again, I know their results off
by heart. Susie and Tom's words play in my memory. An altercation between 'Eddie something' and Robbie, and the rumour
that Robbie was in a relationship with a 'small girl, the pretty
one'.

'Mark?'

He looks up from his phone.

'When we were over in your mum's on Thursday night and
we were talking about Lily Murphy, she mentioned a guy called
Eddie – she said there was some kind of fight between him and
Robbie Murphy?'

'Oh yeah . . . that's right. Robbie ended up with his arm in a
bandage or something.'

'Do you remember Eddie's surname?'

'Hogan. Eddie Hogan.'

Why didn't I ask him sooner? 'Great. And your mum also
said there was a girl, a "small, pretty one" in a relationship with
Robbie Murphy?'

'Yeah.' He sits up straighter. 'I'd forgotten all about that
rumour. Zara was her name. She was a good friend of Fran's.'
His cheeks flush and I wonder again about Mark and Fran, and
it makes me smile to think of him keeping it from me. 'A rumour
went around that Zara got pregnant by Robbie Murphy. That
was awkward. Robbie's child disappears and meanwhile, he's
fathered another one with a teenager.'

'Holy shit.'

'To be honest, I don't know if the pregnancy bit was true – I never heard about her having a kid. But there were very strong rumours about the relationship between them.'

'There was me thinking everyone was very boring back in the eighties . . .'

'Yep. Rowanbrook might look sedate and wholesome, but behind closed doors, it was all going on.' A knowing nod. 'And Robbie and Zara weren't the only ones.'

'Wow, who else?'

'Ah, a lot of it was just rumours,' he backtracks quickly.

'Mark, you can't say something like that and not tell me the rest.'

'Well, there was a woman called Ines O'Brien – the one who brought me home from the park when the babysitter forgot me?' I nod and he continues. 'She was supposedly cheating on her husband left, right and centre. If you believed the rumours at the time, she was somehow having concurrent affairs with Eddie Hogan, Robbie Murphy, Fran Burke's father before he ran off, and even a guy in my class in school. But Ines was Spanish and kind of glamorous compared to everyone else, and she travelled a lot. I don't know if she was really having affairs or if she just looked like someone off *Dynasty* and everyone assumed she must be.'

'OK, go on. Any other affairs or rumours?'

He shakes his head. 'I can't.'

'Mark! I'm your wife, spill.'

'Oh God. OK, this is kind of gross, but there was a rumour about my dad and the babysitter.'

My jaw drops. '*Tom?* You're kidding.'

'It's not true. But if we're talking about *rumours* that went around at the time, that was one of them.'

'Jesus, does Susie know?'

'Do you honestly think that's the kind of thing you ask your mother?' A beat. 'Sorry.'

'You don't have to say sorry.' His misplaced sensitivity is kind, but never fails to make me feel guilty. 'It was a long time ago.'

'Sorry,' he says again. 'Just with that gorse fire in the news all the time, I wasn't sure if you were OK . . . you don't really talk about it.'

For very good reasons. Out loud I say: 'Honestly, it's fine. Tell me more about your dad and this babysitter?'

'Yeah . . . I don't know if Mum heard the rumours back then – I hope she didn't. I heard it at school. Can you imagine being a sixteen-year-old guy and having some fucker come up to you and say your dad's screwing the babysitter?'

'What did you do?'

Mark goes red. 'I punched him.'

'Mark!'

'Yeah. He was this guy who lived here in Rowanbrook. Married someone from here too. Actually, I think he died a few years ago, which is weird to think about now. Gavin was his name. Thought he was God's gift to girls – all stonewashed denim and floppy hair and cigarettes hanging out of his mouth.'

'Mark Stedman, there's a dark side to you! I can't imagine you punching someone.'

'He deserved it, and not just for what he said about Dad and yer one. He was creepy as fuck, always hanging around, watching out of these half-closed too-cool-for-school eyes. Like he thought he was James Dean. He used to watch Mary and Lily all the time apparently – I remember people talking about that. Just *staring.*'

'That's starting to sound like more than just "creepy" – did anyone tell the guards?'

'Ah no, it wasn't anything to do with her disappearance.' Mark stops for a moment, tilting his head. 'Though according to my mother, he was there that day, watching the younger ones play Hide and Seek in the building site.'

I type 'Gavin' into my laptop. 'What's his surname?'

Mark shakes his head. 'Can't remember now. It'll come back.'

I delete Gavin from my Google search bar. There is one more name to try, and I do, wondering about resemblance and nicknames and ages and dates. But as usual, nothing at all comes up. As far as the internet is concerned, Lila Kirk is a ghost.

13

THE CAFE SMELLS OF coffee cake and warm vanilla, and it's busy for a Tuesday morning. Stacks of pancakes and plates of smashed avocado whizz past as I sit reading the menu. I'm early. Cora is right on time. At ten on the dot, she pushes through the door, blinking at the shift from bright sunshine to dimmer interior. Spotting me, she waves enthusiastically, descending on the table as though it's water in the desert.

I smile hello, taking in my new neighbour again. Cora's narrow forehead is mostly unlined but has a translucent, papery quality, hinting at an indoor existence. Her small eyes are like raisins, either side of a sharp nose, and her mouth has a permanently pursed look. She's wearing a bright cerise-pink jumper that fits neither the heatwave nor the twenty-first century, and her pine-green denim jacket.

'Hello! Delighted to see you again!' she says, sitting opposite, gazing at me. 'I have a feeling we're going to get along brilliantly.'

This makes me squirm, but on the scale of things about which I feel guilty, it's pretty low. 'Thanks for meeting me. You know when you're new and you just want to get a sense of the place and the people . . .'

'Oh, I do! I remember when I first moved into the flat in Ranelagh. Let's see . . . that was 2005. Or was it 2004? I'd just started in a call centre, different one to the one I'm in today, and—' Cora is interrupted by a woman who swoops down to take our order. She knows Cora by name and greets her with a smile. She asks her how she's settling back to Rowanbrook, then swishes away. Giving silent thanks for the interruption, I jump in.

'Yes, so, I'm looking forward to hearing about Rowanbrook, and especially what it was like back when you were growing up. I imagine it was idyllic – in and out of each other's houses, playing on the green?'

Cora's raisin-eyes narrow. I've gone too far, too soon. The clunk of the coffee grinder and the sound of a baby's cry at a nearby table punctuate an awkward silence. But then Cora smiles.

'Idyllic. That's a nice word.'

'Lots of friends your own age?' I try.

'Oh, friends of all ages. Back then you played with everyone. I didn't have any siblings, so I relied on other kids,' she says, as our drinks arrive. A latte for me and a hot chocolate with whipped cream for her.

'I'm an only child too.' *At least, I am now.* 'Did you ever wish you had siblings?'

Cora picks up the sugar dispenser and pours a teaspoonful. 'Sometimes. I'd have loved a little sister to play with.' She stirs the sugar into her hot chocolate. I wonder how it could possibly require further sweetening. Cora looks up.

'Ines – my mother – wanted another baby, and that felt strange at times.'

'Oh, really?'

'Yes. Strange because *I* would have liked her to have another baby – something to cuddle and love – but I couldn't understand why *she* wanted it so badly; why I wasn't enough. Odd, thinking back on it now, to have had such conflicting feelings . . .'

'I can understand that. I had days when I'd have loved a sibling, and others when I was glad it was just me.' *Be careful what you wish for.* 'But my mother never said anything about wanting another baby, so at least I didn't have to worry that she was sad about it.'

'Mm. Not that my mother ever said she was sad to *me*.' Cora pours a second teaspoonful and dumps it into her cup, stirring vigorously. 'She wasn't one for opening up, but I used to hear my dad talking about it on the phone to his sister, when he thought no one was listening. Sometimes I'd pick up the extension when he was on the phone in his study.' She says this without guile. 'He used to talk to my auntie about being worried for my mother. How my other aunties – my mother's sisters – seemed to just pop them out and how hard it must be for Ines. I always remember him saying that, and imagining babies popping out. Like pricking a pregnant belly as you would a balloon and the baby just *popping*!' Cora smiles and there's something slightly disturbing about it. 'And then somehow word got out and everyone in Rowanbrook knew my mother couldn't have any more children.'

'That must have been hard for her.'

'She kept her head held high, pretended she didn't care that everyone knew so much about her personal life. She was good at that. And she escaped Rowanbrook whenever she could – visiting her family in Spain and going to retreats and health spas. She knew how to look after herself.'

'And who looked after you?'

'Babysitters. And my dad of course, when he wasn't working. It's kind of ironic though, that my mother was desperate for another baby, but hardly spent any time with me. Honestly, sometimes it felt as though she barely remembered my name.' A pause. Her eyes widen. 'Actually, one time she literally *did* forget it, when she was talking to my dad about me – she got my name wrong. Imagine that!' A sigh. 'It all made me feel like I was somehow defective. Forgettable. Not enough. She loved her garden and she loved her cigarillos and she loved her trips. That was it.'

It seems like a lot to disclose to someone she hardly knows, but Cora is unemotional as she sips her hot chocolate. Mark's words ring in my ears – Ines O'Brien and her affairs 'left, right and centre' – and I wonder if this was part of why Ines travelled so much. Perhaps it had nothing to do with Cora. But despite how forthright she's been, it doesn't seem like the kind of thing I can ask and it's not what I'm here for. What I really need to ask is what happened that morning with Lily.

'Cora, I hope you don't mind, but as you might be aware, the house we bought is the one where Robbie and Mary Murphy used to live. And I know—'

She holds up her hand. 'Stop.'

'Oh. I'm sorry.'

Her mouth is set, and for a moment, there's silence.

'Yes, I was with her that morning,' she says eventually, 'but I don't know anything about what happened to her and I made a pact with myself a long time ago that I wouldn't talk about it, so I'm sorry, but you're going to have to accept that.'

'Of course. I understand. It's just that—' How do I explain? How do I tell her I have a personal interest, that it's not morbid curiosity?

Cora shakes her head and her hand goes up again.

'Sorry, but no. What happened that day destroyed my family, and I won't talk about it.'

'You mean . . . your dad?'

'How did you know?'

I can't tell her I was googling her parents. 'Someone said it . . . Mark's originally from Rowanbrook and his parents mentioned—'

'So you know the police came to our house?'

I nod.

'It was horrible. Two guards, tramping around inside, asking questions. And it turns out it wasn't even—' She stops and it's very clear she's changed her mind about something she was going to say. 'Anyway. It happened. Then of course, as it always does in Rowanbrook, word got out. Victor O'Brien suspected of doing something to Lily Murphy. It followed him everywhere, it affected his business and their marriage, and eventually . . .'

Eventually Victor O'Brien drove off a bridge. I don't need her to say it. And as much as I want to know what happened, I can't do this to her any more.

'I'm sorry. I didn't mean to pry. It was just a shock finding out that the little girl used to live in our house. I need to stop obsessing! You know, I'd love to hear more about the Residents' Association?'

'Yes!' Cora brightens immediately and it's as though she's forgotten everything we just discussed. 'You should join the RA. They're always looking for new members, apparently. My other neighbour, Liz, said she might join too. She's just a bit busy right now but she's going to come back to me.'

I hide my smile. Liz would be completely allergic to joining the RA.

'And it would give us a chance to get to know each other properly,' Cora continues. 'I think we're going to be great friends.' She reaches across the table to touch my arm. 'Really great friends.'

14

May 1985

MARY WATCHED ABSENTMINDEDLY AS Cora O'Brien pulled her babysitter's hand, eager to move forward in the queue for the ice cream van. Cynthia lit a cigarette and flashed Mary a smile, the gap in her front teeth making her seem somehow childlike. Her long red gingham dress gave her a hippie-ish look, though the hem was frayed and there was a cigarette burn halfway down the skirt. Her eyes had a glassy quality, just like at Lily's party. Suddenly, without knowing why, Mary decided she didn't want Cynthia babysitting Lily any more.

Della Burke, just ahead of Mary in the queue, leaned back to whisper in her ear. 'Did you see the state of Tom Stedman with herself, at Lily's party?' She nodded back towards Cynthia.

Mary smiled. 'I'm sure it's harmless. Tom's devoted to Susie, beneath all that flirting.'

'Oh, I know, but that girl Cynthia is trouble. If you were Ines O'Brien, would you head off on your travels leaving someone like her practically living in your house?' She nudged Mary. 'Sorry, forgot you're married to a saint.'

If only you knew, Mary thought, but kept her smile in place. 'She's not sleeping over in the O'Briens' though, she just does a few hours in the afternoon. I think she has another job too; she's always rushing off whenever she babysits Lily.'

'Fair enough. Anyway, don't say you heard it from me, but apparently, Ines and Victor sleep in separate bedrooms. Cynthia told Susie and Susie told me.'

Mary shook her head, more at the casual sharing of gossip than the O'Briens' sleeping arrangements. Dear God, nothing was sacred with Cynthia snooping around all their houses.

Two other women joined the queue, both wearing sunhats to shield their eyes. None of them ever wore sunglasses, none except Mary, and she knew what they thought about that. *That woman, she thinks she is in Hollywood*, she'd heard Ines say once, when she didn't know Mary could hear. Ines didn't like her. That was OK, Mary didn't really mind, though she sometimes wondered if Ines minded how much time her daughter Cora spent looking after Lily instead of playing with kids her own age.

So, the Rowanbrook women carried on squinting and Mary carried on wearing her sunglasses. Now, she pushed them up the bridge of her nose, and twisted her hair into a bun, for relief from the heat.

'Excuse me!'

Mary and Della turned towards the owner of the voice. Ruth Cavanagh was standing outside her house, glaring over at the queue for the ice cream van.

'Us?' Della's translucent eyebrows rose towards her hairline.

'I want a word with you,' Ruth snapped, beckoning them over.

'I'll mind Lily, you go,' Della said with an eye-roll. 'I dealt with the drama about the bins, it's your turn.'

Mary grimaced, and leaving Lily in the queue with Della, she walked towards their neighbour. Ruth was standing in her drive-way, hands on hips, dressed all in grey: a grey blouse, a stiff grey skirt that looked like a school uniform, and even grey garden-ing gloves. Her old red Micra and a burst of purple foxgloves added the only dash of colour.

'Are you OK, Ruth?' Mary asked.

'I'm certainly not OK. Someone has thrown a stone at one of my back windows.'

'Oh, gosh, is it broken?'

'*Yes*, it's broken, and I can't get a glazier out, so I've had to tape cardboard to it. All because parents around here can't keep their children under control and the schools are afraid to say boo. I can tell you, in my day, the nuns wouldn't have let them get away with any of it. The threat of a crack from a ruler is what children need,' she said, with an emphatic nod.

Mary had no idea what to say or why Ruth was telling her any of this. Perhaps because she lived in the house behind Ruth's? Did she really think Lily was responsible? Though Ruth was staring over at the ice cream van, so perhaps it was Della's twins she had in mind. Mary looked over now too. Della was at the top of the queue, and a few feet behind her, Cora was trying again to pull Cynthia forward.

She turned back to Ruth. 'Have you talked to the Residents' Association?' she tried. 'Maybe they can help?'

Ruth snorted. 'And what exactly do you think those geriatric imbeciles are going to do? This is down to lax parenting.' She launched into a monologue about discipline, and Mary found herself switching off, her eyes drawn back to the queue at the ice cream van. Cora had moved forward and was bending down to say something to Lily. As Mary watched, Della grabbed Lily by the arm and pulled her away from Cora. Mary tried to make out the expression on Della's face, but now Della was busy putting change in her purse and making *calm down* motions to her excitable sons. Lily was licking an ice cream and seemed perfectly fine.

Mary turned back to Ruth Cavanagh.

'I can ask Robbie if he knows a glazier?' she tried, as Lily skipped towards her, licking her ice cream.

'Della bought it for me!' Lily said, a beaming grin splitting her face.

'I owed ya,' Della called over, from her safe spot by the van. Too far away for Mary to see the wink, but she could hear it.

Ruth shook her head, her eyes still on the ice cream queue and Della. 'Spoil them rotten, then wonder why they run riot.'

'Run riot?'

Ruth folded her arms. 'Trespassing and vandalism. You mark my words, this will escalate.'

'Gosh. Well, hopefully not,' Mary said, unsure how to respond to Ruth's prophecy. 'We need to go now, I hope you get a glazier soon.'

She took Lily's hand and walked back towards Della, leaving Ruth staring after them.

'Did something happen at the top of the queue with Cora and Lily?' Mary asked, as they walked back to Rowanbrook Drive to the tune of a buzzing lawn mower.

'Oh. Ah, nothing really. Cora was pretending to eat Lily's ice cream, just a bit of fun, but she was gripping her wrist too tightly. No harm meant, I'd say. Though I wonder too if Cora'd be as well off making a few friends her own age. Might be healthier for her. What did Ruth want?'

'Someone threw a stone and broke her back window. I'm sure it was an accident but you know Ruth, she wants to string everyone up.' They stopped outside Della's house. 'By the way, is

Fran in? I was going to ask if she could watch Lily next Wednesday afternoon?'

'You didn't want to ask Cynthia? Maybe you're worried about Robbie after all?' Della said, winking.

Mary smiled. 'I just don't know if she's the most responsible person to leave taking care of a child. She doesn't seem quite . . . with it?'

'She's ditzy all right.'

'No, it's more than that. Sometimes I wonder if she's on something.'

'*On something?*' Della's eyes widened. 'Do you mean drugs?'

'Maybe. I could be wrong. Perhaps she's just a little odd.'

'Speaking of odd' – Della did an exaggerated double-take – 'is that Gavin Bowman mowing your lawn?'

'Yes. Robbie arranged it as some kind of lead-in to doing work experience at his office. I'm not sure he knows what he's doing though. He doesn't look as though he's ever used a lawn mower before.'

'Do him no harm at all – that boy could do with a dose of honest, hard work. I reckon Robbie was absolutely right,' Della said, sounding not unlike Ruth Cavanagh.

Gavin's inexperience with gardening became more than apparent half an hour later when he tripped over the hedge trimmer cable and landed in a bramble bush. Lily came inside to tell Mary, with a scratched and bruised Gavin following behind.

'Oh, goodness! Let me get some ointment and some gauze.' Mary reached for the first-aid box, and set about cleaning Gavin's scratches. He sat silently on a kitchen chair, his arm resting on the table, watching as she dabbed and cleaned. After a while, Mary, although not given to chatter, began to feel awkward. Even when Lily made a cup of pretend tea for

Gavin, he took it wordlessly, never taking his eyes off Mary's hands.

'Now!' she said brightly, as soon as she was done. 'I think you're good to go.'

He stood, lightly touching the Band-Aids on his arm, and looked up at her.

'I'll come back tomorrow to do some more,' he said.

'There's really no need. I think maybe your gardening days are done. I'll explain to Robbie.'

'I'll be here.' That was all he said, before turning and leaving through the back door.

He came back the following day, and the day after, and the day after that. And each afternoon, he found a reason to come inside the house – a glass of water, a splinter in his thumb, a request to wash his hands. Lily made pretend tea for him whenever he came in, and each time, he took it without saying a word.

'He's in the kitchen more often than he's in the garden,' Mary confided in Della, towards the end of the week. 'I'd rather he stayed outdoors, but how do I say that?'

'You just say it,' was Della's response. 'Be direct. You're too nice, that's your problem. I bet while in your head you're wishing he'd leave, on the outside, you're smiling and welcoming and filling his glass. Am I right?'

She was right. But it was awkward. 'Be direct', as Mary knew, after five years of marriage to Robbie, was easier said than done.

15

June 2018

'JUST THINKING, YOU HAVE therapy tonight, don't you?' Mark says when he arrives in from work on Tuesday evening. 'Maybe you could bring up Lily Murphy with Dr Kinsella and try to exorcise some ghosts?'

I hesitate, guilt eating away at me, and Mark mistakes it for something else.

'I know you see her because of what happened to your parents, but I'm sure she wouldn't mind you bringing up the whole Lily thing and the new house and how it's making you feel? Maybe there's a link even – your own childhood trauma rearing up because you're thinking about what happened to Lily?'

A link. I wish it was as simple as a link.

'Look, I can see it's going around and around in your head and I think you need to do something proactive now,' he continues. 'Or nothing will change, it'll just keep driving you mad. And surely Dr Kinsella is the person to advise?'

I nod and promise I'll do as he suggests.

Do something proactive. Those are the words that are running through my head as I drive towards Woodbine Street on Tuesday evening. Mark is right. Thinking and worrying and googling is getting me nowhere. The more I look at photos of Lily, the more I see a resemblance; she's familiar now because I keep examining the same pictures. But the date . . . that's more concrete. I know Lila was three when she came to us. And I know I was nine, which makes it 1985. Was it July? I'm not sure. But I'm certain of the year, and maybe I need to start asking direct questions now, to the people who were there back then – people like Susie and Cora and Fran. I need to know if Lily was my sister. If Lila was Lily.

Not too *direct though*, warns a voice in my head. No questions that could raise suspicions or lead back to me. I just want the truth, so I can move on.

I start with Susie, calling her from the car on my way to Woodbine Street.

'Joanna! So nice to hear from you. Is everything OK?'

'Yeah, I'm on my way to Dr Kinsella, and I still have that whole Lily Murphy story rumbling around in my head, so I wanted to ask you a few things about it, if that's OK?'

'Well, of course!'

'I was wondering if anyone ever called Lily by a nickname?'

'Mmm. Her mother called her Lilybug, sometimes. Mary was American. That always seemed like a very American nickname to me.'

'Any other names? Lila maybe?'

'*Lila?* No. It doesn't ring a bell. But then this was thirty years ago. And I couldn't say what other names Mary and Robbie might have called her at home. I used to call Mark all sorts of things. I remember—'

I jump in quickly before she goes down memory lane. 'Oh, I'm nearly at Dr Kinsella's – can I just check something else with you real quick. Did Lily have any health issues – an illness?'

'Illness? She got colds like anyone else, I'm sure, and I

remember she had a fever a few weeks before she went missing. Is that the kind of thing you mean?'

'No, I meant like a long-term condition?'

'Gosh, not that I know of. I suppose she might have had something Mary didn't mention . . . Where's all this coming from?'

'Just research. Things I found online about kids who might be Lily.'

'But darling, if the police can't find out what happened to her, you'll hardly find it on the internet.'

'I know. Just an itch I need to scratch, to help feel more settled in the new house. I'd better go, I'm at Dr Kinsella's now.'

She says goodbye as I find a parking spot just opposite Kinsella House. I'm early and wondering if there's time to call Cora or Fran, though perhaps it's better to ask them in person. The irony doesn't escape me. If there's anywhere I should be able to figure things out, it's here, tonight, right inside this building. I sit staring at it. The three-storey, flat-roof complex; so modern, I imagine, when it was first designed. Now, surrounded by taller, glossier blocks of offices and apartments, Kinsella House looks dated. I force myself to get out of the car, conscious, as always, of the paradox: it's a struggle to make myself turn up here, and yet I can't stay away. Week in, week out, the same internal discord. Anyway. I'm here now and she's expecting me. I lock the car and cross Woodbine Street towards the main door. Yes, this is exactly where I should be able to sort it all out. But for now, that's a step too far.

On Wednesday morning, when I come back from the school run, Fran is in her garden, deadheading roses.

'Hi, Fran, I'm glad I caught you. I'm still mulling over the whole Lily Murphy thing and I was wondering if you could help me with a few questions?'

Fran stops. 'What kind of questions?'

'Did anyone have a nickname for Lily?'

'Ha. I used to call her Liliput. I forgot about that.' She squints in the sunlight. 'And Mary used to call her Lilybug, which made me cringe back then. I don't know why. Teenagers are so judgy. No idea if anyone else had a nickname for her though.'

'Did anyone call her Lila?'

Fran shakes her head. 'Not that I remember . . . But I wouldn't have thought "Lila" was a nickname for "Lily"?'

'True. And was Lily ill at all – any health conditions?'

'I'm sure she was sick from time to time but nothing that stands out.' Fran picks up a rake and begins dragging it through a patch of brown grass. 'What's with all the questions?'

'Something I saw online . . . speculation about a child some random commenter had seen. He thought she had a long-term illness that required medication and the parents were calling her Lila, and she had dimples like Lily and—'

'Ah, come on. Dimples and a name that's not even Lily? Sure plenty of children have dimples. There must have been some other reason this internet person thought the child was Lily?'

'I suppose . . . I've no idea what though.' My cheeks heat up and I switch to a safer subject. 'I don't suppose you know a good tree surgeon? The trees at the very back of our garden are blocking the sunlight quite early each evening.'

'They're not yours,' Fran says, still whacking the brown grass.

'I'm sorry?'

'The tallest trees – the ones that block the light – they're in the garden *behind* yours.'

'Oh.'

'This goes way back to when the Murphys were here. The woman who lived behind them was called Ruth Cavanagh, and good God, she wasn't a woman given to finding joy, but she got as close as she ever could when it came to those trees, and telling Robbie Murphy she wouldn't top them.'

'She sounds great craic.'

'Ha. She was our local Miss Trunchbull. A retired school teacher whose favourite method of teaching was intimidation. The smaller kids thought she was a witch – people used to say she made poison out of foxgloves in her garden.' Fran leans on the rake. 'Always giving out, never more happy than when she was judging. You know the type. My pal Zara was her niece and Jesus, when she found out—' Fran stops suddenly. 'Anyway, not a very nice person.'

I nod. I'm guessing she'd been about to mention the Robbie-Zara-pregnancy rumour and I want to ask about it, but I can't think of a way to do it without sounding gossipy. Instead, I ask her about Saturday night.

'Oh – I saw you in The Wine Cask the other evening. I went over to say hi but I just missed you.' Fran looks disconcerted all of a sudden and although I don't know what I've done wrong, I find myself rushing to cover the awkwardness. 'I love that we're walking distance from The Wine Cask now, it's nice to be able to leave the car at home and have a glass of wine.'

'Indeed. Anyway, I need to get on,' is all she says, before turning away and walking indoors.

16

'MORE TEA, FWAN-CES?' LILY pushed the pink plastic teacup towards Fran's mouth before she had time to reply – to say, *I'm OK thanks, Lily, fourteen cups is my limit.* How on earth did Mary ever get a minute's peace? They were sitting on a bench, in the shadow of the huge evergreen trees at the end of the garden. Fran had made sure Lily was safely in the shade but had positioned the bench strategically, so that she could have her own legs in the sun. She needed a bit of colour before the J-1 summer. Americans, as everyone knew, were very tanned.

The day was still and the sky a deep denim blue, with not even the tops of the trees swaying, which was why the sudden crackle of twigs stood out, she supposed, when she thought about it afterwards.

A crackle, followed by a hurried rustling, then more cracking, as though someone had stepped on twigs, then done so again in their haste to retreat.

It was coming from behind her, beyond the trees.

Fran stood up from the bench. Could it have been an animal? It was too loud to be a bird. A dog? A fox? A human?

She stood still for a moment, listening.

Nothing.

But she had the strongest sensation that someone else was standing still, listening too.

She shook herself. How could there be someone there? Nobody could get into the back garden without coming through the house. Unless they'd come through the side gate . . . Mary had told her it would be unlocked, so Gavin could let himself in to mow the lawn.

'Let's go back inside, Liliput,' she said to Lily, taking her by the hand. 'Because Mammy and Daddy will be home soon,' she added, for the benefit of anyone who might be listening.

Lily wanted to look at books in her bedroom and, reluctant to leave her alone (or to be alone herself, perhaps), Fran joined her, sitting on the floor, her back against the bed, her feet against the radiator under the window. She examined her runners as Lily turned pages. Shabby and yellowing, where they'd once been pristine white. No matter. In Virginia Beach, she'd live in flip-flops. Four more weeks, then goodbye Dublin. Her eyes travelled beyond the radiator to the Holly Hobbie wallpaper that was peeling off near the skirting board. She looked more closely, her attention caught by something dark, and realized that beneath the colourful paper, the wall was painted black. How odd, she thought. Reaching out, she lifted the corner of the wallpaper where it had already come unstuck. The wall underneath was indeed black, but only in that one patch. Like someone had coloured it in with thick marker. Carefully, she lifted the paper further – it came away easily, already unstuck. The coloured-in patch of black was actually part of a bigger picture. Fran leaned closer, examining it. The thick black oval shape, the white circle inside, the black circle inside that.

It was an eye.

And it was staring at her.

Feeling suddenly on edge, she smoothed down the wallpaper to cover the eye, and stood.

'Maybe we'll bring the book downstairs,' she said, taking Lily by the hand. *Maybe we'll go hang out in my house.* Mary hadn't left her a key to get back in if they went out, but Della kept a spare for Mary next door. She could use that. And if she was lucky, Della might mind Lily for a few minutes while Fran took a break from all the pretend tea.

When Mary arrived back that Wednesday evening, Lily was sitting in front of the television.

'I just put it on now,' Fran explained, cursing herself. She's spent all day entertaining the child, and as soon as she turned on the telly, Mary arrived back. But Mary didn't seem worried. If anything, she was distracted, half listening while Fran told her about their day.

'Actually,' Fran said, as Mary rummaged through her purse for money, 'there was one strange thing – when we were on the bench in the garden, there was a noise. As though there was someone there, hiding among the trees. I was thinking after, it might have been someone in the garden behind?'

Mary looked up from her purse.

'I mean, I was a bit spooked at the time,' Fran continued, 'but there obviously couldn't have been someone in *your* garden, so it must have been someone in Ruth Cavanagh's?'

'There's a pathway between the gardens,' Mary said. 'It's very narrow, only a few feet wide. A kind of dirt track between the trees. I think the builders used it for access and it was meant to be closed off after they finished Rowanbrook, but it never was.'

'Really? I had no idea!' Fran said. 'You mean, right behind our house too?'

'Yes, but you have that big, high wall at the end of your garden, so you can't see it.'

True. For reasons now lost to history, her father had built a twelve-foot wall at the end of their garden, so instead of the gently swaying evergreens everyone else looked out at, her family had grey concrete. An apt legacy from the man who had added no value whatsoever to any of their lives.

'So, you think someone might have been walking along that path when I was out there with Lily? Watching and listening?'

'Perhaps kids passing through,' Mary said. 'They do that sometimes, to get to the green. Maybe it was Ellen from next door. Now, this is for you.' She passed a five-pound note to Fran. Creepy noises and evil eyes notwithstanding, this was easily the best paid babysitting job around.

Later that night, on the phone to Zara, Fran filled her in on her afternoon next door.

'I found this weird drawing under the wallpaper in Lily's room,' she said, keeping her voice low while dragging the phone into her bedroom. 'Some kind of evil eye type thing.'

'God. Like a curse? Do you think Mary and Robbie know about it?' Zara's family had a telephone extension in her parents' bedroom, so she had all the privacy she wanted.

'I don't know . . . I didn't say anything because I assumed it was them who put it there, but maybe it wasn't.'

'Hmm. I could see Mary believing in that kind of thing, definitely. Not Robbie though,' Zara mused. 'He's far too smart. Have you ever heard him talk about politics? He makes the Anglo-Irish agreement sound interesting. One time, on our way home from babysitting—'

And she was off. As Zara zipped from subject to subject – Robbie, fake ID for America, dresses to bring to Virginia

Beach – Fran let her chatter uninterrupted. Virginia Beach was exactly what Zara needed to fix her broken heart. And even though the Robbie infatuation was silly – so ridiculously silly – it was harmless most of the time. If it got Zara through her break-up, and as long as she didn't actually act on it, what harm could it do?

As Zara moved on to the topic of free drinks on the transatlantic flight, Fran pulled the phone across her room towards her bookshelves. Every book she'd ever owned was still there – a row of *Sweet Valley High* paperbacks, a half-dozen Robert Ludlum spy novels, and all her Stephen Kings. On its own, at the end of the bottom shelf, sat the big red hardback encyclopaedia she used to use for schoolwork. She picked it up and sat on her narrow bed, leafing through the 'E' section as Zara kept talking.

Fran traced her finger down the page. There. *The evil eye is a curse or legend believed to be cast by a malevolent glare, usually given to a person when they are unaware.*

Fran stared. Was someone trying to curse Lily? Or the whole family? Should she say something? She shook herself. She was being silly – it was all nonsense. Nobody believed in curses and evil eyes, Fran decided, as she closed the book and tuned back into Zara. There was no need to say anything.

Three weeks later, that thought came back to haunt her.

17

June 2018

IT'S ALMOST TIME TO collect Sophie from preschool and I'm still trying to work out how best to ask Cora the questions about Lily. She'll more than likely be at work right now, and I don't know her well enough to phone her out of the blue, so I opt for a message instead.

> Hi Cora, so nice to do coffee yesterday. I hope you don't mind me asking but I found some interesting stuff online about Lily Murphy, rumours that she had a long-term illness and people used to call her 'Lila' as a nickname – do you know if any of that is true? Susie (my MIL) and Fran Burke next door couldn't remember but thought you might know. Joanna x

The blue ticks are immediate. Then *Cora is typing*. Then *Cora is online*. And again, *Cora is typing*. This continues for so long, it's time to pick up Sophie. Cora's answer finally comes through as I'm walking up the driveway of Sophie's preschool.

> Hi Joanna. As mentioned, I won't talk about that morning. But if you say you're asking your questions to others as well, I'll take

you at your word. I don't remember any nickname. Or illness. Sorry can't be of more assistance. Cora.

I can't help wondering how it took her fifteen minutes to compose a message that's basically 'sorry, no' but perhaps if she's at work, she's trying to type without being seen. Either way, it's another dead end.

A message from Susie pops up on my phone just as I'm about to walk through the nursery doors.

Hi Joanna, I found some old photographs and videos from Mark's childhood. Some pics of neighbours and Lily Murphy there too. Call by when you can and I'll show you, Sx

A fizz of anticipation bubbles up as I type the reply.

I can come tonight or tomorrow morning when kids at school?

Her response is swift.

Sorry, out tonight and golf tomorrow. Maybe Friday morning?

It will have to do.

Two hours later, I have all three kids and we're walking back to Rowanbrook with Adana and her three, for an impromptu coffee and playdate. This is the part of being at home I like most. The afternoons supervising homework, less so. As soon as this thought hits, I feel guilty. The whole point of taking time out from work is to spend afternoons supervising homework, and five weeks is a little soon for the novelty to wear off.

Five of the kids are walking ahead and Adana is pushing her youngest in the buggy, filling me in on a newspaper piece she read online last night – an interview with Mary Murphy a week after Lily disappeared.

'God, that poor woman. Imagine trying to speak to a journalist. Imagine your child being gone a week . . .'

'I know. Horrific,' Adana says. 'And imagine wondering if one of the people helping you search is actually responsible.'

'Do you think so? Really?'

Adana shrugs as we turn into Rowanbrook Drive.

'I don't know. The thing is, everyone believes she fell in the river. But then why didn't they find her? It sounds like it's little more than a shallow stream. Well, *you'd* know, you live here – it's not a raging white-water rapid, is it?'

I fish for my key as we approach Number Six.

'I don't actually, I haven't been there. We could have a look?'

Without answering, Adana turns the buggy and calls her two older kids.

'OK gang, we're going on a walk,' she says as they run towards her, Sophie in between them, Ben and Emily trailing behind.

A shiver runs down my bare arms, despite the warm sunshine.

'But everyone be careful, it's a bit dangerous,' I warn, leading the way towards the green and the woods and the river beyond.

'See those red-brick houses there,' I say to Adana as she pushes the buggy across the dry, spindly grass, 'they're the ones that were being built when Lily went missing. At least that's what I figure from reading the Wikipedia page.'

'So, Mary and the other women were somewhere there, I guess,' Adana says, pointing back to the edge of the green, 'and the kids were playing over there in the trees.' She shields her eyes to look ahead towards the wooded area into which our children have just disappeared.

'And in the building site too. The kids kept sneaking in there, apparently.'

'Speaking of kids, we'd better keep up with ours,' Adana says, pushing the buggy towards the trees. 'Imagine the headlines: Women exploring mystery disappearance manage to lose six kids of their own.'

'Well, we've only lost five,' I remind her, nodding towards the buggy. 'We're doing OK.'

Inside the woods, the light is different. Even when the sun makes it through the trees, it's a quieter light somehow. A colder light. And even with the noise of the kids as they crash through branches, there's something eerie about this place that makes me shiver. Maybe it's the contrast with the sunlight, or maybe it's the silence. Or maybe it's because we know what happened here. Adana glances over, and I'm waiting for a customary wisecrack, but none is forthcoming. Solemn is the word that comes to mind. The woods feel solemn.

Without speaking, we push on, following the flash of blue that is Sophie's t-shirt. Whoops and shouts reach our ears as the kids spot the river. When Adana and I catch up, the five children are hunkered at the water's edge. Ben has found a stick and is testing to see how deep it is. Adana's kids are throwing stones into it, and Sophie is throwing daisies. Emily just watches, as the copper-coloured water flows past. It's little more than a stream, really; 'river' is far too grand a term. Could a child get swept away in it? Hardly likely. It looks about six inches deep, no more, if Ben's poking is anything to go by.

'Not a white-water rapid then,' Adana says, rocking the buggy gently back and forth.

I watch as Sophie plucks a fresh handful of daisies and begins throwing them one by one into the water, trying, I think, to hit a rock that juts up in the middle of the stream.

'No. Unless it was a lot bigger back then, it seems weird that anyone would even suggest it was dangerous.'

'And the parents would hardly have let the kids play here if it was a hazard.'

'Exactly.'

'So, where does that leave us?'

I shake my head, watching as Sophie leans forward to grab at something in the water.

'Be careful, you're too close to the edge.'

You're such a worry wart. Lighten up, says a little voice in my head. I am. I know I am. But I can't help myself.

'Sophie, did you hear me?'

Sophie ignores me completely, still trying to reach a daisy – one she threw in herself, just moments earlier.

'Sophie, can you please move back from the edge?'

I take a few steps towards her and later, I wonder if it is this, perhaps, that causes it – Sophie glances back, loses her balance and falls in, hitting her head on the mid-stream rock.

For a second, I'm frozen. My body lets me down, my limbs don't move. Then adrenaline kicks in and I run to the river and I'm shin-deep in water, scooping her out.

'Sophie!'

Blood seeps from a small cut on her forehead and at first, she's too shocked to cry. I hug her wet body into me, then pull away to check the cut. There's a lot of blood but it's not deep. Sophie coughs and blinks as water streams from her nose, then her eyes widen and she bursts into loud sobs.

'You got a fright, that's all, you'll be OK,' I whisper, pulling her into a hug again. *I'm sorry, I'm sorry, I'm sorry.'*

Adana hunkers down and hands me a tissue to press against the cut. 'It's just a graze, she'll be fine,' she says gently.

'Is she OK, Mum?' Ben asks, hovering above us, a worried expression on his small face.

I clear my throat. 'She is. Sorry, love, I'm over-reacting. Why don't we go home and get a plaster, and I have ice-pops for everyone.'

This elicits a cheer from the uninjured children, and a small nod from Sophie.

And off we go, trooping through the woods, me carrying Sophie, Adana pushing the buggy, the other children running ahead, back across the green, on down to Rowanbrook Drive, and into Number Six.

'So,' Adana says, when the kids are safely in the garden eating their ice-pops.

'So,' I reply, scrubbing blood from my white t-shirt.

'I guess if she fell in the water and no one was around, she might have been too shocked to get herself out?' Adana says. 'Especially if she hit her head?'

I swallow, batting away an image of Lily toppling into the stream. A Sophie-sized Lily, but all alone. I don't want this to be true. I really don't. But if it is, it means I didn't do it. Lila was not Lily, and I'm not responsible for Lily's death. Then again, does it really make any difference? Lila is still dead, whether she was Lily or not. Nothing changes that.

'But if she fell in the water, why didn't they find a body?'

'I don't know . . .' Adana says. 'Will we keep looking?'

I nod, open the laptop and key 'Lily Murphy Disappearance' into Google. On autopilot, I click on the first link.

Adana shakes her head. 'There's no point in going into Wikipedia again. That's going to say the same thing it says every day. Check the news tab instead.'

'Yes, boss,' I mutter, but she's right. I'm not holding out much hope for anything fresh in the news tab either, but the first search result is, in fact, something we haven't seen before.

'Another Deep Dive blog post . . .'

Heads together, we begin to read.

Lily Murphy and the Locked Room
Google 'killer kids' and you might be surprised at what you find. Evil is everywhere and it can start surprisingly young. Even in a quiet Dublin suburb, in 1985?

Well, yes and no. Sometimes they don't mean harm but once things have gone past a certain point, there's no going back.

Every once in a while, there's a kid who takes things too far. And there are parents who protect their children when they do wrong. Was that what happened in Edenvale? And was it fully investigated at the time? Probably not. The parents didn't want to talk, and it's easier to blame strangers. But if no one even asked the question, will we ever have the answer?

Killer kids. My breathing is short and fast now, and I'm trying to slow it down before Adana notices. *Get a grip, Joanna.* This Deep Dive guy can't be talking about me. I've never told, and the only other person who knows is never going to tell. This is not about me. *Breathe.*

'OK, this just got really interesting,' Adana says, still looking at the screen. She's oblivious and I'm grateful. 'What do you think it means? And what's the "locked room" reference in the title?'

'I . . . I don't know. I could try asking Cora . . . though she doesn't want to talk about that day.'

'Who's Cora again?'

'She was with Lily during the game of Hide and Seek,' I remind her.

'Oh yeah. The last person to see Lily alive.'

As soon as Adana leaves, I start to type a second comment on Deep Dive.

> Hi, I commented recently to say I'm interested in the Lily Murphy case. Reading up on it, I can see that it's clear she drowned. No need to reply, thanks.

It's not a delete button, but it will have to do. Just as I hit Submit, my phone rings. Cora O'Brien. Not sure what to expect, I answer with a tentative 'Hello?'

'Joanna, hi' – she rushes on without waiting for a return greeting – 'I keep thinking about the questions you asked me in your text earlier. Where did you get the name Lila? I've searched online and I can't see any reference to it or a link between the names Lily Murphy and Lila?'

Shit. Scrambling for an answer, I come up with something that is immediately clearly ridiculous.

'Oh. Well you see, a good few years ago, I saw a little girl when we were on holidays. Blonde hair and blue eyes and dimples like Lily Murphy. And her mother was calling her Lila. It always stuck with me, but realistically it was probably because it was around the ten-year anniversary of her disappearance so her photo was in the newspapers again.'

'But if it was the ten-year anniversary, how would she have been a little girl? She'd have been thirteen?'

I'm an idiot. 'Yeah sorry, I meant a girl around thirteen. Don't mind me, I'm just addled from all the googling. Forget the Lila thing.'

'OK.'

I wait for more, but Cora has disconnected the call.

18

June 2018

THE TEXT FROM CORA early on Thursday morning catches me by surprise.

> Joanna. I've been thinking more about our coffee the other day.
> I was a bit quick to stop you when you asked about the morning
> Lily disappeared. It might be good to talk. I've called in sick to
> work today. Do you want to stop by for coffee?

I reply immediately, telling her I'll be there as soon as I'm back from the school run.

Mark must see something in my expression.

'All OK?' he asks, between mouthfuls of toast.

'Yeah, grand – have you seen Emily's water bottle anywhere?'

'No, but just use the spare one.'

'It's in one of the boxes I haven't unpacked yet,' I say, rummaging for the third time through her school bag, as though the bottle will suddenly appear.

'Mum!' Emily shouts from upstairs. 'Ben is taking like an *hour* to brush his teeth, can you tell him to get out?' Mark and I exchange an eye-roll. Ben is no great fan of teeth-brushing so this has all the hallmarks of a deliberate provocation. But

Sophie needs help with her shoes and I'm trying to get lunches into school bags and fill missing water bottles.

'Mark, could you go up and referee Emily and Ben – just hurry him up a bit?'

'Sorry, I gotta go before traffic gets too heavy,' Mark says, planting a kiss on my forehead. He's gone before I can answer. I let out a sigh. When I was working, I had to be in earlier than he did, leaving him to hand over to our childminder every single morning, and after years of dealing with bathroom wars and lunchboxes and shoes, I can't blame him for making his escape now that he can. *This is what you signed up for*, I remind myself as the sound of Emily pounding on the bathroom door filters down the stairs – this is all part of 'spending more time with the kids'.

It's a full hour before I get them all to school and arrive back in Rowanbrook, but finally, I'm in Cora's kitchen.

'It's not in great shape,' she says, matter-of-factly. 'My mother arranged to have it rented out when she went into a nursing home, and the last lot left it in a mess.'

To me, the mess looks less about bad tenants or wear and tear, and more about dirty dishes in the sink and open cans of food on the counter top. There's a musty smell, something like clothes that have been washed but not dried, and beneath that, I realize, there's a smell of stale smoke. It makes my skin crawl, reminding me of another place, just as it always does. So when Cora suggests we take our coffees outside, I don't hesitate.

The garden is a different vista entirely. Huge leafy hedges border the sides, and tall trees like ours line the back. Raised flower beds, edged with stone, run the length of the garden, one on each side, and at the end there's one more raised bed, this one a blaze of wildflower colour with tulips, foxgloves and poppies.

'What a beautiful garden.'

'Yes. My mother insisted on doing it herself, and once she went into the nursing home, she made me promise to keep it tidy and tended. Every time I visited, she'd be over at the window, smoking those disgusting black cigarillos of hers, rasping away at me. "How is my garden, Cora? You must look after it." That woman never cared about anything other than herself and this garden.' She doesn't sound bitter. Just resigned.

We take seats, side by side, on a wooden bench that faces the sun.

'So, Joanna. I think we can say we're friends now, yes?'

I'm a little taken aback and glad we're side by side so she can't see my face.

'Of course.'

'I was premature when we talked on Tuesday. I may even have come across abrupt or rude when you asked about that morning. People tell me I can be abrupt.'

'God no, not at all,' I say, remembering how she held her hand up to stop me mid-sentence. 'Totally understand. I shouldn't have asked.'

'I've thought it over, and I think it's time to talk.'

I tense on the bench, trying not to look eager, wondering what's brought on this change of mind.

'There's no big secret,' she continues. 'The thing is, I wasn't actually there when Lily disappeared. I'd gone to another girl's house to get a drink of water – a girl called Aoife who was a few years older than me. When I got back, I couldn't see Lily where I'd left her. But it was Hide and Seek, people were always moving places. I just found another spot and stayed there until it was time to go home for lunch.'

She turns to face me and it's going to be weird if I don't meet her gaze, even though it means we're so close I can smell the coffee on her breath.

'I see,' is all I say, because really, what is there to say? I don't know what I was hoping and she was hardly going to confide in me thirty years on that she saw someone kidnap Lily, but this feels anticlimactic.

'I don't like talking about it because people are so nosy. Always wanting to know what it was like to be the last person to see her alive.' She doesn't sound worried or guilty or sad, but perhaps that's what thirty years does. 'And the irony is, what happened that morning is nothing compared to what happened afterwards. It destroyed my family.' There's a tinge of anger in her voice now. I stay quiet.

'After word went around that the police had interviewed my dad, people would *not stop* talking about it. It followed him everywhere. "That man who did something to Lily." "No smoke without a fire." And there were no grounds for it. No reason to interview him, even. It was so *wrong*.'

I'm trying to put myself in her shoes. It must have been dreadful. And maybe I'd have felt the same. But some part of me thinks any logical person would understand that the police had to investigate. And they must have had good reason for interviewing Victor O'Brien.

'The thing is . . .' She pauses. 'The thing is, what happened was all my fault.'

19

June 2018

CORA IS JUST INCHES from my face, staring straight at me, and I have no idea how to respond to what she's just said. *What happened was all my fault.* Does she mean because she was with Lily that morning and left her alone? Or something else entirely? Did she see something? Or *do* something? The silence goes on too long, demanding a reply. I clear my throat.

'Cora, it wasn't your fault. You were only a child.'

'That's not what I mean. It's something my mother told me shortly before she died.'

'Oh?'

'The police never interviewed my dad. They came to our house a number of times, but it was always to speak to me.'

'Because you were the last one with her, I presume?'

'No, it was more than that.' Her skin flushes. 'Someone – I don't know who – reported me. Said I was hurting Lily.'

My mouth drops open but I have absolutely no idea what to say.

Cora keeps talking, her voice laced with anger.

'I never knew at the time. I remember the police coming and I think I remember them speaking to me, but as far as I understood, they were here to see my dad. That's what *she* told everyone.'

'Who?'

'My mother. She may not have bothered with hugs or affection, but appearances mattered. She didn't want people saying I did something to Lily. She didn't want it tainting me for the rest of my life, preventing me from becoming a doctor or lawyer or finding the right husband.' A wry smile now. 'So when people noticed the police car at the house and started gossiping, she made my dad step up. She let people think the police were here to see him.'

'Oh God.'

'I think she assumed that because my dad was a successful businessman, people wouldn't take it seriously, but it blew up and spread like wildfire.'

'I'm so sorry.'

'Those months after Lily disappeared were awful. My mother was as cold as ever and my dad just drank more, and neither of them talked to each other or to me. The little bits I knew, I learned from listening to their conversations with other people.'

Again, no compunction about eavesdropping. Cora is, by any definition, unlike anyone I've ever met. Or perhaps she's just more honest.

'It sounds like the whole thing had a dreadful impact on your family,' I say, thinking about her father's death. 'But it still wasn't your fault. It was your mother's decision to muddy the truth. You were a child.' I can't help wondering about the report that she was hurting Lily but I'm not going to ask. Instead I say: 'People don't realize, I suppose, about the wider impact of Lily's disappearance. They think about Mary and Robbie and Lily, but not the effect it had on the Rowanbrook community too?'

'Exactly. And you can see why I didn't want to speak about it – any of it; the morning it happened, the police, the claim that I was hurting Lily, my dad's death . . . But now, I realize I need to be the one to break the cycle. So I decided rather than leaving you in the dark, like *I* was in the dark, I'll talk.'

This has the air of a rehearsed speech – a conjured-up piece of psychobabble – but I'm not going to argue.

'Perhaps,' she says, 'after all these years, you and I might be the ones to solve this?'

'Maybe . . .' This is dangerous ground. I need my questions answered but I really don't want Cora or anyone else asking their own questions.

'We could start with the things you found online about Lily – the stuff about her being ill, and the name Lila. Will we have a look on those websites together?'

Oh crap. 'Sure. I can't remember now where I saw them, but how about I look tonight on my laptop and send you the links?'

A pause. 'OK then. I want to get to the bottom of this. For my dad's sake. He drank himself to death over what happened. It wasn't the bridge that killed him, he was gone long before then. If I can find out what happened to Lily, I'll have justice for my dad. It won't bring him back, but seeing the right person pay will help.'

I swallow, unable to think of anything to say. And together we sit, staring at the flower beds and the riot of colour under the hot June sun, the idyllic scene belying everything going on inside my mind.

My head is pounding when I leave Cora's garden – too much sun or too much coffee or perhaps just too much ricocheting around in my brain. The headache is still there that night when Mark texts to say he'll be late home, and I don't mean to take it out on the kids but when Ben puts his uneaten pasta on to Emily's plate and Emily throws it back towards his, missing it and hitting the floor, I lose it.

'Stop!' It comes out in a roar. Three stunned faces look up at me. 'For God's sake, can we please have one dinner in peace? One dinner where nobody fights?'

They nod in silence. My headache is worse. No parenting medals for me tonight. I *hate* this. I hate shouting at them. Being unpredictable. Losing control. My one and only wish for my kids is to keep them safe from the kind of upbringing I had. And yet, here we are.

'I can help clean up,' Ben says quietly. Always the quickest to read the room.

Even Emily, usually slower to back down, begins gathering plates. Sophie, chin to chest, doesn't move.

'I'm sorry for shouting. It's been a long day.'

'But you're not working at your job any more?' Ben says, and all I can do is shake my head.

As the kids slink out of the room to the refuge of their devices, a text pings through on mine. It's from Cora, and it leaves me hot and cold all at once.

I've worked it out. I know why you were asking about Lily and the name 'Lila'. We need to talk.

20

June 1985

MARY FELT HER JAW tighten as Gavin's familiar shape passed the kitchen window. He didn't ring the doorbell any more to announce his arrival but seemed to come and go whenever suited him. No lawn needed that much tending and this certainly wasn't what Robbie had envisaged when he offered Gavin 'work experience' – Mary was sure of that. But there didn't seem to be any polite way to make it stop either. She found herself pulling drapes and blinds for privacy and keeping Lily indoors, though she couldn't quite say why he made her so uncomfortable. It wasn't anything he said. He rarely spoke at all, in fact. It was more the way he looked at her. The silent, intense gaze. And his very presence. Home was the one place you could expect some privacy, some space to be yourself. She reached up and pulled the kitchen blind.

'Can I get a glass of water?'

His voice caught her off guard, and she smacked her head on the open icebox door when she straightened without thinking. Tears sprang up as she bit back a yelp of pain.

'Let me help you.' His hands were on her arms now, leading her to a kitchen chair, sitting her down.

'I'm fine, just dazed.'

A bag of frozen peas, pressed to her head. Lily running in, asking what was wrong.

'It's OK, Lilybug, Mommy's just hurt herself.'

'Will I get the special cream? The one you putted on my sore knee before?' Lily paused to remember the name, screwing up her face. 'Arnica!' she said then, pleased with herself.

'No, sweetheart, the frozen peas are all I need.'

'Is he helping you?' Lily asked, pointing at Gavin.

'Yes, but I'm fine now. Thank you, Gavin, I'm fine.'

Lily frowned at Gavin. 'Daddy's good at helping too.'

Mary laughed. 'Of course he is.' She stood up, ducking out from under the bag of peas. 'Thanks again, Gavin, but I'd better let you get back to the garden.'

Gavin nodded, watched her for a moment longer, then walked over to fill himself a glass of water just as Susie Stedman knocked and let herself in through the back door.

'Oh!' she said. 'I didn't realize you had company.'

'Gavin's just getting some water. Come through to the living room.'

'So, does Gavin spend a lot of time here during the day?' Susie asked with a gleam in her eye, as soon as the living room door was closed.

Mary felt her cheeks heat up.

'I wish he wouldn't. Robbie arranged it, when Gavin's parents asked for some work experience. That's what they were talking about at Lily's birthday party.'

'Ah yes, of course! That makes sense now. The Bowmans were telling everyone at the golf club on Saturday what a great man Robbie is, insisting on buying drinks for him all night. I wasn't sure what it was about, but I can tell you, they seem only

delighted to have an "in" with Rowanbrook's golden couple.'
She nudged Mary and Mary broke out the expected smile.

'Hardly golden. I'm sitting here with a throbbing head, looking like goodness knows what. That's why Gavin was in the
kitchen. I bashed my head on the icebox,' she added.

'Well, Gavin wouldn't be my favourite person, but lucky he
was here to help. And you'll have a lovely tidy garden once he
eventually figures out what he's doing.' Susie shook her head.
'Robbie's so good to arrange it for them – I'd say Tom would
run a mile if the Bowmans asked him. But then with six kids of
our own, we don't have the time to take on other people's. It's
different when you've just the one.'

Mary bit her lip. 'Of course. Can I ask, why do you say he's
not your favourite person?'

'Oh, it's nothing really. But Mark's in his year in school and
he says Gavin's trouble.'

'What kind of trouble?'

'The usual – not turning up to class, smoking, and apparently' – she lowered her voice – 'a little bit of a thing with their
science teacher last year. Young, pretty woman who should have
known better. Not sure how true it was but the Bowmans were
called in about it. Cynthia babysat the younger brother the day
of the meeting and overheard them talking about it.'

'Oh. I see. None of this is making me feel any better about
having him here!' Mary laughed to lighten it.

'Then tell him to stop coming.'

'But Robbie arranged it and the Bowmans are so pleased . . .'

'I'm sure they are, but would Robbie like it if he knew about
the science teacher? And that you were feeling uncomfortable?
If I were you, I'd just tell Gavin to stop calling.'

Mary sighed. 'But how do I say it?'

'You just say it. Sometimes you have to be direct. You're too

ANDREA MARA

nice. Take a leaf out of Ines's book. She wouldn't be long sending him off. "You must go now."'

They both laughed at Susie's dreadful attempt at a Spanish accent.

'I'm no Ines O'Brien.'

'And all the better for it,' Susie said.

'Poor Ines. It's funny. Or not funny, so much as strange.'

'What is?'

'That we're all supposedly friends, but nobody really likes her. Robbie can't stand her.'

Susie gave Mary an odd look. 'Yes. Well.' She stopped then as though thinking the better of what she was about to say.

'Oh – does that sound terrible?' Mary asked. 'I should be more charitable. She's had a tough time.'

'You mean the infertility?'

Mary nodded.

Susie tilted her head. 'Was she all that devastated by the news though? She's not exactly a doting mother with Cora.'

'But you said it yourself – you said Victor told Tom they were deeply upset by it?'

'He did,' Susie conceded. 'But maybe she just *thinks* she wants another child. It's all about optics with that woman.'

Mary smiled to herself. Susie wasn't above the 'optics' of parading her six smartly dressed children down the centre aisle at Mass every Sunday.

'By the way,' Susie said, lowering her voice, 'did I hear there was a police car parked outside the Burkes' the other night? Tom thought he saw something when he was out walking?'

'Oh.' Mary's cheeks heated up. 'I didn't see anything . . .'

'Mm. One of the older two in some kind of trouble maybe, hardly Fran or the twins. Not easy for Della on her own.'

'I really don't think Della's kids would—'

124

Susie cut her off. '*That* is because you're too nice. Anyway,' she went on, as they heard the sound of the back door closing, 'back to Gavin – if you want him gone, you need to say so.'

In the end, it was Lily who inadvertently saved the day. She mentioned to Robbie that she was making tea for her new friend Gavin. Robbie wanted to know more and Lily explained that the three of them – Mary, Lily and Gavin – had tea together every afternoon at the kitchen table. This wasn't quite an accurate description of events but it was the end of the gardening. Gavin was promised a week in Robbie's office in July, and he hung up his gardening gloves for good.

He didn't go away though. At night, when Mary closed the curtains, he was there, leaning against the lamp post across the street from her house. In the mornings, when she was out walking with Lily, he was walking too. Or sitting, or leaning or standing or smoking. Sometimes with Della's twins and Ellen next door and Aoife from the Grove and the other kids from round and about. Sometimes on his own. Headphones on. Hands in pockets. Watching. Always watching.

21

June 2018

I STRUGGLE TO MATCH Susie's wide smile when I arrive on her door-step on Friday morning. Cora's text from last night is still imprinted on my brain.

I know why you were asking about Lily.

I haven't replied and she hasn't texted again.

Yet.

'Joanna, where are the kids? Oh yes, I'd forgotten they'd be in school. What a pity. Hopefully you'll bring them to visit more now that you're nearby. We keep forgetting what they look like!'

I nod and agree to bring the kids next time as she leads me through to her beautifully decorated living room. It's a visual feast of cream – cream carpet, cream walls, cream sofas and a cream rug. Susie regularly begs us to bring the kids more often but once they're here, she spends the entire time worrying about her cream living room and hinting that it might be time to go.

There's a tray with a cafetière and some lemon cake already sitting on the glass-topped coffee table, and on the floor beside it a dark brown lidded box, marked '1982–1986'.

The radio is on, tuned to news headlines: more gorse fires, a funeral for the couple who died, and a delay on the DART train line this morning after an 'incident'. Susie makes a face and switches it off.

'We all know what "incident" means – some poor soul jumped, I'll bet. And you've heard quite enough about fires lately. Anyway! I was thinking about all your questions and your . . . anxiety? Yes, anxiety about living in the Murphys' old house, and I thought looking through some old photos might help. Yes? Yes.' She pours coffee into two delicate china cups. 'You'll get a kick out of it too – Mark's in lots of them. He's a bit older than Ben but the spitting image of him. Right, let's see . . .'

She pulls off the lid and I'm gripped by an urge to tell her to stop. To replace the lid, to walk away. But I need to know. Especially if Cora is about to expose the truth.

'I went through them last night,' Susie is saying, 'to find as many of Lily and her family as I could. I got some of Eddie too, the man who had a fight with Robbie. Still can't remember his surname.'

'Hogan. Mark remembered.'

'Of course! Eddie Hogan. Dreadful bull of a man. You'll see. And it was his daughter rumoured to be sleeping with Robbie, I'd forgotten that. Pretty little thing but trouble, I'd say. Quite flighty. I can't imagine Robbie was sleeping with her.' She purses her lips in a way that tells me she doesn't quite buy into her own certainty. 'But the Hogans moved away soon after, and Tom and I had already moved by then, so there were very few of the old crowd left. Everything changed after Lily disappeared.' She sounds wistful. 'It was almost like no one could bear to live there any more.'

'So it was just Mary and Robbie left?'

'And then poor Robbie died, and Mary had to sell.'

'Where did she move to?'

Susie blinks, looking sheepish. 'Somewhere in the city centre

I think, and then I believe she eventually went back to the States, though where exactly I'm not sure . . . I'm afraid we lost touch. That doesn't cast me in a very good light, does it?'

'Oh. I'm sure it was difficult.'

'Well yes, it was. They became very reclusive in their grief and we didn't really know what to say. I used to send Tom over with casseroles but Della Burke and Ruth Cavanagh were sending food too, so it seemed unnecessary. Ruth, in particular, made rather excellent lamb casseroles with vegetables from her own garden. So my paltry efforts were a bit pointless. I was never much of a cook. And . . . it was easier to give them space, you know?'

I nod, reassuring her that I'm not judging. I'm in no position to judge anyone.

'Anyway, we're getting sidetracked. Let's look at the photos.'

The first image shows what looks like a picnic. I recognize Susie, her blonde hair gleaming in the sun, legs demurely curled under her short, check dress. Beside her is Mary Murphy, with a newborn baby in her arms, and then Robbie. Mary is wearing a long white summer dress and huge sunglasses, while Robbie looks a little overheated in suit trousers and a shirt.

'Is that Lily in her arms?' I ask.

'Exactly.' Susie checks the date on the back of the photo. 'June 1982, so she was about four weeks old. That's Victor O'Brien on the next blanket, with Cora.'

Like Robbie, Victor is wearing a suit, and looks deeply uncomfortable sitting on a rug. Cora's small, pale face is solemn.

'Was it a picnic on the green in Rowanbrook?'

'Yes. Our annual "Summer Fun Day". We used to do a clean-up in the morning and have a picnic in the afternoon. Now, see that man standing behind everyone? That's Eddie Hogan.'

He was indeed a bull of a man – his white shirt stretched

across broad, muscular shoulders, his hair cropped close to his scalp. His back is to the camera, but his head is turned to look at something, so his face is visible in side-profile. In one fist, he holds a bottle of stout. Nothing about him looks familiar to me.

'Loved a drink, did Eddie. I remember that.'

'He's huge.'

'Used to be a boxer when he was younger.' Susie's curled lip leaves me in no doubt about what she thinks of people who used to be boxers. 'Worked as a builder on the site in Rowan-brook until they went bust.'

She flips to the next photograph. 'This one's taken on the same day and look, you can see Mark!'

My husband, or the thirteen-year-old version of him, is leaning against a tree with a familiar expression on his face – it's the same one I get from Ben when I try to take his picture.

'Mark hated us taking his picture. Always so embarrassed about everything at that age.'

'Who's that beside him?' I ask, pointing at a dark-haired girl. She's grinning at the camera, far less shy about it than Mark.

'Oh, that's the girl we were talking about – Zara Hogan. The one who' – she lowers her voice – 'slept with Robbie Murphy. *Supposedly* slept with him, I mean.'

'My God, she's just a kid. She can't be more than thirteen or fourteen?'

Susie nods. 'Now, bear in mind, the rumours only started just before Lily disappeared. Three years later. So she'd have been seventeen then.'

'But Robbie was an adult.'

'Oh, I know. But she was absolutely gorgeous, and aren't men easily tempted?'

That's not what I mean at all, and there's so much I could say right now but I let it go as Susie flips to the next photo. Again, it's of Mark and Zara, but Tom, or whoever took the photo, has moved back and there's a third person visible now too, someone I recognize as Fran. And in the background, a little way away, a boy around the same age as Mark. He's on his own, leaning against another tree, hands in pockets, looking over at the trio posing for the photo. He's a good-looking kid, wearing an expression of disinterest and condescension remarkably well.

'Who's that?' I ask.

'A boy called Gavin.' Susie's cheeks flush. 'Awful person. He married a girl from Rowanbrook, if I remember. I don't know what she or anyone else saw in him.'

As I watch her face bloom pink, it strikes me now that she possibly *does* know about the rumours that went around; about Tom and the babysitter, about Mark punching Gavin.

This is my first time seeing Gavin but there's nothing about him that rings any bells. I couldn't say I've never met him any more than I can say I've never met Eddie Hogan or Robbie Murphy or Victor O'Brien, but really, they're just faces that mean nothing. In fact, the only person who looks in any way familiar – and it may be because I know her now as an adult – is Cora.

'Can I see a photo of Cora again?'

'Yes, I have a better one actually. Hold on.' Susie sifts through the pile. 'I was looking at them last night and one in particular stood out. The glum face on Cora, the bored, grumpy expression on her dad . . . He had absolutely no interest in being there and didn't try to hide it.'

'Where was her mother?'

'Oh, she was always off jet-setting around the place. Visiting her mother in Spain, if I remember, but to be honest, I suspect it had more to do with the Spanish sunshine and avoiding the tedium of parenthood than anything else. I shouldn't really say this – Ines and Victor were our friends – but' – she looks at me over her glasses – 'she wasn't exactly the most attentive mother.' She looks down at the pictures again. 'Ah, here it is.'

She passes the photo to me, pointing at the small girl at its centre. 'Look at poor Cora. Solemn little thing. A bit quirky if you ask me, but hardly surprising given the upbringing she had. And she was harmless, really. And Victor – he couldn't be less interested if he tried.'

On some level, I can still hear her words.

But my breath is stuck in my chest and my eyes are rooted to the photo.

Not on the girl, not on the man, but on the other person in the picture.

Susie is still talking and the room is swimming now and my head is filled with white noise. I stare at the image, my throat dry.

And suddenly, it all comes crashing down.

Suddenly, I know.

22

June 1985

SPLASHES OF WATER BURST high into the cloudless sky, then back down, rippling across the surface of the paddling pool, and Lily laughed. Mary watched. It was so easy to make her happy. Two parents who loved her. Some fun in her day. A story at night. It was that simple. And as long as Mary kept it like that, Lily would stay happy. At the drinks table, Fran and Zara were lining up glasses and straightening bottles. They'd shown up in white shirts and black skirts; a catering uniform of sorts that caused Mary to smile.

'It's just a few neighbours, nothing fancy,' she'd reassured them, hoping, as she said it, that she was correct. The neighbours had come to expect so much from their parties and she was never quite sure if she'd struck the right tone. Or theme. Or dress.

'You're so effortlessly glamorous,' Della had said recently. 'And so calm and serene. Like a swan among us ugly ducklings,' she'd added with a self-deprecating laugh.

A swan, serene on the surface, but paddling furiously beneath – where no one can see, Mary wanted to say. The outsider, expected to know how to act. How to *be*. How to throw a birthday party or a dinner party, or, as was the case today, a wedding anniversary party. Imagine if their guests knew the level of Robbie's commitment to his vows.

'Five years is a big milestone!' Robbie had said, without irony, 'and I want to show you off to everyone.' And so here she was, on a sunny Saturday afternoon in June, in a full-length cream sundress, waiting for their guests, hoping she'd got everything just right.

Ines and Victor were the first to arrive, Cora trailing meekly behind. Mary smiled hello as Fran led them through to the back garden. Ines flashed a rare smile back, but there was nothing friendly in it. There never was.

'How was your trip to Spain?' Mary asked. 'You're home earlier than expected?'

'Yes. There were some problems. My mother is very ill.'

'Oh, I'm sorry.'

Ines clicked her tongue impatiently. 'Why are you sorry? You did not make her ill.'

'I just meant—'

'My mother is old. It is not a big surprise that she is sick and that she will die. Why must people make such a drama of these things. Death comes for all of us.'

Mary, whose mother had died in her forties, wasn't sure how to respond, so she switched to a more practical topic. 'Do you need to get back over there? I could help take care of Cora if you like?'

Ines eyed her up and down. 'Cynthia will look after Cora.' A pause. Then: 'The Stedmans – will they be here?'

'Yes, they should be coming, and their younger kids too, so Cora will have someone to play with.'

Cora hovered behind Ines, her eyes trained on the paddling pool.

Mary looked down and smiled.

'Do you want to get in, Cora? Lily would love to play – do you have a swimming costume on?'

Cora nodded and took off her dress before stepping carefully into the water.

'Can I make you chief sitter and lifeguard now, Cora?' Mary asked.

Cora nodded vehemently.

'Good.' Mary turned to smile again at Ines and Victor, her back to the pool.

Over the next half an hour, they all arrived. The Stedmans with three of their children and their ever-present babysitter, Cynthia. Della with an apple pie. Ellen from next door, slipping through the gap in the fence. Her mother might be in later, she said, taking a seat on the swing. Aoife was away for the weekend and Ellen looked a little lost without her constant companion.

'The twins will be in soon,' Della told her, 'then you'll have someone to talk to.'

'I'm not sure they will, Mam,' Fran said, pouring a glass of white wine for her mother. 'Gavin Bowman called in earlier and he's up in their room with them.'

Della's face creased into a frown. 'He's too old to be hanging around with the twins. He must be sixteen if he's a day.' She turned to Mary. 'How's he getting on with the gardening?'

'Oh. He's finished. I don't think gardening is his strong suit.'

Susie Stedman joined them and Mary remembered Ines's question. 'Susie, Ines was looking for you earlier.' She spotted Ines at the drinks table with Cynthia, and waved her over. 'Ines, Susie's here now.'

Ines tossed her head impatiently. 'Why are you telling me this?'

'Oh. You asked about Susie?'

'I wanted to know if they were coming because I need to speak with Cynthia. I do not need to speak with Susie.' She stalked off back to Cynthia, leaving Mary open-mouthed.

'Don't mind her,' Susie said. 'She's the most disagreeable person I've ever met.'

'She said her mother's ill,' Mary murmured. 'She's trying to organize a sitter so she can travel back to Spain. I imagine she's stressed.'

'Stressed she won't have a bolthole in Spain to run to if her mother dies, you mean,' Della said. 'Though maybe her mother will leave her the house and she'll be gone for good.'

Susie threw back her head and laughed, her blonde bob flashing in the sun. Mary bit her lip, trying not to smile. Della's comment was mean, but then again, Ines made it difficult to be nice.

Robbie emerged through the patio doors, a bottle of wine in hand, and strode down the garden, followed by Victor.

'Drink up, everyone,' Robbie announced, 'this is a celebration!' He put his arm around Mary's waist and kissed her temple, then held up the bottle.

'Oh, go on so, I'll have another glass, thanks,' Susie said. 'Cynthia's looking after the kids – I may as well enjoy myself.'

Mary glanced over to see Cynthia had moved away from Ines, and was now chatting with Tom Stedman down near the end of the garden. At a distance, she looked almost goddess-like. Long, wavy butterscotch hair, contrasting with her white broderie-anglaise dress. Like a midsummer fairy. At a distance, at least.

The three Stedman children were running towards the pool now, cannonballing into the water as soon as their t-shirts were off. Susie brushed water droplets from her neat, pink dress, and frowned, looking around the garden, searching for her less than attentive babysitter, perhaps. Her gaze settled on Cynthia and

Tom and she immediately looked away, smiling around at every-one else.

Mary jumped in. 'Should we move away from the pool before we get wet? We could sit?' She pointed at the white garden chairs, set up around small tables, a little way away from the pool.

'We'll have to move the chairs soon,' Robbie said, squinting at the sky and the trees at the end of the garden. 'We lose the sun very quickly in the afternoon.'

'Can't you top those trees?' Victor said impatiently, somehow making it sound like a criticism. 'I'll give you the name of a tree surgeon.'

'They're not our trees,' Robbie said. 'The tallest are in Ruth Cavanagh's garden. We've gone in I don't know how many times, offered to pay for all of it, but she's so *stubborn*.'

'She's a cranky so-and-so, that's for sure,' Della said.

Susie put her finger to her lips. 'Della, you've a voice like a foghorn. She might be in her garden.'

'Ah look, she'll never hear me at this distance.' Della turned to Mary. 'Will Lily be OK in there? It's deep for a paddling pool – the water must be up to her waist?'

'It is, but she's in capable hands, Cora is so good with her,' Mary said, smiling at Ines, who had joined them again.

Ines nodded and sipped her wine as the sound of splashing and laughter drifted over from the pool. Lily was trying to copy Cora now, lying down in the water beside her. Cora's voice lifted above the shrieks and yells of the Stedman boys' game. *You have to stay down for longer. Five seconds now, OK?*

The sun blasted down from the mid-afternoon sky and the conversation moved from Ruth Cavanagh to Ines's mother to Victor's business; the lazy buzz of summer – insects and lawn mowers and thick heat and wine muffling words. Tom and

Cynthia joined them, Tom taking his place beside his wife, his arm around her waist. Mary smiled at Cynthia and asked how she was doing. Cynthia flashed a gap-toothed smile back and ran her hands through her hair. Up close, the goddess mirage evaporated. Up close, Cynthia smelled of unwashed skin and cigarettes. Her long, white dress was stained yellow under the arms, and her breath was a mix of coffee and wine. Up close, Cynthia was glassy and jittery and unsettling.

'Do you have vodka?' Cynthia asked Mary, shaking her empty wine glass.

'Oh. I'm not sure,' Mary said. She *was* sure, she knew they did, but she couldn't quite work out if it was OK to offer it to an on-duty babysitter. Susie and Tom were talking to Victor and didn't seem to notice.

'We do indeed have vodka,' Robbie said, chiming in. 'Come on inside and I'll get you some.'

Mary watched as Robbie placed an arm lightly over Cynthia's bare shoulders to steer her indoors.

Fran hid a smile as Zara stared open-mouthed after Robbie and Cynthia.

'Oh my God, tell me he's not interested in *that*,' Zara whispered, uncorking a fresh bottle of white wine.

Fran shook her head. 'He's getting her a drink, that's all.'

'That's *our* job. I don't know why he'd be bringing her into the house to do something he's literally paying us to do? I mean—' Zara stopped suddenly, and Fran noticed she was swaying a little. 'Oh God.'

'What is it?'

'The smell of the wine. Jesus. It's making my stomach turn.'

'Is it gone off?' Fran leaned in and took a sniff. 'It smells fine to me.'

'Ugh. God. I need to go in and get a glass of water. Can you manage without me?'

Fran looked around at the small clusters of guests dotted across the lawn. 'Yeah, I think I can handle the hordes for five minutes,' she said with a grin. She picked up Zara's abandoned bottle of white wine and made her way down the garden. Why Mary felt the need to have 'staff' at something like this was beyond her, but if she wanted to pay good money to have them dress like waitresses and top up wine, Fran was more than happy to do it. All the more dollars for Virginia Beach.

Down near the paddling pool, she hovered beside a group of chattering guests – her mother, the Stedmans, the O'Briens and Mary Murphy. Nobody paid her any attention and she made an executive decision that their glasses were sufficiently full. She sat on a vacant chair a little to the side of the group, taking a moment to enjoy the sun.

Something drew her attention to the pool. The noise? No, the lack of noise – the splashing had stopped. Cora and Lily were lying side by side. Cora's arm across Lily's chest. Both girls' faces just below the surface. The water calm and quiet. The thought came to Fran subconsciously at first, casually in tune with the lazy, summer afternoon. Why weren't they splashing any more?

She sat up straight.

Why aren't they splashing?

How long had Lily been under the water?

Fran zipped off the chair as time slowed down. She ran, conscious of the contrast: the background hum of conversation and the total silence from the girls. Sunlight dappled still water. Two figures shimmered beneath the surface. Fran stooped at the side of the pool. On her knees, she pushed Cora's arm off Lily and pulled Lily by the shoulder, so her face was out of the water.

Lily's eyes were closed, her lips pale. Fran shook her and Lily blinked in the sunlight, beginning to cough. Mary's voice came from behind.

'Oh! Is she all right?'

Ines arrived too, crouching down beside Fran and Lily.

'She simply swallowed some water,' Ines said, reaching out to rub Lily's back. 'She was splashing and some got in her mouth.'

'Sweetheart,' Mary said softly, pulling Lily out of the pool and into her arms. Lily's coughing began to subside. 'Thank you,' Mary said to Fran and Ines, over Lily's tiny shoulder.

'Of course,' Ines said, 'but maybe she is too small for this pool of yours.'

'And thank you too, for watching her,' Mary said to Cora.

Cora blinked, trailing her hands in the speckled water, saying nothing at all.

Mary carried Lily across the lawn and into the house, rubbing her back. How quickly it had happened. How easily, even in shallow water, her daughter had slipped under.

'Let's get you into dry clothes,' she whispered, bringing Lily through the hallway. As she passed the living room door, Robbie and Cynthia's voices wafted out – Robbie telling Cynthia about the three different types of vodka they had. Cynthia probably didn't care which type she drank, Mary thought, as long as her glass was full.

Upstairs, inside Lily's room, Mary dried her off and put her in a clean dress. Lily's eyelids drooped as she sat on the bed, tired from the afternoon sun and the drama, perhaps. Mary laid her down.

'If you want to sleep for a bit, that's OK?'

'Stay, Mama?' Lily said, grasping her hand, and Mary did, quietly glad of the chance to escape the small talk outside.

It must have been twenty minutes later when she heard their voices; Della and Susie coming up the stairs to use the bathroom.

'Did you spot Cynthia with Robbie in the living room?' Susie was saying. 'Fawning all over him, taking twenty minutes to get one drink.'

Mary stiffened.

'Ah yeah, but I'd say Robbie's having none of it,' Della said loyally.

'Hmm. He might not have a choice. She's a hussy, that one,' Susie replied. 'And Robbie's not above a little extra-curricular activity in that department.'

'What? You're not serious. Not Robbie. He's one of the good ones.'

'Oh, listen, I *love* Robbie – he's great fun, an absolute charmer, and the neighbourhood would be a boring place without him,' Susie said. 'But he's not immune to the lure of a cheeky little affair, I'll tell you that.'

'Ah stop. There's no way he'd cheat on Mary.'

'Whatever you say. But if Cynthia has her way, Robbie won't have a choice.'

23

June 2018

I STARE AT THE photo in Susie's hands. At the dirty-blonde hair and gap-toothed smile, beaming out from 1982.

'Who's that?' I keep my voice neutral.

'The babysitter, Cynthia.' Susie's tone is light. Breezy. 'Honestly, Mark is probably right, she wasn't a great babysitter. But never tell him I told you so.' She smiles.

'But . . .'

I don't know where to start. I stop and begin again.

'Why is she in the photo?'

'Oh, let me see . . . She would have been looking after Cora around then. Ines was off on one of her jaunts to Spain. I'd had Luke a few weeks before Lily was born, and I remember Mary and I discussing it, thinking it must have been hard on Ines seeing everyone around her having babies. God love her, it can't have been easy.'

'Cynthia was there – in Rowanbrook, all that time?'

'She used to do afternoons when Cora came out of school. Victor was around at night, of course. Now, you might well ask what Cynthia was doing at a Rowanbrook picnic on a Saturday afternoon. Victor should have been perfectly capable of looking after Cora himself.' Susie shakes her head. 'I'd say Cynthia liked the cash, and she liked mingling with people here in Rowan-brook. But she didn't like to be seen as the babysitter – as a lowly employee. She wanted to be one of the guests.'

On some level, I can hear the snobbery in her words, but I don't process it. I can't take my eyes off Cynthia. I suck in a slow, quiet breath to steady myself before I speak again.

'This is 1982, yes? Was she still around in the years following this photo?' I ask it this way because I can't yet ask the more direct question.

'Oh God, yes. Part of the furniture. She used to mind mine – I had six, as you know, I needed all the help I could get. And she minded Cora a lot, and Lily too, until Mary stopped asking her.'

'Why did Mary do that?'

Susie picks at the hem of her skirt. 'She got it into her head that Cynthia wasn't quite reliable. That she was on drugs. At least that's what Della told me.' Susie laughs. 'As if anyone was on drugs in Ireland in the eighties. And as if I'd let some drug addict mind my children.' She laughs again, but it sounds forced.

'So you kept using her, even after Mary stopped?'

'Well, no. Not long after, she became unavailable. She stopped coming.'

'And when was that?'

'Goodness, why so many questions about Cynthia?'

Deep breaths. Slow breaths. 'She just looks familiar,' I say, choosing my words. 'I'm trying to work out where I might have seen her.'

'Well, she stopped babysitting when Luke was three, so pretty much three years after this photo was taken. Yes, I remember it as a particularly difficult summer. I had to keep turning down lunches and dropping out of tennis matches because I had nobody to mind the children and Luke was such a handful.

Mark was off in Irish College and the girls were on a French exchange and it was just so stressful on my own with the smaller ones.'

'If Cynthia stopped coming when Luke was three, I guess that was also when Lily was three?'

'Yes, that must be right.'

'So the summer Lily disappeared?'

'Gosh, yes. Oh. When I say it was a difficult summer, obviously there were much bigger things going on than my tennis matches. Goodness, how must I sound.' Her cheeks pinken.

But I'm not worried about Susie's memories of her dismantled social life. I'm worried about the woman in the photo, and why her time in Rowanbrook ended when Lily disappeared.

24

June 2018

MY HEADACHE IS BACK on Friday afternoon and the kids are tiptoe-ing around me in a way that makes me feel guilty and grateful all at once. I should do something with them – something that counts as quality time; the kind of things I thought I'd do when I finished up at work. But my mind is full of Cynthia. And the text from Cora. *We need to talk.*

I'm lying on my bed with my eyes closed when the doorbell rings, and it's Cora I think of first. *Oh God.* Is that her? This is what I get for ignoring her text. What does she know? What is she going to ask me and what am I going to say? Lightheaded, I pull myself off the bed, psyching myself up to answer the door. To face her. But Emily gets there first.

'Mum?' she calls up the stairs. 'The police are here.'

The police? Why on earth would the police— I freeze, my hand on the bedroom door handle.

Cora's told them.

I think I'm going to be sick.

There are two of them. Detective Sergeant McCarthy and Detective Garda Walsh. Without asking why they're here, I lead them through to the living room and close the door, telling a confused Emily to keep Ben and Sophie in the kitchen.

I gesture for them to sit, my hand shaking as I do. The one called McCarthy takes a seat on the bigger of the two sofas. A wisp of hair has escaped her bun, and she pushes it behind her ear. The garda called Walsh stands by the fireplace. White noise whirrs in my ears as I wait for them to speak. What am I going to tell Mark? Tell the kids? How did I think this would all stay secret for ever? A child died. A life ended. It was always going to come out. Dizzy now, I reach behind me, feeling for the seat of the smaller couch, and lower myself on to it.

'Mrs Stedman, are you OK?' McCarthy asks, half rising from the sofa. 'Are you ill?'

I shake my head.

'OK then. We're here about a woman called Cora O'Brien,' McCarthy says, settling back on the couch.

I force a small nod.

'I'm afraid to inform you that Ms O'Brien has been involved in a fatal accident.'

'What?'

'I'm very sorry.'

'I don't— What happened?'

'An accident on a railway line, I'm afraid.' McCarthy tries to hide her grimace, but I see it. Dear God. The incident on the DART tracks. Cora.

'Ms O'Brien was on her way to work in the city centre early this morning. The platform was crowded with rush-hour commuters and just as the train was pulling into the station, she was propelled forward in the surge, and knocked on to the tracks.' She sounds robotic almost, as though she has spoken these same words a number of times today. 'There was no way for the driver to do anything, I'm afraid.'

Oh God, poor Cora. Tears well up.

'Was she . . . did she—' I can't finish the sentence.

'She would have more than likely died instantly,' McCarthy says.

I nod, gripping the couch cushion, rocking back and forth. For a moment, nobody says anything, and it's in that silence that the next thought arrives.

Why are they telling me this?

I wasn't close to Cora. Even without parents or siblings or children, there must be others they should be informing? But I can't think how to ask that. So I sit and rock and wait.

'You hadn't heard about it already?' McCarthy asks then.

'I heard it on the radio this morning.' My voice is shaking. 'I didn't know it was Cora though.'

'Did you know her well?'

'Not at all.' The answer comes out quickly. 'I only met her for the first time last Friday,' I tell her, forcing some composure. 'We had a housewarming and she came with a mum from the school, Liz Landry. She and Cora are neighbours.'

Walsh is flipping pages in a notebook and nods at McCarthy as if confirming what I've said.

'And have you had any interactions with her since?'

'Yes. I messaged her on Monday night and we went for coffee on Tuesday.'

McCarthy cocks her head, as though waiting for more, her grey eyes boring into mine. What is she looking for? Why is she here?

'I wanted to get to know the neighbours and I've recently finished up in my job, so I'm at a loose end during the day sometimes.' I give a small smile. McCarthy doesn't smile back.

'So coffee on Tuesday – and any communication since then?'

'I . . .' Jesus. Do I say it or not? What if they take my phone? 'I messaged her on Wednesday.'

'About?'

Fuck. 'About . . . well, it's a long and not very interesting story, but I found out last week that this house used to belong to the parents of Lily Murphy, a little girl who disappeared in 1985.'

McCarthy nods, giving nothing away.

'Go on.'

'It's been on my mind ever since. It's a bit unsettling, living here, knowing she was never found. I'm sure she drowned, just as the police at the time thought—' I break off, waiting for perhaps a nod of confirmation. *Yes, she drowned, no, you did not kill her.* But there's no nod. 'Anyway, I've been doing a lot of googling to try to understand what happened. And I—' *Tread carefully.* 'I asked Cora about it in a text. She had said she didn't want to talk about it – when we met for coffee. She was the last one to see Lily alive, so you can understand why she's uncomfortable.'

A nod.

'So what was in this text?'

I think about lying. But they can check my phone. They can check her phone, if it's not crushed under a train. *God.*

'I asked if she'd ever heard anyone call Lily any nicknames or other names.'

'Why did you ask that?'

'I . . . I saw a child on holidays once and thought she looked like Lily Murphy, but about ten years later. Ten years older, you know? I'm sure you hear of sightings like this all the time?'

A non-committal nod.

'Anyway, it was a moot point, Cora had never heard anyone call Lily any nicknames.'

'And this child you saw' – there's something in the way she says it, as though she doesn't quite believe my story – 'was there a specific name you heard used? A name you then asked Cora about?'

I hesitate but there's no way out of this. If I lie, they'll find out and then they'll wonder why I'm lying.

'Lila.'

It comes out in a whisper. I wait for a response, for the axe to fall. But McCarthy's face is neutral, her eyes giving nothing away. Walsh writes something in his notebook.

'Lila. OK. And did you ask anything else of Ms O'Brien?'

For the love of God, why did I ask those stupid questions? Why couldn't I just leave it alone?

'Mrs Stedman? Anything you can tell us will help with our inquiry.'

'But wasn't it an accident? Cora's death?' *Please let it not be suicide.*

McCarthy doesn't answer my question. 'Did you say anything else in your text to Ms O'Brien?'

'I asked her if Lily had any illnesses.'

McCarthy looks like I've just confirmed something she already knew and I'm relieved that I told the truth.

'Why did you ask that?'

This is dangerous territory.

'Stuff I saw online.' The answer comes to me in a rush. 'Rumours on various true-crime forums. People speculate all sorts of things on those boards. Someone said they saw a child that looked like Lily, but this child had very severe asthma. As far as I know from asking around, Lily didn't have asthma, so I don't think it was her.' That actually sounds plausible, I think, and it is this small jolt of confidence that inspires me to try a question of my own. 'Is there a reason you're asking all this? I can't imagine it has any-thing to do with what happened to Cora?'

McCarthy says nothing for a moment, then seems to make up her mind.

'We found a notebook in Ms O'Brien's bag. She'd written

down your name, and the words you've just mentioned – "Lily/ Lila" and "illness" – followed by a question mark. Do you know why Cora might have done that?'

I shake my head. 'I've no idea.' This time I'm telling the truth. 'Was there anything else in the notebook?'

Another pause. 'That's all for now, we'll be back if we need more,' McCarthy says, sidestepping my question. And, I realize, I have inadvertently sidestepped hers. I've not been asked if I saw Cora again since Tuesday. Which means they don't know I was in her house yesterday morning. While I'm trying to work out whether it's better to say it or not, they're getting up to leave. I say nothing and see them out.

The story of Cora's death is spreading like wildfire. Once the gardaí leave, I see messages from Liz Landry and Fran, and three missed calls from Mark. My finger hovers over the number to phone him back but I stop before pressing Call. I need a minute. The news has flattened me. It seems impossible that she was alive yesterday when I had coffee in her garden. Alive this morning – eating breakfast, I imagine, like any other day; listening to the radio, planning her weekend – and now, in the most grotesque way, she's dead. Lying in a morgue. And with no immediate family to mourn her, she's desperately alone. I hardly knew her and I can't quite fathom why this is hitting me so badly, but it is. I pick up my phone again to call Mark but now I can't get through. I try Liz Landry next, and she answers.

'Joanna, Jesus, it's awful, isn't it?'

'I don't even know why I'm phoning, but I'm sitting here in the house trying not to let the kids find out and I just feel like I need to talk to someone. Anyone who knew her.'

'I'm the same. And I hardly knew her at all, to be honest. But, God, it's horrendous. I'm just . . . shell-shocked.'

'Do you know anything more about how it happened? Did she . . .'

'Jump? God, I don't think so. That's not the impression I got from the guards. Why, did you think she was . . . well, suicidal?'

'No, not at all. I had coffee with her yesterday and I mean, I don't know her, but she seemed fine.'

'I'm sure it was an accident. And the guards are investigating. I suppose if it was suicide, they'd tell us? They do, don't they?'

I nod into the phone though I suspect we're both grasping at straws, afraid we missed something in Cora's behaviour or demeanour.

'So the guards called to you too?' I ask, after a bit.

'How do you mean?'

'You said the impression you got from the guards.'

'Ah. No, they called at Cora's door, looking for a next of kin, but got no answer. I came out to see what was up and got most of the story.' A beat. 'Wait, do you mean they called to you?'

'No, I— Oh, Liz, sorry, the kids are arguing in the kitchen – I'd better go. I'll see you at the school.'

25

MARK IS LATE HOME on Friday night and I can't go to Kinsella House, which is the one place I need to be right now. It's not Tuesday, she might not be there anyway, I tell myself, as I pour a glass of wine. And what would I even say? How would I ask what I need to ask, without mentioning the thing we don't talk about? The guilt about Lila never goes away, but on nights like this, it surges up, overwhelms me. I sit, refreshing news coverage of Cora's death, waiting for Mark to come home and ignoring the fresh headache that's setting in. The updates are scant. A body on the tracks isn't common in Dublin, but it's not headline news either. Most people view it as a tragic accident. But I keep thinking about the police visit earlier. If it was a tragic accident, why were they here? Do they think I somehow drove her to suicide? I couldn't have. My mind casts back to our coffee yesterday. She was certainly angry about how Lily's disappearance had affected her family, determined to get justice. Cold. Fearless even? Not suicidal. But then, what would I know?

Mark finally arrives and we sit together in the garden, me on my third glass of wine as he starts his first. There's still heat in the low evening sun and the artistry of the pink-gold sky is at odds with everything that's gone on today. My head is pounding now.

'How're you doing?' he asks.

'I'm OK – I didn't really know her or anything . . . it's just very weird to have seen someone so recently and now she's dead. You know?'

'Yeah. I've never known anyone who died suddenly like that,' Mark says. 'It's really hit me in a way I didn't expect. God, I can't even begin to imagine what it was like for you with the fire. I always knew it was this awful thing that happened to you but when I think how shocked I am about Cora, someone I hardly knew – Jesus, your *parents*!'

Oh God, I need to stop this. I need to say it. *There was no fire!* I want to scream it into the evening sky. But how can I? It's gone on too long. It's in the foundations of our relationship. Crack that and everything breaks.

'It's OK, it was a long time ago. And it's normal to be shocked by what happened to Cora. In the next few days, the shock will lessen and soon – it sounds harsh – we'll hardly think about it at all. I promise.' I top up his wine and force brightness into my voice for the next bit of what I need to say. 'On a more upbeat note, I called to your mum this morning, and she showed me a whole bunch of childhood photos!'

Mark groans.

'Hey, you were a pretty cute kid, don't worry. The funny thing was, that babysitter you mentioned was in a few of them. Like, part of the furniture. Or part of the family – families plural.' *Like a parasite.* 'Cynthia was her name?'

He nods. 'Yeah, that's right.'

'Do you think there's any truth in the whole thing with her and your dad?'

'Nah, it was just flirting. She used to flirt with Robbie Murphy too apparently, and even tried with Victor O'Brien, though he was always very sour, if I remember.'

My head is really thumping now. I put down my glass and press my fingers against my temples.

'Headache?'

'Yeah. Pretty bad.'

'Would you not just take a painkiller and go to bed? One tablet won't hurt. Even martyrs have their limits.'

'No. I'll be fine.'

'I don't get why you have this thing about medicine. It's not a sign of failure to take a painkiller or a Rennie or the odd throat lozenge. I know you like to be "strong" but I promise you, suffering on for no reason doesn't make you strong.'

'I – I'll be fine,' I say again, pressing harder against the sides of my head. 'Anyway, what was she like, this woman who seems to have inserted herself in every family in Rowanbrook?'

'When I was smaller, I thought she was fun. Younger than my mother, way more relaxed about everything, let me do whatever I wanted. She was pretty too, I remember that. But then when I was older, I saw her differently. She was kind of . . . grotty? Like, dirt under her fingernails, bad breath sometimes, a kind of musty smell from her hair? I guess teenage-me saw her with different eyes.' He laughs a little self-consciously. 'She even tried it on with me in front of my mates once. I nearly died.'

'Tried it on?' My jaw is tight and I have to consciously work to unclench my teeth as Cynthia's face swims in front of my eyes.

'Oh God, silly stuff. She'd put her arms around me, kiss my cheek, tell me if I needed drink or slightly less legal substances, she could get them for me, that kind of thing. To be honest, I was glad when she stopped coming around.'

'Which was when Luke was three?'

He shrugs.

'Same summer as Lily disappeared?' I try.

'Actually it was, I think. I remember Cynthia asking me if I was single, giving me advice, and being quite full-on for a bit, and the next minute she was gone – not coming around any more, leaving poor Mum to look after her own kids, God help her.'

'Advice?'

'I use the term loosely. It mostly seemed to involve me giving her money to buy drink for my mates, and her taking a cut of the cash *and* the beer.'

That, I think, sounds exactly like Cynthia.

I park on Woodbine Street opposite Kinsella House and sit for a moment, composing myself. I have cake with me. She doesn't eat. Not regular food like regular people. But she likes cake. Takes tiny bird-like nibbles, picking with her narrow fingers, pincer-gripping crumbs with her long nails. So I have cake. And an excuse for calling on a Saturday.

At the front door, I press the buzzer, half hoping she won't be there. Mostly hoping she won't be there. But she answers; a hoarse, nicotine-soaked 'Hello?'

'It's Joanna. I was nearby so thought I'd stop in. I have cake.'

Her reply comes in the form of the buzzer, and the click of the front door.

Her apartment door is ajar. I push it, not sure why I'm expecting it to be different to any other time. It's not. The dark, dust-covered furniture, the half-closed green velvet drapes, the faded oriental rug, the smell of stale smoke that makes my skin crawl – everything is exactly the same as always. She's lying on the couch, her head on a cushion, her bare feet resting on the arm, a cigarette between her fingers. She blows smoke rings towards the ceiling, then turns her head to face me. I take her in with fresh eyes, comparing her to the photo in Susie's house.

Her hair, white-blonde, is piled on top of her head in a bun, no longer flowing down her back. Her skin is cracked from age and nicotine but her eyes are just as blue as they were back then. Her teeth are stained yellow now, the gap as prominent as ever. Cute, no doubt, back in her heyday. Less so today. Sixty-two now, Cynthia could pass for forty-five on a good day and at other times – on bad days, at her most hungover, after her rages – she becomes a shell inside her own skin and could be eighty. She still favours the same kind of long dresses she wore when she was young, and today she's wearing something that looks like a white Grecian robe. A blonde Cleopatra, reclining. Waiting for an explanation.

'Why are you really here?' she asks, eyeing me with suspicion.

'Nice to see you too, Mother,' I say with a quiet sigh, and take a seat.

26

June 2018

I SHIFT ON THE chair opposite as she takes me in, the beginnings of a frown on her forehead.

'You're looking for something. I can tell. You were the same as a child, too timid to say what you were thinking. Just speak up!'

A spark of annoyance now, and I'm tempted to change tack – to tell her I'm here because Mark has noticed how expensive my fictional therapy sessions are. To say that I'm not earning now, and the 'Dr Kinsella' payments have to stop. That she'll need a new source of income to pay for her cigarettes and whiskey and other substances of choice. But I don't. I stay on track.

'You know we moved house?'

'No. How would I know that?'

'Well, we moved house. To a place called Rowanbrook.'

I watch for her reaction but there's none. Or is that a slight narrowing of eyes?

'Good for you.' She says it in a way that makes it clear she does not in fact mean 'good for you'.

'Have you ever been there?'

'Are you inviting me?' A sly smile now. A cat eyeing up a mouse. 'Would you like to bring me over to meet your fine, upstanding husband and your fine, upstanding children?'

She has no interest in meeting them, I know that. She does this to torture me. I call her bluff, as I always do.

'Absolutely. You should come for Sunday dinner.'

A bark of a laugh. 'Some day, I might just do that. And then your little house of cards will come tumbling down, won't it.' She stubs her cigarette and immediately lights a fresh one, her hand shaking as she holds the lighter to the tip. 'You think I'm joking but I'd quite like to see it – Joanna Kirk in her nice but boring house with her nice but boring husband. I'm guessing your kids are nice but boring too?'

I bite my lip.

She nods slowly. 'I bet they're the kind of kids who try to please everyone – the sort who are no fun at all. I bet they end up walking around the school yard on their own every lunchtime. You were like that – remember?'

My cheeks colour but I'm still not rising to it.

She nods. 'I remember. You whimpering that you had no friends. Nobody to talk to.' A deep drag of her cigarette, eyes on mine. 'Maybe lighten up a bit?' she says through her exhale. 'Maybe try not being such a drip all the time, then you'd have friends?'

'I have friends.'

'Not back then you didn't. Never invited to parties, never asked over to anyone's house. The clues were there.' A laugh that turns into a cough as she breathes out blue smoke. 'Tell you what, invite me over and I'll teach your kids how to be fun.'

God, this woman. 'Absolutely. Mark would love to meet you. So would his mother, I'm sure. Susie Stedman is her name.'

A slight frown that quickly clears.

'Do you know her?' I ask.

'How would I know your husband's mother. This is boring. Pour me a drink.'

I should say no. I should tell her to get her own drink. But somehow, we always revert to parent and child when I'm here. She demands – drinks, cigarettes, attention – and I comply. I fix her a whiskey and stand just close enough to hand it to her, then try again with my questions.

'It's just, I saw a photograph of you. From 1982, at a picnic with Susie Stedman.' That's enough for now.

'I have no idea who this woman is but, who knows.' She shrugs. 'The eighties are a blur. Good times.'

Christ. I was six years old when that photo was taken. Six years old and home alone while she was leeching off the Rowanbrook residents. Drinking their wine and taking their cash and half minding their kids. Half minding at best. A 'blur'? She could be talking about a night out, not a decade of negligence.

'You were their babysitter.'

'Was I?' She sits up, swinging her legs around. Her feet are cracked and caked in grime. 'I babysat your husband?' She throws back her head and laughs.

'More so his younger siblings, and some other kids in Rowanbrook. A girl called Cora, and . . . and a girl called Lily.' Again, I watch. And again, there's a slight crease in her forehead. So tiny, only someone who's known her forty-two years would spot it.

'If you say so.'

She flops back on the couch, eyes half closed. Sleepy and bored.

I sit, watching. Where to go from here? I can't bring up what happened. She'll never, ever forgive me for that. I can't even say her name without bringing on a rage. But I need to know. Was Lila Lily? Was the sister I killed actually Lily Murphy? And if so, what was she doing here with us, while her heartbroken family searched?

27

June 2018

I LEAVE CYNTHIA AS she's finishing her second drink, before she has a chance to ask me for a third. It's impossible to say no to her. I couldn't then and I still can't now. Guilt and loyalty and a warped kind of love keep me paying her bills, and coming back, week after week. Often – mostly – I can't bear her, but I can't bear to cut the tie either. So I turn up and do my duty and fill her drinks and bring her cake. But I don't stay long. And now I go, back into lazy Saturday morning traffic, home from what Mark thinks is a coffee with Adana.

On the way, I stop in to Susie. She's surprised to see me again so soon.

'Joanna, we are honoured. Twice in two days. Come in!'

'I won't stay, Susie, I just wanted to ask if I could borrow some of those old photos from yesterday? I'll take good care of them.'

'Of course, darling. Come through and choose any you like. I heard what happened to poor Cora O'Brien. Awful situation. It was on the news all day yesterday and I had no idea it was her. Imagine, it could have been any of us. I was at the DART station on Tuesday. It could have been me.'

This is very Susie. I remember once there was a news story

about a bomb in northern Spain and for months after, she kept referring to the time she'd been in Madrid six years prior – hundreds of miles from the bomb site. But to listen to her, you'd think Susie had been seconds from death.

'It's awful,' I say. 'Poor Cora. She had quite a tragic life, didn't she?' I kneel beside the box of photos and lift the lid.

'A tragic end for sure, but her life wasn't particularly awful, was it?'

'I mean the rumours about her dad after Lily went missing. And his death . . .'

I rummage through the photos as Susie clicks her tongue.

'Poor Victor. Those dreadful stories suggesting he did something to Lily. Honestly, I know it's hard to understand when you weren't there, but Ines and Victor were our friends. Not the most charismatic pair, to be frank, but our friends nonetheless. And he was a *businessman*, they had plenty of money, good backgrounds. There's *no way* he had anything to do with it.'

Again, this is very Susie. If you're from the right place, you couldn't possibly be guilty of any wrongdoing.

'If you ask me,' she goes on, 'the police never looked into Eddie Hogan properly. When he heard his daughter was supposedly pregnant with Robbie's baby, he hit the roof. Hit *Robbie*, to be more specific. That's where you should be looking.'

'And *was* she pregnant with Robbie's baby?'

She purses her lips. 'Robbie said it wasn't true, and that should be good enough for everyone. I know who *I* believe. Certainly not that Eddie Hogan.'

'Do you know where I'd find him or anything about him?'

'Gosh no. We weren't friendly with the Hogans. They didn't quite fit in. Did I mention he used to be a boxer?'

Oh, Susie.

The photo of Cora, Victor and Cynthia is at the bottom of the pile and I put it in my bag now. That's all I came for really, but as an afterthought, I decide to take the one of Mark, Fran and Zara too – the one with Gavin in the background. And one of Susie with Mary, Robbie and newborn Lily.

I slip them into my bag and say goodbye, promising to bring the kids over soon.

When I pull into the driveway, Fran is in her front garden again, watering shrubs.

'It's a watering can!' she calls across. I must look confused because she elaborates. 'The hosepipe ban. I'm sticking to the rules.'

'Oh, of course. I forgot. My brain's addled.'

'The news about Cora?'

I nod.

'Me too. I didn't know her really, but still.'

This seems to be true of all of us. Who actually knew Cora?

'Some folks are saying she jumped . . . I wonder was it guilt,' Fran says now. 'If she covered up for her father.'

'I doubt it. She was eight. And—' I pause for a moment, wondering if it's my place to tell. With everyone dead, it probably doesn't matter. 'Cora says the police never interviewed her dad at all – it was Cora they came to see.'

Fran's eyes widen. 'Really?'

'I guess it may or may not be true. Her mother told her before she died. It was because someone reported that Cora was hurting Lily.'

Fran folds her arms, nodding slowly, and I can't help feeling I've just confirmed something she already guessed.

'Anyway, we shouldn't speak ill of the dead,' I continue, 'and my mother-in-law was just saying it's far more likely it was that man Eddie Hogan, or at least that the police should have asked him more questions. He had a go at Robbie apparently, for allegedly getting his daughter pregnant.'

'Bullshit.' Fran's tone has changed completely.

'Sorry?'

'This has nothing whatsoever to do with the Hogans.'

'But was it true? Was Zara Hogan pregnant with Robbie Murphy's baby?'

Fran's mouth is set in a tight line.

'You mentioned that she's your friend,' I go on. 'Could I talk to her?'

'Absolutely not. Why are you raking all this up? Hasn't there been enough upset around here?' And with that, Fran turns her back and walks away.

28

June 1985

As THE DOOR CLOSED behind Robbie and Mary on Saturday night, Fran switched on the TV, and Zara began poking around in the kitchen. Lily was already asleep. *Thank God.* The best kind of babysitting was the one without the baby.

Zara stuck her head around the door. 'Wagon Wheels *and* Penguins!' she said, brandishing multipacks. 'Can I open both?'

Fran nodded, and slipped Zara's bootleg copy of *A Nightmare on Elm Street* into the video recorder. Tonight, for once, would be easy money.

Four hours later, Fran woke with a start. Confused, she looked around with bleary eyes. On the television screen, black-and-white fuzz told her the film was long over, and beside her on the couch, Zara snored gently. White noise buzzed in Fran's ears. She couldn't shake the feeling that something had woken her. A bump? From upstairs? Had Lily fallen out of bed?

There it was again. A creak, as though someone had stood on a floorboard.

She listened for a cry but there was nothing. Was that good or bad? Fran pulled herself off the couch and walked out to the hall. At the bottom of the stairs she stood, listening.

Silence.

163

She held her breath, suddenly sensing that someone else was doing exactly that – holding their breath, listening for her. Ridiculous. The horror film was getting to her. She started up the stairs, slowly and carefully, and paused again at the top to listen. Nothing.

She made her way along the landing and gently pushed Lily's door. The room was in pitch darkness. On tiptoe, she crossed the bedroom floor towards the bed at the window. As her eyes adjusted to the dark, she could make out a shape.

A dark, upright shape.

Her blood froze.

Then a voice. Lily's voice. It was Lily, standing on her bed.

'Hide and Seek!' Lily said.

Fran let out a long breath.

'Lily! You gave me a fright. It's sleepy time now, you can't play Hide and Seek. Maybe next time?'

'Hide and Seek!' Lily said again.

'No, you have to lie down now, Liliput.'

Fran reached for her. She could feel Lily's warm arms going around her neck, waiting to be picked up, but in one practised move, Fran had her lying flat in the bed.

'Hide and Seek with my friend,' Lily murmured, but she'd given in. She didn't try to get up again. Fran sat on the other bed, waiting to make sure she settled. Her eyes roamed around the room as shadows took shape. The huge wardrobe with one door hanging open, the bookcase of battered books, the floor-length velvet curtains covering the window, and the evil eye symbol beneath. Fran shivered.

From the smaller bed came the soft, even sound of sleep. Carefully, Fran stood, wincing as the bed creaked when she moved. Lily didn't stir. In fairness, Fran acknowledged, when

Lily was asleep, she was really asleep – nothing would wake her. Except tonight, when something had.

Fran made her way out of the bedroom and through to the main bathroom, locking the door behind her. She usually used the downstairs loo when she was here and took a moment now to take in the colourful Spanish tiles and the ornate clawfoot tub. Quite a departure from the functional avocado-coloured bathroom in her own house. In the oval mirror above the sink, Fran's face was pale and drawn, with the crease mark of a couch cushion lining one cheek. Perhaps not the best look for an alert and capable babysitter. She turned on the tap, running the water until it was properly cold, then splashed it on her face. Better. Just about. As she turned off the tap, a noise elsewhere in the house caught her attention. Zara?

She unlocked the bathroom door and stood on the landing listening, and again couldn't shake the feeling that someone else was listening too. God, what if this was a dream? What if she was inside her own dream? *Bloody Freddy Krueger.*

As she stood listening, she heard it. Faint at first. Then a little louder. A creak from downstairs. Like a door opening. Like a hinge that needed oil. Like someone trying not to make noise. Louder now, jarring in the otherwise silence. Hairs stood on the back of her neck as she held her breath. Not moving.

Footsteps.

Slow.

Quiet.

But clear.

Someone was down there.

Fran moved to the top of the stairs and gripped the bannister. She had to go down – Zara was on her own, asleep in the living room. She put her foot on the top step of the stairs and stopped to listen. Which way were the footsteps going? Then came the sound of a door. The kitchen door? She took another step. Then stopped, at the sound of something breaking, followed by the noise of another door closing. Was it Zara? Going out the back for a smoke? She raced down the rest of the stairs and into the living room. Zara was still asleep on the couch. It wasn't Zara. Then who?

Zara was sceptical. 'It's the film getting inside your head, don't worry about it. Is there any more chocolate? What time are Robbie and Mary coming home?' she asked with a wide yawn.

'I didn't imagine it. I definitely heard noises, and something breaking.' Fran looked around but couldn't see what it might have been. 'There was someone in the house. They were upstairs, and then when I was in the bathroom, they went downstairs.'

'But how would they have got in? Think about it. You watched a scary film, fell asleep, then woke up thinking you heard someone in the house – what would you say if someone else told you that story?'

Zara had a point. But the noises were so vivid, she couldn't have imagined them. Could she?

'What were you doing in Lily's room anyway?'

'I was checking on her – she was looking to play Hide and Seek, at one o'clock in the morning.' Fran rolled her eyes.

'God, is it that late?'

'Yeah. You can head on if you want? I'll wait for Robbie and Mary.' As soon as the words were out, she knew she didn't mean them. The last thing she wanted was to be on her own in the house.

Zara's eyebrows went up. 'What, and miss the chance of my walk home with Robbie? I don't think so.'

Fran shook her head in mock exasperation.

'Grand. I'll make coffee to keep us awake. I don't want to be flaked on the couch when they get in.'

Zara followed her into the kitchen and hitched herself up on to the counter top while Fran took out a jar of Maxwell House and two mugs.

'Don't make one for me. My stomach's still not right,' Zara said. 'Coffee's making me gag at the moment.'

Something about the way she said it – the forced lightness – made Fran look up.

'Are you OK?'

'Yes!'

'Zara. That's your lying face. What's going on?'

'It's nothing.' A beat. 'It's probably nothing. I'm late.'

'Oh shit.'

'It's nothing. I'm sure of it. I'm just late.'

'Zara.'

She slid off the counter and threw up her hands.

'Oh God, I wish I'd said nothing now. You're going to turn this into a thing.'

'It *is* a thing. Can you do a test?'

A sigh. 'I should. I will. Just to shut you up, OK?'

'You can buy tests in the pharmacy now, you don't even have to go to the doctor. I heard my mam talking about it. So, no excuse.'

Zara made a Scout's honour sign.

'I'm sure it'll be fine,' Fran added, gentler now. 'How could you be pregnant anyway – you're not going out with anyone. It would be the Immaculate Conception, part two.'

'Well, it could—' Zara stopped herself and made a lip-zipping motion. 'Anyway, as long as my parents never know we even uttered these words, I'll be fine.'

A creak from the hall made them both look up.

'It's nothing,' Zara said after a moment. 'God, I'm getting as jittery as you.'

That's when Fran noticed something on the floor. A little Alice in Wonderland figurine, in three pieces. Was that the noise she'd heard?

'Did you knock this?' she asked Zara.

Zara looked offended. 'Oh, come on, I just woke up. And if I broke something, I wouldn't leave it there. It was probably Lily.'

Fran picked up the pieces. Zara was right, it was probably Lily. She didn't feel it was her place to throw it away though and maybe it could be fixed. She lifted a souvenir plate from its stand on the windowsill and laid it flat, then put the figurine pieces safely on top. Beside the plate, the sill was discoloured in two patches – a pair of neat round circles, one larger than the other. As though, perhaps, other souvenirs and knick-knacks had once sat there and been removed. The Alice figurine accounted for one spot, and Fran looked around now to see if something else had fallen, but there was nothing on the floor.

She returned to the task of making coffee, her hand still shaking slightly as she spooned powder into her mug. Nobody could have got into the house. Her eyes travelled over to the back door. The Murphys were careful. Always locking the side gate and the doors, in case Lily got out. So, the door would be locked. *Should* be locked. Unless someone was in the house, in which case . . . She stepped forward and reached out to touch the handle. But she couldn't do it. If the door opened, she'd know. And suddenly, she really didn't want to know.

'Where are you going?' Zara asked. 'Out for a smoke?'

'No. Just . . .'

'We'll have one up the chimney,' Zara decided for both of them. 'Too dark and spooky out there, with those huge trees at the back.' She shivered. 'I got the fright of my life on the way over here, actually. I was just about to turn into the driveway when I almost crashed headfirst into Gavin Bowman. He was leaning against the pillar. Just standing there, for no reason at all. God, he'd be so hot if he wasn't so sullen. The way he looks at people, with his eyes half closed and that beanie hat he wears. It's kind of sexy, isn't it? Doesn't he remind you of Matt Dillon?'

'No. Well, maybe a bit but ... I don't know, he gives me the shivers. And not in a nice, Matt Dillon way. Did he say anything?'

'No. He just stood there, smoking. I kept walking.'

'He's probably bored out of his mind. There's nothing to do in Edenvale, especially in summer.'

'True. Anyway, soon none of it will matter, because we'll be gone to Virginia Beach. We're nearly there now, Fran. Nothing can stop us.'

Fran nodded. *Unless you're pregnant.* That would be the end of everything.

29

June 2018

'Mum, look, aren't they gorgeous?' Emily points at a pair of trainers on her tablet. 'And they're only €120 which is way cheaper than the Air Jordans I was showing you last week.'

'*Only* €120 for a pair of runners – are you mad in the head, child,' Mark says, opening the patio door and stepping outside. A light breeze flickers through the stifling heat in the kitchen.

'But the ones I'm wearing have a hole in them,' Emily calls after him. 'You don't want me going to school with holes in my shoes, do you?'

Ben chimes in. 'Oh – you mean the hole you made with the scissors, so you could get new ones?'

'Oh my God, Ben, shut up. As if.'

'Don't say shut up,' I tell her, on autopilot. 'It's not nice.' It's Saturday evening and Mark is thinking about putting on the barbecue, and now Emily wants to show me a new jacket she'd like too, and I smile and agree and admire and promise but I can't concentrate on any of it. *My mother kidnapped Lily Murphy.* There is no other logical conclusion. I keep playing it over and over in my mind. The photographs of Lily online. The sharp shock of resemblance. The cold light of day telling me no, Lily is surely not Lila. The search for a connection – the hope that there was none. And then

170

there she was. My mother, sitting on a picnic blanket, in Rowan-brook, in 1982. Still there in Rowanbrook in 1985. Still there during Lily's final days. But why would she take her? She didn't look after the daughter she had – leaving me alone in the flat on Woodbine Street; five miles and an entire world away from her life in Edenvale. Leaving me alone while she was working and partying and drinking and leeching. Leeching off the people of Rowanbrook, and then taking one of their own. But why?

'Mark?' I call, through the open patio door. The smell of grill-ing burgers wafts in. Someone – Fran maybe – is using a hedge trimmer. The sky is a midday blue, though it's already six o'clock.

Mark looks up from the barbecue.

'This is a little random, but did anyone ever ask for a ransom for Lily Murphy?'

'A ransom? Not that I know of. Though I suppose I wouldn't know . . . And I'm just thinking now, if the Murphys got a ransom request they'd be warned not to tell the police, right? Like on TV?'

'Maybe . . . though if they paid a ransom, I suppose she'd have been returned.'

'Not necessarily. On TV they're always double-crossing – taking the ransom but killing the person anyway.'

My chest tightens at that. *Breathe.* 'I wonder if there's any way to find out if there was a ransom request?' On some level, a stepped-back level, I can't help marvelling at how calm I sound. 'Or where Mary Murphy is now? You don't know where she moved to, do you?'

'Not a clue. Maybe our solicitor or estate agent would have some kind of record? There'd have to be a contact address on the legal docs when they sold . . . Who's that friend of yours who's an estate agent, would she know?'

'Liz Landry. She might.'

*

Mark carries on grilling and I sit at the kitchen table staring at my phone, trying to decide whether to message Liz now, interrupting her Saturday evening with a work-ish question, or to wait till Monday on the school run. Before I can decide, an email from an unfamiliar address pops through.

Joanna, thanks for your interest in the Lily Murphy case. I saw your first comment, but wasn't sure about responding as I'm wary of giving up anonymity. It gives me the freedom to write what I want to write. But your second comment really caught my attention. What has made you decide Lily drowned after all? I was surprised to see it. In my experience, the more you dig into this case, the less likely it seems she drowned . . . Let me know what led you to this? Deep Dive.

Damn. Why did I ever write that first comment? Now there's no easy way to close this Pandora's box. I think for a moment then start to type.

Hi, thanks for getting back. It's a long story, mostly based on research on true-crime websites. Maybe we could chat by phone?

The less I put in writing, the better. And maybe this person Deep Dive has some insight, something that will help me find out for sure if my mother took Lily. Jesus. Even thinking those words feels bizarre. Bizarre and sick. Which sums up Cynthia perfectly.

Cynthia. There's no getting away from it. I need to go back there to find out more. *You need to confront her,* says a little voice in my head. *Ask her directly.* But if avoiding confrontation were a superpower, I'd be running the world. And never more so than when it comes to my mother. We can't talk about my childhood (a 'blur' or 'so boring' or 'Joanna, let it go' are her stock responses) and we can't talk about my father ('a one-night stand' or 'I don't even know' or 'Joanna, let it go') and we can never, ever talk about Lila. I tried once, about six years after it happened. I asked her why Lila only came to us aged three. She was calm at first. Lila was with her dad, she said, but he didn't want her any more. She looked wistful and almost sad and this was perhaps what lulled me into a false sense of closeness. Of reconciliation. Redemption.

I'm sorry, I said, *for what happened to Lila.*

And that was it. She stood, taller than me still, her hands, her bony fingers digging into my arms, as strong as when I was ten, the night it happened.

Don't you ever, ever mention her name again. You lost the right when you did what you did.

And she pushed me so hard I fell to the floor. It comes back to me now clearly. Viscerally. Viciously. Lying on our grotty carpet, staring up at her furious face. I should have left then. Walked away. But she was my mother. And I wanted her love. If not love, then acceptance. So instead of leaving, I nodded and promised. I'd never speak of Lila again.

'Mum?'

Ben's voice pulls me back to the present. 'Yes?'

He's standing at the open patio door. 'Dad says dinner's nearly ready.' He tilts his head to one side. 'Mum, are you OK?'

'Of course! Why?'

'You look sad all the time.'

I shake my head and gesture to him to come over for a hug. 'I'm not sad, pet, I'm fine. But thanks for asking.' I kiss his ear. 'Now, grab the ketchup and let's get the table set.' I look at him sideways as he extracts himself from the hug. 'That is, unless you'd prefer some . . . puréed broccoli on your burger?'

He shrieks in mock horror and I tickle him, prompting squeals of laughter.

'Stop! Stop!' he says breathlessly and I do. 'Do it again!' he says immediately, just as he always does. Nine-year-olds get so much joy out of the simplest everyday interactions.

And suddenly Lila's on my mind again. Lila who never got to be nine. Lila who never got to go to school like my kids do. Who never got to make friends or play video games or eat barbecues.

God, I need to sort this out, I think, pulling Ben back into my arms for another tight hug.

Mark is calling us outside for burgers. I send Ben for the ketchup and glance at my phone one last time before dinner. There's a reply from Deep Dive already.

> I don't like the phone. Let's meet in person. Blackrock Park tomorrow at 11?

There is only one answer. And it's either the solution to everything, or a huge mistake.

30

June 1985

TALL CHURCH CANDLES FLICKERED on the altar as the smell of incense rolled across the pews. The sermon was about rich men getting into heaven. Mary watched as the parishioners listened. They didn't see themselves as rich men. They didn't think this sermon was about them. But they'd put ten pounds in the collection plate and walk outside to get into their Volvos and BMWs and go home to their more than comfortable five-bedroom Edenvale houses with their gardeners and nannies and cleaners. What was that, if not rich? On Mary's lap, Lily squirmed, and beside her, Robbie pretended to listen to the priest as his eyelids slipped ever lower. Susie and Tom sat in the next pew, with the three younger children in tow; fidgeting and nudging and pushing and whispering. No Cynthia today. Even Susie couldn't justify paying a babysitter to come to Mass. On the other side of the aisle, Ines and Victor sat a few rows ahead. Ines in a pink coat, not unlike Mary's, her hair pulled back in a tight, dark bun. Victor, as always, in a suit, his back stiff like his wife's. Rigid, tense people who never seemed to relax. Cora, head bowed, sat quietly beside her dad.

Outside, blinking in the sunlight, Susie and Tom Stedman joined Mary and Robbie on the steps of the church.

Tom clapped Robbie on the back and kissed Mary on the cheek, pulling her close, enveloping her in the smell of his cologne.

'All still on for dinner tonight?' Robbie asked.

'We cannot *wait*. Mark and the girls are away, and the smaller ones are an absolute handful without the bigger ones. As you can see,' Susie said, gripping Luke's hand as he tried to pull away. 'So I *badly* need a night out.'

'Excellent. We'll see you at eight so,' Robbie said, rubbing his hands together.

'Wonderful. And our turn next, for sure. As soon as we're properly settled over in Oakbrook,' Susie said. 'Did you hear about Ines's mother?'

They hadn't.

'Oh. She passed away this morning. Ines is trying to get a flight to Spain.'

Mary clapped a hand to her mouth. 'That's awful. Are they still here? I saw them in the church.'

'No, they've gone on home. She's trying to get over there as soon as she can.'

'So they won't be at the dinner tonight?' Robbie said, sounding a little put out.

Mary winced.

Susie gave him a funny look. 'I'd guess not.'

And that was how, Mary thought later, Ruth Cavanagh ended up at the dinner. The flap of the butterfly's wings that changed everything.

'That child will get fat.'

Mary turned, startled, as Ruth Cavanagh emerged from behind a tree in her garden, shears in hand. Mary and Robbie stopped at her gate as Lily skipped ahead, then turned back too, a lollipop in her mouth.

'Ah, it's just a Sunday treat, Ruth, it won't kill her,' Robbie said. 'We always stop into the shop after Mass.'

'Mass.' She sniffed. 'Full of hypocrites. When I was teaching, every child in the class could tell me they'd been to Mass on Sunday but not one of them knew their Bible.'

Lily, oblivious to Ruth's mood, had slipped into the driveway, still sucking on her lollipop.

Ruth turned to stare at Mary. 'If anyone thinks they're something when they're not, they deceive themselves. Galatians 6:3.'

Mary felt a wave of heat crawl over her skin. An itch to get away. She glanced up the road towards home, spotting Ellen, Aoife and Gavin at the edge of the green. Ellen's blonde ponytail bobbed up and down in the sunlight as she hopped from foot to foot. Aoife was saying something to Gavin, trying to convince him to come with them, pointing over towards the building site. The Rowanbrook residents didn't like that – kids hanging out in the building site. But as far as Mary could tell, there was nowhere much for them to go. As she watched, she saw Gavin shake his head. Then he turned slightly and locked eyes with her. She looked away.

'We should go,' she said. 'Lily, time to go!' It was only then that she registered Lily was hunkered down at the bed of flowers that bordered Ruth's lawn. 'Lily! Come away from those, foxgloves are dangerous!'

Lily obediently slipped back out of the driveway as Ruth made a 'pah' noise and muttered something about 'foreigners'. Mary wasn't quite sure how being 'foreign' made her any less likely to know about gardening, and felt a rare compulsion to defend herself.

'My mother studied flowers and herbs and she taught me,' she said quietly. 'I was never allowed near foxgloves – it's dangerous to have them around children.'

'Lucky I don't have any children then, isn't it,' was Ruth's response to that.

Children might stray into your garden, Mary wanted to say, but this wasn't a strong argument. Ruth's property was, after all, Ruth's property.

'We'll go on, Ruth,' Robbie said cheerfully, seemingly oblivious to her mood. 'We should leave you to your gardening. And if you ever change your mind about those trees at the back, I'd be happy to contribute towards a tree surgeon.' He paused. 'Actually, if you're free tonight, we're having a little dinner party at ours? You'd be more than welcome?'

Ruth looked like she was about to say no, but then suddenly nodded yes, before turning back to her gardening.

Mary closed the oven door and turned the temperature down, her mind already on tonight's dinner. *Just a little dinner party.* For Robbie, yes. But for her, cooking for six, getting it right, fitting in with the social rules of Rowanbrook – there was nothing *little* about it. Outside, Robbie and Lily were playing – Lily inside the paddling pool, Robbie on the lawn beside it. Golden sunlight sparkled on the water's surface as Lily sat wriggling her toes, smiling at her dad. Mary watched, her mind shifting from tonight's dinner to Ruth Cavanagh's Bible quote to Gavin's increasingly unsettling presence. She turned to take her recipe notebook from the windowsill. As she did, she stopped suddenly, her hand hovering halfway. The souvenir plate – the one with the illustration of Santa Cruz Wharf – was lying flat on the windowsill, instead of standing as it usually did. Her Alice in Wonderland figurine was in three pieces, sitting on the plate. And her Santa Cruz lighthouse wasn't there at all. She stared at the discoloured patches where the souvenirs had sat. Then she picked up one piece of Alice. It looked eerie in her hand, this body-less ceramic head, smiling back at her. How did it break? Lily couldn't reach this high, not even if she climbed on a chair. Mary put down the smiling Alice-head and picked up the body, turning it over in her hand. Maybe Fran had done it? She had seemed a little off when they came home last night, jittery almost, but Mary had put it down to the late hour. Perhaps Fran had somehow knocked the figurine off the sill and didn't want to admit what she'd done. Or perhaps it was Zara; Zara whose breath whispered of whiskey once or twice, Zara who lapped attention from Robbie, Zara who thought Mary didn't notice her face light up each time Robbie offered to walk her home.

She scooped the figurine into her hand and crossed the kitchen.

Pieces of Alice. Into the trash. Just like that.

Had the girls smashed the lighthouse too? Mary peered into the trash. Chocolate wrappers, empty potato chip packets, but no lighthouse. It didn't matter, not really. It was just a cheap souvenir. But it reminded her of home. Gave her comfort. Why they threw it away and not the figurine, she wasn't sure. Then again, she didn't really understand these Irish girls with their clumpy shoes and awkward ways.

'Have you seen my watch?' Robbie asked that evening, as they got ready for their dinner guests' imminent arrival. 'I couldn't find it this morning.'

'I haven't seen it . . . were you wearing it when we were out last night?'

'No, I'd left it on the dresser but when I looked this morning it wasn't there,' he said, buttoning his shirt. 'I thought it'd show up during the day, but it hasn't. Strange.'

He walked out to the bathroom and Mary stood in the middle of the bedroom. Thinking. Scanning. She moved to the dresser. Her perfume bottles stood where they always stood, and her powder puff rested on her compact, exactly where she'd left it last night. Her lipstick, usually upright, lay flat. She reached to pick it up, and on instinct, removed the lid. Inside was half a lipstick. Someone had broken it. Someone had broken it *after* she used it at seven o'clock yesterday evening. She looked around the room, at the floor beneath the dresser, under the bed, beside the door. But it was nowhere. Who might have broken it? Lily? Fran and Zara? And where was Robbie's watch?

She shook her head.

The lipstick was old. The watch would show up. She sat on the bed and took a steadying breath. Everything would be OK.

31

June 2018

NOW THAT I'M IN Blackrock Park, I'm uneasy. What if Deep Dive is some kind of fraudster or psychopath? I pull my blazer tighter and glance around. Maybe I shouldn't have come on my own. But who else could I have brought? Mark thinks I'm walking the pier with Adana, and Adana's on her own with the kids this weekend. Beyond those two, there is no one.

I'm sitting on a bench near the pond, just as Deep Dive instructed. He'll find me, apparently.

The sky is grey for the first time in weeks and the park is unusually quiet for a Sunday morning. A little way away, a child of about three is throwing bread for the ducks. A small, blonde child who reminds me of Sophie but then just as quickly, of Lila. Of Lily.

I turn my head to scan the handful of people walking through the park. A woman in her thirties, pushing a pram. An elderly lady with a tiny dog. Two teenage girls in shorts, both on phones. A man in a baseball cap and dark glasses. My eyes stay on him. He's walking faster than the people around him and seems to be coming in my direction. I sit forward on the bench, torn between fleeing and staying put, and I'm so fixated on him, I don't notice at first that someone is sitting beside me.

'Joanna?' says a woman's voice.

'Yes?'

'It's me. I'm me,' says the woman, and gives a small laugh. 'Obviously I'm me,' she adds, 'but I mean I write the blog.'

The man in the dark glasses passes by and, still confused, I shake the woman's hand. Deep Dive is *not* what I was expecting. A couple of years older than me, petite and pale, with black-rimmed glasses and blonde hair. She's wearing a simple white shirt with light grey jeans, flat sandals and no make-up. With tiny pearls in her ears, and a burgundy scarf around her neck, she looks wholly unremarkable and her first impression is somehow insipid, completely at odds with the authoritative voice behind Deep Dive.

'I'm not what you expected,' says the woman, reading my mind.

I rearrange my face.

'In the blog posts, you sound quite . . .' I trail off, unable to find the right word.

'Assertive?' suggests the woman. 'Yes. The blog is where I get to rant a little, say what I really want to say. Maybe be the person I wish I was. And to write about Lily, of course.'

I can't imagine this unassuming woman ranting; not out loud, not online. But here she is, in the flesh, and she might know something about what happened that day.

'What prompted you to write about her?'

The woman sighs. 'A combination of things. My husband died and—'

'Oh, I'm so sorry.'

'Thank you. And my daughter had moved to London, so I was at a bit of a loose end.'

Now I'm scrutinizing her face, trying to work out how she has a daughter old enough to move to London. She can't be more than a year or two older than me.

'I've always liked writing,' the woman continues, 'but I've never been brave enough to let anyone read. My husband used to take my journal and narrate it out loud. It was terribly embarrassing. If I couldn't handle him reading, how could I let anyone else?'

I nod, wondering what kind of husband reads his wife's journal.

'Then one night, after a second glass of wine, I googled "how to start a blog" and in the end, it was so easy. I realized that being anonymous was the key. I could write whatever I wanted without worrying what people would think. At first it was about anything and everything, but then the thirty-year anniversary of Lily's disappearance came along, and suddenly, that's all I wanted to write about.'

She stops to take a breath, gasping slightly. I have the odd impression that the woman isn't used to talking.

'So, you did some digging? Looked up old articles?' I prompt.

The woman looks at me strangely. 'Yes. Lots of that. But it was mostly trying to remember.'

'Remember?'

'And talking to Aoife. Well, *listening* to Aoife.' Her eyes look sad. 'Hearing things I wish I'd known back then.' She shakes herself. 'It's all very blurry. Fragments of memories. Like watching a home movie.' She touches my knee. 'Think back to when you were thirteen, how much do you remember? Your thirteenth birthday? Or Christmas Day that year?'

'Snippets, I suppose, more than clear memories,' I say quietly.

'Exactly. Same here. And now that Aoife and I have talked, some of the memories are crystallizing, though it's hard to tell if that's because we keep talking about them, making them real, or if they were real to begin with.'

'Sorry, who is Aoife?'

'Another woman from Rowanbrook. Well, she doesn't live there any more.'

And suddenly I understand. I look at the woman's face, at the white-blonde hair, the small, neat features. I remember her now as she was in the video at Lily's birthday party thirty-three years earlier; at the end of the line, accepting her fate. Pretty, yes, but not as striking as Aoife.

'You're Ellen.'

'I'm so sorry, I forgot you didn't have my name. Yes, of course. I'm Ellen.'

32

'OH MY GOD, YOU lived in Rowanbrook back then . . . next door to the Murphys.' I stare at Ellen, seeing it so clearly now.

'Yes. I knew Lily her whole life. I was too young to babysit, but I used to pop through the gap between our gardens to play with her.' She smiles. 'I had two brothers but no sisters so I guess I kind of adopted Lily as a stand-in.'

'And you were at Lily's birthday party – I saw you in the video.'

'Goodness, I didn't even know there was a video of that day. I'd love to see it.'

'And the day it happened?'

'I was there. I was playing Hide and Seek that morning. I helped search. I listened to the adults talking in whispers about drownings and kidnappers. I saw the looks they gave that little girl Cora and her mother. I listened on the extension phone when my mum told my gran about a neighbour called Eddie Hogan fighting with Lily's father, and about the guards interviewing Cora's dad.'

'Victor.'

'That's it. I couldn't remember his name at first but then Aoife did, and we found an article about his death. Awful.' She swallows. 'It was a really horrible time in Rowanbrook. People were

185

shell-shocked about Lily, and of course the rumours started then. About Victor and why the guards interviewed him. About Eddie Hogan, and why he was so angry with Robbie Murphy.'

I nod. I know these stories.

Ellen continues: 'One minute, Rowanbrook was the most normal place in the world; full of very ordinary, boring people – at least in my thirteen-year-old opinion. Then suddenly, it was turned upside down and all sorts came out.' She shakes her head. 'I guess you never know what people are hiding behind their smiles and their cheery good mornings.'

I nod again. I know *this* story – this existence – only too well.

She shakes herself. 'But yes, anyway, here we are thirty-three years later, still trying to figure out what happened.'

This gives me a jolt – somehow I've forgotten she's here to find out what happened to Lily. I need to take care.

'I've been asking the neighbours and googling to find out more,' I say carefully, 'but it seems likely she drowned.'

'Yes – you'll read next to nothing online beyond the generally accepted conclusion that she drowned. But I found out something recently that suggests that's not true.'

My stomach twists. 'Oh?'

'I think it's important to say, I was just a child myself. But. Having lived through it – the rumours, the whispers, the stories about Victor O'Brien and Eddie Hogan – it feels like there *had* to be more to it. And even though it's all very blurry, between Aoife and myself, we've managed to piece together a good chunk of what was going on that morning.' She pauses. 'As I say, sometimes it's hard to tell if we're really remembering or creating memories. But something happened that day, something that was never made public at the time, and it wasn't anything to do with Eddie Hogan or Victor O'Brien.'

33

June 2018

SHE TAKES A DEEP breath and I steel myself for whatever she's about to say.

'This is going to sound bad . . . I found out recently that Gavin took a key to Mary Murphy's house and let himself in one night when they were out.'

Ellen is talking again as though I know all these people. Presumably she means Gavin Bowman, the boy who Mark punched, so I don't interrupt her.

'Gavin was fixated on Mary. She'd been nice to him once when he was doing their garden, and that was it, he was infatuated. Even though he was sixteen and she was an adult. And married. And a mother.'

'Ugh. That's a bit odd.'

Ellen gives me a funny look. 'It was harmless enough until he broke into her house. He took the key from the Burkes next door – they used to keep a spare. He wanted to take something from Mary's room. A keepsake. Stupid, really. But we were kids.'

I nod, though this doesn't seem like any kind of normal behaviour to me.

'He got the wrong room though. He ended up in Lily's

bedroom and when she woke and saw him, he hid in the wardrobe. He told us all about it the next day.'

This is taking a very different direction from what I expected. I want to ask about Cynthia but I hold back.

'You think Gavin did something to Lily? To stop her telling that she saw him in her room?'

Ellen sighs. 'Yes. Maybe. A sixteen-year-old boy in a three-year-old's bedroom doesn't look good, no matter what way you spin it. And there's such a lot I don't think was properly looked into at the time.'

'So people back then didn't know Gavin broke into the Murphys' house?'

'Exactly. But more than that. Things I didn't know at the time. Things I only found out when he was gone.'

'Gone where?'

Ellen looks puzzled, then smiles. 'Sorry, I've done it again. I keep forgetting how little I put on the blog. Gavin is dead. We were married for twenty years, and then one morning, he just didn't wake up.' Her voice is clear. Dispassionate, almost. As though she is used to telling this story, or she's warning her audience not to get emotional.

'I'm so sorry.'

She waves it away. 'That's when I found out.'

'Found out?'

A neat, careful intake of breath. 'In his will, Gavin left an old but expensive watch, a little ceramic lighthouse, and a significant financial bequest for Lily Murphy, if she was ever found. With very specific wording – an instruction to tell her "I'm so sorry for what I did, I should never have locked you in."'

'Wow. Do you know what he was talking about?'

She nods. 'After Gavin died, Aoife came to stay with me for a bit, and we were reminiscing about old times, the good bits and the bad. How Gavin was back then, the way he obsessed over Mary Murphy that summer. I used to see him from my bedroom window, standing outside their house. Then Aoife reminded me of the morning Lily went missing; that we saw Gavin in the building site, talking to her. To Lily.'

'Oh?'

She nods. 'I remembered it then, as soon as Aoife said it – Cora was a bit behind, following Lily as usual, calling her. But all of Lily's attention was on Gavin. She had her arms out, as though she wanted to hold his hand or get him to pick her up. We couldn't hear what they were saying, but suddenly Lily's arms dropped, and she started to cry. Gavin didn't stay to ask what was wrong or comfort her, he just turned and walked away.' She pauses, composing herself. 'That's when I realized he didn't need to ask what was wrong – he'd *caused* the tears. I'd forgotten about it but as soon as Aoife said it, it was there, clear as day. Then Aoife said something about the door with the barrels, and I had no idea what she was talking about.'

'The door with the barrels?'

'She kept saying, "Remember, we saw Gavin pushing the wooden pallet and the barrels in front of the door?" but I couldn't. After a while, she realized I wasn't with her. I think she was shocked when she worked out that I'd never been part of this huge thing that had happened.'

She stops, looking at her hands.

'What was the huge thing?'

'She told me that when we were all playing Hide and Seek, she'd seen Gavin blocking a door in one of those half-finished houses on the building site. She didn't really think anything of it until later, when people realized Lily was properly missing. She went back to the house where she'd seen him, but Mary and Robbie Murphy were already there, along with a man called

Tom something and Della Burke and her daughter Fran. Fran was the neighbour I mentioned earlier, the one who was minding Lily the night Gavin broke in.'

I nod but don't interrupt.

'Anyway, they'd moved the barrels and there was nobody inside. She says she remembers Mary Murphy looking out of the window, shining a torch out there, and the sheer terror on her face as the search went on. But Aoife couldn't stop thinking about the way Gavin made Lily cry, and then seeing him block the door.'

'Why didn't she tell anyone?'

'She did. She told her parents, who went to Gavin's parents. And they said there was no need for anyone to take it further, since Lily clearly wasn't in that room. And that was that. That's what I mean about things not being properly investigated.'

'So you decided to reveal it in a blog post, thirty-three years later?'

'Kind of, but I couldn't do it in the end. Whatever he may have done, Gavin was my husband. I wrote posts hinting that there's more to the story, but stopped short of telling what Gavin did that morning during the game of Hide and Seek.'

'Is that what you meant in the blog post title – "The Locked Room"?'

'Exactly.'

Not my locked room. Not me at all.

But as much as I want to cling to this idea – that somebody else did something, that it wasn't Cynthia and it wasn't me – I can't escape the facts.

'The thing is though,' I say carefully, 'Lily wasn't in that room . . .'

'I know, but he clearly locked her in. And nobody looked into it.'

'But then she'd have been found there . . .?'

'Not if she climbed out the window. There was scaffolding and planks of wood outside, but what if she fell off that and someone hid her body?'

I shiver.

'Or what if she managed to get down to the ground and then fell in the river?' Ellen's voice cracks. 'It would still be Gavin's fault for trapping her there.'

I put my hand on her arm, looking for the right thing to say, but I can't quite order my thoughts or find the words.

Because if Gavin caused Lily's death, then Lila wasn't Lily. And I didn't kill her.

Somehow, this doesn't give me any peace at all.

34

June 1985

FRAN WAS PAGING THROUGH a magazine in her kitchen on Sunday evening when Della lowered herself into a chair, a curious look on her face.

'So, were you going to tell me about Zara?' she asked.

'What about Zara?'

'Come on, Fran.'

Fran stared. 'Mam, I have no idea what you're talking about.'

'You really don't know?'

'Know what?' God, her mother could drive her crazy.

'About the *baby*.' Della whispered the last word, though there was nobody else in the house.

Fran's blood ran cold. 'Baby?'

'She's expecting. Did she really not tell you?'

'No! I mean yes, but she couldn't be, Mam. She doesn't even have a boyfriend. Her period's late, that's all. Who told you?'

'Her mother. She phoned me to give me a dressing-down. All my fault, and your fault, apparently.'

'*What?*'

Della sighed. 'I couldn't make much sense of it. She ranted and raved that you were a bad influence and I've no control

192

over you, and no wonder I'd been left on my own with five children and did they even have the same dad.'

'Jesus Christ.'

'Fran. Language.'

'Sorry, but come on.'

'I know. Look, I need you to tell me. What is her mam on about? Why does she think this has anything to do with you?'

Fran shook her head. None of it made any sense. But she needed to talk to Zara.

Shoulders hunched, head bent, Zara marched down her driveway as Fran followed a few steps behind. Zara didn't stop until she got to the green, where she lowered herself on to the grass at the entrance to the building site. Fran sat beside her, wishing she'd worn something warmer than shorts.

'What's going on?' she asked her friend.

'You tell me.'

'My mam said you're expecting? The test was positive?'

'Yes, the test was positive.'

Jesus. Poor Zara. Fran reached for her hand. Zara snatched it away.

'But whose is—' A glare from Zara stopped Fran finishing her sentence. 'I take it your parents went mad?' she said instead.

'Yes.' Zara's eyes were wet now. 'How could you do it, Fran? And for God's sake, why?'

'Me?'

'Why did you tell my parents?'

'I didn't tell your parents! Why on earth would you think that?'

'Because you're the only one I told about being late.'

'Zara, I swear to God I didn't tell. Are your parents claiming it was me?'

'No,' Zara conceded. 'They got a note. They won't show it to me or tell me who it's from.'

'Oh God. What did it say?'

' "Congratulations on your future grandchild. Will it be an accountant like its dad or a slapper like its mam?" ' Zara spat the words. Angry. Embarrassed. 'When they read the note, they went mad. Tore through my room, searching for God knows what. A diary, love letters, I don't know. And they found my journal, and saw I'd been doodling on it.'

'And?'

'Look, same as any of us. I'd been writing my name with his name, drawing love-hearts, the usual stupid stuff we all do. Putting our names with the surnames of boys we like.'

An accountant like its dad. 'Oh, Zara. You were writing "Zara Murphy" on your journal?'

'Yep. And "Zara Hogan loves Robbie Murphy". And "Robbie Murphy loves Zara Hogan". But the worst bit was the sketches I'd done of him. Pornography, my mother said.'

Fran clapped her hand to her mouth.

'I know. It would be funny if it wasn't so horrible. My dad's threatening to call in to Robbie and beat him "black and blue". My mam's trying to talk him down – she said if he does something like that, everyone will turn against our family and it's going to be hard enough dealing with me being branded a "whore" and having a "bastard" child. Her biggest concern is, of course, Mass. How's she going to go to Mass once people find out – what's the priest going to say?'

'I'm so sorry.'

'Yeah. And the worst thing is – among many worst things – no J-1 summer.'

Fran thought she might cry. Though how would that look – if after hearing all Zara's bad news, the thing that set her off was losing her travel buddy. She swallowed.

'I'm not going without you.'

'Ah stop, you're not cancelling. You'd lose your money, and think of all our plans – perfecting our American accents and kissing American boys and coming home mahogany after a whole summer on the beach? No *way* are you cancelling.'

No way am I going alone, Fran thought, biting her lip, still trying not to cry. And yet staying here for the whole summer . . . *God*.

'So now we just need to pray my dad doesn't see Robbie any time soon. Or God knows what he'll do.'

'You believe me that I didn't send that note, right?'

'Yeah. Sorry.' She paused, picking daisies from the damp grass. 'OK, I need to tell you the truth.'

Mary smiled around at their guests that Sunday night, wondering what they'd think if they knew how little she wanted to be there. Wondering where Robbie's watch was and who broke her Alice figurine and why she had seated herself beside Ruth Cavanagh.

She can't be any less craic than Ines or Victor, Robbie had whispered just before they opened the door. That, indeed, was true, but Ruth was giving them a run for their money. She'd hardly said a word all night and had sniffed at Mary's Mexican platters, asking if there was any 'Irish' food. 'A boiled egg?' Tom Stedman had suggested with a grin, earning him a dig in the ribs from Susie.

'The food is wonderful, Mary. So *exotic*,' Susie said. 'And the place settings. And what an unusual piece,' she added, pointing at a star-shaped candleholder in the middle of the table. 'I saw something similar in my catalogue. Is it from the Kays catalogue?'

'No, it was my mother's. She was into symbols and talismans and that kind of thing. One of many quirky belongings passed on to me when she died.'

'So it's from California!' Susie was more impressed now. 'Like your painting up there?' She pointed at the photograph of Santa Cruz Wharf that hung on the dining room wall. Mary glanced up.

'That one's actually a photo, but yes.'

'It's wonderful. Like the food, *so different*. So much more exciting than Dublin. You're a lucky man,' she said, turning to Mary's husband. 'All this fabulous foreign cooking.'

'Don't I know it,' Robbie said with a wink. 'Poor old Dublin can't live up to the glamour of California, though Mary does a good job of hiding her feelings.' He put his arm around Mary's shoulder and squeezed. Her smile tightened.

Ruth snorted.

Susie looked over at her, flashing a strained smile. 'Ruth, have you had any luck fixing that broken window?'

'Eventually.' The response was curt, snappy – as though it was Susie's fault her window was broken. Della lifted her napkin to her face to hide an eye-roll.

'Does anyone know if Ines managed to get a flight to Spain?' Susie asked, changing the subject again.

'She's hoping to fly out tomorrow,' Della said. 'Victor and Cora are staying here.'

'Who'll mind Cora?' Susie asked.

'Cynthia, as far as I know.'

'Oh great, there goes my childcare,' Susie said.

Mary and Della exchanged tiny smiles. Susie had a way of making everything about herself.

She seemed to realize what she'd said. 'Of course, they need Cynthia far more than I do, I understand that. But with the younger kids off school now and Mark and the girls away, dear God, the summer seems long.'

Mary nodded in agreement, though with Lily not yet at school, it really made no difference.

Ruth spoke up then. 'What's the point, Susie, in having six children, if you don't actually want to raise them yourself?'

Susie's mouth dropped open. Mary squirmed. What on earth had possessed Robbie to invite Ruth?

'It's so we'll be guaranteed a good nursing home,' Tom quipped, dispelling the tension. Everyone laughed far more loudly than necessary.

'We're screwed so,' Robbie said, 'with just the one child. We didn't think that through, did we, Mary! Then again, we wouldn't want to ruin your figure.' He gave her a squeeze and got up then to open a bottle of expensive whiskey he'd been saving for just this occasion, and as the others oohed and aahed over it and held their glasses to be filled, Ruth shook her head and pushed back her chair.

'I'll leave you to it,' she said. 'I've enough to be getting on with and this kind of get-together isn't to my taste.'

But before she left the table, to Mary's surprise, she leaned down and whispered something in her ear.

Four words that changed everything.

And then came the hammering on the door.

35

June 2018

IT'S SUNDAY AFTERNOON AND Mark wants to know how my walk on the pier with Adana went. He doesn't really want to know, he's just being polite, making small talk, the way couples do. But suddenly it feels as though he knows I was sitting on a bench in Blackrock Park this morning, and not with Adana at all. I've lied to him for so long now, this additional fabrication shouldn't feel any worse, and yet it does. The walk was good, I tell him, though Adana couldn't stay long – because somehow if the fictional walk was short, that feels closer to the truth.

This news about Gavin Bowman and the locked room has knocked me. Between what Ellen's friend Aoife saw that morning in the building site and the bequest in Gavin's will, it seems clear he definitely locked Lily in that room. So maybe Cynthia didn't do anything. Maybe I have it all wrong. Skewed and confused by years of hazy memories. Guilt distorting and contorting. Tricking me.

But Cynthia was *there*, in Rowanbrook, in the early eighties. I know that for sure. And Lila appeared out of nowhere; a sister who'd been 'living with her dad'. A sister I'd never known about. So, locked room or not, I'm still at square one. Could there be some link between Gavin and Cynthia? If he liked older women and she liked younger boys – flirting with Mark and his friends? Cynthia was around the same age as Mary, who by Ellen's account was the object of Gavin's attention. More than attention.

Mark is bustling around the kitchen making a Sunday roast, and the kids are in their rooms, pretending they're not on various electronic devices. Sitting at the kitchen table, I tilt my laptop screen away from Mark and type 'Gavin Bowman' into the search bar.

Facebook, Twitter, LinkedIn. A death notice. Some newspaper features about his various roles in various charities. Looks like Gavin went from moody teen to giving back to society. Or at least, very well-paid giving back to society. I dig and I dig, and search their names together, but there's nothing to suggest a link between Gavin and my mother.

I try 'Cynthia Kirk' on its own. I know what comes up, I've googled her many times before. Her court appearances for social welfare fraud. Her conviction for possession of a controlled substance. Her suspended sentence that kept me out of care. No social media for Cynthia. Two photographs, both linked to her court dates. A semi-smart version of my mother, in a suit she must have borrowed.

I try 'Lila Kirk' though I already know nothing will show. My sister is, and always has been, a ghost. I flick to a photo of Lily, open in another tab. A photograph of Lila would help . . . Maybe it's not possible to tell if they're the same person but perhaps there'll be something that rules her out; some birthmark or feature I've forgotten. In two days, I'm due to visit Cynthia. Maybe it's time to stay a little longer. Maybe after enough whiskey or recreational painkillers, she'll sleep, and I can look around the flat. Look for photographs, evidence that my mind is playing tricks. That Lila was someone else entirely.

My phone rings suddenly, jolting me. A Dublin number, but not one I've saved in my contacts.

'Hi, Joanna speaking?'

'Mrs Stedman, this is Detective Sergeant McCarthy with Blackrock Garda Station. Do you have a moment?'

'Yes.' It comes out in a whisper. *Dammit. Get a grip.* 'Yes.' Clearer now.

'We're just going back over the notes from our chat with you on Friday and I wanted to check – did you say Tuesday was the last time you saw Ms O'Brien?'

Shit. Why didn't I just tell them? Mark is looking over now, making an *all OK?* face. I nod and walk into the living room.

'Oh, actually I had coffee with her on Thursday in her garden. A quick visit. That was the last time I saw her.'

'And you didn't think to mention that when we spoke to you?'

'I think we got talking about something else and then you left. I thought about it after and wondered if I should phone but it didn't seem important.'

Silence. Maybe she's writing it down. Maybe she's judging me. *I* would judge me. Lying by omission – I'm pretty sure that's what it's called.

'It was maybe fifteen minutes, in her garden. That's all,' I continue, filling the gap. I bet this is what they do – stay quiet so dumbass people like me keep blabbing.

'What did you talk about?'

'Um . . . she was telling me a bit about her family and her house – she said her mother rented out their house in Rowanbrook when she went into a nursing home, that the tenants left it in a mess. We talked about the garden – it's beautiful, really well maintained.' I'm over-eager to share now, to show that I'm willing to help.

'Did she talk about Lily Murphy, the little girl who dis-appeared?'

'A . . . a little. She felt it had destroyed her family.'

'And was she trying to do something about that?'

This has the feel of a very specifically worded question.

'She said she wanted to find out what really happened, to clear her father's name.'

'And what made her think she could do that now, all these years later? When the gardaí haven't managed to?'

Is that a hint of defensiveness?

'I suppose because I brought it up . . . old memories surfaced maybe, when I started asking questions. She was kind of fired up.' From the kitchen comes the clatter of dishes. 'But,' I add quickly, 'it seems clear Lily Murphy drowned, so I guess she might have given up again pretty soon.' Yes, Joanna, *that's* how to distract the police. Just remind them that Lily drowned and they'll forget all about it.

'Guys! Dinner!' Mark calls from the kitchen, giving me my escape.

'Detective Sergeant McCarthy, I have to go now, if that's all you need?'

'We may call you to come in so we can ask again about that visit on Thursday. By all accounts, you were the last one to speak to her in any great depth before she died.'

'Of course.' I want to ask why. If it was an accident, why all the questions? If it was suicide . . . I really don't want to think about that. Not when I was the last one to speak to her. Not when I was the one who resurrected the story that destroyed her family. 'Any time, bye now,' I say instead, and disconnect the call.

It's after six when I decide to bite the bullet and call in to Fran. Sunday evening is not an ideal time but I don't like how we left things yesterday morning, after I asked her about Eddie Hogan and her friend Zara. It's not so much that I owe her an apology, but perhaps an olive branch. Her expression when she answers the door is a mix of surprise and irritation, and it makes me want to turn on my heel and go home. But I stay.

'Fran, I'm sorry about yesterday, when I was asking about your friend Zara. It's none of my business. And it can't have been easy having her dad gossiped about. I saw first-hand how it upset Cora, and maybe didn't appreciate it would have been every bit as hard for your friend.'

Fran appraises me for a moment, then nods – an unspoken and not terribly clear acceptance of my olive branch, I think.

'I discovered something that might be of interest,' I continue, with the same impulse to please that I felt on the phone to McCarthy. 'I met with a woman called Ellen, who used to live in the house on our other side?'

Her eyes widen. 'Ellen! My God, I haven't seen her in years. That's a blast from the past.'

'Yes. She ended up marrying a guy from around here. Gavin Bowman?'

Fran nods. 'I remember. They were practically teenagers when they got married. He's dead now, isn't he?'

'Yes. The thing is, Ellen found out recently that Gavin did something that morning. He locked Lily in a room in the building site.'

'What? Jesus, are you serious? Do you want to come in?' She pulls the door wide. Olive branch accepted. I step in and follow her through to the kitchen, taking in my surroundings as Fran makes tea. I didn't see in here the morning I watched the video of Lily's party, but like the living room, it's a shrine to 1980s decor: pine cupboard doors, faux-marble counter tops, tile-effect linoleum floor. The smell of lemons, but not the fresh kind. Clutter, everywhere. Piles of papers on the worktop. Ornaments and knick-knacks and mugs of pens on the windowsill. I take a seat at the kitchen table.

'Now, tell me more about this locked room?' Fran says, putting two empty mugs on the table as the kettle thunders to its crescendo.

I fill her in – Gavin's fixation on Mary, the break-in at the Murphys', Lily waking up, and Aoife's recollection of the locked room with the barrels in front of the door.

Fran's mouth drops open. 'Oh my God,' she says. 'That's right. The night I babysat, the weekend before she went missing, I thought I heard noises.'

'Oh?'

'I went up to check, and Lily was awake and I remember now, she wanted to play Hide and Seek.' She closes her eyes, as though trying to conjure up the memory. 'I remember telling Zara afterwards. Lily kept pointing at something. Good God. So you're saying Gavin was there – hiding? While I was checking what the noise was?'

The thought turns my stomach. As a child, I was always afraid to get out of bed after dark, in case a hand shot out from under my bed and grabbed my ankle. As an adult, I thought I knew better – that this was the stuff of horror films, not real life. But if a teenage boy can so easily take a spare key from a neighbour and let himself in to creep around, then anything is possible.

'I guess that's what happened. He broke in, got caught by Lily, threatened her that morning in the building site, then locked her in the room by pushing barrels in front of the door. That's what Aoife told Ellen, but only recently. She saw him pushing the barrels, though she didn't know why. Jesus. The thoughts of that little girl locked inside and nobody realizing.' I clear my throat. 'You say you saw the room with the barrels – so you were there, searching that day?'

'All day, yes. We all were.'

We all were. Including the parasite babysitter? 'Who exactly was there?'

'My mam, Mary and Robbie obviously, the Hogans.' She pauses, as though daring me to bring up Zara and Robbie again. I don't. 'Your in-laws, all the kids from around the area too. Cora was there, crying a lot, because people kept asking her where she'd last seen Lily, and muttering about why she'd left her alone. She was really upset, and she didn't even have her parents with her, now that I think about it.'

'She was out helping with the search on her own?'

'Her mother had gone to Spain for a funeral, and her dad was at work at least until evening time, I suppose, so she was with her babysitter.'

Cynthia. Of course.

36

On MONDAY MORNING, I linger at the school gate pretending to look at my phone, watching out for Liz Landry. My mind is in overdrive, whirring with everything I discovered yesterday. No matter how I look at it, regardless of what Gavin Bowman did, there's no getting away from it: Cynthia was there that morning. My mother was in Rowanbrook when Lily disappeared. And sometime around then, she introduced me to a new sister. But why? Why would she want another child when she couldn't look after the one she had? There had to be a reason.

Liz emerges through the school gate. She greets me with a half-smile, and we fall into step.

'Walking back to Rowanbrook?' she asks, and I nod, adding something about the weather. Today Liz is wearing office clothes – a black shift dress with smart tan sandals and matching tote bag. Her earrings – rose-gold crosses with tiny embedded crystals – coordinate perfectly with a delicate chain around her neck. I look down at my own leggings and trainers and have a sudden yearning for office clothes and my old job. And maybe my old house too, and life – imperfect though it was – before discovering Lily Murphy's story.

'I'm still struggling to get my head around what happened to Cora,' Liz says, pushing Prada sunglasses to the crown of her head. 'I didn't know her at all really, but I can't stop thinking about it. The horror of how it happened. And wondering if she jumped.'

'Same.'

'Not that I thought she had any reason to,' Liz adds hurriedly. 'If anything, she was full of . . . vigour? Is that a weird word? I bumped into her on Thursday afternoon. Maybe that's why the whole thing has left me so shocked – that I saw her hours before she died.'

So I wasn't the last one to speak to her. *Thank you, Jesus.* The thought is out before I can box it away.

'Do . . . do the guards know you bumped into her on Thursday?'

Liz gives me a funny look.

'It's just that they thought I was the last one to speak to her. I wondered if they knew . . . not that it matters,' I hurry to add.

'I mentioned it to them on Friday when they told me what happened, yes. But it was a very brief chat at the garden wall. She was on some mission to clear her dad's name over the whole Lily Murphy thing. She said she had a "lead", as she called it.'

'Did she say what it was?'

'No, but she was excited.'

'Actually, Liz, on the subject of Lily, I wanted to ask you – with your estate agent hat on – is there any way to find out the forwarding address of a previous owner, when someone moves house?'

'If both parties are happy to do so, the estate agent can put them in touch with each other. You want to contact the person who sold you your house?'

We skirt through busy Monday morning traffic to cross the road and turn into Rowanbrook.

'I'm more thinking about Mary Murphy, wondering if there's a way to track *her* down. Mark and I were talking about it over the weekend and speculating about a ransom demand.' Liz looks at me quizzically. 'I just want to find out what I can and lay the story to rest. Peace of mind.'

'God, I don't know how you'd get the address. The information would be confidential; there's no way your solicitor would pass it on without permission, and Mary might have moved on again since. I actually thought she went to the States. But no harm in asking. Start with your solicitor. If you need help from any of the estate agents involved over the years, I'll see if I can do something. Everyone knows everyone.'

'Great. Thanks a million.' We stop at the turn for Rowanbrook Drive.

'No problem. Whatever it takes to get you some peace of mind. And I'm sure your husband will be glad to move on.'

'Sorry?'

'I mean, to be off the hook – you were saying you couldn't believe he didn't know it was the same house?'

'Oh. Yes.' That seems like a million years ago.

'For what it's worth, when I was showing the house that became my home, to the person who became my husband, I had absolutely no idea that Lily Murphy had lived in Rowanbrook. So, while the story is well known, the address probably isn't. Does that get him out of the doghouse?' She grins.

I put on the smile she expects. 'Just about.'

Oh, how I want to live in a world where Mark's memory is my only problem.

'Well, this is me. I'm in work at ten so I'd better get going.'

She goes her way and I go mine: home to rattle around 6 Rowanbrook Drive, just me and Lily's ghost.

*

Susie is there when I arrive, waiting on my doorstep, fanning herself against the morning heat.

'Joanna, darling! You know, you really shouldn't let yourself go now that you're not working any more,' she says, eyeing up my leggings. 'In my day, we never wore sportswear other than when we played sports! Or are you on your way to the gym?'

I'm heartily tempted to tell her I am, but instead, I invite her in.

'Goodness,' she says as we walk through to the kitchen. 'How do you stand the gloom!'

'We'll get to painting it – we just haven't had time yet.'

'Too busy obsessing over Lily Murphy, I bet. You have to let it go. It's not good for you.' She puts her handbag on the table, a tan leather Michael Kors, and scans the kitchen. 'It's strange to be here again, all these years later. I remember the birthday parties for Lily, the dinner parties, the card nights. *Big* into socializing, they were. More so Robbie, to be honest. Mary could be shy. Or aloof, depending on who you talked to. A bit like you, Joanna. "Hostess with the mostess", but not great at letting people in.'

My mouth drops open.

'Yes, just like you,' she continues. 'Very warm and welcoming and saying all the right things, but not quite letting the guard down. If you ever want to talk, by the way, I'm here. Not a replacement for your own mother, of course, but still.'

If only she knew.

She walks across the kitchen and stands at the window, looking out. 'Gosh, the garden is huge, isn't it? Such *potential*. I suppose that's what sold it to them, too. The Murphys, I mean. Their old house had a much smaller garden. A "scrubby little yard", as Mary used to call it.'

'Susie, would you like coffee?' She's not going any time soon; we may as well be caffeinated.

'Please. Mind you, the main reason they moved was showing off, to be honest.'

'Oh?'

'Robbie liked the idea of a grand home. "Every man wants a castle," he'd say. And this' – she waves a hand around my kitchen – 'this was his castle. They had one child and didn't plan on having more, so you'd wonder why they needed a five-bedroom house with a huge garden. But the old house was a bungalow with a postage-stamp patch of grass – wouldn't have suited the garden parties.' She rolls her eyes, but there's affection in it. 'They did have one dinner in the old house and it was a little, shall we say, below par.'

'You knew them before they lived here?' I pass her a coffee.

'Well, yes. They were in Rowanbrook then too. A little bungalow in the Grove. Mary called it "Santa Cruz", after her hometown.'

'Santa Cruz? I feel like I've heard of it.'

'Oh yes, it's quite a big town on the west coast of America.'

I smile. 'No, I meant a house called Santa Cruz.'

'Ah, of course. Will you name this house? Maybe you could choose something linked to your childhood – your home in London? If it's not too painful of course.' A sad headshake, a touch of the arm. *Oh, why did I ever start this.* 'Or use your family name maybe? Kirk? How about . . . Kirkwood. Kirkville?'

Oh Lord. 'Hmm. It doesn't sound quite as pretty as Santa Cruz . . . Oh – I remember now where I heard it – a mum from Ben's class who was here at our housewarming. She lives in it now.'

'Did I meet her?'

'Liz Landry is her name?'

'No. But maybe don't tell her I called her garden a scrubby little yard,' she says with a grin.

Even Susie, it turns out, sometimes has a filter.

37

June 1985

THE HAMMERING ON THE front door caught everyone by surprise – it wasn't the kind of thing you expected in Rowanbrook on a sunny Sunday evening, in the middle of a perfectly civil dinner party. Mary felt a chill as Robbie got up and walked out to the hall. The banging stopped for a second or two, then resumed, but louder. And now a voice, shouting Robbie's name.

'That's Eddie bloody Hogan,' Tom Stedman said in surprise. 'What on earth's up with him?'

As a unit, they sat quietly around the dining table, holding a collective breath – all but Ruth, who was standing, ready to leave. On some level, Mary knew that she should get up and close the dining room door and pour more wine and start conversation, but she was riveted to the spot as Eddie's words rang through from outside.

'I know you're in there, Murphy. Come out and show your face!'

'Whatever it is, it can wait till you're calmer,' Robbie called through the closed front door.

'Don't you dare tell me what to do!' Eddie roared. 'After what you did?'

'I don't know what you think I did, but it sounds like something to discuss when you're sober.'

'*You condescending fuck.*' More banging. 'Maybe we need to get the guards involved. How would you like that?'

Through the doorway, Mary could see Robbie shaking his head.

'You're drunk, go home. We have guests and you're making a fool of yourself.'

'Oh, you have *guests*, do you. Maybe your guests would like to know you got my daughter pregnant, would they? Would your high-and-mighty wife like to know that?'

Mary felt the room tip. Della put a hand on her arm. The Stedmans exchanged a look that was part horror, part *Schadenfreude*. Ruth Cavanagh, still standing behind her chair, pursed her lips.

Robbie, to his credit, remained calm.

'Eddie, I don't know where you got that idea, but—'

'I'll tell you where I got it. Gavin Bowman,' Eddie shouted. 'And if anyone's sniffing around your house often enough to spot what's going on, it's Gavin Bowman. So open the fucking door and tell me what you're going to do about this baby!'

Della got up now and quietly closed the dining room door, immediately muffling Eddie's shouts.

'That man would want to lay off the drink,' she said loyally, patting Mary's arm. The Stedmans nodded vigorously.

'I believe he's quick with his fists,' Susie said. 'Robbie's absolutely right not to open that door.'

From upstairs came the sound of a small voice calling. Lily.

Mary pushed back her chair, feeling a weakness in her legs as she stood.

'Yes. Leave him on the doorstep to cool off,' Tom agreed. 'He'll slink away when he gets no reaction.'

Della looked sceptical and Tom caught it.

'You don't think so?'

'I think,' Della said heavily, 'if he really believes, incorrectly, of course' – she patted Mary's arm – 'that Zara is pregnant and Robbie's the father, he won't leave it at this. He'll be back.'

Fran couldn't sleep. Poor Zara, bloody hell, a baby. At seventeen. The end of Zara's everything. And the end of Fran's summer in the States. A minor but not inconsiderable detail. She tossed in the narrow bed, wishing the sheet was cooler. At half twelve, she gave in and got up to get a glass of water, and to cool her feet on the kitchen floor. The house was quiet, everyone asleep. That's what made the sudden noise all the more shocking. A banging on the front door. She froze. Should she answer? It took another moment to realize it was too far away. It wasn't her front door. It was the Murphys'. Shouting, then. Zara's dad, roaring for Robbie to come out and face him. *Oh God.* Should she wake Della? Go out and get Zara's mother? Call the police? Eddie'd clearly been drinking for hours and God knows what he'd do. She slipped into the downstairs bathroom and cracked the window. The banging subsided, but started again. Then another sound. The sound of Lily crying.

38

June 2018

TUESDAY NIGHT. MY WEEKLY visit to Kinsella House. My penance. I'm gone from here twenty years – my suitcase packed the day my very first pay from my very first job hit my account. Enough for a tiny room in a house-share in Glasnevin. Enough to pull away from Cynthia. But not enough to ease the guilt. No money in the world could do that. I killed her daughter. So I keep coming back. I send her money. I pour her whiskey. I do my duty.

The flat is dim, with just a thin slice of yellow sun casting through the gap in the heavy curtains. Cynthia is reclining; goddess of her own couch. Arm outstretched, empty glass in hand. I get up to fill drink number four, suggesting a fresh glass, taking time to scan the grubby kitchen. There won't be any photographs of Lila here. Thirty years on, why would there be? But I have to start somewhere. The first kitchen drawer holds cutlery. No neat tray with forks and knives in separate sections here – a jumble of everything thrown in together. The next drawer has receipts, torn scraps of paper, and lists and lists of random words in my mother's looped, dramatic handwriting. She is always taking notes.

For when I write my life story, she says. *It'll blow people away.*

It won't blow people away.

It's a sad, squalid, unoriginal story. A woman who loved her narcotic highs too much. A mother who couldn't give them up. A story of neglect and narcissism. A story not of what was done *to* her but *by* her. She won't see it that way, of course, in the story she'll never write. Because it is *all* about her. And always has been. Back when I was six, at home alone, wondering if she'd ever return. Told to look after myself, to clean the flat while she was gone. *Six is old enough*, she'd say, pulling the door after her. The lean months when we couldn't pay the electricity bill. The better months, when things were easier, but I still went to school in a too-small uniform. The days we feasted on pizza, because she was hungry. The days we had nothing to eat, because for her, wine and whiskey were enough. The days I stole food from other kids' school bags. The days I didn't go to school at all. Those days won't make it into her imaginary book. Her child might not even make it in there. And what of the other child? The ghost?

I check the third drawer. A jungle of musty plastic bags, pharmacy receipts, more notes, half a dozen syringes still in their packaging, another three open, possibly used, and six white plastic bottles of pills. I pull one out. OxyContin. No prescription sticker. I put it back and close the drawer. That's when I notice the pestle and mortar on the counter top, and the white powder residue inside.

'Joanna! Where's my drink?'

Back in the living room, I put the fresh drink in her hand, and sit opposite.

'What's the OxyContin for?'

'My back pain. You have no idea how bad it is.'

'I noticed there's no pharmacy sticker. Did you get a prescription for it?'

'Oh Joanna, you're such a goody two-shoes. You never change. You were like this as a kid too – everyone your age out sneaking smokes and getting drunk on their parents' vodka, and you, hunched over your books, all alone in your room.' A smile and a faux-sympathetic headshake. 'No wonder you had no friends.'

I had no friends because I couldn't bear to bring anyone here – to meet you, to see how we lived, I want to scream at her, but there's no point. She'll never get it. Instead I pull her back on topic.

'We're talking about you now, not me, and about the pain-killers. Did you get them from a pharmacy?'

A sigh. 'Who cares? Lighten up. I have few small pleasures left.'

This, from the woman who spent my childhood partying.

'OK, just promise me you'll stop injecting. It hits your system far too quickly.'

'That, Joanna, is precisely the point.' She lies back, eyes closed.

God, she's impossible. Why do I still care? After everything she's done, why on earth do I care? I need to get what I came for, and go.

'I was wondering . . .' I say carefully.

She looks at me, her lids half closed.

'One of the kids has a project at school to make a family tree. And they need photographs of me as a child. Would you have any still?'

A lazy blink that tells me nothing.

'Remember there was a box of old photos in the bottom of your wardrobe?'

'Oh yes!' She sits up now. 'I'd forgotten. I was quite good, wasn't I? Quite an eye. I should have kept taking photos.'

'You were good. I remember.' Like every new infatuation, her love of photography burnt from obsession to complete disinterest almost overnight. Like sketching. Like writing. *Like Lila.*

I, on the other hand, never warranted the obsession part.

'I'd love to see them again. Can I check in your wardrobe?'

She flops back on the couch, waving her hand. *Go, go.*

*

The box is smaller than I remember, and far less exotic. A shallow, square tin that once contained shortbread biscuits. The lid comes away easily and inside, just like in the cutlery drawer, the contents are in disarray. Photographs in a variety of sizes; some black and white, some colour, all bleached with age. My fingers fumble and the photos slip when I try to take them out. *This is it.* This is where I'll find the truth. Lila was locked in when Cynthia went out – for her own safety, she said – but when the three of us were here, Lila was free to run around the flat. There won't be any day-trip photos in this box; no visits to the zoo, no playgrounds or beaches. But Lila played here and my mother took her photograph. And some of them might be in this box.

'What the hell are you doing!'

My head snaps up.

Cynthia is framed in the doorway, her hands on the woodwork, her eyes cold.

Suddenly I'm eight again. Caught sneaking cold pizza after she fell asleep.

'You . . . you said it was OK? Photos for a project?'

Momentary confusion. A whiskey-soaked softening.

'Did I?'

I nod.

'Take what you want and go, I'm too tired for this.'

She sways in the doorway, watching.

I take a handful and close the box.

At home, on autopilot, Mark asks me how it went with Dr Kinsella. If he ever looks her up online, he'll find two therapists called Kinsella in Dublin; one based, as it happens, not far from Woodbine Street. But to date, he never has. Why would he, I suppose. Why would any man suspect his wife of lying about years of therapy? I tell him it went well, just as I always do, and not long after, he says he's going to bed. As soon as he's gone, I begin to sift through the photos, spreading them out on the living room floor. Memories swarm as I look at them. Me, lying on the carpet, my arms wishboned behind my head, in a pose my mother made me do for what felt like hours. Me, at around eight or nine, wearing one of her dresses and a pair of her battered ankle boots. My mother, gazing at herself in the mirror. The huge grey cat I used to feed, before it went back to its owner. And then, there she is. Lila.

It's a black-and-white photo, taken in her bedroom. Lila is lying on her narrow bed, her chin resting on her hands, her face visible in side-profile as she stares straight ahead at something out of shot. I examine her face. She might have been four by then, though I never remember her having a birthday. She's smiling but looks sad. Jesus, what a life she had. Locked in that room whenever Cynthia went out. Hidden in a way that I should have questioned at the time. And then all too soon, she was gone. Familiar guilt rises up and threatens to overwhelm me, but this is not the time for self-indulgent wallowing.

My Mac is still open on the tab with Lily's photo. I hold Lila's photo against it.

Is it her? Some of the baby chubbiness has gone from her cheeks, though it may be due to the pose, and I can only see her in side-profile. The dimple is still there. Her hair is longer. Maybe darker too, or perhaps it just looks like that in a black-and-white photograph. I try to age Lily in my imagination and yes, it's possible she's Lila. There's still a seed of doubt . . . but every day it's getting smaller.

39

July 1985

ON MONDAY 1 JULY, Della's voice seared through the last fragments of Fran's sleep long before she was ready to get up.

'Aren't you babysitting for Mary at nine?'

Jesus, she'd forgotten. What had possessed her to say yes to
early morning babysitting? She sighed as she pulled on jeans
and a t-shirt, last night's various dramas hitting her again one
by one. Zara's pregnancy. *Zara's pregnancy.* How were those
words even possible? Eddie Hogan banging on the Murphys'
door. And Lily's cry.

Mary would only be an hour, she said, but would Fran mind
taking Lily out for some air? Fran *would* mind, if she was being
honest – she was wrecked – but she nodded and smiled and
agreed that air would do her good. Which was how she found
herself out on the green that sunny Monday morning, at the
ungodly hour of quarter past nine, sitting on the grass – yet
again – this time making daisy chains with Lily. She reached
across to slip a daisy into Lily's hair. 'Now, isn't that pretty?'

Lily didn't look up or smile. She'd been quiet since Fran
arrived, with none of the usual non-stop chatter, and in spite of
herself, Fran missed it.

'Are you OK, Liliput? Tired?'

Lily looked up at her, then back down at the daisies in her hand.

From the corner of her eye, Fran spotted a figure coming out of the building site. Who was out at this time of morning? Squinting, she watched as he crossed the green. Gavin Bowman. *That fella Gavin*, as her mother would say. Lily looked over as he drew closer. And to Fran's surprise, her face lit up and she smiled for the first time that morning.

'Hide and Seek!' she said, stretching her arms towards Gavin.

Fran opened her mouth to say something, then closed it again, curious to see his reaction.

'We play Hide and Seek now!' Lily said, arms still outstretched.

Gavin stopped, just feet away from them. His face was a question mark, his mouth an undecided O.

'We play again? Hide and Seek?' Lily asked, undeterred by the lack of response.

Gavin stood for another moment, head tilted, watching Lily, a strange look on his face. There was something about him. Primal. Yet polished. A pin-up boy with pieces missing. Cracks beneath the surface, caked in something dark and grimy. Suddenly, Fran wanted him gone.

Lily broke the silence.

'Play?'

A slow smile slid across Gavin's face. 'Maybe we will.'

Fran reached down and took Lily's hand, pulling her to her feet.

'We have to go now, Lily – your mammy will be back any minute.'

Still, Gavin stood where he was, watching Lily; one hand in his jeans pocket, the other rolling and kneading what looked like a small ceramic lighthouse. It seemed familiar but Fran couldn't remember where she'd seen it. She gripped Lily's hand. Their route back across the green to Rowanbrook Drive wasn't blocked as such, but they'd have to skirt around Gavin to get there. And why should they? She wasn't scared of him. He was a year younger than her, for God's sake. Though he was tall. Even taller than Fran, who had spent her whole life wishing she could shrink. She busied herself smoothing the skirt of Lily's dress and re-buckling one red shoe. This was ridiculous. She stood up straight again. Gavin moved his gaze from Lily to Fran, then slowly turned and walked away.

Fran let out a breath. She was conscious of two other girls watching from a distance; Aoife and Ellen she thought, though she didn't look over. She waited until Gavin disappeared up Rowanbrook Road, his sloped shoulders and stonewashed jacket fading in the distance. Fran really didn't care who her brothers hung out with. But she might just say something about Gavin to her mother.

And then she gently squeezed Lily's hand and they walked together towards Number Six for the very last time.

40

WHEN MARY ARRIVED BACK that morning, she seemed distracted. Jittery. Fran noticed then that her eyes were red with dark circles beneath and her hand shook as she took her purse from her handbag to pay for the babysitting. Fran bit her lip. This had to be down to Eddie Hogan's late-night visit. Mary must know why he was hammering on her door. God. What a mess. Should Fran say something? It wasn't really her place though. And the whole thing was very awkward. She wondered too if she should say something about Gavin on the green just now. But what was there to say? Gavin Bowman was hanging around and behaving strangely – that wasn't news to anyone. So in the end, she said nothing, took her money and left. As she walked away, Lily was asking Mary to go back out to the green. Determined, it seemed, to play a game of Hide and Seek.

There was nothing. No sign. No portent in the wide blue sky.

Just a normal, everyday midday in Rowanbrook. Warmer than usual, yes. And maybe that had something to do with it. Maybe if it hadn't been so warm, Mary would have gone in sooner. Taken Lily in. But the sun on her skin reminded her of home and she needed it. More than ever, that morning, she needed it. So, she stayed. Listening to Della's chatter. Half listening. Half watching, her eyes on the green in front of them, her mind somewhere else entirely.

A tall, blond boy darted from behind a tree, yelling 'Caught you!' at a crouching child. Skittish laughter. Sunlight dancing on small brown limbs. Another one bites the dust. The tall boy – one of Della's twins – continued his prowl, parting bushes, crawling into spaces under low-hanging branches. A flash of red, dashing from the trees, heading for the half-built houses beyond the green. Mary watched from behind her sunglasses. Serene as ever on the outside; paddling furiously beneath the surface.

'I wish to God they wouldn't go into that building site,' Della muttered, squinting, shielding her eyes against the sun. 'It's a bloody hazard.'

Mary nodded.

'Where's Lily?' Della asked.

'Cora's with her, helping her hide. They're somewhere in there,' Mary answered, pointing towards the wooded area at the back of the green.

'Hmm. Cora could really do with finding some friends her own age . . .'

'I think she likes looking after the little ones. I guess she'd love a brother or sister.'

'True, and probably has no idea it won't be happening. Poor Ines. And now her mother dead as well. Did she fly out this morning, do you know?'

Mary wasn't sure.

'The dinner last night was lovely, by the way,' Della added carefully. 'I hope you weren't too upset by . . .' She trailed off.

Mary nodded but a tightness in her throat stopped any reply.

'Are you OK?' Della asked, angling her head to take stock. 'You look pale this morning.'

Again, Mary tried to answer, but all she could do was nod. If words would come, maybe this was her chance. Maybe she could tell Della what was really going on. But no words came. And then Della was speaking again.

'Listen, Eddie's an awful man for the drink. I wouldn't pay a blind bit of notice to what he says.' Della folded her arms, a clear full stop on the subject, and the moment had passed for ever.

Two other women joined them, one pushing a buggy, both holding toddlers by the hand, and the conversation turned to the weather. Mary nodded and smiled, just as she always did, but her mind was on last night. And high in the sky above, the sun kept beating down, giving no hint at all of what was about to unfold.

'Oh, Ines must have gone,' Della said suddenly, 'Cynthia's here.'

Mary turned to look. Cynthia was making her way across the green towards them, her hair hanging loose around her shoulders, a long white skirt trailing slightly on the grass.

'Is Cora here?' she asked when she drew level with them, smiling at each woman in turn.

'Yes, they're all there playing Hide and Seek – Cora's helping Lily to hide,' Della said, nodding towards the woods.

A sigh, as though Cynthia didn't relish the idea of expending any more energy finding her charge.

'Will you send Cora home when you see her?' she said, turning on the smile again. Always engaging but never quite engaged herself, Mary thought.

Della looked at her watch, a thin, gold bracelet on her sturdy, freckled arm.

'I'm going to get my lads in now.' She cupped her hands to her mouth and roared their names.

Like greyhounds, the twins darted out of the building site towards their mother.

Four other boys followed, their pudding-bowl haircuts flying as they ran. Aoife and Ellen bounced out from behind the trees, chanting something about winning and *first the worst, second the best.*

'You didn't win,' one of the boys said to the girls as they drew close. 'The game ended when my mam called us for lunch. No winner.' He planted his feet, arms folded.

'No, we win, you never found us!' Ellen said, blonde ponytail silver-white in the sun.

'It doesn't matter,' Della said, circling her arms around her boys, 'the hiders *and* the seekers are going home.'

Mary craned her neck, looking for Lily and Cora, but they hadn't come out yet.

'Hey, where's Gavin?' one of the twins asked.

Aoife and Ellen looked at one another, eyes locked in what struck Mary as an unspoken message.

Aoife shrugged. 'Who knows.'

And with that, they all began to walk away. The two girls. The twins. The four boys who belonged to the women with the toddlers. Some older kids from Oakbrook. Mary looked at their backs as they moved further into the distance, sudden unease slipping over her skin.

Wait! she wanted to call. *You didn't find Lily yet, you can't leave while she's still hiding – it's your job to find her!*

But that was silly. Lily was with Cora, and they'd come out now too and they'd all go home.

'Oh – I see Cora now.' Cynthia squinted back towards the road. 'She must have taken the shortcut through the woods.' She shook her head. 'Her mother hates that. Says there could be rats or anything there.' She shrugged and smiled at Mary. 'I won't tell if you don't.'

Mary stood, feet rooted to the ground. Staring. Staring at the small figure of eight-year-old Cora O'Brien as she walked along Rowanbrook Avenue towards her house.

All on her own.

41

July 1985

MARY FROZE, AS CORA grew smaller in the distance.

Cora can't go home, she's playing with Lily. Why are they all leaving – they have to find Lily first!

Helplessly, she turned to Cynthia.

'Cora was with Lily – is she going home without her?'

Even as she asked, she knew it was a nonsense question. Cora was clearly on her own.

Cynthia pulled her hair into a low ponytail, frowning slightly.

'I'm sure Lily's still hiding. You just need to go into the woods and pick her up.' She turned to walk away.

'Cynthia, please could you stay here just for a moment? In case Lily comes out and I don't see her?'

Hesitation. Then the high-wattage smile. 'Sure. Anything for that sweet little one. I miss looking after her, you know.'

'Thank you,' Mary said, walking quickly towards the woods.

Inside the wooded canopy, shade replaced sun, sucking up light and sound. Mary stood to listen but heard only silence. The grass grew longer there, where the lawn mowers couldn't reach, and it brushed the back of her bare legs, spidery against her skin.

'Lily!' she tried again, blood roaring in her ears.

She'll be fine, she'll be crouched down looking at flowers, it's nothing. There is nothing to worry about.

'Lily! Come on now! The game's over.'

Nothing.

She moved deeper into the trees, denser now, no light at all, and other than the snap of twigs beneath her feet, no sound. Mounds of earth, clusters of daisies and buttercups, gnarled roots of ancient oaks. Not a sound.

'Is she there? I kind of have to go . . .' Cynthia called. She had walked across the green to the edge of the woods.

'I can't find her yet,' Mary called back, voice hoarse, heart pounding. 'Please can you ask Cora where they were?'

She could see Cynthia's outline just beyond the woods, her white skirt bright between the trees.

Hesitation. For just a second.

'OK.'

And then she was gone.

Mary kept calling, searching. Crouching low in long grass, standing straight to scan again. What was Lily wearing? A lilac skirt, red shoes. Little white socks with frills on the turndown. An unnecessary blue hairclip in her short curls.

'Lily!' Why wasn't she answering?

Mary closed her eyes, quelling rising panic. It would be fine. They'd find her.

She looked back and saw Cynthia coming through the trees with Cora trailing behind. Cora looked apprehensive, her small, pale features pinched.

Behind Cynthia came Della, with the twins.

'Cynthia told us. We'll find her in no time,' Della said. 'Now, Cora, love, where were you?'

Cora looked like she might cry.

Mary moved towards her. Forced her words to sound calm.

'Cora, can you tell me where you two were hiding?'

Cora bit her lip and tucked herself behind Cynthia. Cynthia turned and took hold of her arms to dislodge her.

Behind Della, Mary was half aware of more mothers and children approaching, and Ruth Cavanagh just behind. She ignored them all, focusing on Cora.

'Cora, please sweetheart, can you show me where were you hiding?'

Cora looked at the ground, kicking a pebble with her sandalled foot. She whispered something.

'What was that?' Della asked.

But Mary had heard. She started to run towards the building site.

42

MARY STUMBLED AS SHE raced between the trees, but somehow stayed upright. Ahead, the building site loomed grey and dusty against the skyline, its half-built walls like robot teeth. It was big. Too big. Too big for a small girl.

'Lily!' she shouted, pushing through a gap in the fence. Behind her came the others, not running, not yet, but walking fast now. Calling Lily's name. Della and her twins. Cynthia holding Cora's hand. Aoife and Ellen, ponytails bouncing. Ruth Cavanagh, frowning and sour.

The ground underfoot was cracked and uneven, littered with planks of wood and scraps of torn-off labels. Half-full sacks of sand blocked the way and Mary stumbled again, trying to steer around one. And again, she kept going. The building nearest to her, the one at the edge of the site, was little more than foundations. It was easy to see there was nobody there, but she stopped to look anyway, as though Lily could somehow appear if she just stared hard and willed it to happen.

Beyond the foundations was the start of another house – knee-high walls, a cement mixer, a wheelbarrow. Further along, three barrels. Mary stared at them.

'Lily!' she shouted, running towards them. All open-topped, all empty, save for small pools of moisture. Lily wouldn't get into something like that, of course she wouldn't. And Cora wouldn't have let her.

Cora.

Mary looked back. Cora was staring at the foundations of the first house.

'Cora, where is she?'

The little girl looked down at her feet. Mary moved towards her, but Della got there first.

'Cora, lovey, you're not in any trouble, you just need to show us where you and Lily were hiding.'

Cora looked up at Della, her small face scared. She pointed at the foundations.

'There. It wasn't a very good place to hide but we could hear them coming so we just jumped in and ducked down.'

Mary scanned the expanse of soil and stone.

'She can't have gone far then, it's only been a few minutes.' She cupped her mouth. 'Lily! Lily!'

Cora looked uncomfortable.

'Cora, there's something else, isn't there?' Della asked.

A tear slid down Cora's cheek.

'I needed to get a drink of water.'

'That's OK,' Della said. 'When was that?'

'I don't know. I don't have a watch. But I was really thirsty.' Her cheeks flamed.

'So, where did you go?' Della asked.

'I was going to go to my house, but I met Aoife on the way and she said we could go to her house cos it's nearer.'

Aoife spoke up.

'Yeah, she came to my house, my mum doesn't mind me bringing people home. Then she left my house and I stayed at home for a bit longer to change into shorts.' Informative. Authoritative, or as authoritative as a thirteen-year-old can be.

'OK,' Della said, beckoning Aoife forward. 'So, do you know what time it was?'

Aoife looked down at a blue plastic strap on her wrist, then off to the left, and suddenly Mary knew she was going to give an answer whether she knew what time it had been or not.

'Oh, it was . . . ten. Ten o'clock.'

Della shook her head. 'No, pet, we weren't even out here yet at ten. Maybe your watch is wrong. Would you have a feeling about how long it was?'

Aoife put her head to one side in a display of serious thinking and Mary wanted to shake her.

'Half an hour?' Aoife said eventually, her finger on her lower lip. 'Or an hour?'

Mary put her face in her hands. 'Oh God.'

Della glanced at her, still speaking to the girls.

'Now, I don't think it was an hour. Mary and I saw Cora and Lily maybe forty-five minutes ago. But we need to assume she could have gone a bit further than we realized. I think maybe we'll spread out and search, but girls, if you think of anything, come find me or another grown-up immediately, OK?'

Aoife nodded solemnly, Cora tearfully.

Mary was shaking her head, frozen to the small patch of stony soil on which she stood. Della stepped forward and rubbed her arm.

'She's here, of course she's here, we'll find her. Let's split up and cover the whole site.'

And they did – Della and her twins, Cynthia and a sobbing Cora, Aoife and Ellen, Ruth Cavanagh with her downturned, sour mouth, and Mary, trying to hold it together. Certain – all of them certain – that they would find her. Until they didn't.

43

July 1985

ONE AND A HALF hours missing. People everywhere. Combing. Roaming like ants. Police. Neighbours. Strangers. Blurred faces, eyes not meeting hers. The children – the other children, the not-missing children – so many gone home now, eating lunch and watching TV. *Is it a bit dangerous to have the smaller ones here?* one of the women had asked, and maybe it was, but Mary wanted to scream all the same: *What about Lily? How could you leave her?*

The call to Robbie at the office, the rush home from work. His face, pale and shocked, etched in her mind. Searching and searching and searching. The other men still searching too. Some of the women at home with the children. But not Della, who was holding her up now.

'The guards know what they're doing, they'll find her,' Della was saying, over and over. 'You need to take a break. Just for five minutes. You're shaking. You'll collapse.'

Della was right, but how could she stop searching?

'Mrs Murphy?'

'Yes,' she whispered, turning to face a police officer.

'I'm Detective Sergeant Branagh. I know my colleague has already asked you some of these questions, but I need to ask you again. Does Lily know her address?'

'I don't think so,' she said, still whispering. 'She always says she lives in "Edenvale, Ireland" if she's asked. I don't know why we didn't teach her the address.' Tears threatening.

'And do you have a phone in the house?'

She nodded.

'She wouldn't know the phone number, would she?'

A headshake.

'And . . .' He paused and swallowed visibly. 'Does she know how to swim?'

At that, Della gripped Mary's arm, sensing perhaps that Mary was having difficulty staying upright.

'No.' She said it so quietly, Branagh had to ask again.

'She can't swim?'

'She's three. She can't swim,' Della said, taking over. 'But that river is so shallow this time of year – if she fell in, she'd be knee-deep at most?'

'We're just gathering as much information as we can,' was all he'd say. 'And, going back to when she was last seen – what time was that?'

'Around midday,' Della said.

'Is that correct, Mrs Murphy?'

Mary nodded.

'And she was playing in the wooded area beside the building site?'

Another nod.

'Without adult supervision?'

'Of course there was adult supervision,' Della said. 'We were standing on the green, watching. But it was Hide and Seek, so they were hiding.'

'And Lily was on her own with the bigger children?'

Again, Branagh addressed the question to Mary, and again, Della answered.

'She was with Cora O'Brien.'

'And how old is Cora?'

'Eight,' Della said, and now Mary could hear how wrong it sounded.

'And the older children – all from here in Rowanbrook?'

'Yes. Mostly. We get kids from Oakbrook coming here, because of the green and the woods.'

'And the building site,' said Branagh.

'Yes.'

'We heard reports from some of your neighbours about trouble recently – broken windows, young people creeping around at night?' Branagh asked, looking from Della to Mary and back again. Mary opened her mouth to speak but still nothing came out.

'I heard the same,' Della was saying, 'but I doubt it's anyone from here doing it.'

'And you, Mrs Murphy?'

'I've heard about broken windows, yes. But not our windows . . . There's been—' She stopped, unsure.

'What is it, Mrs Murphy?'

'I . . . I noticed some things missing from my house over the last two days, and wondered if someone broke in. But I don't know. Nothing of real value was taken, other than my husband's watch. And it may just be misplaced.'

'Right. Have you noticed any strangers in the vicinity?' Branagh prompted. 'Any men who aren't from Rowanbrook hanging around?'

Mary thought she might be sick. She sagged against Della, closing her eyes.

'No, no strangers,' Della said to Branagh. She put her arms around Mary, as Branagh moved away.

*

'Listen, Mary, there's no stranger taking children, we'd have seen him. There's no way on earth someone pulled up here, walked by us on the green, and took Lily right back past us. Do you hear me?' She hugged her tightly.

Mary nodded, desperate to believe her.

'But what about the other side,' she whispered, 'the shortcut Cora took through the trees. What if a car stopped at the end of the pathway and someone went in and took Lily? No one would even see—' She broke off and put her hand to her mouth.

Della shook her head, lost for words.

Behind them, the woods and the building site filled with more and more searchers, word of mouth bringing neighbours from all over Rowanbrook and beyond. Only Ruth Cavanagh was idle, hovering near the entrance to the site. Della looked over at Ruth and shook her head. 'If she thinks she's going to slope off home,' Della muttered, 'she has another think coming. We need every pair of hands we can get.' Out loud, she called, 'Ruth, thanks for helping. Can you go with Mary to the houses down towards the back, and I'll work on the middle row?'

Ruth nodded and moved wordlessly towards them. Della squeezed Mary's arm and walked ahead. She wasn't going to the middle row of houses, Mary knew that. She was going to the shortcut, the pathway through the trees, and trying to shield Mary from what she might find.

44

July 1985

FRAN SAT ON HER bed to tie her laces. Three hours missing. Poor little Lily, she'd be terrified, wherever she was. Fran could hear her mother's voice wafting in from the hall, through her open bedroom door – Della on the phone to her sister.

'The whole neighbourhood's out,' she was saying. 'Though I think I caught Ruth Cavanagh trying to skive off, miserable thing that she is. You'd swear her walk was more important than helping out with the search.'

Fran tuned out. Once her mother got going on the subject of Ruth Cavanagh, there was no stopping her. Then something her mother was saying caught her attention.

'I just don't know if I should say anything,' Della said. 'I mean, Cora's only eight. But she *was* the last one with her.'

Curious now, Fran slipped off her bed and tiptoed to the doorway to hear better.

'No, it was more than once,' Della continued, in response to something her sister had said. 'I wish I'd said something to Mary now, but I didn't want to jump to conclusions.' She sighed. 'God, how many awful things happen because people don't want to jump to conclusions?'

A pause. Fran strained to listen, but her aunt's voice was tinny and indistinct.

'Yes, Cora definitely hurt Lily that morning in the queue for ice cream. I couldn't tell if it was on purpose, but she hurt her all right.'

Another pause as Della's sister responded.

'She's desperate for affection, I suppose, and that can warp you. Right, we'd better get back out there. I'll ring you later. Bye now, bye.'

Her mother put her head around Fran's bedroom door, coming nose to nose with her daughter.

'Oh. Are you ready?'

'Mam, did you see Cora hurting Lily?'

Della put her hand to her cheek.

'Ah. Look, I don't know if it was on purpose. But it happened more than once. I'm certain it has nothing to do with today, but it's bothering me now.'

'It's just . . . the day of the party in their garden – the paddling pool . . . I saw something too.'

Fran followed Della, as they pushed forward through the building site.

'Lily!' she shouted, along with the rest of them. 'Come out now, the game's over!' In the distance, she could see Mary Murphy and Ruth Cavanagh going into one of the houses and she was relieved they were too far away to see her. What do you say to someone whose child is missing?

She followed Della towards another of the half-built houses and they paused a few feet from the doorway, scanning the outside. Scaffolding hugged unfinished walls and a wooden walkway circled the perimeter, just above the yawning downstairs windows.

They moved inside. The concrete floors were cool and dusty, littered with sandbags and sandwich wrappers. Fran shivered.

'Lily!' Della called, as they walked through to another empty room. 'She's not here,' she said to Fran. 'Let's try the next house.'

'Could she be upstairs?'

They both looked up.

'There's no stairs yet,' Della said. 'She wouldn't have been able to get up there. Come on.'

The next house was the same – high scaffolding, dark windows, empty rooms, no stairs.

From all directions, voices echoed, calling Lily's name. In the distance, Robbie emerged from the shortcut through the woods. Fran watched as he put one hand to his eyes, scanning. Then she noticed his other arm.

'Mam, Robbie's got his arm in a sling – do you know what happened?'

Della pursed her lips. 'No.' She looked like she was going to say something else but decided against it.

'Only, I heard Zara's dad bashing on their door around midnight last night . . .'

Della made a clicking sound with her tongue. 'I knew he'd be back,' she said, under her breath. Then, out loud: 'Come on, less chat, more searching.'

Behind them, Cynthia moved towards a house Della had already checked, Cora trotting beside her. Fran and Della went on to search six more houses, and in the last one, they found stairs.

Fran went up first, with Della following.

At the top was a broad landing with six doorways, all empty, except the one straight ahead, which was blocked by a large wooden pallet and two blue barrels.

Fran walked through to the first room on the left.

Della followed as Fran moved to the window.

Outside, she could see Aoife and Ellen talking to Gavin and the twins. The group were huddled together a little distance away, and she couldn't see their faces but Gavin was talking earnestly about something. Beyond the huddle of kids, she could see the brown-gold flash of river – glittering in the summer sun, grazing the riverbank reeds as it slipped past.

'Come on,' her mother said, 'we'll check the other rooms.'

At the boarded-up doorway, they stopped. Fran reached to push one of the barrels. It didn't budge.

'She can't be in there,' Della said. 'She wouldn't have been able to move that barrel. Let's go.'

'We've already searched there,' Della said to Susie Stedman, when they bumped into her outside a house down by the river.

'I know, I just want to be doing something. This is *awful*.'

'Dreadful.'

'Poor Mary and Robbie, they look shattered. Did you see Robbie's arm's in a sling? Got a wallop off someone last night.' Susie lowered her voice. 'Eddie Hogan, I bet. I wonder if he came back after we'd all left the dinner party?'

Della glanced at Fran then back to Susie. 'Who knows,' she said, sidestepping the question.

'You don't think there's truth in this thing with Eddie's daughter and Robbie, do you?' Susie asked.

Fran stiffened.

'I doubt it. Anyway, best we focus on the search.' Della glanced over to where Cora was sitting on a low stone wall, drawing something in the dirt with a stick. Beside her, Cynthia smoked a cigarette. It seemed to make up Della's mind. 'Susie, is that police van still at the entrance?'

*

Half an hour later, the sound of shouting rang out across the building site. Fran froze, then began moving towards the noise. Della followed, half walking, half running. Ahead, near the river, Fran could see a group gathering. Her brothers. Ellen and Aoife, hopping from foot to foot. Gavin, hanging back, disinterested, or trying to look disinterested. Tom Stedman, running his hand through his hair. Robbie Murphy, still like a statue. Cynthia, smoking another cigarette. Some men and women Fran didn't know. And Susie Stedman, who turned as they approached.

'A shoe,' she said, her voice shaking. 'Fran, your brother found a shoe.'

Fran sucked in a breath. At the centre of the group stood Mary. One hand at her mouth, holding in a scream. And in the other hand, a little red shoe.

45

July 1985

DUSK NOW. DOGS. FRESH panic. Solemn faces. White noise in her ears. Tight fear in her throat. Cold dread seeping into her bones. Mary couldn't tell how much time had gone by; how long they'd been sitting, rocking on the ground. She shook herself.

'We should be searching. My God, what are we doing?' she whispered, stumbling to her feet.

'It's OK, it was a five-minute break, that's all,' Della said, holding her. 'You've been out here for hours with nothing to eat and no break until now. You needed it.'

'And you,' Mary whispered. 'You've been here all that time too.'

'I'm as strong as an ox, you know that. Besides, I ate when I ran home to check on the kids.'

'You went home? I don't even remember that . . .' Mary shook her head.

'Just for a short time, when you were with Ruth. Not that Ruth bothered hanging around for long once I got back,' Della added, muttering the last bit. 'You find out who your friends are in a crisis.'

Mary nodded, leaning against her as they walked back across the green and into the trees. Della shone a torch on the ground ahead of them.

'Will we look here? Or in the building site?' She didn't add the word 'again', but Mary heard it anyway. They'd looked here. They'd looked everywhere.

'Let's head over to the site,' Della said, answering her own question.

The torches were fireflies, flitting around the dark hulk of the building site. Shouts for Lily broke the otherwise silence; nobody had the energy or inclination to chat. Mary and Della retraced their steps, checking inside every half-built house, inside every room, in every corner. Mechanical searching. Holding hands to hold one another up. Not speaking. Not even calling her name.

Fran, Della's daughter, joined them. A whispered greeting, reassurance that the twins were fine, then more silent searching.

Inside a house that had proper stairs, they heard voices from the first floor. Robbie, and Tom Stedman. Mary began her ascent on shaky legs, followed closely by Della who seemed braced to catch her. But Mary wouldn't fall. Now was not the time for falling.

At the top of the stairs, Robbie put his good arm around Mary, whispering into her hair.

'We'll find her, we'll find her.'

Mary leaned into him and nodded, not trusting her voice.

Della was saying something to Fran. Mary turned to listen.

'I was just saying, I was here earlier and couldn't get into that room,' Della repeated, louder now, pointing at a doorway and at a wide, wooden pallet that was leaning against the wall. 'Two barrels were blocking the pallet and the pallet was blocking the doorway. Who moved them? Was there anything inside?'

'Just another empty room,' Tom said. 'I don't know why it was blocked off.'

'I need to see,' Mary said quietly, walking through the doorway. Robbie followed, holding a torch. He swung it slowly about the room, lighting up the floor and then the walls. Mary turned like a music box ballerina, following the light. Nothing. No sign that anyone had been there. At the window, she stood looking out, the night breeze blowing wisps of hair into her eyes. The scaffolding beneath the window ran the width of the house but it was too dark to see beyond the surface immediately below.

She turned to her husband. 'Can you shine the torch out here.' Her voice shook. Robbie did as she asked. The beam swept all the way along the wooden pathway, first one side, then the other. Nothing.

'Let's go back down,' Robbie said, putting his good arm around her shoulder, which made the shaking worse.

'Mary, love, I think you should go home. You're freezing and exhausted. Will you go for even an hour? Della, would you be able to bring her?'

'Of course. Fran will mind the twins, I can stay with Mary all night.'

Her husband passed her to her friend, and Mary, limp now, allowed it.

Tom bowed his head, like a mourner at a funeral. *They've given up*, Mary realized. *They're still searching, but in their minds, they've given up.* Hands shaking, legs loose, she reached for Della. She would not fall.

46

It's 3 a.m. and I can't sleep. Instead, I'm roaming through the house, rewinding Ellen's words – *the door with the barrels . . . the locked room* – retracing Mary's steps. Lily's steps. Shadows on walls, worn floorboards creaking under bare feet. The house is asleep. Emily, curled foetal-style under her duvet. Ben, star-fished on top of his. And then there's Sophie's room. I lean to kiss Sophie's head and sit on the floor for a moment, running my fingers across the floorboards, listening. Sophie's breath has that almost soundless quality of deep sleep. Safe, secure sleep under a safe, secure roof with parents whose love she's never doubted for a second of her three years on earth. Unlike Lila, whose world was everything Sophie's isn't. Unpredictable. Controlled. Cold. Over.

My fingers trace the floorboards, the knotholes and ridges, as far as the corner by the radiator, where I pull back a strip of wallpaper, exposing the Holly Hobbie print beneath. The strip tapers off to nothing almost immediately and comes away in my hand. I pull another strip, and this time some of the Holly Hobbie paper peels off too. Beneath that is something else entirely. Something black that looks hand-drawn. I get up to push the bedroom door wider, letting in light from the landing, and crouch again by the radiator.

Someone has drawn an eye on the wall. A dark, eye-shaped outline, with a black circle inside. It's neat, not like a child's doodle, and somehow ominous. I sit back. What does it mean? I have no idea, but I don't like to think of it in Sophie's bedroom, watching her. I need paint.

'Morning,' I call across to Fran as I arrive back with my purchases. She's on her way out to her car and lifts a hand in salute.

'Getting started on a bit of DIY,' I say, lifting a paint pot. 'Sophie's room, to begin with.'

Fran just nods. There's no invitation to elaborate, but I do anyway.

'I found this drawing of an eye under the wallpaper. And I know it could have been done by anyone at any stage, but I wonder if it was Lily's room and if the eye had something to do with her . . .'

Now she's interested. 'Oh. God, that's a blast from the past. The "evil eye".' Fran puts the words in air quotes and moves closer to the dividing wall.

'You know about it?'

'I saw it once. I can still see it in my mind's eye, no pun intended. It really stuck, freaked me out. It was when I was babysitting one afternoon, sitting on the floor in Lily's room – you're right, by the way, the room with the eye was Lily's.'

Even though I guessed as much, this still gives me the shivers.

'I wonder who put it there and why?'

'No idea. But I remember I went home and looked it up, found some stuff in an encyclopaedia about evil eye curses and decided I didn't want to know any more.'

'Why would someone want to put a curse on the poor child? Mary would hardly do that, would she?'

Fran shakes her head. 'I doubt it. Though it's an odd thing to put on a child's wall, if you believe in curses and the like. Anyway' – she looks at her watch and clicks her key fob to unlock her car – 'I'd better go. Yoga at eleven.'

As soon as I open the front door, I know I don't want to be here. Leaving the pot of paint in the hall, I grab my Mac and head back out, going on foot to The Sugar Tree cafe. If I'm going to spend the morning staring at photos of Lily and my sister, I may as well be somewhere with other people and fresh coffee. And the walk there will do me good.

I'm surprised to see Fran there when I enter the cafe half an hour later. This doesn't look like 'yoga'. She's sitting with the same woman she was with in The Wine Cask the Saturday night before last, and a dark-haired woman in her fifties. Fran is deep in conversation and doesn't notice me approaching as I make my way towards an empty table at the back.

'Hiya,' I say, turning as I pass.

Her mouth drops open. 'Oh. Joanna. Hi.'

'Yoga cancelled?'

Her face flushes.

'*Yoga!*' says the younger of her two companions. 'Since when do you do yoga?' The woman turns to look up at me. 'I think I need to hear more about this.' Her smile is bright, mischievous. The other woman is staring at her coffee, shoulders hunched. I've clearly interrupted something or put my foot in it, but I can't work out how.

'My mistake,' I say. 'It was another neighbour doing yoga.'

'You're Auntie Fran's neighbour? I need *all* the goss, immediately. I'm Saoirse.' She sticks out her hand.

'I'm Joanna,' I say. 'Nice to meet you. And yes, I live next door to your aunt.'

'She's not really my aunt, she's my godmother, but also fairy godmother, and my mother's best friend in the world, and since I have no actual, literal aunts, she may as well be.'

The dark-haired woman is still looking down at her coffee and it's gone from odd to awkward. If she's Fran's best friend, does that make her Zara? Meaning Saoirse is Robbie's daughter? And Lily's half-sister? I can't help staring at her now, looking for resemblances to Lily. There's something familiar about the turn of her mouth, the shape of her jaw, maybe, but then I've spent so much time staring at photos in the last twelve hours, everyone is starting to look like everyone.

'I'd better leave you to it,' I say, as we all pretend it's not weird that the dark-haired woman hasn't looked up or introduced herself. Fran and Saoirse say goodbye, and I take a seat at an empty table.

47

June 2018

ON THURSDAY AFTERNOON, I'M buttering crackers for Sophie when she bursts in from the garden, shouting. At first, I can't make out the words.

'Slow down! What is it?'

Sophie takes a breath and starts again.

'There's a ghost in our garden! Or a monster maybe.' Eyes wide, she climbs up on a kitchen chair. 'I'll stay here and you check, OK?'

I hand her a cracker. 'OK, I'll go hunt the ghost.'

As I approach the trampoline, shielding my eyes against the sunlight, I hear what Sophie heard. Yowling and scratching coming from the coal bunker. Something is trapped in there. That slows me down. I'm not entirely sure how I feel about unleashing whatever creature is inside. Sure enough, the hatch is down; something got in and can't get out. A fox maybe? I move closer. Listening. Foxes don't yowl. At least, not as far as I know. It's a cat. Has to be. I step closer, reach forward to slide up the hatch, and jump back. A ball of black fur springs out and sprints across the garden, up on to the dividing wall. Fran's cat, blacker than ever now that he's covered in soot. Poor thing, we really should do something with the coal bunker. But as I'm about to slide the hatch back into place, something catches my eye.

It's covered in soot and barely visible. Hidden in the coal, a shape that's at odds with everything else. It's square. A box. An old, metal box. It slides awkwardly through the hatch and I rub it in the grass to clean off some of the soot. It's an old tobacco tin, I realize, as the words 'Navy Cut' appear. I give it a small shake and something moves inside. It could be anything. It could be nothing more than dead insects and bits of old coal. I shake it again. The contents move but don't rattle. It's something soft, not hard or metal or sharp. But what? There's only one way to find out. I dig my nails under the metal rim of the lid and work to get it open. It doesn't budge. I need a knife.

Inside the kitchen, I set the tin on a tea towel and use a butter knife to prise the lid. This time, it opens and now I can see the contents. A single envelope. Thick and yellowed and covered in fine coal dust. It's not sealed and inside is a small stack of Polaroid photographs, held together with an elastic band. The first picture shows a little girl outdoors, facing away from the camera, looking towards tall trees at the end of a garden. They look just like the trees at the end of our garden. Is it Lily, before she went missing? It's hard to tell, but the child has blonde curly hair, just like Lily's. She's wearing a navy duffle coat and dark tights and red wellington boots.

Something doesn't quite fit, but I can't put my finger on it.

Sophie comes into the kitchen, her small face worried.

'Is the monster gone?'

'It was a cat! Can you believe it? Now, we have to pick up Ben soon – can you put on your shoes?' I kiss the top of her head, and hoosh her from the room.

I look down at the Polaroid again. There's definitely something off about this photo, but I can't work out what it is. I set it to one side and begin to examine the next one. This time, the photographer has moved to the other side of the garden and the child is facing the camera. And this time, I'm certain it's Lily. I can see her face now. I can make out a red dress beneath the navy coat, and a matching red-and-white polka-dot bow in her hair. Behind Lily is the house, lit by low winter sun. How surreal to see my own house like this, thirty-three years earlier. But again, there's something not quite right.

Then it hits me.

The house is the wrong way around. The back door is on the right, when it should be on the left. And the kitchen window has also moved. My eyes travel across the cream paintwork and up to the second storey. The bathroom window is in the wrong place too.

It's not my house.

It's someone else's.

I look back at the small child, and suddenly I know.

48

June 2018

I STARE AT THE photo. It's definitely not my house in the backdrop, but that's not what's wrong.

It's the trees.

I lean closer to examine the trees that line the side of the garden that is not mine. Apple trees maybe, or pear. Bare branches against a bleached sky. A pale winter sky.

And a child who looks around Sophie's age. Three, possibly four.

But during her last winter in Rowanbrook, Lily was only two years old. She turned three the following May, not long before she went missing. I squint at the photo. Could it be a particularly cold day in early summer? One that required a duffle coat and tights? No. The branches are bare. This is not just-turned-three Lily on a cold day in early summer. This is Lily, some time in the winter of 1985–1986, months after she went missing.

But whose garden? And who put the tin in the coal bunker? Robbie or Mary? Although – I look out of the window, then back at the photo – the coal bunker is right at the bottom edge of the garden and accessible from the passageway behind. And,

I realize, accessible through the gap with the property next door; the house that used to be Ellen's. So maybe not Robbie or Mary. It could have been anyone in Rowanbrook. Or outside Rowanbrook. But why?

From upstairs comes a call from Sophie – something about her socks. I slip the photos into my back pocket and put the tin under the sink.

Fran's car is in her driveway when I get back from the school, the photo of Lily still burning a hole in my pocket. If anyone can help me work out which house is in the picture, Fran can. But I don't want to leave the kids on their own, so I sit on my hands, figuratively, and at one point – during a particularly fraught piece of Irish reading homework – literally, until Mark gets home from work, then I run next door and ring Fran's bell.

She looks irritated. I've upset her, I suspect, though I'm not sure how. But when I show her the photos, curiosity takes over and she invites me through to her back garden.

Five minutes later, over cups of tarry coffee on the sunny patio, I tell her the story of the tin in the coal bunker, and my theory that this means Lily was alive after the day she went missing.

I spread the photos across the small, wrought-iron table, turning them to face Fran.

'I was hoping you might know whose house it is. It's the inverse of our house; like yours actually – with the back door on the opposite side. It's so similar, I think it has to be a Rowanbrook house.'

Fran peers at them.

'Any ideas?'

She picks up the one showing the back of the house and Lily's face. Pulling her glasses down from the top of her head, her eyes scan the photo, over and back, over and back. Giving nothing away.

Eventually she looks up, a curious expression on her face. 'Yes. In fact . . . Yes. I know whose house it is.'

49

I sit forward. 'Are you serious? You think you know?'

Fran points at the photo, at the top corner of the back of the house.

'Do you see that?'

I lean closer.

'The window?'

'Yes. Look at the upper part of the window, the small panel that opens out.'

I'm squinting now. 'It's hard to see . . .'

'Look below it then, at the rest of the window.'

'I can't really make anything out – there's a glare on the glass from the sun, I guess.'

'Exactly. There's no glare at the top. No glass. The top part is broken, covered over with cardboard.'

'OK, you're going to have to spell this out for me.'

She points at the photo, stabbing at the picture of the house and the tiny broken window. 'Ruth Cavanagh was always complaining about having her windows broken. To be honest, she was such a wagon, I think some of the local kids targeted her house deliberately. So unless I'm way off, that's Ruth Cavanagh's house.'

This is not what I was expecting.

'The lady who wouldn't cut down her trees – your friend Zara's aunt? But why would she steal a child?'

Fran shrugs and raises her hands.

'That's the million-dollar question.'

'Hmm. It doesn't really add up. We know Gavin locked Lily in that room, and we know that the O'Briens were questioned by police, and we know that' – I hesitate, then push on – 'that Eddie Hogan had an argument with Robbie Murphy. But Ruth Cavanagh? It makes no sense.'

'She wasn't a very nice person . . .' Fran says, as though that explains it.

'But sure, every neighbourhood has someone like that. They might not give your football back but they don't usually kidnap your child.'

Fran looks at the photo again.

'Maybe we're wrong about the whole thing – maybe Lily is only two in this and it was taken the year before.'

'No. The more I look at it, the more certain I am. It's winter in that photo, and that's not a two-year-old child. God, if she did do it, it's awful to think Ruth Cavanagh may have taken her crimes to her grave.'

'Oh, Ruth's not dead.'

'What?'

'She's not dead, she lives in a nursing home.'

I'm tingling now, breathing faster.

'But this means we might find out what happened to Lily.' *And if she's Lila.* 'Do you know what nursing home? Could we ask your friend Zara?'

'I suppose . . . shouldn't we go to the police though?'

Oh God, no. Not yet. 'I don't know . . .' I say carefully. 'A photo of some leafless trees and an old lady in a nursing home . . . I feel like they'd laugh us out of the place.' I force a grin.

'Yeah, you're probably right. Fine, I'll check with Zara.'

I shouldn't ask, but curiosity gets the better of me. 'Was that her yesterday morning in the cafe?'

A small nod.

'And, was that her daughter? Robbie's daughter?'

Tight-lipped silence. I rush to explain.

'It's just, there's something familiar about her and I've been looking at so many photos of Lily, and I couldn't help wondering if Saoirse is Lily's half-sister?'

'Look, this is none of your business and it's not my place to say, but no, Zara did not have Robbie's baby. Now, can we drop it?'

'I'm sorry.' In a quiet voice, I add: 'Is it still OK for you to ask Zara which nursing home she's in?'

A sigh. But one of agreement.

I get up to go home, and despite Fran's denial, Saoirse's face is still etched on my mind.

50

June 2018

IT'S LATE THURSDAY NIGHT by the time Fran texts me the name of the nursing home. I google their visiting hours, and as soon as the kids are at school on Friday morning, I'm driving towards St Teresa's Nursing Home in Dún Laoghaire. I've driven past it many times on my way to and from the kids' school when we lived in our old house, but I've never been inside. Shiny laminate wood floors and the smell of disinfectant greet me when I push through the glass doors to the foyer. I sign in at the desk, tell the receptionist that Ruth is my aunt and that I'm home visiting briefly from America. My face is on fire as I say it and I'm convinced she'll know I'm lying, but she doesn't seem remotely perturbed and I'm taken by a care assistant to Room 26 on the second floor.

I'm not sure what I was expecting, but after all the talk of a Trunchbull-style creature, I'm surprised to find a thin, wizened lady sitting in an armchair by the window. Her hair is the colour of storm clouds, and her dark-framed glasses take over most of her face. She smells of lavender and looks lost inside an over sized floral nightdress, like a diminutive walnut. Her bright

257

blue eyes, resting on me, are surprisingly clear. But she does not look like a kidnapper, and suddenly I feel very foolish.

'I'll leave you to it, I'm just down the hall if you need anything,' the care assistant says, and pulls the door after her.

'Do I know you?' Ruth Cavanagh asks, in a voice that crackles with age.

I had considered many options on my journey here but in the end, I'd decided honesty is best.

'You don't, but I live in the house once owned by Lily Murphy's parents.' I'm watching carefully for a reaction. Ruth's expression doesn't change. Her eyes stay on me, betraying nothing. On her lap, she clasps her hands together.

'Do you remember Lily and her parents?' I try, removing my phone from my handbag and placing the bag on the floor beside the bed. It's hot in the room and I'm suddenly thirsty. On the nightstand, there's a glass of water that looks like it's gathering dust, and a full plastic jug beside it. A framed photo shows a man dressed in a suit, his face unsmiling. Mr Cavanagh, perhaps. A small silver dish sits in front of the photo, like an offering at an altar. In it are two emerald rings, a Miraculous Medal, a string of blue plastic rosary beads, and an earring in the shape of a cross. A memorial card – for Mr Cavanagh, maybe, faded with age. A dark red leather-bound notebook takes up the rest of the nightstand surface, and on top lies a silver pen.

I take a seat on the plastic chair opposite Ruth and try again. 'Do you remember Lily?'

Ruth smiles. 'Oh yes, a singer I believe. Back in the forties. Goodness, I loved her music.'

'No, not a singer – she lived in the house behind you and went missing in 1985.'

Ruth shakes her head dreamily. 'I don't, I'm afraid. But I've just realized who you are. I met you at the newsagent's yesterday, didn't I? When I was buying my cigarettes? The shop on Kilburn High Road, the small one with the canopy.' She claps her hands together and smiles triumphantly.

I smile back.

'You might be mixing me up with someone else. But look' – I hold up the Polaroid – 'that's your house, and that's Lily Murphy. Do you remember?'

Ruth shakes her head.

'Did you take this photo maybe?'

'No, not me.'

'Did someone else take it? Maybe someone sneaked into your garden and took the photo?'

'Perhaps. Yes, I think so.' Ruth still sounds dreamy but I decide to take her reply at face value.

'Do you mean somebody may have sneaked into your garden, smuggled Lily in and taken her photo, all without you or her grieving parents hearing anything?' I keep watching for a reaction. 'The houses are back to back, remember, you can hear everything.'

'That sounds lovely, dear. How's your sister? I remember her when she was young, such a beautiful girl.'

'I don't have a sister,' I say gently. 'I'm here because of Lily.'

'Ah good, and your mother?' Ruth goes on, as though she hasn't heard. 'How's she?'

'She's fine.'

'And your father?'

'I don't have a father, I'm afraid, I'm not much use to you. I have a father-in-law though! And he forgets things too.'

Ruth claps her hands together again. 'How nice. Tell me more about him!'

'Oh. Well. He's funny and a bit politically incorrect and he's getting forgetful, though sometimes I think he's putting it on to get out of things he doesn't want to do.' Abruptly, I stop and look at Ruth, staring at the clear blue eyes. Ruth stares back, unblinking.

'You know' – I hold up the Polaroid again – 'I can't help thinking about *where* these were found.'

Ruth smiles benignly but just under the surface, there's something sharper now. She doesn't say anything.

'Neatly placed in an envelope, carefully sealed inside a watertight tin. I mean, it doesn't scream kidnapper.'

Still Ruth says nothing, but her eyes are clear and fixed on me. Listening.

From down the hall comes the sound of a door opening, a murmur of voices. The room is stiflingly hot with sun streaming through slatted blinds and – I touch the radiator under the window – the central heating is on too.

'Mrs Cavanagh, I found a symbol on the wall just beside the radiator in what was Lily's room. An "evil eye".' This feels wrong. Ruth is so old now, and on the surface at least, it looks like dementia has her in its grip. But there's something below that surface, something telling me Ruth might know what she's talking about. A small chance, but still. And I'm so close now.

From out in the corridor comes the swish of a floor cleaner and soft footsteps. How long until someone asks me to leave?

'Mrs Cavanagh. I keep thinking about the evil eye. Was Mary doing something to Lily? Was Lily in danger?' I sit forward in the chair, just inches from her now. 'Did Mary hurt her? Is that why you took her? To save her?'

Ruth grips the arms of the chair but doesn't reply. I know it's not OK to question an elderly lady like this, but I can't stop now.

'Mary and Robbie Murphy, the so-called golden couple of Rowanbrook – but maybe Mary wasn't quite as perfect as everyone thought? What exactly went on back then? And did Robbie Murphy die thinking his daughter was dead? Did you let him go to his grave without knowing she was safe and well?'

'That man does not deserve your pity.' Ruth spits the words and she no longer sounds like an elderly dementia patient; her voice is clear as a bell and blistering with anger. I stop talking, ready to listen. And finally, thirty-three years on, Ruth Cavanagh tells her story.

51

May 1985

MARY CLOSED THE DOOR on the last straggling birthday guests and leaned against it. From outside, Susie Stedman's voice wafted in as she and Della walked away.

That was lovely, but they really indulge that child, she was saying. *Imagine how they'd cope if they had six, like I do! Robbie's a great father, though, isn't he?*

Mary closed her eyes.

The voices disappeared with their owners, and Mary made her way slowly to the kitchen. Through the window, she could see Robbie walking around the garden with Lily, pointing out flowers. Lily's small hand in his, her face lit up.

Mary began filling the sink, piling in cake plates and chocolate-muddied forks. On the windowsill, her Santa Cruz lighthouse glistened in the sunlight, calling her home. Home. She turned off the faucet. *This is home now. You made your bed.*

Much later, when Lily was asleep and the kitchen was finally spotlessly clean, Mary joined Robbie in the living room. Wind whistled down the chimney as she picked up her book and curled her bare feet beneath her on the armchair. The clock on the mantlepiece ticked towards nine, the second hand moving slowly, inexorably, round and round. Tick tick tick. The lights flickered. She kept her eyes trained on her book. Robbie glanced up from his paper.

'So that was a good day,' he said, his voice light.

She nodded. 'Lily loved it.'

'Though how on earth did you mess up something as simple as serving jelly and ice cream?' His voice still light, but not in a good way.

She bit her lip. Debating. Reply or don't reply. The memory of his hand on her shoulder still branded on her brain; his fingers digging into her skin while he smiled and said it didn't matter. Always the perfect host.

'It made us look cheap. Like we're trying to pass off a jar of jam as dessert. I saw Ines whispering about it to Victor.' He smoothed the newspaper on his lap. 'Mind you, anything that annoys Ines tends to cheer me up.' He laughed now.

Mary nodded. Safer territory. The clock ticked as though there was nothing to worry about. *Nothing to see here.*

'I'd say Victor's delighted she's heading off to Spain again,' Robbie continued. 'I don't know how he puts up with that woman.'

Still the clock ticked. But this was smooth, even ground. On the subject of Ines O'Brien they were in agreement, and that made it a *good* topic.

'She's always so rude.' Mary shook her head.

'She's jealous of you.'

'Oh, I don't think so.'

'She is. She was Queen Bee until you arrived. Rowanbrook's one and only half-glamorous resident. Think of the competition – Della looks like she was dragged through a hedge, and Susie thinks she's a model but she's pushed out six kids; she's well past it.'

Mary nodded, forcing her fading smile to stay in place. Robbie picked up the paper again and patted the couch. 'Come sit beside me.'

She uncurled her legs and moved to the couch, her book still in her hand.

'What's the book?' he asked.

This was new. Robbie didn't like novels. Fiction was made up, a waste of time. And people who read novels were pretentious, according to him; making out they were smarter than everyone else. He was never interested in what she was reading. Everything else, yes. Her friends, where she went while he was at work, her interactions with neighbours. But never her novels.

She lifted the front cover to show him as the clock ticked louder.

He tilted his head to read, then reached to take it from her hand and turned it over to read the back. His brow furrowed, two deep troughs between his eyes.

Bad troughs.

Trouble clouds.

Warning signs.

She tensed. A familiar trickle of unease unfurled inside her stomach. Crawled into her chest. Seeped across her shoulders. Down her arms.

Robbie cleared his throat and began to read aloud from the back of the book.

' "Could she tell anyone what was going on, and if she did, would anyone believe her?" Interesting.' He looked at her. 'What's the book about?'

She swallowed. 'Oh. It's a silly one I picked up at the bookstore. I didn't even read the back.'

'Well, you're halfway through now, according to your bookmark. So, tell me, what's it about?'

She opened her mouth to speak, but no words took shape.

'I'm waiting.' Robbie dropped the book to the floor. He swivelled on the couch so he was facing her.

She swallowed again. 'It's about a woman, struggling in her marriage, who meets someone new.'

'Why is she struggling in her marriage?'

'They just . . . they just don't get along.'

'Because?'

'Because . . . they're incompatible.'

'I can't help feeling you're not telling me the whole story.' Robbie wrapped his fingers around her wrist. Gently. No pressure. For now. 'The back suggests there's more to it.' He pointed towards the book on the floor. He wasn't talking about the words of the blurb, she knew that. He was talking about the opaque image behind the words. The woman's haunted face, the purple skin around her eye, the tiny spill of blood at the corner of her lip.

'Her husband has a stressful job and sometimes . . . loses his cool.'

'And she goes off with someone else?'

Mary nodded. A tiny, shuddered movement.

'And what do you think of that?'

It bloomed inside now, just as it always did. The terror. The tell-tale heart ticking loud.

'You think that's a reasonable thing to do? To walk out on your husband because he gets a bit stressed from time to time?'

She tried to say no. But he wasn't listening. He stood, yanking her off the couch by her wrist.

'Is this your way of telling me?'

'No, that's not it. It's just a silly book. I'm not going any —'

The slap caught her off guard. She'd been here a hundred times before, but he always avoided her face.

'Now look what you've made me do!' He was yelling.

'Lily, don't wake her . . . she'll be frightened . . .' she whispered, putting her free hand to her stinging cheek. He smacked it away.

'Oh, that'd suit you. Make me the bad guy, frightening the child. On her birthday, of all days. You've ruined it. You've fucking ruined it.' He threw her then, like a rag doll. She landed on the living room floor, cracking her head against the corner of the fireplace. Stunned for a moment, she didn't move. He hovered above her. Quivering. She braced herself for a kick, tucking her legs, trying to cover her ribs. He always went for her legs or her ribs. But not this time. This time he raised his foot and stamped down on her hand. She put her other hand to her mouth, to stifle the scream. Lily must not see this. Lily must never see this.

52

MY THROAT IS TIGHT as I listen to Ruth's stories, as everything is turned on its head. I don't want to interrupt now that Ruth is finally talking but when she pauses to drink some water, I ask a question.

'What about the evil eye? I'd started to wonder if Mary was a bit unhinged. If she was harming Lily.'

'With a drawing on a wall? Really?'

Now that Ruth says it, it feels silly.

'But why put an evil eye on her daughter's wall? Isn't that like putting a curse on her?'

'It doesn't put a curse on anyone, quite the opposite. Where did you get that from?'

'Frances Burke said it. She looked it up after she saw it.'

'Frances. If that one had a brain, she'd be dangerous. If she did her research properly, she'd know that the evil eye relates to putting a curse on someone, but the evil eye *symbol* provides protection against that curse,' Ruth continues. 'At least if you believe in all that. People who *do* believe often wear an evil-eye bracelet to protect them from harm. Mary didn't want to put a bracelet on' – she stops, as though about to say something else, then starts again – 'on the little one, so she drew it on the wall

267

instead. To protect her. Mary could take anything as long as Lily was safe.'

'And did she believe in it?'

'I think you could say she *hoped* in it.'

'And you?'

'I'm not against using the resources nature provides to solve insurmountable problems. Let's put it like that.'

I have the distinct impression Ruth is telling me something, but I have no idea what. I stay silent, hoping for elaboration.

'Enough about that, let me tell you some more about Mary and her life with Robbie. I think then you'll understand.'

53

June 1985

'WELL, THE PADDLING POOL certainly went down well with the kids – the whole party seems to have been a great success,' Robbie said, closing the door on Della and the Stedmans. 'Did you see the look on Ines O'Brien's face when she saw the bottles of champagne lined up on the drinks table?'

Mary shook her head.

'Watch now, they'll have a garden party next week with twice as much champagne. Such one-upmanship. That woman gives me a pain in my face.'

Mary nodded and ducked her head into the living room to check on Lily. Fast asleep on the couch. She'd never sleep tonight. But Mary hadn't the heart to wake her.

'Come on, we'll have a cuppa while it's quiet,' Robbie said, leading the way down the hall to the kitchen.

If she could only have this Robbie all the time. This amiable version who threw the best parties in Rowanbrook and brought her a cup of tea every morning in bed. The perfect father. The husband who bought her perfume and paid her compliments. The good moods that made her think they'd turned a corner. That he'd changed. Because how could this charming man be the same one who hit her? The same one who sometimes hated her?

She followed him into the kitchen and sat. He set about brewing a pot of tea and she continued living in hope.

'Did you see yer one Cynthia draped all over Tom again.' Robbie shook his head, in an approximation of judgement that sounded like envy.

'I did. I feel for Susie.' Mary didn't like gossiping about their friends, but she wasn't above joining Robbie in his favourite pastime if it meant keeping him onside.

Robbie had his back to her, pouring boiling water into the teapot. 'I tell you, Ines is a brave woman, leaving her husband with Cynthia while she goes off to Spain.'

'If Della's to be believed, it's Ines who's to be watched!' Mary said, hating herself for stooping to his level but needing the peace it tended to bring.

'Really?' Robbie turned around.

'Oh, you know Della. She probably heard it from her hairdresser's cousin. I wouldn't repeat that. Anyway, I think Lily had a great day – she loves that paddling pool. Cora had great fun in it too.'

'Yeah.' Robbie put the teapot on the table and a mug in front of Mary. 'I don't know about that child. She's odd. Always watching, saying nothing.'

'She's quiet, yes. I was probably a bit like that as a kid. Maybe I still am – the oddball American who doesn't quite fit.' She laughed but Robbie didn't.

'It's more than that. Did you see when Fran ran over to pull her away from Lily in the pool? I was in the kitchen and even I could see there was something strange going on.'

'Oh, I really don't think so, they were just playing,' Mary said as Robbie poured the tea.

'Do you think I'm making it up?' he asked, still pouring.

'Gosh! No, not at all. Just that I think Cora is harmless.'

'So, you *do* think I'm making it up.' The tea was close to the rim of the mug now and Robbie hadn't noticed. He was still pouring. She put her hand out to signal *enough*. Before she knew what was happening, Robbie had moved the teapot. Just a fraction of an inch. The boiling tea hit her skin, stunning her. She pulled away her hand, clutching it against her chest. But Robbie kept pouring. On to her lap, soaking through her light summer dress. She pushed her chair back and it crashed against the radiator behind, her skin stinging.

'You should be more careful,' Robbie said, before placing the teapot on the table and walking out of the room.

54

June 2018

I LISTEN IN SILENCE to Ruth's stories, my hands clasped tightly on my lap, my fingernails digging into my skin. For what feels like hours, but is probably only thirty or forty minutes, I sit and listen, nodding but not speaking until Ruth asks me a question.

'Do you see now?'

I nod.

'But why didn't Mary tell anyone? Wouldn't Della have noticed?'

Ruth laughs softly. 'Della didn't know. Nobody knew. Robbie was very, very careful. Never hit her anywhere anyone would notice. Ribs and stomach and legs. No visible bruises. Endless tubes of arnica cream to heal the hidden ones and Mary always in long dresses. Nobody knew a thing.'

'God. What a fucker.' I look up at Ruth. 'Sorry.'

'That's all right. I might have said the same thing myself once upon a time.'

'But still . . . How did nobody know? I thought they were all friends.'

'Do you tell your friends everything?'

'I . . . no.' *Good God, no.*

'It's not an easy thing to admit,' Ruth continues. 'That your

272

marriage is a nightmare, that your husband is a vicious, controlling sociopath. That you made a mistake. That you moved continent for a life of misery. That you brought a child into that miserable life and couldn't keep her safe. That's what pushed her over the edge.'

A soft knock interrupts us and a nurse pops her head around the door.

'Time for your meds, Ruth. And if you're getting tired, you'll let us know, won't you?' She glances meaningfully at me and I feel like a naughty child.

'I can go if you're tired . . .' I say, hoping I sound sincere.

Ruth says nothing, sitting quietly as the nurse administers three coloured pills, each swallowed with a small cup of water.

The nurse – Tracy according to her name badge – straightens the top sheet and cover on the bed and refills the glass of water on the bedside locker. She stands, hands on hips, squinting at the television set that's suspended from a metal arm attached to the wall.

'Is that in the right spot for you? Will I move it?' she asks.

'Oh, thank you. *Glenroe* will be on television tonight, won't it?'

'*Glenroe* is long gone, more's the pity,' Tracy says, reaching to tilt the TV set towards the bed. She throws a sympathetic look towards Ruth, and a smile at me. *God love her*, she mouths, shaking her head.

I smile, marvelling. Ruth has them all eating out of her hand.

Tracy leaves, pulling the door behind her, and I give Ruth a hard stare.

'Mrs Cavanagh, I don't know how to ask this politely, but why are you faking dementia?'

For the first time since I arrived, Ruth grins. Not the dreamy half-smile she gave the nurse, but a proper, knowing grin.

'I'm as dothery as can be; I'm ninety-three, for goodness' sake. Just you wait and see how hard it is to grasp the right words when you're my age.'

'Dothery is one thing, but you seem very capable of slipping in and out at will.'

'Well, people leave you in peace if they think you're not compos mentis. Less inane chit-chat. And I may have needed to deteriorate a little when you started asking your questions.' She blinks. 'You can do that at ninety-three and nobody bats an eyelid. Now, where were we?'

I lean forward. 'You mentioned that something tipped Mary over the edge?'

'Ah yes, that was the night of the dinner party.'

55

June 1985

MARY SMILED AND SMILED and smiled. For Robbie's video camera. For the dinner guests. For the applause. They were applauding her Mexican food, and at the same time eyeing it with suspicion. *Make them something exotic*, Robbie had said. *Mexican. None of them will ever have had Mexican food before. They'll be talking about it for months.* He was walking backwards now, away from the table, and finally – she hoped – switching off the camera.

'Ruth,' she said, passing the older lady a bowl of refried rice, 'will you try some of this?'

'Certainly not,' Ruth said, passing the rice to Tom Stedman.

'Can I make you something else?' Mary asked. 'I'm sorry, I should have asked what people like.'

'It's fine,' Ruth said, with a pronounced sigh.

'Some bread even?'

Ruth turned to her and locked eyes. 'No.' She sipped her water; the conversation, apparently, over. Mary bit her lip and tried to tune back into the chat around the table.

'It's great to have us all here together,' Tom was saying. 'I hope nobody told the burglars though. Prime time to break in when we're all at Robbie's getting sozzled!'

'Do you think there are burglars around?' Mary asked.

'Ah, there are always break-ins every now and then,' Tom said, taking a swallow of his whiskey.

'Only, I noticed some things missing today. And some things moved.'

'Probably just the babysitters,' Robbie said, passing a plate of chicken to Susie.

Della looked up sharply.

'Not on purpose,' Robbie added hurriedly. 'Fran and Zara are great. But they might have moved things accidentally and not put them back in the right place.'

Mary thought about her smashed Alice figurine and the broken lipstick and Robbie's missing watch. Could it really have been an accident?

The conversation moved on then, to Ruth's broken window and Ines O'Brien's mother and what on earth Susie was going to do with six kids for the long summer holidays. Robbie opened a bottle of Midleton Very Rare whiskey and managed to drop into conversation how much it cost.

'Isn't he a perfect host,' Susie said. 'I know so many would keep the good stuff for themselves.'

At that point, after declaring the get-together not to 'her taste', Ruth was the first to say she was leaving.

She pushed back her chair, then leaned down and to Mary's astonishment, she whispered in her ear. Four words Mary would never forget. Four words that gave her permission. Four words that gave her strength.

'He doesn't fool me.'

And then she heard the hammering on the door.

56

MORNING IS SLIPPING BY and I'm conscious of the school run, but I can't leave, not now. I pick up my phone and text Adana, asking if she could collect the kids and at the same time, I ask Ruth a question. 'You said there was a turning point for Mary – something about keeping Lily safe?'

Ruth nods. 'Yes. Eddie Hogan called at the door that night, raging that his daughter was pregnant by Robbie. Robbie was angry and embarrassed about the whole thing, that's for sure. But what was worse – in his mind anyway – was what Eddie Hogan said about Gavin Bowman.'

'Oh?'

'We could all hear Eddie shouting. Mary was like a deer in the headlights and the rest of them just sat there, delighted with the drama, I'm sure. Eddie said that if anyone knew what was going on with the Murphys, it was Gavin, because he was always "sniffing around" Mary.'

'Ah. I heard something about that all right.'

'I don't think Robbie really minded the accusation of sleeping with Zara. On some level he was proud of it, I suspect. But the bit about Gavin sniffing around Mary was humiliating. Gavin had been in and out of their house, doing the garden, but by all accounts, finding any excuse to sit in the kitchen with Mary. And Robbie didn't like that one bit.'

'So he took it out on Mary?'

Ruth nods. 'Robbie lost it after everyone left that night; kicked her, hit her, then he punched a framed picture in the dining room – a photograph of Mary's hometown if I remember correctly – and threatened her with a shard of broken glass. He ended up with his arm in a sling because of it – bruised knuckles and a sprained wrist.' Ruth shakes her head. 'Everyone blamed Eddie Hogan for that.'

'God, poor Mary. Putting up with all that and nobody to confide in. Della right next door, with no idea what was going on.'

'Della had five children of her own, there wasn't an ounce of peace in that house. The earth could have opened up and swallowed Mary's house and Della wouldn't have heard it. And you can't see in the windows of Number Six from next door.'

There's something about the way she says it.

'Wait, do you mean you can see in the windows from somewhere else? From your old house?'

Ruth smiles but it's tinged with sadness. 'The irony is, Robbie was always obsessed with cutting those treetops to get more sun, but if you went down to the bottom of my garden, you could see right through the middle, where the trees were thinner. You could see the Murphys' garden clear as day, and all the way into the windows at the back of the house. The kitchen, the dining room. Their bedroom.'

'Ah.'

'I saw all sorts, once I started paying attention. Sometimes they were on the bench at the end of their garden, and I was only twenty feet away in mine. They never knew I was there. I could hear everything if they were outside or even if they had the patio doors open. The arguments, the odd push, the look on her face when his tone changed. The boring conversations about dinner that would suddenly take a turn towards anger. Or not. That was the thing. I never knew which way it would go. Mary never knew. That was the hardest bit, I think. She could never tell if or when he'd turn on her, or how to steer the conversation so it wouldn't happen.'

'Life on eggshells. On a knife blade.' I grew up in a house like that – watching every word that came out of my mouth, waiting nervously for a reaction.

'And there was no answer, no magic trick to avoid upsetting Robbie. It seemed to be utterly on a whim.'

'Did Mary never call the police?'

'No. She was terrified. And a foreigner with no family network. It's not as easy as you might think to go to the authorities.'

I nod. This too is something I know well. I wonder then if Ruth ever contacted the police, but there's no way to ask without sounding accusatory.

'I went to the gardaí once,' Ruth says, reading my mind. 'They sent a car around. I remember now, Tom Stedman saw it and thought it was parked outside the Burkes'. Poor Della's ears were burning.'

'But what happened? Did the police do anything?'

'Robbie charmed the pants off them, Mary said it must be someone trying to stir trouble, and it never came to anything. He carried on as always, his mood changing as quick as the garden breeze. And I carried on listening.'

'And they had no idea you were there, witnessing all of this?'

'No idea. When Mary finally told me the full story, she said she'd no clue. Though Fran did get a fright when she was babysitting one afternoon and heard rustling. Mary told me later she was worried there was someone creeping around. Much later, I mean. After.'

'After?'

'After the day Lily went missing . . .'

I sit up straighter. Finally, I'm going to get some answers.

57

MARY WAS CURLED IN a ball on the dining room floor when she heard the steps on the stairs. Winded, clutching her stomach, she tried to tell him.

'Lily's coming.' It came out in a gasp.

Above her, Robbie nursed his bruised fist, rage still pulsing in his temples, the shard of glass still in his hand. The framed photo of Santa Cruz Wharf, lying on the floor.

'Look what you made me do, you stupid bitch!' He hadn't heard what she'd said.

'Lily,' Mary tried again. She could see her now, tiny in her long nightdress, standing at the dining room door.

'Robbie, Lily's—' The kick, aimed squarely at her stomach, made contact before the next word could leave her mouth. She tried desperately to claw through the pain, to keep her eyes open, to will Lily back up the stairs. But it was too late. She'd seen. She was coming over.

Mary opened her eyes to see Lily pull on Robbie's shirt.

'Daddy, Daddy, I thirsty, can you bring me water?' Pulling him away, perhaps, or maybe she really wanted water.

On some level, Mary was conscious of banging on the front door now, and shouting outside, and that Eddie Hogan was back, but in that moment, the only thing that mattered was Lily, who was still tugging at Robbie's shirt.

'Stop!' Robbie roared, and shoved Lily off him. Her tiny, light body flew across the floor. At first, there was no sound, then a scream of shock or pain or both cut through the air. Mary scrambled to all fours and crawled to her daughter. Lily screamed again and Mary took her into her arms, comforting and shushing.

Robbie stood over them. Glass still in hand.

'Jesus. Is she OK? I didn't think she'd . . . It was an accident. Lily, come up now, you're OK.'

From the hall came more shouting and banging, and Robbie seemed to register it for the first time. He closed the dining room door.

'She's OK, Mary. Don't over-react. She tripped over her own legs when I was trying to get her to give me a second's peace.'

'Sorry, Daddy,' Lily said in a tiny voice, and a heavy dread settled around Mary. Lily had seen glimpses of her father's anger – outbursts that left her quiet and subdued. But this was the first time he'd hurt her. And now, she was apologizing for it. This was how it started.

At the front door, the banging and shouting persisted, but Robbie ignored it. He looked stunned.

'Jesus.' He stood, still running his hand through his hair. Then he turned and walked through to the living room, and closed the door. Mary checked Lily's arms and legs, running her hands up and down tiny limbs. No cuts, no lumps, no bumps. She lifted her t-shirt then, and there it was. On her back. A blazing red mark on Lily's skin. *Dear God.* She pulled Lily up into her arms and stood by the dining room window, staring out. Lily nuzzled into her neck, and outside, at the end of the garden, the treetops swayed against the midnight sky. Beyond the trees, the back of Ruth's house was lit up: lights on in every window. Mary pulled Lily closer. She'd have to confront Robbie. To face him head on. No matter what the outcome. And with Ruth's words ringing in her ears, for the first time, Mary thought she could.

He doesn't fool me.

58

July 1985

THE NEXT MORNING, IN a turn of events neither of them could have predicted, Ruth was by Mary's side, combing the building site. Twelve short hours, but a lifetime beyond the dinner party. *He doesn't fool me.* Now Ruth stayed with Mary as they searched for Lily.

Up and down the building site, Della Burke and Susie Stedman and their children shouted Lily's name, but Mary didn't have any voice left. And deep inside, below her panic, beneath her terror, she was grateful for Ruth's calm presence.

It was the position of the barrels that caught their attention. Even in her near hysteria, Mary could see there was something deliberate about the way they had been placed, blocking the doorway. Beside her, Ruth tensed.

Without speaking, they moved together towards the first barrel and pushed it aside. The second one was heavier, but between them they got it out of the way. Still silent, they each gripped a side of the wooden pallet and lifted. Mary walked through, sick with fear and dread and hope. Her eyes skittered this way and that, her voice stuck in her throat. But there was nobody there.

On her arm, she felt Ruth's fingers and only then realized she was slipping towards the floor.

'Not now,' Ruth was saying. 'This is no time for fainting fits.'

Mary leaned against Ruth, taking a moment to steady herself.

'I was so sure . . .'

'Yes. Well. She's not here and we're wasting time.'

Mary nodded and turned back to the empty doorway.

But something stopped her.

Later, she never knew what. A sound? An instinct? The tug of an invisible maternal cord? She turned back to the window and moved towards it. Not a window, a space where a window would at some point be. A long, low window, just a couple of inches from the floor. Outside there was scaffolding, with a timber deck for the now-gone builders to access the upper part of the house.

And something else.

Huddled on the timber floor, like a bundle of rags.

Lily.

Holding her breath, Mary stepped out on to the scaffolding and crouched to scoop up her daughter. Lily's eyes were closed, her face pale, her limbs slack. White noise roared in Mary's ears as her hand covered her daughter's face, chest, wrists, neck; checking, checking, not able to think about what she was checking.

Movement. A twitch of a leg, a turn of a lip. Enough to tell her Lily was alive. Asleep. But alive.

'She might be injured, stay there,' Ruth was saying. She climbed out on to the scaffolding too, and on some level Mary wondered if it was safe, if it could bear their weight, but she couldn't move, not yet.

'Let me have a look.' Ruth hunkered down, surprisingly nimble, and began running her hands over Lily, checking limbs, neck, forehead. It was then Mary noticed that Lily's face was streaked with tears. Her poor child. Had she climbed out of the window on her own? Who had locked her in the room? She must have been terrified. Mary blinked and hot tears spilled out, a mix of horror and fury and relief. She touched her daughter's cheek, and now Lily's eyes fluttered open.

'Mama,' was all she said, curling on her side, sinking her little body further into her mother's lap.

'Just a minute, I'm nearly done,' Ruth said brusquely, lifting Lily's t-shirt, checking her front and then turning her over. The bruises on her back were dark purple now.

Silence.

A thousand explanations ran through Mary's head as her face flushed red but no words came out.

'I don't think these are from today,' Ruth said quietly, quashing every one of the thousand explanations.

'I . . .'

'Mary.'

'I know. I have to do something. And I will. I'll get her away,' she whispered. 'We'll leave together. Tonight.'

'He'll stop you.'

'I . . . but I have to try.'

'Even if you manage to sneak out of the house, he'll find you. He'll chase you for the rest of your lives.'

'We can hide.'

'Where? Mary, if Robbie knows you took Lily; if he knows you two are out there together, he'll dedicate the rest of his life to finding you.'

'But what else can I do?'

Ruth said nothing for a moment. In silence, she looked down at Lily's bruised skin, and out at the building site below and the woods just beyond. In the distance, they could hear people shouting Lily's name.

'We'd better tell them we found her,' Mary said, beginning the process of standing up, still holding Lily.

'No.' Ruth put out a hand. 'Wait.'

Afterwards, it always seemed like a jumble of words and movements that Mary could never quite order correctly. Like cobbled-together scenes from a very old home movie. Had she given in immediately to Ruth's suggestion or had they sat there for an eternity, debating in hurried whispers? She liked to tell herself it was the latter. That she'd put thought and reason into it; that she hadn't taken the decision lightly. That Ruth had tried to convince her while she held out. Appalled at first. But she was never quite sure. Ruth was offering an escape hatch and in her occasional lucid memories of that day, Mary suspected she'd jumped at it.

'I'll go home and get my car. I'll park it at the end of the pathway – the shortcut through the woods. I'll come back here to get her then. If I take her out the back door and through the woods,' Ruth said, 'nobody will see me.'

'What if they see her in your car?'

'She can crouch down in the footwell and I'll cover her with a blanket. I'll tell her it's a game of Hide and Seek.'

'And I'll wait here?' Mary asked.

Ruth thought for a moment, then reached down and slipped off one of Lily's little red shoes. She handed it to Mary.

'Put that in your pocket. When I'm back after getting the car, you go down and leave the shoe beside the river.' She paused. Waiting, perhaps, for Mary to understand. To be OK with what she was suggesting. Mary nodded, her throat tight.

'You must leave it somewhere it will be seen, and quickly. But you can't find it yourself, in case it leads to suspicion later.'

Later. God. Was she really going to do this?

'You'll have to be smart about it. Just grab whoever is nearby and ask them to search the area with you, but let them find the shoe. Yes?'

'Yes.'

'And then you must scream, shout, draw attention. Get everyone to the riverbank. That's when I'll take her out the back door and through the woods to the car.'

'But what if someone catches you?'

'Worst case scenario, if they do, I explain I just found her, I'm taking her to find you. Nobody is going to think a cranky sixty-year-old woman is kidnapping a child.'

Kidnap. Was that what this was? A kidnap? A crime? Of course it was a crime. Mary looked at Lily, at her sleepy, tear-stained face, at the purple bruises still visible under the hem of her t-shirt. A crime, yes. And an escape hatch.

In the end, the first part was easiest, though it didn't feel that way at the time. Mary stayed with Lily while Ruth got her car. She held Lily close, terrified someone would find them before Ruth got back, but half hoping too that at any moment Robbie or Della would burst through the door, and she wouldn't have any choice. She wouldn't have to do this thing that Ruth was suggesting.

But when someone did come up the stairs, it was Ruth, nodding to let Mary know all was OK. She'd parked the car and no one had seen. The next bit was harder. Passing Lily into Ruth's arms, and walking away. But she did it. She ran down the stairs, out into the building site and over to the riverbank, knowing Ruth could see her through the window. She checked nobody else was watching, hunkered down and slipped the shoe from her dress pocket, behind a mound of scrubby grass. She looked for Della then, or Susie, but neither of them was nearby. Should she wait? She couldn't wait. Ruth needed her to act. Lily needed her to act. One of the Burke twins was a little way down the riverbank.

'Will you help me search this area?' she called to him and he nodded, glad, she thought, to be able to contribute in a concrete way. 'If you look around here,' she indicated with her hand, 'I'll go further along.'

She moved quickly away from the shoe and began a search of the tall reeds that lined the riverbank. The shout went up even sooner than she'd hoped.

'I found something!' he called. She turned. In his hand was the little red shoe. After that, it got blurry again. Shouts and running and panicked faces. A shoe by a riverbank was not good. Eddie Hogan rushed over, Susie and Cynthia and Cora, the other Burke twin, Ellen and Aoife. Neighbours, strangers, two gardaí. And Robbie. Mary felt sick. She put her hands to her face, telling herself to stay calm. If Robbie was here – if everyone was here – nobody would see Ruth take Lily through the woods. And this might work. Deep breaths. She could do this.

Hours later, Mary was back in the half-built house with the barrels in front of the door, and still she had no idea who had locked Lily in. Lily, now safe in Ruth's house. *Dear God, let her be safe.* Mary, going through the motions, playing a part. An impossible yet impossibly simple part to play. Shaking. Anxious. Sick. And back where it started, but without Ruth this time. This time, with Della and Fran and Tom. And Robbie. The searchers. The ones who must be convinced. Back at the room with the barrels.

'I need to see,' Mary said quietly, walking through the doorway. Robbie followed, holding a torch. He swung it slowly about the room, lighting up the floor and then the walls. Mary

ANDREA MARA

turned like a music box ballerina, following the light. Nothing. No sign that anyone had been there. At the window, she stood looking out, the night breeze blowing wisps of hair into her eyes. The scaffolding beneath the window ran the width of the house but it was too dark to see beyond the surface immediately below.

She turned to her husband. 'Can you shine the torch out here.' Her voice shook. Robbie did as she asked. The beam swept all the way along the wooden pathway, first one side, then the other. Nothing. Nobody. No sign anyone had been there at all.

'Let's go back down,' Robbie said, putting his good arm around her shoulder, which made the shaking worse. *Don't let him guess. Dear God, don't let him guess what I've done.*

'Mary, love, I think you should go home. You're freezing and exhausted. Will you go for even an hour? Della, would you be able to bring her?'

'Of course. Fran will mind the twins, I can stay with Mary all night.'

Her husband passed her to her friend, and Mary, limp now, allowed it.

Tom bowed his head, like a mourner at a funeral. *They've given up,* Mary realized. *They're still searching, but in their minds, they've given up.* Hands shaking, legs loose, she reached for Della, relief making her weak. She could do this. She would not fall.

59

June 2018

'OH MY GOD.' *I didn't kill Lily Murphy.*

'Yes.'

'It was Mary? She kidnapped her own child?' *Not Cynthia?*

Ruth purses her lips.

'Well, technically *I* kidnapped the child. And as I kept saying to Mary, in her many, many moments of anxiety, she *saved* Lily. The law's the law, yes, and legally it was a crime, perhaps morally too. Who are we to take these godlike decisions?' She folds her arms. 'But I wouldn't change a thing.'

'But I don't get it – from everything I've read about the case, Mary and Robbie continued their search together for months. There was nothing about Mary leaving?'

'She didn't leave. She continued the search that day, went home that night, started again at first light the following morning. Lily was safely with me, in my house.'

'Wow. So Mary knew where Lily was but played the part of the distraught mother? Every single day?'

'She didn't think she could do it at first. But after years of pretending her marriage was fine, that Robbie was the golden boy everyone thought he was, lying about this came easily. And the stakes were high. Life or death, I'd say.'

'Jesus.'

'Indeed. It meant I had to stay in the house, couldn't join the search. My ears were burning for weeks.' Ruth grimaces. 'The Rowanbrook old guard couldn't believe I wasn't bothered helping look for Lily. But I'm a tough old boot.'

'And what did you tell Lily?'

'That there was a problem with the electrics in her house and she was staying with me. Mary used to come by every day through a gap in the fence at the end of her back garden. Sometimes early in the morning, sometimes late at night, and as time went on and Robbie went back to work, she'd come and stay all day. She got me a Polaroid camera and I used to take photos of Lily and put them in an old tobacco tin in their coal bunker. She'd write notes to Lily and leave them in there for me to pick up. Anything that made her feel closer during the hours she couldn't be with her.' She looks wistful. 'We were a happy little bunch when we could be together, Mary, Lily and me. It might be hard to believe, but they were good times. I loved having her there. Loved keeping her safe from *him*.'

'But Mary was still living with him?'

'That broke my heart. There was a small reprieve – a week or two during the search when he didn't go near her with his fists. She even started to worry she'd made a mistake. Imagine thinking that. *My husband hasn't knocked me to the floor in a fortnight, maybe I was wrong about him.* But that's how it is, I suppose. Hard for any of us who haven't been through it to understand that desperate need to believe he's not a monster. But then one morning she slipped into my house and I could tell from the way she was holding herself something was wrong. Cradling her ribcage, lowering herself so slowly to the chair, wincing when Lily jumped into her arms. The monster was back.'

'The poor woman.'

'And it only got worse. He stopped caring about hiding the cuts and bruises, she stopped going out. They became recluses – at night and at weekends, they stayed indoors. He took it all out on her. It was her fault Lily had disappeared: she hadn't been taking proper care, he knew Cora wasn't to be trusted – he'd said so and Mary hadn't listened, he claimed. And it was all her fault for letting Lily out of her sight.'

'Jesus. And then he had his heart attack and Mary was free.'

Ruth gives me a funny look.

'Yes. Mary was better off. She and Lily went to stay over on the other side of the city, with a new name for Lily.'

'What did she call her?'

A sidelong glance. 'No need for you to know that.'

'Wait, do you know where she is now? Are you still in touch?'

'Mary passed away, unfortunately.' Ruth's eyes glisten as she says it. 'Bloody cancer. And here's me, lingering on at ninety-three. Life's very unfair.' She shakes her head.

'I'm sorry. But I meant' – I hesitate – 'I meant Lily. Is she alive?'

No response.

'Please. Is she alive? Do you know where she is?'

Ruth smiles and the dreamy look is back.

'It must be time for *Glenroe*. Will you put on the television on your way out?'

Ruth has picked up a book from the windowsill and is turning the pages as though searching for her place. But it's fake, it's all fake. She's not really looking for her page, she's waiting for me to walk out. The air is thick, buzzing with told and untold stories.

'Can you at least let me know she's not dead? I've spent every hour of the last few weeks thinking about her, searching for answers. Haven't I earned the right to know?'

Still paging through the book, Ruth doesn't look up when she answers but her voice is clear.

'That's fair. Yes, she's alive.'

'Oh, thank God.' *Certainty, finally.*

Ruth looks surprised, wondering, I suppose, why I'm so invested in this.

'That little girl, I felt so sad for her, and now she's . . . I'm just happy.'

'And she's happy too, and you need to leave her in peace.'

'You know where she is? You're in contact with her?'

A hesitation, then a nod.

'Wait, even now? Even with her mother gone? Does she know who she is?'

'No, she doesn't know anything about her early childhood.'

'Who does she think you are?'

Ruth looks up. 'I'm Aunt Ruth, of course. I've been Aunt Ruth since she was three years old.' Her voice cracks, just a little, and there's a glimmer of emotion. But just as quickly, the chink closes. 'And that's all you need to know.'

'Does she live here in Dublin?'

No reply.

'Wait, do you still see her – does she visit you here in the nursing home?'

Still no reply. Ruth is back to turning pages in her book.

'Oh my God, she does, doesn't she?'

'You should go now, I'm tired.'

'Don't you have a duty to tell?'

Ruth looks up from the book. 'Duty to who?'

This leaves me momentarily stuck for words. I look around the neat room, at the slants of afternoon sunlight coming through the venetian blind. At the print on the wall, Jesus and the Apostles at the Last Supper – had Ruth brought it with her? At the neat bedspread and the turned-down top sheet. At the spare slippers, under the bed. At the nightstand with its glass of water and dish of jewellery. The rings, the Miraculous Medal, the string of beads. Rosary beads. The earring in the shape of a cross. The memorial card.

'I hope you don't mind me saying this, but you seem like a religious person?'

Ruth nods. 'I don't mind at all.'

'So don't you have a duty to truth? I see why you did it, and I'd like to think I'd be brave enough to help a friend like you did. But isn't it time to tell the truth? Now that Robbie's gone and Mary's gone and Lily's safe?'

'Who would it serve? How would it help her? And – this will sound selfish – I've got this far, I don't think I'd like to spend my final years in jail. This room may not look like much, but it's better than a prison cell.' Her eyes twinkle and I can't help smiling.

'Come on. They're not going to put a ninety-three-year-old in jail.'

'Maybe not. But it doesn't serve me or' – she stops – 'or Lily to have the truth come out now.'

'You were going to say her other name, weren't you.'

'It's time to move on, Joanna. Know that Lily was saved by the bravest woman I ever met. That your house is free of black clouds and curses and evil eyes. That Mary only ever had love for Lily, that she did everything she could to protect her. That Lily is safe.'

I stand up and move towards the door. I take one last look around the room – a room that is indeed much nicer than any hypothetical prison cell – and nod at Ruth.

'I'll leave you in peace.'

60

June 2018

I DIDN'T KILL LILY. *Lily is not Lila.*

But I did kill Lila. And for the first time in thirty years, I'm ready to ask questions. If Mary could risk everything for her daughter, I can surely stand up to my mother. It's too late for Lila, but I owe it to her memory to find out the truth.

Cynthia is asleep on the couch when I arrive on Saturday morning, and annoyed at being woken.

'It's eleven a.m.,' I tell her, and she looks surprised. At the time or at my retort, I can't tell. She's not used to retorts.

'The kids need more photos for the family tree project. Could I take some from the tin in your wardrobe – or maybe the whole box?' I chance.

Head tilted, an amused look on her face, she folds her arms. 'I'm not stupid. This isn't for any project. What are you up to?'

The impulse to tell her is so strong. To let it all out, finally.

She shakes her head, a smirk on her dry lips. 'You were a creepy little mouse when you were young, always hovering on the edge. Tiptoeing around everyone, afraid of your own shadow. Afraid to speak up. And you haven't changed a bit, have you. Go on, show a bit of backbone for once. Spill. Why do you want the photos?'

'I'd like to know where she came from. If she was really my sister.'

The smirk disappears.

'Don't you dare bring her up. After what you did? *Don't you dare.*'

'I'm sorry.'

'Sorry? What good is that? You *killed* her.' Her voice goes up a notch. ' "Sorry" doesn't bring her back!'

'I know. But I was ten. A child.'

'What are you trying to say? That it was my fault for leaving you in charge? I had to work!'

This. This has always been her story, and for years, long before Lila came to us, I pictured her working every hour to pay the bills. Not swanning around Rowanbrook, drinking wine and going on picnics. Anger is taking over now, invading the spot where guilt has lived for more than thirty years.

'You can't leave a child in charge of another child! This is like when people blamed Cora O'Brien for what happened to Lily Murphy.' I lock eyes with her. 'Why did Lila look so much like Lily Murphy? Did you have an affair with Robbie Murphy?'

'Ha! No. No, I did not. I've told you who she was. Now, I've had enough of this. Get me a drink and get out of my flat.'

I stand my ground. 'Yes, you've told me who she was but I don't believe you any more. She looks like Lily, and I know you were in Rowanbrook in the eighties. Did you sleep with Robbie?'

She shakes her head. 'Look at your prissy face, judging me. Holier than thou, Joanna Kirk, who never put a foot wrong.' She leans forward, warming to her theme. 'You know that people don't actually like spending time with someone who thinks they're better than everyone, don't you? You know that's why you had no friends growing up – because you're a judgemental prig.'

'Oh, for God's sake, I don't care who you slept with. I'm not judging you – I'm just asking if you slept with Robbie Murphy.'

'No, I didn't. Now get out, I've had enough of your patronizing for today.'

'Fine. I'm going to the police.'

She laughs, a harsh sound that turns into a cough, and lights a cigarette.

'And what exactly are you going to tell the police?'

'That you left a ten-year-old in charge of a four-year-old. That I was put in a position where I had to administer what turned out to be lethal medication. That's negligence.' I've never said these words out loud, never even consciously thought them until now, and it feels good.

Her eyes flicker as blue smoke circles slowly to the nicotine-stained ceiling.

'I mean it. I'll go to the police. You had me terrified I'd go to some kind of detention centre; be taken away from you. It's *you* who'd have been in trouble though, isn't it? For leaving me home alone for days at a time. For locking her in. Why was she locked in?'

A blink, but no reply.

'Fine. I'm going down to Blackrock Garda Station. There are two gardaí there I've got to know pretty well in the last few days – they'll be very interested to hear what you were doing.'

I turn and put my hand on the door handle.

'Stop.'

I face her again.

'Sit.'

The armchair is dusty and there's a food stain on the cushion but this barely registers. The truth is coming.

She fills a dirty glass from the whiskey bottle by the couch and takes a long swallow.

'Lila wasn't mine.'

Oh my God.

'She wasn't your sister. I was asked to mind her. Just for a few weeks. Then weeks became months and then – well, you know what happened. You ended it.' A barked, cold laugh. 'That was the end of the money too.'

Jesus Christ. 'You did this for money? But who was she? And why were you asked to mind her?'

She shakes her head and zips her lips.

'No, that's all you get. I signed a non-disclosure agreement. If I give any details about her parents, I'll have to return all the money and I don't have it.'

'You can't be serious. It was thirty years ago! Who's going to come looking for money from you now? You're utterly deluded,' I add, and on some level, I enjoy the surprise on her face.

She shakes her head. 'I'm not taking any chances.'

'Can I see a copy of the agreement?'

'I don't have one. There was just the original and' – she pauses – 'the mother took it with her.'

'But what kind of mother gives up her child?' *Is that any worse than a mother who leaves her child alone, neglected?*

'Oh, you'd be surprised. That woman. She really thought she was something. With her money and her clothes and her accent. Looking down on me because I didn't have a husband and a big house like she did.' She takes a deep drag of her cigarette. 'She thought she was so glamorous, with her long nails and her long hair and those stupid black cigarettes she smoked. Bitch. Served her right, what happened.' She smiles.

Black cigarettes. Cora's words come back to me. *Those disgusting black cigarillos of hers.*

And suddenly, it all makes sense.

61

June 2018

'INES O'BRIEN.'

This wipes the smile from her face.

'What do you know about Ines O'Brien?'

'Her daughter Cora mentioned she smoked cigarillos. "Her money and her clothes and her accent" you said – Ines O'Brien was Lila's mother?'

Cynthia is sitting up straight now, her mouth moving to form a response.

'Mother,' I say, the dynamics shifting, 'for the love of God, they're all dead. There's nobody coming for your money. So, as you put it so eloquently yourself – spill.'

She lies back against the couch, the fight gone out of her. At least momentarily.

'OK,' I say, 'let's start with an easy question – why did Ines O'Brien give you her child?' Something flickers in my memory then. 'Wait – are you sure you have the story right? I thought she couldn't have any more children after Cora?'

'It was her husband who couldn't have more kids.'

'Victor?'

'Yes. They did all these tests, and it turned out he had fertility problems. He broke down one night in the bar and told Tom

Stedman that they couldn't have any more children. Sloshed when he said it. Realized too late that he hadn't really intended to tell the world about his infertility.' She reaches for her cigarette packet and taps another one out. 'He backtracked then and told Tom it was Ines who couldn't have any more children. That ridiculous man – thought people would pity him and couldn't hack being anything other than this successful, virile businessman. Anyway, word went around – soon everyone in Rowanbrook knew that Ines couldn't have any more children.'

'And Ines wasn't tempted to set the record straight?'

Cynthia shrugs, lighting her fresh cigarette from the tip of her last one. 'As long as she could come and go as she pleased and live off Victor's money, he could say whatever he wanted.'

'And then Ines got pregnant?'

'Yes. An affair. Awkward, right?' She smiles and her meanness shines. 'Whatever the rest of Rowanbrook might have thought, she certainly couldn't let her infertile husband find out she was up the duff.'

'And Robbie was the father? That's why Lila looked so like Lily?'

'Yes. He never knew though. The affair was long over by the time she realized she was pregnant – she was so far gone, going to Liverpool wasn't an option.'

Going to Liverpool. Cynthia loved using that one on me. *I should have gone to Liverpool for an abortion.*

'But surely people spotted she was pregnant?'

'No.' A long drag before she elaborates. 'By the time she started to show, she'd gone to Spain to visit her mother. She stayed long enough to have the baby, then left her there.'

'What?'

'She left her with her mother in Spain. She didn't want to raise her, couldn't let Victor find out – they were sleeping in separate bedrooms but that wouldn't have stopped him throwing her out if he knew.'

'Jesus.' I'm trying to imagine leaving one of my children with someone else to raise.

'It's no different to adoption,' Cynthia says, reading my mind. 'Don't be so fucking judgemental.'

This, from the woman who locked a small child in a bedroom, and left an only slightly older child alone for hours on end.

'But how did Lila end up with you?' I use her name deliberately this time, testing new boundaries. She doesn't flinch.

'The grandmother – Ines's mother – she got sick. She died in 1985 – just before Lily Murphy disappeared, I think. I remember I was minding Cora that day, during the search. Ines had flown to Spain that morning for the funeral.'

'And to bring Lila back?'

A nod. 'There was nobody there to look after her any more. And even Ines wasn't cold enough to abandon her child with no one to take care of her.'

'How nice of her. And how did she end up with you?'

'Ines was used to me, I suppose. Knew how good I was with kids.'

This makes me laugh and Cynthia has the nerve to look hurt.

'I was good at my job. I was fun. Not like those po-faced mothers who never let their kids do anything.' A mean smile slides across her face. 'I bet that's what you're like. Overprotective and overbearing. Needy? Neurotic? I'm right, aren't I? But kids *liked* me and Ines knew that.'

Give me strength.

'She just *gave* you her child?'

'Well, no – we agreed it in advance, obviously, and it was temporary. She came home when her mother was sick, and took me aside at a garden party at the Murphys'. Laid it all out, how much she'd pay, what she'd need from me, mentioned Lila's diabetes and so on. It was only supposed to be for a few weeks, and the pay was very good.' She taps ash on to a filthy saucer. 'Like, *very* good. I was what you might call an off-site babysitter? But weeks turned into months, and Ines never found a more permanent solution. And she couldn't risk Victor finding out. Divorce wasn't legal yet here but it wouldn't have stopped him cutting her off.'

'So he knew nothing?'

'Not then. He found out just before he died. Lila was dead by then.'

There isn't an ounce of emotion when she says it. All these years, she hasn't let me so much as say her name – too traumatic, too painful – and now, just like that: *Lila was dead by then.*

'Did Ines visit? I don't remember seeing anyone here . . .'

'No, never. I had to give her updates; how Lila was doing, with her health issues, and so on.'

Health issues. What a neat term.

'Wasn't she worried about the diabetes?'

'No. I was managing it.' She stubs out her cigarette and takes a long slug of whiskey. 'Until you messed up.'

'I was ten!'

'Don't get all stroppy about it now. What you did ruined everything – it was the end of the money.'

'Are you for real?'

'Joanna, she wasn't my child. It was a business transaction. A long-term babysitting arrangement. And when you gave her that insulin, you cut off our income.'

'Jesus Christ. How can you say that? A child died!'

'Oh, believe me, I know it.' She lifts the glass to her lips again, and pauses. 'You know, on some level, I think Ines was relieved. So maybe you did her a favour.'

62

June 2018

I'M GOING THROUGH THE motions.

Up. Breakfast. School drop. Smile.

Inside, I can think of nothing but Lila. Not Lily, Lily's OK – wherever she is – but Lila. Left to the monster that is my mother, a woman who thought it perfectly fine to leave a ten-year-old in charge of a four-year-old. A woman who had no compunction about reminding me, over and over, that I'd killed my sister. I wondered, on Saturday night and all day yesterday, if that changes anything – is it any less awful now that I know she wasn't my sister? It's not. Somehow it's worse. She wasn't even born into our family, and irrational though it is, that makes it seem more unfair. What chance did she have with someone as inept as Cynthia Kirk looking after her? Cynthia Kirk, and me. *How could Ines do it?* I think, as I wave Ben off in the school yard. Smiling and waving, like my world hasn't been turned upside down, yet again.

Liz Landry sees me from across the yard and raises her hand in a gesture that means *hang on*. As she approaches, neat in her work dress and heels, I can see there's something wrong.

'Hey, what's up?'

'I was wondering if you heard anything more about Cora?' A

304

strand of hair has caught in the chain around her neck and she works to undo it, frowning. 'About what happened to her?'

'No, why?'

She lowers her voice. 'Adana was telling me she heard they're saying it was suicide.'

My throat tightens. 'Oh God. Who's "they"? The police?'

'No, not the police. It's just word that's going round. People who were in the DART station that morning, saying it was busy but there was no "surge" when the train arrived. That it was just Cora. That she must have jumped.'

'Oh no.' I think I'm going to cry now, right here in the middle of the school yard.

'I can't stop thinking about it,' Liz is saying, 'wondering if there was something I could have spotted.'

'Me too. God. Liz, I was asking her all sorts of questions about Lily and about her dad.' I swallow. 'Do you think . . .'

She puts her hand on my arm. 'Stop. There's no *way* that was it.'

We both know she's just being nice. There's no way to know that wasn't it either.

I dial the number. I can't believe I'm doing this but I need to know. Someone puts me through to DS McCarthy and I ask outright if it was suicide.

'We can't discuss that, I'm afraid.'

'Please. I was one of the last people to talk to her, as far as I know. If I said something that caused her to . . .' Jesus Christ. Another death on my conscience.

'I'm sorry, Mrs Stedman. We're investigating and there'll be an inquest, but I can't share anything with you right now. You'll have to wait.'

'Please.'

A pause.

'Look, I can tell you one thing if it helps – you weren't the last person she spoke to.'

'I know that – I know she saw Liz Landry later on Thursday but only very briefly, and I can't stop thinking—'

'There was someone else too. That's all I can say.'

Adana calls by on Monday afternoon, and I'm still on autopilot. Brewing. Chatting. Nodding. Smiling. Adana's my oldest friend, my best friend, but where do you even start?

My childhood is a fiction.

I never lived in London.

There was no fire.

My parents didn't die.

My mother is a monster.

I killed a child.

'Another coffee?' is what I say instead.

'Sure. Are you feeling any more settled in the house since you met the Deep Dive blogger person?' she asks.

Ellen. That seems like a million years ago.

'A bit. Though it's horrible to think of Gavin locking Lily in that room.' And good to know she was rescued, but I'll keep that secret.

'Poor little thing. I wonder will they ever find her body. Everyone deserves a grave. A headstone. A cross. Some kind of marking.'

I sit up straighter.

'What is it?'

I'm not sure. Something in what she just said . . . A *headstone.* A *cross.* But it's slipping away again.

I shake my head. And smile. And go through the motions.

63

June 2018

TUESDAY NIGHT. VISITING HOUR. But it's a whole different world now, knowing what I know. Cynthia is unperturbed. Draped in her usual spot on the sofa, drink lolling in her hand.

'I have more questions,' I tell her, sitting opposite.

'I'm not promising anything. Make me a drink first.'

I do and she takes a deep swallow before indicating I can go ahead.

'Why did you lock her in the room?'

She looks at me as if I'm stupid. 'It was just easier. She was only four. What if she'd got out? Cut herself on something or got through the front door and into traffic?'

'You cared enough to keep her safe from traffic but not enough to question the ethics of what you were doing?'

Her eyes widen slightly at the unfamiliar tone. 'Get over yourself, Little Miss Perfect. I was paid to look after a child, and that's exactly what I did. There's nothing illegal about it.'

I have no idea if that's true or not, but part of me wonders if she's right. We pay people to mind our children when we're at work or out at night – who's to say there's anything unlawful about a longer-term arrangement? But the on-paper version of

307

the story doesn't mesh well with the stark reality – a child locked in a room, starved of daylight and friends and school.

'She was well looked after and you know it,' Cynthia adds. 'There was always good food.'

This is true. During the months Lila was here, there was money, and there was food. I don't know why I never made that connection before. Payment for minding her. Hiding her away.

'Next question – where is she buried? Why wasn't I allowed to go to her funeral?'

'Make me another drink.'

Suppressing a sigh, I bring the bottle in from the kitchen and fill her glass to the brim with the cheap supermarket whiskey.

It's two-thirds gone before she answers, and when she does, it isn't an answer at all.

'She's buried somewhere safe.'

'Where though? I'd . . . I'd like to visit her grave. You never let me.' The plaintive tone of my voice grates on me but I can't help it.

'You can't visit. Anyway, she wasn't your sister, so let it go.'

Dismissed earlier than usual, I'm letting myself out of the door of her flat when I pause outside the bedroom. Lila's bedroom. I haven't been in there since the night she died – Cynthia kept it locked even after Lila was gone. Can I bring myself to go in there now? Cynthia is almost but not quite asleep on the couch. This is as good a chance as I'll get.

The handle turns easily. The door is stiff at first, but one gentle push is enough to get me quietly inside. The room is dark and musty and full of dust. It looks untouched. As though nobody has cleaned it in thirty years. A cough lurches in my throat and I swallow it back as I make my way across to the bed. Yellowing sheets and a brown coverlet, stenched with the passage of three decades. Had she even washed them after Lila died? The sheets are crumpled, the coverlet pulled to one side. Maybe she hadn't. On the floor beside the bed lies an empty glass, the water long gone. Bits of paper. Sweet wrappers. Medicinal sugar for when she was low. Notebooks; some mine, some Lila's. Her still-baby letters drawn so carefully. My attempts at playing teacher. A hairbrush. An illustrated copy of *Charlotte's Web*. Tears rear up as I remember reading it to her. Beside the book is a vial and syringe and this is the sight that overwhelms me. Before I know what's happening, I'm kneeling on the floor, sobbing. Quiet, gulping sobs for the little girl who died. And the other little girl, who didn't mean to kill her. I pick up the vial of insulin. The vial that once contained insulin – there's nothing in it now. How can one liquid be so necessary for survival and so lethal? I think back to the daily injections I'd seen my mother give. Three times every day, once before each meal. At least at first. As time went by, she didn't always think of it. Sometimes she was too busy injecting herself with whatever her various dealers supplied that week. And sometimes she wasn't here at all. I remember asking her about it. Why did Lila need insulin? For her blood sugar, my mother said. Is it medicine? Is she sick? I'd asked. A sigh. Yes, it's medicine, yes, she's sick. Now stop with all the questions.

I remember the times Lila's blood sugar was low. Now, I know it's called hypoglycaemia, but I didn't have that word when I was ten. I just knew it was dangerous. And now, I know that low blood sugar requires glucose to bring the levels back up, but I didn't know that back then either. Back when I was ten, and left in charge of a child. Back when her blood sugar fell one night, while Cynthia was out. Out at a party or out with a man. I don't remember. I just remember panicking. Lila was low and my mother out. Low blood sugar was dangerous, Lila was ill. She needed her medicine. I'd seen Cynthia do it a hundred times by then. Could I manage it? I filled the syringe, just as she always did. How many units she needed, I had no idea; I just knew I had to do something to save her. I injected her stomach, exactly as Cynthia always did. And I waited. Waited for her to come back. Only she never did.

My mother screamed when she arrived home. Then she grabbed me by the shoulders and shook me till my teeth rattled.

'Jesus Christ, Joanna, what did you do?'

'Her blood sugar was low so I gave her the medicine . . .'

'You gave her insulin when her blood sugar was low? Insulin brings it even lower! You stupid, stupid fucking idiot girl, what have you done? You've killed her!'

The words that have reverberated around my head for more than thirty years. *You've killed her.*

I'm sitting on the floor now, oblivious to the smell, leaning my head against the mattress. Lila deserved so much more than this room in her short life. And the way it's been left, abandoned for thirty years, unwashed and unclean, is an insult to her. That night, Cynthia ranted and railed at me for what I did; told me I'd ruined her life, ruined everything. And yet, she couldn't even clean the room. I should never have been left in charge of a small child. Yes, it was my fault; yes, I injected the insulin; but no, I shouldn't have been minding a four-year-old. I shouldn't have been administering medicine or insulin or anything at all. I was ten. I was ten years old and for the first time since that night, I can accept that it wasn't my fault.

Angry now, I stand and pull off the covers, rolling them into a ball. What kind of woman lives for thirty years with an unmade death bed in her home? I pull the pillow off the bed, stripping its cover. The mattress, bare now, is stained in patches, dusty and mouldy. I lift that too, and shove it to the far side of the bed. For three decades, I've felt only guilt and sadness. Now I'm furious.

'What are you doing?'

She's standing in the doorway, wide awake now.

'You couldn't even clean the room? You just locked the door and walked away?'

'Oh, don't be such a drama queen. What difference does it make?'

'What difference? My sister died here!'

'She wasn't your sister.'

'For fuck's sake! That doesn't change anything! You left me in charge of a child when I was just a child myself. How could you do that?'

'How was I to know you'd inject her? I never told you to do that.'

'I panicked. I was on my own and she was having a hypo. I thought I was doing the right thing. I was ten! And you blamed me.'

'Who else was to blame?' A shrug.

'You! You were to blame. Just as much as I was. You were the adult! I've spent all this time dealing with the fact that I killed my sister and never once did you try to help me or share the blame.' I'm crying now. Angry, frustrated, long-held tears.

Something softens in her eyes. 'Come on out of here, this room stinks.' She reaches for me. 'Come, I'll get you a drink.'

I don't accept her hand or touch her, but I follow her to the living room and sit on the armchair again. She hands me a whiskey in an almost-clean glass.

'I don't drink whiskey.'

'It'll help.'

To my surprise, I knock back half of it in one go and it does help. I want to be numb. I want oblivion. Cynthia sits on the couch, but perched at the edge now, hands clasped on her knees, waiting for my questions.

'Why wasn't I taken off you?' I ask. 'Surely it was negligence that a child died in your care?'

'Ines sorted it.'

'How?'

'She felt that it would be . . . complicated to report the death. Because the birth hadn't been registered here.'

'What?'

'She brought Lila home from Spain and I took over her care pretty much immediately. There was no need to register the birth here. I'm not sure it even struck Ines to do it. But it would have made registering the death complicated. And explaining why Lila was here and not with her.'

'Oh, what happened to "it's just a babysitting service"?'

She shrugs. 'It wasn't against the law. But it might have been hard to explain if people found out.'

'You don't say.' I take another sip of whiskey. 'What do you mean she "sorted it"?'

'She arranged the burial. We did it on private property.'

'Hold on, so there was no funeral? She's not in a cemetery?'

'Exactly.'

'Jesus Christ. It's like she never existed. Where's she buried?'

'In Rowanbrook. In Ines O'Brien's garden.'

My legs are unsteady when I make my way across the hall outside her flat. I shouldn't have had the whiskey; now I have to drive home. Shit. I can't think straight. Lila, buried in Cora's garden. Lila with no headstone, no cross, no name. Like she never existed. I'm trying to open the main door, but I can't find the right button and now I'm rattling the handle as though that will help. I don't notice the woman opening her door until she speaks.

'Are you OK? You look ill?'

'I'm fine, thanks, just need some fresh air.'

'I heard the rattling and thought it was the other woman back again.'

'Sorry, I couldn't find the button, though I've been here a thousand times.'

'You're Cynthia's daughter?'

'No. I'm not.' It doesn't even feel like a lie now.

'The other woman was in a right state. I'm glad it's not her again. Maybe *she* was the daughter.'

'What other woman?'

'A week or two ago, on a Thursday evening. Some woman banging on the door like a lunatic. Cynthia didn't open it for ages, I was going to call the police. Then finally, she let her in.'

'This woman – what did she look like?'

'She was short, shorter than you, I see that now. Curly hair, like a bird's nest. And wearing a green denim jacket.'

I let go of the front door handle and turn back to Cynthia's flat.

64

June 2018

'WHY WAS CORA O'BRIEN here?'

'I have no idea what you're talking about. I have a headache now and it's time you left. Again.'

'Don't lie to me.' I step closer and the smell of whiskey on her breath turns my stomach. 'I know it was her. Your neighbour just described her to a tee.'

'Oh, for God's sake. Always the drama queen. Fine. Sit.'

I do. Again.

'It's your fault,' she starts, and though I have no idea what she means, I'm not surprised. It is somehow always my fault. 'You started asking her those questions. If Lily had a nickname or any kind of illness.'

'But Cora said she didn't know the answer to those questions.'

'She didn't. But it reminded her of a fight she'd heard between her parents, the night her father died. She was quite the eavesdropper, Cora. Always listening in on extension phones or hovering outside doors. Never a good idea.'

'What did she hear?'

'She told me she heard Victor say to Ines, "How could you do that to your own child." It stuck with her because she had never heard her dad speak up for her before. I think she was quite pleased.'

'OK. And?'

'It was Ines's reply that confused her. Ines apparently said, "Lila was well looked after by Cynthia." Cora couldn't understand why her mother used the name "Lila", she said. Her mother was cold and absent, but she certainly wouldn't have forgotten her own daughter's name. So it stayed with Cora all these years; a name that made no sense but didn't matter in the bigger scheme of things. The main thing for her was that her dad had stood up for her, just hours before he died.'

'So Victor must have found out about Lila? And her death?'

'He wasn't supposed to be there. Ines had planned the burial for a night he was due to be away, checking on a factory down in Limerick. But there was a huge storm forecast, and he turned back. No mobile phones then – people didn't text to say they were on their way. So suddenly, there he was. Standing on the patio. And there we were, filling in her grave.'

'I think I'm going to be sick.'

'Is it the whiskey? It's not the best brand . . .'

No, it's not the whiskey. Christ.

'It all came out then. There was no way to hide her body from him, and any explanation we could have conjured up was worse than the truth, to be honest. So Ines told him everything. He drank half a bottle of vodka, told her to be gone by morning, got into his car, and that was that.'

'He drove off a bridge.'

She shrugs. 'Honestly, I don't know if it was the vodka or the storm. Roofs blew off houses that night, trees down everywhere. It might just have been the storm.'

'Or it might have been the discovery that his wife was a monster.' The words slur slightly.

'Oh Joanna, have another drink and get over yourself.'

She gets up to go into the kitchen for another bottle. The clattering of glass and the opening and closing of cupboards lulls me into a stupor and seems to go on for a lot longer than it should. Maybe she doesn't want to tell me any more. When she eventually arrives with a fresh bottle, I shake my head but accept the drink anyway.

'Tell me the rest.'

'I'm sure you can work it out – when you asked Cora if she'd ever heard Lily called "Lila", it rang a bell. She remembered her mother saying, "Lila was well looked after by Cynthia," and wondered if this was all tied up with Lily's disappearance. She was adamant she wanted to prove her father's innocence.'

'How did she find you?'

'Easy, unfortunately. Google "Cynthia Kirk" and my address is there in the reports on my court appearances.' She shakes her head. 'There she was, banging on my door till I gave in and opened it. Little Cora O'Brien, all grown up, demanding answers.'

'And?'

'She laid it all out – your questions, the overheard conversation between her parents – and then she accused me of kidnapping Lily Murphy.' A laugh. 'What the fuck would I want with kidnapping a child?'

'So what did you tell her?'

'That she was wrong. That Lila was someone else. I didn't tell her Lila was her sister.' A self-satisfied nod. 'She was adamant though. Kept insisting she knew I'd done something, that she was going to the police. I got worried then. I don't know how these things work – statute of limitations or whatever. I could still get done for Lila's death, even though it was technically you. And the illegal burial. Or even taking Lila, since I have no way to prove it was agreed with Ines.' She pauses and smiles. 'Also, Cora was bugging the shit out of me. I had enough.'

'What do you mean?'

'I followed her on Friday morning. I wasn't quite sure what I was going to do, but it was ridiculously easy in the end. Those train station platforms get so crowded at rush hour. A well-timed shove was all it took. Nobody was going to suspect the nice lady with the dreamy smile and the hippie hair.'

I'm crying now, tears choking my throat and running down my face. Crying for all of it: Lila who deserved so much more than she got, Cora who was trying to fix the past, and me – thirty years of blaming myself. Cynthia slips off the couch and kneels in front of me, arms outstretched. She's a reptile, a monster, a snake. I don't want her arms around me. But the lost child in me takes over, and I don't resist.

The sting is so light, I almost don't feel it. Almost.

65

June 2018

'WHAT DID YOU DO?' I'm rubbing my shoulder and the sting is gone now, but whatever she put in me is not. 'Cynthia, what was that?'

'It won't hurt, baby. Shush now.' She wraps her arms tighter around me, pulling me gently on to the floor. 'You'll see. You'll just feel blissfully happy and then float away. I promise.'

'Cynthia.' I try pushing her off me. 'What have you done?'

'Shh. Just go to sleep and it'll all be over.' She's rocking me and I'm struggling to unlatch her arms, to shove her off, but I can't. My head is light and dizzy and my breathing feels too slow and I'm so, so tired. Why is she so strong and why can't I get her off me? Why can't I move?

I know why. The sting in my arm, the drug in my veins. Dizzy and dark and light and hot and cold and so, so sad. Oh my God. I'll never see them again. Emily and Ben and Sophie and Mark. The only family I have, the only ones who matter. They don't know about this, about her. They don't know she exists. They won't know I'm here. They'll think I just disappeared. Like Lily. Like Lila. I try again to push her off but there is nothing left. Only black.

*

And all around, on Tuesday night, life in Rowanbrook continues, its residents oblivious. In Number 6 Rowanbrook Drive, Ben and Emily retreat to the den to watch YouTube. Sophie brushes her teeth without being asked, and instructs Mark to send a message to Joanna to tell her the news. Mark is finishing a work email and wondering if Joanna will be back from therapy soon – they might have time for an episode of the series with the subtitles. He looks at his watch. She's running late. He lines up the show and presses pause. He'll wait.

Next door, Fran is standing at her wardrobe choosing an outfit for Cora's funeral. Something colourful. Fran doesn't like black. For the hundredth time this week, she thinks back to what she and Della did, reporting Cora. Was it the right thing to do? They thought so at the time. But then Victor took the fall. And nothing came of what they said about Cora. All the better, she thinks now in hindsight. Whatever they thought they saw back then, Cora was only eight.

Over in Oakbrook, Susie, too, is choosing a dress for the funeral. Her second-favourite black funeral dress is laid out on the bed and she's hunting for patent heels. Is Joanna going to the funeral, she wonders. Perhaps they can go together. She picks up her phone to call Joanna but it rings out. She must be still at therapy. Some might say it's a bit of an indulgence, all this therapy . . . especially at those prices. But anyway, that's none of Susie's business, she thinks, as she finally locates her shoes.

DS McCarthy stares at the computer screen. Her routine background check on Joanna Stedman just got interesting. Joanna Stedman née Joanna Kirk. McCarthy sits back, thinking. Kirk is Joanna's maiden name, and the woman who was referenced in

Cora's notebook is Cynthia Kirk. *Kirk.* Not an extraordinarily unusual name in Ireland, but not at all common. She waves at Walsh to come over to her desk. They'd called to Cynthia Kirk's flat on Saturday, explaining that her name and address were in Cora's notebook. Cynthia denied that Cora had contacted her; said she had no idea what they were talking about. And there was nothing they could do – an address in Cora's notebook wasn't enough. But the surnames are the same. That can't be a coincidence. Walsh is making his way to her desk. McCarthy picks up her keys and gestures for him to follow. Time to chat to Cynthia Kirk again.

66

June 2018

WHEN I WAKE, THE black is gone. Now it's white. Everything is white. Bright lights and a smell that tells me it will be OK. A hospital smell. A nurse calling a doctor. Checks and muttered words and reassuring nods. It's going to be OK. I go back to sleep.

The next time I wake, Mark is there, holding my hand. I can't talk at first, I'm crying too much, trying to ask to see the kids, but choked with tears. He's shushing me, promising he'll bring them soon. What day is it? It's Thursday, he says, I've been here since Tuesday night. An overdose of OxyContin; crushed and dissolved and injected by the woman who gave birth to me.

It takes a while to understand what happened, to piece it all together from what Mark tells me. The police had found Cynthia's address in Cora's notebook, along with the notes she made on my questions. Cynthia's denial that Cora had called could not be disproved: CCTV showed that Cora had gone to the building and gone through the main door but not where she'd been beyond that. Maybe Cora had called when she was out, Cynthia had said. She knew nothing about this Cora person. Sorry she couldn't be of more help.

It might have been left at that, but when I phoned DS McCarthy on Monday, worried about suicide, she logged my call, and on Tuesday, she decided to do some digging into my background. It felt a little odd when Mark told me that – imagining a police detective looking into me. But a good thing she did, because apparently, on Tuesday night, she discovered my maiden name was Kirk, and linked me with Cynthia. She and Walsh went back to Cynthia's apartment but nobody answered their repeated knocks. The neighbour had been *very* cross this time, according to Mark, and had come out to have a word with the two gardaí. She was adamant that a woman had been rattling the front door and had gone back into Cynthia's flat not fifteen minutes earlier. Nobody had left since, she told them, there were definitely two people inside. Maybe Cynthia was in trouble? the neighbour speculated.

Not Cynthia though. Me. Lying on the floor, dying in her arms.

McCarthy and Walsh kept knocking and eventually broke through the door. There we were on the dirty carpet. Me unconscious, Cynthia calmly rubbing my hair. McCarthy called an ambulance, and a paramedic with a syringe of something called Naloxone saved my life. I need to thank the woman next door. And McCarthy and Walsh. And the paramedic. And I need to see my babies. But God, poor Cora. Trying to clear her father's name. And Lila. Lila who did nothing at all.

Mark, understandably, wants to know what I was doing there. Why I lied about going to a fictional Dr Kinsella all these years. Who this woman Cynthia is. Why she injected me with a lethal dose of painkillers. It is the longest story in the world, the one I've never been able to tell him, but now I'm lying in a hospital bed, and we have all day. I start at the beginning, dismantling the fiction, filling in facts. He is baffled and hurt and can't understand why I made it all up. Invented a tragedy. A fire. The made-up parents and their made-up deaths. Because it was better, I tell him. Even a tragic fire was better than the truth of my childhood: the mother who didn't care, the girl whose death I caused. He still doesn't get it, but Mark was brought up in a safe and happy house. He's never had to invent anything at all. And now he's bruised. Betrayed. I understand that. We talk and we talk and we talk. We work out what to tell the kids and what to keep to ourselves. He's hurt. Curt at times. And sometimes, the way he looks at me, I wonder if he'll ever really trust me again. But we hold hands even as he struggles to understand. He's still there for me.

'They found her burial site,' he tells me on Saturday. 'Right where you said, in the garden of the O'Brien house. It looked like a flower bed.'

And although I knew she died that night long ago, it hits me all over again. Even with Cynthia arrested and Lily alive, there is no happy ending. Not for Lila. She was betrayed by everyone around her.

'Her death is unacceptable,' I say to Mark through fresh tears. 'She was a vulnerable, defenceless child.'

'So were you,' he says, squeezing my hand. 'You were ten. You were trying to save her. You have to forgive yourself. It was an accident. A horrible, horrible accident.'

I don't know if I can forgive myself, but I *can* accept that Cynthia should never have put me in that position. And maybe that's a start.

'She'll get a proper burial now,' Mark says.

I nod, remembering Adana's words. *Everyone deserves a grave. A headstone. A cross.* That's when I realize what's been niggling at me. And now I have the last piece of the puzzle.

I know where Lily is.

67

June 2018

IT'S OVERCAST OUTSIDE AND the nursing home room is cooler this evening. Ruth is in her chair by the window, and pleased, I think, to see me. Though she is soon horrified by the story I tell her, about Cynthia, and Lila who was not Lily.

'Mrs Cavanagh, I wanted to ask you something else – why do you have just one earring?'

'Pardon?'

'The earring shaped like a cross, the one on your nightstand – there's just one. Why not a pair?'

'What an odd question!' Ruth says, but her eyes are darting now, between the nightstand and me.

'And, I hope you won't mind me saying this, but' – I pick up the earring, 'a rose-gold cross with embedded crystals doesn't seem quite the thing for a lady of your vintage? No offence.'

'None taken. I'm a woman of eclectic tastes. As I said to you last time, you can get away with all sorts when you're ninety-three.'

'It's an unusual earring though. And I've seen it before. But on someone else.'

Ruth looks caught off guard but recovers quickly, shakes her head and looks back down at her book.

I turn the earring over in my palm. 'I'm pretty sure about this actually. It belongs to a woman called Liz. Liz Landry?'

Now Ruth's head jerks up and it's written all over her face.

'Am I right?'

'How do you know Liz?' Ruth asks, giving nothing and everything away.

'She lives in Rowanbrook and her kids go to the same school as mine. But you must know that she lives there, right?'

A pause. A long pause, as Ruth stares, and I can almost see the battle going on inside her head. Eventually she sighs.

'Sit.'

I do as I'm told.

Ruth places the book back on the windowsill and clasps her hands together on her lap. It feels like a long time passes before she speaks. I can hear everything – every tick of the clock on the wall, every rustle of leaves outside the window, each time the evening breeze picks up. But I say nothing, resisting the urge to fill the silence. Eventually, Ruth begins the final part of her story.

'Mary chose her mother's name, Elizabeth, for Lily, when she moved out of my house and they started a new life away from Rowanbrook. It was also Lily's middle name. Evolving from "Lily" to "Lizzie" wasn't too difficult when she was three, and then as she got older, she became Liz. Mary reverted to her maiden name after Robbie died and started calling herself Mary-Ann, which was her birth name and on her passport. So, Mary Murphy was Mary-Ann Holborn, and Lilian Elizabeth Murphy became Lizzy Holborn, who then married and became Liz Landry.'

'And Mary stayed in Ireland all that time? Didn't she want to get further away? Back home to the US?'

'She couldn't risk flying. It was easier to get passports back then, and children flew on their parents' passports, but even still, she was terrified they'd be caught. So she stayed here. For Lizzie.'

'And you were the only one who knew who they really were?'

Ruth nods. 'Mary never told a soul. Oh, now, she built a good life for the two of them; they had friends, they had a house, it was all very normal, don't worry.'

'And they had you.'

'Yes.'

'Where did they live?'

'I thought she should go down the country, live in the middle of nowhere, away from prying eyes. But Mary's from California, and she always said cities are the best place to be anonymous. The easiest place to hide.'

'So, they stayed here in Dublin?'

'They did. I thought she was mad, but she proved me wrong. To begin with, they moved to a convent in North Dublin; an order I knew from my time teaching. They lived with the nuns for a few years, keeping their heads down, then they lived in Marino, not far from the city centre. In a huge but perfectly nice, normal housing estate where people are friendly but leave each other in peace. Mary said she was a "single mom" who'd split from her husband in Canada and was starting a new life here. Nobody ever questioned it. Lizzie was older by then; her hair had grown longer and much darker, light brown instead of blonde. I still thought people would recognize her, but over time I began to relax.'

'But what about the media? The police?'

'None of the journalists ever found her – the years in the convent were enough to break all links between Mary Murphy and Mary-Ann Holborn. Word went around that she'd moved back to the States, and over time, that became the accepted story.'

'But surely the police had to stay in touch with her?'

'They did. They gave her updates every now and then, or rather, news that there was no news. But she always called to the station to meet with them. They never saw her house, never saw Lizzie. They believed Lily had drowned and that Mary was a grieving mother – they had no reason to think she'd taken her own child.'

'So you were the only one who knew.'

'Yes, and during the early years, I was terrified they'd be caught. But they moved house twice after they left the convent, and by the time Lizzie started secondary school out in Swords, even I had to admit nobody would ever guess that tall, athletic, cheeky, dark-haired Liz Holborn was really little blonde Lily Murphy.' Ruth smiles and there's such fondness in it, I find I'm welling up.

'Little blonde Lily Murphy, missing, presumed drowned.' The words are out of my mouth before I can stop myself, and I regret them immediately.

'Yes. Well. It wasn't perfect. I can't pretend I was comfortable knowing people were still searching, gardaí wasting time. But we couldn't risk telling anyone. Mary might have gone to jail. I could have handled prison, I had no children or husband to worry about. But she needed to be here for Lizzie. So we stuck to the plan.'

'And you saw them over the years?'

'Oh yes. I used to call to them regularly, it was the highlight of my week. Always in their house, of course. They never came back to Rowanbrook.'

'Well, until Liz moved there. Jesus. You must have got a shock when that happened?'

Ruth laughs softly. 'That's as close as I ever came to having a heart attack.'

I stop for a moment, remembering a conversation with Liz.

'I'd forgotten this, but she told me that when she was starting out as an estate agent, her now-husband was viewing a house in Rowanbrook, and she swapped with a colleague so she could show it to him, because she fancied him. Jeez. What are the chances.'

Ruth looks surprised.

'I think you picked it up wrong. She *did* switch with a colleague. But it was to see the house, not the man. Santa Cruz.'

'Oh. But why?'

Ruth sighs. 'Mary got rid of almost everything when she sold Number Six. Letters, photographs, videos – things she couldn't risk bringing with her in case Lizzie found them. She wouldn't leave them with me, she didn't want there to be any concrete links between us.'

I nod but don't interrupt.

'She was very careful. So meticulous in everything she did, all the hiding and covering up, but when she died and Lizzie went through her old stuff, there was one rogue letter. A letter from one of her cousins back home, addressed to Mary-Ann Holborn in Santa Cruz, Rowanbrook Grove – the house Mary and Robbie lived in before Number Six. Mary named it after her hometown.'

'Ah, of course,' I say, thinking of the framed photograph I found in the attic.

'Yes. Lizzie asked me about it when she found the letter and I was completely caught off guard. What could I say? I remember feeling so flustered, blurting out something about her mother renting there when she was younger. She was baffled, couldn't understand how neither her mother nor I had ever mentioned that we lived in the same place at one point, but then she forgot all about it. Or so I thought.'

'She forgot about it until she saw it was for sale?'

'Exactly. When she realized it was on view that morning, she swapped with her colleague out of sheer curiosity – she wanted to see inside the house her mother had once lived in. A fairly benign event really – it's not like anyone in Rowanbrook was going to see this adult estate agent and think, "There's little Lily Murphy" – but then she fell hook, line and sinker for the man who was viewing the house and what should have been a twenty-minute nose around her mother's old home became something entirely different.'

I nod, remembering now what Liz had said. *You never know when a tiny and slightly sneaky manipulation of a work schedule can change your life.*

'Wow. You must have been anxious when she moved in?'

'I was terrified. Afraid she'd remember something. Afraid someone would spot a resemblance, afraid someone would put the very disjointed pieces together. But nobody did. Until now.'

'Shit. Sorry.'

'Indeed.' Ruth unclasps her hands and sits forward. 'And this is where we need to have a very serious conversation.'

I shrink a little in the chair, suddenly seeing the Ruth Cavanagh who terrified Rowanbrook children back in the day.

'Liz must never find out.'

I swallow.

'Do you understand?'

'But doesn't she have a right to know? Morally? Ethically?'

'Maybe. But right now, she has happy childhood memories of a mother who loved her, a strong woman who brought her up on her own after her husband walked out on her, back in Canada. Does it help Lizzie to know that actually her father was an abusive monster, and that her mother resorted to kidnapping to save her? That her mother endured years of beatings, and that she cut herself off from almost everyone she knew, to give a better life to her daughter?'

I shake my head.

'Believe me, it's not a comfortable thing. Knowing this secret, keeping it from her. It's not right. But it's more right than wrong. And it's the price I pay for what I did. Now it's the price you pay. For all your searching. Can you handle that?'

'I can.'

'And the ghosts are gone. Your house is your own. Your family can enjoy it, *should* enjoy it – make it the happy home it should have been for Mary and for Liz. For Lily, I mean.'

'No, for Liz,' I say softly, my throat tight. 'Lily is gone. Thank you.'

I get up, smile a silent goodbye, and walk out of the room. It's late evening now, and the kids are waiting in their forever house. I'm ready to go home.

68

Six weeks later

'I DON'T GET WHY we're having another housewarming,' Emily says for the hundredth time. Mark and I exchange glances. Mark knows why. I meant it when I told Ruth I'd keep her secret, but spouses are excluded from such promises, I'd decided. Especially spouses from whom too many secrets had been kept already. And Mark won't tell. Now it's *his* turn to play a part: for the kids and for his parents and for everyone else in our lives, he's acting just as he always does. With me, he's wary. Distant, at times, after all the lies. But he's trying to build back trust, and for now, that's all I can ask.

'Because first time round,' I explain to Emily, 'I was obsessing over Lily Murphy's disappearance, and now I'm not. And we've painted the rooms and the house isn't gloomy any more, and that seems like an excuse for a do-over,' I tell her, earning her an eye-roll. But Emily doesn't really mind – parties mean endless bowls of crisps and unobservant parents and unmonitored screen time, so she's happy.

I decided against making jugs of Aperol Spritz this time, and instead, people are helping themselves to bottles of beer from an ice-filled bucket. Mark is flipping burgers on the barbecue, in the company of Liz Landry's husband. Ellen is sitting on her own on the bench at the end of the garden, staring up at the house next door. Her childhood home.

'Happy memories?' I ask, sitting beside her.

'Yes,' Ellen says. 'Actually, yes. I didn't know if I could say that, after everything that happened then and since, but I was happy here.' She turns to me. 'You seem happy too. I just wish we knew what happened to poor Lily.'

I brace myself. I've practised this with Ruth, I have her blessing. But even so, every time I've told the story – to Adana, to Fran, to Susie, and especially to Liz – I've been anxious, afraid of arousing suspicion.

'Well,' I start, 'I did some digging, and found out more. Not the full story, but enough. I found out that Robbie was abusive, and that Mary took Lily.'

Ellen's jaw drops.

'I know. Incredible. She managed to get her back to the States, and though there's no way to trace Lily now, by all accounts she was, and is, happy.'

'Oh my goodness!' Ellen's eyes fill with tears. 'She's alive?'

I nod.

'So she was OK? What Gavin did – he wasn't responsible? She didn't . . . she was OK?'

'Yes. She was OK.' I stop short of pointing out that Gavin *did* lock her in a room and threaten her, even if the outcome wasn't the tragedy Ellen feared.

'How did you find out?'

'I can't really say much . . . but Mary had help from someone who is still alive today and doesn't want to be discovered for what they did. I'm sure you understand the need for keeping all of this confidential, and why I can't say who told me the truth.'

Ellen nods emphatically, though I'm sure she'd love to know more.

'And of course, we don't want the police going looking for Mary and Lily now, so we need to keep all of this to ourselves.'

'Absolutely. I'm just so relieved it wasn't Gavin,' she says, and smiles. 'Thank you, Joanna, for doing everything you did.' She reaches into her bag and pulls out something. 'I wonder if you'd like to take this.' In her hand is a small ceramic lighthouse. 'It doesn't feel right for me to have it, knowing now why Gavin took it, but it would be wrong to throw it away. It should be somewhere safe, with someone else who cared about Mary and Lily's story.'

Nodding, I take the lighthouse. 'I'll keep it safe in their memory, I promise.'

I make my way towards Fran who's standing under a pear tree, chatting to Susie.

'We were just saying, you did a good job with your detective work,' Fran says. 'I can't believe what was happening to Mary right under our noses. That poor woman. And that awful man. God, I remember Zara fancying him. I feel sick thinking about it now.'

'Has Zara been in to see Ruth since?' I ask, wondering if Ruth is keeping up appearances.

'She has, and she told her that Lily is alive. I suppose we'll never know if it was really Ruth's house in that photo. If it was, do you think she knew Mary somehow got Lily away from Robbie?'

I shrug. 'No idea, but I doubt it. They weren't exactly friends, those two.'

'True. So Lily's all grown up and safely in America. That's kind of surreal. Funny, sometimes I'd see people on the street and wonder if it was her.'

'Oh, me too.' I laugh. 'I even wondered – just for a heartbeat – if your god-daughter Saoirse was somehow Lily.'

'Ah, stop. What did you think, that I'd kidnapped her? That I loved babysitting so much, I took the child?'

'I didn't *really* think it, but there was something familiar about Saoirse and I was seeing Lily everywhere. Something about the set of her mouth and the line of her jaw.' *And if Saoirse and Lily are both Robbie's daughters . . .* I shake my head. Fran's going to get annoyed if I go down this route again. 'Anyway, it was just a moment of madness, and all's well that ends well.'

Susie shakes her head. 'I can't believe all these years we thought it was down to that man Eddie Hogan.'

I throw her a warning look.

'Well, he did attack Robbie that night, broke his arm,' she says defensively.

I feel a little bit sorry for Eddie Hogan, wherever he is now, but I don't correct her.

'And it had nothing to do with Victor O'Brien or Cora either,' Fran says. 'I feel bad for them now.'

Me too.

'Goodness, it was never anything to do with Cora,' Susie says, clicking her tongue. 'Why on earth would you think that?'

'It's ancient history now, but I thought I saw her hurt Lily once and my mam said the same.'

'Nonsense.' Susie shakes her head. 'Cora was a little over-enthusiastic at times, that's for sure, but there was never a bit of harm in it. She grew out of it as she got older. Gosh, there's no such thing as a bad child. Nurture might corrupt over time but all humans start out good.'

Fran looks suitably chastised.

'Poor Cora,' Susie continues, with a shake of her head. 'God rest her soul. Did you hear they're saying it was actually murder, not suicide at all?'

I feign shock, mirroring Fran's genuine response. There'll be

334

a trial of course – Cynthia's been charged with Cora's murder and is being investigated for Lila's death. I'll have to talk to the police again too, about my part in it, about what I remember. And when it goes to court, it'll be in the papers. But Mark is still the only person who knows the truth about my upbringing, and I'm hoping nobody I know will connect me to Cynthia. Secrets are bad for the soul, but some truths are too much.

'Anyway, good that Victor O'Brien and even that bull of a man, Eddie Hogan, are officially exonerated after all these years.' Susie raises a glass.

I raise mine though it's not at all official, since neither Ruth nor I have told the police the new story – the truth about Mary and Lily – but I don't say any of this.

I pop over to Mark who is still turning burgers.

'Do you want me to take over so you can mingle?'

'With my parents, and our next-door neighbour who's still pretending she doesn't remember me? You're all right, thanks.' He grins.

'Fran? Did you introduce yourself?'

'Yep, and she just looked blankly at me. Maybe I've aged badly.'

'Not one bit,' I tell him, kissing him on the cheek.

Liz is inside, filling a glass of water at the sink. She points through the window, to where her children and mine are sitting in a circle at the end of the garden. Heads together, deep in conversation.

'Wonder what they're up to,' she says.

'Plotting something, no doubt. How to get more crisps. How to sneak on to the Nintendo without us noticing.'

'As long as they're not nicking the wine yet, it's all good,' Liz says with a grin. 'I'm just delighted mine have someone to play with. They can meet on the green during the summer, and maybe play in the woods too. I've never been keen on the woods and the river, after what happened to Lily Murphy, but now that we know she didn't drown, it feels like a weight lifted somehow. A shadow gone.'

I roll the lighthouse in my hand. 'That it does.'

'Do you think she's happy?' Liz asks. 'I suppose there's no way to know, but I'd like to think she is.'

I place the lighthouse on the kitchen windowsill as I choose my words.

'I think . . . I think that thanks to the bravery of the strong women in her life, there's a very good chance she's happy,' I say, swallowing the lump in my throat. 'In fact, I'm almost sure.'

Fran sits across from Zara, sipping her wine. The bar is busy and bustling but the wine is making her sleepy, after Joanna's do-over housewarming this afternoon.

'So how was it? Did you meet you-know-who?'

'I did. Pretended I didn't remember him. It's driving him mad, I'd say.'

'What's he like now?'

'You know what he's like, I showed you the photo I took at their first housewarming.'

'No, I mean what kind of person is he.'

'Actually, he seems like he turned out OK. If you decide to tell him, I reckon it would go well.'

Zara smiles. 'You're never going to stop pushing me to do this, are you.'

'Wouldn't it be nice for Saoirse to know her dad?'

'Maybe.'

'That's the first time you've gone from a flat "no" to maybe. Progress.' Fran clinks glasses.

'Does he look like Saoirse?'

Fran nods. Zara looks anxious.

'Like, really obviously? Would Joanna guess? Would Saoirse, if she saw him?'

Fran pictures Mark Stedman – the boy who broke Zara's heart all those years ago, and the husband, the father, he is now. 'No, not obvious unless you know already. Then you can see it. In the set of the mouth and the line of the jaw.'

In her room in St Teresa's Nursing Home, Ruth Cavanagh watches as Tracy tucks her flowers into a vase.

'They're beautiful, Ruth! What are they – foxgloves?'

'Goodness, no. You should never give anyone foxgloves. They're poisonous, didn't you know that?'

'No! Really?'

'To pets and to humans. Now, you have to eat them, really, for it to be fatal. A pet might eat the leaves but a human wouldn't. Unless of course it's served to them in a lamb casserole, by someone they trust.'

Tracy shakes her head. 'Ruth, you're giving me the shivers. Too many of those Agatha Christie books, I reckon.'

'I'm just passing on some age-old advice. A casserole like that will kill a man. And funnily enough, it would go undetected. It would look just like a heart attack.'

Acknowledgements

Thank you to my fantastic editor, Finn Cotton, whose wisdom and expertise whipped this book into shape and ready for bookshelves. Thank you to the equally fantastic Imogen Nelson for looking after it during the in-between time, and also to the equally fantastic Tash Barsby who was there for the start. I feel very lucky to have had three incredible editors work on this book!

Thank you to all at Transworld, Penguin Random House and Penguin Ireland who worked on *Hide and Seek* (and on *All Her Fault* – I wrote the acknowledgements too early last time and missed some people): Becky Short, Louis Patel, Beci Kelly, Vivien Thompson, Tom Chicken, Laura Garrod, Laura Ricchetti, Emily Harvey, Natasha Photiou, Ella Horne, Ruth Richardson, Hana Sparks, Aimee Johnson, Laura Dermody, Sophie Dwyer, Fíodhna Ní Ghríofa and Claire Gatzen. Thank you also to Frankie Gray, Larry Finlay, Bill Scott-Kerr and everyone at the Transworld office for the incredible welcome when I finally made it over earlier this year.

Thank you to my incredible agent, Diana Beaumont, without whom none of this would be possible. You are the BEST.

Like *All Her Fault*, *Hide and Seek* was inspired by a real-life event, so I want to thank my kids for spending the last ten years giving me heart failure and giving me writing inspiration in equal measure. In this case, thank you specifically to my son for going missing during the game of Hide and Seek that sparked this story, but much more importantly, thank you for eventually turning up.

Parts of this book were inspired by my own childhood spent playing on the green, playing in the woods, and playing in a building site in Carrigaline, Co. Cork. (It was the eighties so it was perfectly safe to spend all day playing among cement mixers and diggers.) It has been particularly lovely that through social media and writing I've had the opportunity to get back in touch with people I grew up with in Carrigaline. The sun always shone on those childhood days.

Thank you to Trina Beakey-Wise for answering my random house-purchase questions at the school gate, thank you to Stephen and Allen for the police questions, and thank you Deirdre Fitzgerald, Niamh Kiely and Sinead McCormack for medical answers. All errors are mine!

Thank you to the Irish writing community (as ever, I'm not risking listing names in case I forget someone) and to the book-sellers who kept authors and readers going during lockdown.

Thank you to the absolutely gorgeous community of readers and bookstagrammers on Instagram: thank you for your support and your beautiful photos. Particular thanks to Sinead Cuddihy – join her Tired Mammy Book Club on Instagram if you haven't already! And a big shoutout too to BooKPunK – thank you for all your support.

Thank you as always to OfficeMum readers on Facebook, which is where it all began. Thank you especially for your company during lockdown, which is when I wrote *Hide and Seek*.

I was delighted to get to know two authors at my own school gate over the last year – there's nothing quite like having a local tribe who can meet IRL for coffee and support. Big thanks and

ACKNOWLEDGEMENTS

hugs to Amanda Cassidy and Linda O'Sullivan for all the chats, advice and almond croissants.

Thanks to my Sion Hill pals for your unending support and all the craic in between. Thanks to my sisters and first readers, Nicola, Elaine and Dee. Thank you Dad and Eithne for all the support, and for keeping local booksellers in business!

Thank you to Damien, Elissa, Nia, Matthew and new addition – Lola the dog. Lola didn't really do anything on *Hide and Seek* to be honest, but the other four (variously) read, brainstormed, suggested, proof-read, critiqued and provided baked goods. The baked goods are crucial, as every writer knows.

And thank you, dear reader, for reading this book.

About the Author

Andrea Mara is a *Sunday Times* and *Irish Times* Top Ten bestselling author, and has been shortlisted for a number of awards, including Irish Crime Novel of the Year. She lives in Dublin, Ireland, with her husband and three young children, and also runs multi-award-winning parent and lifestyle blog, OfficeMum.ie. *Hide and Seek* is her second thriller to be published in the UK and internationally.

Also by Andrea Mara

The Other Side of the Wall
One Click
The Sleeper Lies
All Her Fault

If you loved *Hide and Seek*, look out for Andrea Mara's twisty new thriller

Coming soon and available to pre-order now
Read on for an exclusive, early extract

Chapter 1

If only Sive hadn't told the girls to run ahead.

If only her editor hadn't picked that moment to phone.

If only she hadn't slowed to look at her screen.

If only she'd used the baby carrier instead of the expensive but cumbersome pram – fine for suburban Dublin but completely unsuitable for the London Underground on a humid August Monday morning.

If only.

As with most disasters, it isn't one single event or decision or misalignment of stars that causes it, but a myriad of tiny twists and turns over the course of the morning.

If they hadn't picked that day to go for brunch.

If they hadn't picked that week to go to London.

If Aaron's friends hadn't needed a twenty-year-reunion to see who was winning at life.

If, if, if.

But here she is, pushing the pram with one hand, manoeuvring it out of the lift and on to the hot, crowded rush-hour platform, trying to see who is phoning her at 8:30 a.m. when she's supposed to be off work.

'Keep going, Faye – jump on with Bea!' she calls after her six-year-old daughter as the two girls, hand in hand, approach the open Tube doors. 'I'm right behind you!'

Her phone continues to buzz and she squints at the screen. Her reading glasses – a new and unwelcome necessity – are back in the hotel room, but she can just about make out the caller's name. Caroline. Her editor. Her editor who knows she's away but has conveniently forgotten. Still pushing the pram with one hand, she swipes awkwardly to decline the call, but it has already ended of its own accord. Phone signal lost, perhaps, now that they're underground. She glances up to see where her daughters are. Two pink denim jackets, one small, one smaller, visible just ahead. The platform is heaving with rushing commuters, pushing forwards to get on to the train. Sive tries to squeeze through the crowd, murmuring 'excuse me' and 'sorry' while at the same time aware that this tourist-level politeness is not what's called for here. And pushing through isn't really an option – instead she's pulled forwards in the surge towards the doors, a few feet behind her children. Through a narrow gap in the sea of passengers, Sive sees Faye climb on to the Tube, holding Bea's hand as the two-year-old clambers on, too.

And then, just like that, the doors slide shut.

Her children inside looking out.

Sive outside looking in.

Heart in mouth, she rushes forwards. The pram, so awkward just moments earlier, makes an efficient battering ram now as she barges through commuters, shouting her children's names. But it's no good. The train begins to slide away from the platform and Faye's eyes widen, understanding now what's happening.

Sive roars, 'Get off at the next stop! Faye, next stop!' She points forwards and down, in some approximation of a signal for 'next stop', knowing there's no way Faye can hear her or understand, but hoping another passenger will read it correctly and get the children off the train.

And so, the Tube pulls away with six-year-old Faye and

two-year-old Bea on board, leaving Sive on the platform, help-less and terrified.

Whatever adrenaline or presence of mind had pushed her to shout after Faye deserts her now. Her limbs are somehow loose and frozen all at once, as she stares blindly at the rear lights of the departing Tube. *Jesus Christ.* Her children are on a train, in a city of eight million people, on a rush-hour Monday morning. Without her. Without any adult. What the hell is she supposed to do – try to get to the next station? Run there? With the pram? Hail a taxi? Call the police? Leaving this station feels counterintuitive. What if they come back here and she's gone? But how would they get back here? Would someone on the Tube see what happened and return them to her? Did people do that kind of thing? Is there anyone here who can help? Someone is talking to her. A woman beside her on the plat-form. With huge effort, Sive makes herself tune in to what the woman is saying.

'. . . so you stay here, I'll find someone to help,' the woman says. 'OK?'

Sive nods dumbly.

'The man beside your little one on the Tube heard you. You saw that, yes?'

Sive hadn't.

'A man. He saw you shouting. He gave a thumbs-up. He'll get your child off at the next stop. So we just need to get you there, and find someone to radio ahead.'

Again, Sive nods, confused and grateful and terrified.

'The next train is due in four minutes. I'm going to get some-one now, you stay here.'

Sive does as she's told, rocking the pram on autopilot, staring down the track as though her children might magically reappear if she wishes hard enough. She glances up at the train information. Three minutes until the next one. She can do this. Where is the woman? She looks around. Where are the staff? All about, commuters swarm to the platform, jostling and rushing. The heat is stifling and, in the pram, the baby starts to whimper. Sive removes his blanket and continues to rock. *Dear God, dear God, dear God.* Let them be OK. Let them not be lost in this huge city. Suddenly, staying here seems wrong. How can she stand here on the platform when her children are whizzing down the track towards another place entirely? She needs to get there. She turns the pram, just as a man in a bright orange jacket arrives beside her on the platform.

'Your child is on the Central Line train that just left for Oxford Circus, madam? Can you give me the child's name and age?' Matter of fact. No nonsense. Exactly what's needed.

'Two children.' Breathless. 'Faye is six and Bea is two.'

He lifts his radio. 'Can you describe them – what are they wearing?'

Christ, what are they wearing? Her mind is blank. *Breathe. Focus.* This is not the time to fall apart. She slows her mind and pictures her children as she saw them, just minutes earlier. 'They're both wearing pink denim jackets. Matching.' The man nods for her to keep going. 'Faye has bright blonde hair. Bea has light brown hair like mine.' She stops. How else can she describe them? Fun and funny and cute and irritating and adorable and infuriating. And gone. 'They're both wearing dresses under the jackets. Faye's is light grey. Bea's is purple. And they're wearing tan sandals. Faye has a *Frozen II* backpack. Bea has a *PAW Patrol* backpack.'

The man isn't listening any more. He has a radio to his mouth and he's telling someone else everything Sive just said. Two children, six and two. All alone in Oxford Circus. Or not. *Fuck.*

One minute to go until the next Tube arrives. Sive is rocking the pram harder now.

'Would you like me to do that?' the woman asks. Sive takes her in for the first time. She's a little older than Sive, in her mid-forties, maybe, with curly brown hair and kind brown eyes.

'Oh, I don't want to keep you – you're probably on your way to work?' Sive says, taking in the lanyard hanging around the woman's neck.

'I'm early, it's fine. And your train will be here any second now. Would you like me to come with you?'

'Oh God, I can't ask you to do that,' Sive says emphatically, desperately wishing the woman would do exactly that.

The man with the radio has his back to them but turns around now. A train is pulling into the platform and the woman begins pushing the pram towards the opening door, queuing behind a scramble of passengers. The man smiles at Sive and gives her a thumbs-up. 'They got them,' he says. 'Go straight to the next stop. Oxford Circus. My colleagues there will help you, madam.'

Sive's legs almost give way, but the woman is calling her now, urging her on to the train.

And the doors are closing and the woman is waving and the man is smiling. Everything is going to be OK.

The journey is the longest of her life, though it can't be more than a minute. It's OK. They're fine. They got them. They'll stay with them. They're not going to leave two little girls alone on the platform to wait for their mother. Their *imbecile* of a mother. Jesus Christ, how is she going to explain this to Aaron? It doesn't matter. All that matters is getting there and seeing them again. It's hot and sticky and hard to breathe, and Sive feels dizzy. Sick. More and more nauseous with every shallow breath. All around her, commuters hold on to bars and read phones, oblivious to her plight. Oblivious to her desperate need for the train to hurry the fuck up and get her to Oxford Circus. And then suddenly, she's there. The doors slide open. She pushes the pram on to the platform, into throngs of commuters. Where are they? Shit, she should have asked the man where to go once she got here. Maybe the staff will find her? Is there some kind of office? A meeting point for missing children? And then she sees it. Down towards the end of the platform. A flash of pale pink denim and light brown curls. She starts to run.

'Bea!' she grabs her two-year-old, and whisks her into her arms, burying her head in toddler curls. 'I'm so sorry, sweetie. Did you get a terrible fright? Did Faye mind you?'

A woman in an orange jacket smiles at the reunion.

'Hi, love. I'm Rita,' she says, clearly delighted to be part of the happy ending. Gently, she pats Bea's shoulder and Sive smiles back.

Will Rita or the other security people need proof that Sive is the girls' mother? Bea's hug is probably proof enough. And at six, Faye is old enough to confirm who Sive is.

Faye.

Sive looks around.

'Where's Faye?'

Rita looks confused. 'Who?'

'My other child?'

'There was no other child.'

Sive hears the words but doesn't take them in. The woman can't have said what she just said. Through the roar of descending panic, she tries again, her voice high with fear.

'My six-year-old, Faye. She was with Bea. Where is she?'

Now Rita looks alarmed. 'I was told to look out for a little girl in a pink denim jacket.'

'*Two* little girls in pink denim jackets. Two.' Sive can feel her voice getting louder. Panicky. 'They were together. Faye. Faye is six. She was with Bea.' She turns to Bea who's still in her arms. 'Where is your sister, lovely? Bea, where is Faye?'

'Gone,' Bea says. 'Faye gone.'

Chapter 2

All hell breaks loose. In Sive's head, at least, all hell breaks loose. Rita does not have her daughter. None of the staff at the station have her daughter. Faye is not here. And while Sive's been travelling here on the Tube, her daughter has been disappearing somewhere else entirely. Still on the train or somewhere on the platform? Right out of the station? She wouldn't, though. Surely she wouldn't leave the station. Unless she thought that was the best way to find her mother?

'What about the man on the train?' she asks, panic making her breathless.

Rita looks confused. 'The man?'

'The other woman said there was a man on the train who saw me on the platform and gave a thumbs-up.' It sounds garbled.

'The other woman?'

Sive shuts her eyes briefly and forces herself to slow down. *Stay calm. Panicking isn't going to help.*

'A woman in Bond Street station saw a man on the train. He gestured to show he understood, when I shouted at Faye to get off at the next stop. I thought he must have got them off. That that's why we got the message they were here. That that's how Bea is here. Oh Jesus.'

Rita speaks into her radio. More orange-jacketed staff arrive. An announcement comes out over the PA system, but Sive can't concentrate on any of it. She's flailing. Sick. Panicked. Bea on her hip. Pram by her side. Scanning crowds of commuters. The rush on. The rush off. Another train. Another crowd. Another surge. No sign. No clue. No Faye.

Someone calls the police. Rita maybe, or one of her colleagues. More announcements. More orange jackets. More worried frowns. But still no Faye. A police officer. A request for a photo, one from today if possible. Questions asked. Descriptions given. Notes taken. Photo sent. Blurred faces through terrified tears. *Is there anyone you can call?* Someone asks her. Aaron. She needs to call Aaron.

In the end, she hands her phone to Rita, and it's Rita who makes the terrible call to her husband. *We're doing our best. I'm sure we'll find her in no time. Everyone on the lookout. Any minute now. Pink jacket. Grey dress. Tan sandals. Blonde hair. Do you know where she might go if she's lost? Of course you can speak to your wife.*

Aaron is shouting. Sive needs to stay calm. She tries to explain. She says all the things she doesn't believe herself right now – Faye will turn up, any minute. Any. Minute. Now.

Except she doesn't.

Chapter 3

Tim is his name, the man who got Bea off the train. He is standing in front of Sive now, explaining something, but it's not going in. Rita is speaking into her radio again, and a police officer who introduced herself as PC Denham of the British Transport Police is asking Tim questions. Sive pulls Bea closer and forces herself to tune in to what Tim is saying.

'My girlfriend got off at Bond Street and I was waving goodbye to her when I saw the lady shouting,' he says to the police officer. 'I saw her pointing and looking quite panicked. Then I realized there was a little girl, right in front of me. This little one,' he says, pointing at Bea. 'I guessed what happened and that she was telling her to get off at the next stop.'

'And what about the other little girl?' PC Denham asks.

Tim shakes his head. 'I'm sorry. I didn't see any other little girl.'

Sive is going to throw up.

'But she was right there, too,' she manages to say. 'She got on just ahead of Bea. How did you not see her?'

Tim shrugs and then catches himself. 'Sorry . . . It did take a few seconds to work out what you were shouting, and the carriage was packed, of course.' He lifts his hands apologetically. 'Then I noticed a little girl all on her own, and I asked around if anyone was with her and no one was. And I guessed then what had happened. So I took her off at the next stop.'

'And you were on your way to work, sir?' PC Denham asks.

Sive shuts her eyes briefly. How is this relevant? How will this help find Faye?

'That's right.'

'And where is that, sir?'

'Six years as Head of Fund Accounting at Anderson Pruitt,' Tim says, even though PC Denham hasn't asked what his position is or how long he's been there. Beneath the fog of panic, it strikes Sive as odd.

'And where is that located, sir – somewhere near here?' Denham asks.

Sive sucks in a breath. Seriously, how is this going to help?

'No, Liverpool Street.'

'But you got off here?'

Tim's face flushes red. 'To make sure the little girl was safe. I wasn't going to leave her on the platform on her own.'

'So, you handed her to who, sir?'

'One of the security staff. He knew about it. He'd had a message or a call from Bond Street.'

'And then?'

'I was walking out towards the exit for the stairs and spotted this lady with the little girl, so came back over to . . . you know . . .' He shrugs.

To be part of the happy reunion, Sive thinks. To enjoy some Good Samaritan energy, maybe.

'Thank you,' she says now. 'For what you did. But are you sure you didn't see another little girl? She's six,' – she indicates with her hand to show him how tall Faye is – 'and wearing a jacket just like Bea's. Bright blonde hair. Didn't you see her?'

'I'm sorry,' Tim says helplessly. 'I only saw the little one.'

'Alright, sir, I'll just need your contact details in case we need to speak to you again,' PC Denham says, and Tim calls out a phone number.

Sive pulls Bea away from her shoulder so she can look at her.

'Where is your sister? Where is Faye?'

'Chase,' Bea says solemnly, looking at Tim and then back to Sive. 'Chase on train.'

Chapter 4

Aaron is rushing towards her, pushing through crowds, ignoring disgruntled expressions as he barges past. All six foot three of him, here to help, and Sive instantly feels a lift. Between them they'll fix this.

'Faye?' he says helplessly.

She shakes her head. 'Not yet.' It comes out in a whisper.

'My God.' He looks around the bustling platform, and she feels every inch of it. The crowds. The sheer volume of numbers. The size of the city. The endless entrances and exits. The dark tunnels. The oncoming trains.

'What happened?'

In short, breathless, staccato bursts, she explains.

'But how were you not right there with them, getting on the train?' he asks.

'I was just behind them, pushing the pram out of the lift. Telling them to hurry. And then—'

She closes her eyes.

'And then what, Sive?'

'My phone rang. I was trying to see who it was. Trying to decline the call.'

Aaron shakes his head.

'It didn't take more than a second, but . . .'

'Long enough for the doors to close. I know.' He rubs her arm, and the kindness brings tears to her eyes.

PC Denham clears her throat and addresses Sive. 'Your younger daughter said Faye was chasing someone or something? Does that make any sense to you – can you think of anything that she might run after?'

Sive shakes her head. 'I have no idea. I don't think she would.'

Tim is still standing near by, watching, and Denham turns to him now. 'Did you see anything like that – a child running?'

'No, but the Tube was packed. I don't think anyone could run anywhere.'

Aaron looks confused. 'And you are?' he says to Tim.

'This gentleman took care of your younger daughter, took her off the train and handed her to security staff,' PC Denham explains.

Aaron frowns. 'And you claim you didn't see Faye?'

Claim. Sive bites her lip.

Tim stands a little taller, his cheeks flushed. 'I didn't see your other daughter, no.'

PC Denham interrupts. 'We've covered this, and we have contact details, should we need any further information.' Her tone says *I'll ask the questions here.* 'If we could get back to what your younger daughter said. Sometimes kids chase after things without thinking and lose their way. Like running after a ball or a butterfly?'

'A butterfly on a Tube?' Aaron sounds incredulous and Sive wants to tell him to rein it in – they need all the help they can get, to keep everyone on side.

'Can you think of anything your daughter might chase?' Denham says evenly.

Sive looks at Bea, thinking back on her words. *What if that's not it. What if Faye didn't chase a ball or a butterfly. What if someone chased her?*

'Bea, sweetheart. Did someone run after Faye?'

Bea looks blankly at her. A man dashing for a Tube pushes between them, separating Sive from PC Denham momentarily. Sive tries again. 'Darling, can you point – where is your sister?'

Bea's lower lip wobbles. 'Baw-baw.'

'What was that?' Denham asks, cupping her ear against the clamour of rush hour.

Sive shakes her head. 'She just wants her milk.'

'Do you think she might tell us more eventually?' the police officer asks. 'Maybe she's tired or hungry?'

'She's just turned two,' Aaron says tersely. 'She can't tell us anything.'

Aaron. Sive pleads with him silently. Playing the big man isn't going to help here. This police officer isn't one of his witnesses on the stand. She's a woman trying to do her job, to help them find their child.

'She doesn't have a lot of words yet,' Sive clarifies for PC Denham. 'I don't know how much she'll be able to tell us beyond what she's already said. But what if it means someone chased Faye – someone frightened her and made her run off? Maybe she's still on the train, or hiding in a station?'

'We have officers on the train now, and they're checking each station – London Underground staff are checking too. We'll find her. There's a finite number of stations on this line and we'll get to all of them.'

'But if she's left one of the stations,' Sive whispers.

An announcement booms over the tannoy, and Aaron waits before asking his next question.

'Would there have been time?'

'There was maybe six or seven minutes—' Sive's voice disappears, swallowed by panic. She clears her throat. 'Between waiting for the next Tube and getting here. The security people

358

were already looking for her, but they couldn't have . . . they couldn't have covered every station immediately.'

'Oh my God.' Aaron runs his hand through his hair, turning in a slow circle. He looks back at Sive. 'We're in a city of eight million people, and Faye could be anywhere.'

From the bestselling author of ALL HER FAULT

NO ONE SAW A THING

'Andrea Mara is a star.'
Lee Child

ANDREA MARA

Coming

August 2023

Available to

PRE-ORDER NOW!

Want more from Andrea Mara, the Queen of the unexpected twist?

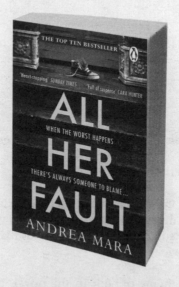

ONE MISSING BOY.

Marissa Irvine arrives at 14 Tudor Grove, expecting to pick up her young son Milo from his first playdate with a boy at his new school. But the woman who answers the door isn't a mother she recognizes. She isn't the nanny. She doesn't have Milo. And so begins every parent's worst nightmare.

FOUR GUILTY WOMEN.

As news of the disappearance filters through the quiet Dublin suburb and an unexpected suspect is named, whispers start to spread about the women most closely connected to the shocking event. Because only one of them may have taken Milo – but they could all be blamed . . .

IN A COMMUNITY FULL OF SECRETS, WHO IS REALLY AT FAULT?

OUT NOW

Reading Group Guide

1. *Hide and Seek* follows two sets of characters in the past and the present – how did the structure of the novel affect your reading experience?

2. Think about the events leading up to Lily Murphy's disappearance. Could the drama that develops from that moment have been prevented? Which characters are to blame for the way in which the tragedy unfolds?

3. Discuss the theme of guilt in the novel. Do you think the characters are justified in acting in the way they do? Would you have made the same choices had you been in their place?

4. Were there any moments you found unexpected or shocking?

5. Consider Ruth's character. How did your opinion of her change over the course of the story and what did you think about the way she acted?

6. Were you surprised by how the final chapters played out? While you were reading, did you have any different ideas for how the novel might end?